METAL

J.F. Lawrence

JFL Press, LLC

ISBN: 978-1-7356301-8-2

Cover design by: J.F. Lawrence

Printed in the United States of America

Contents

DEDICATION

To all the men and women in the Armed Forces, thank you for your service.

CHAPTER ONE

With his sat phone in hand, Professor Terrance Mathison sat chewing on a sliver of beef jerky leaning against the trunk of a moss-covered fir tree half a kilometer from Cascade Locks, the terminus of his two-week camping trip. Wall, as most people called him after he drove a Humvee through three walls of a mud hut in Ethiopia, looked forward to the modern conveniences of civilization and an end to his solo expedition through the wilds of the Cascades. A soft bed, clean clothes, and a fresh meal called him onward.

Yet, he lounged, delaying the end of his trip now that he was so close, contemplating whether to walk a few kilometers back into the woods and set up camp for one last night. Even as tall and trimly muscular as he was, his three remaining protein bars could sustain him until morning. He could hold onto his vacation and the peace it offered for another twelve hours, and the world would keep going as it had for billions of years.

The phone bleeped as it acquired signal.

Sniffing at the air, he knew better than to linger. While smoke from wildfires plagued the entire drought-ridden Pacific Northwest all summer, just like the last few summers, the smell was growing stronger. Staying was the kind of idea that got people the Kazinski Award, named in honor of a grunt who supposedly shot himself in the foot with a Javelin anti-tank weapons system.

Across the field, a portly man in his fifties and an equally unfit woman pulled suitcases up the uneven trail like the other stupid campers he'd seen in the wilderness over the last few days. There must have been an idiot convention somewhere up the trail, a corporate retreat, drawing ignorant city folks into the mountains. Like this couple, perhaps the most inept of them all, they kept clear of Wall, not even saying, "Hi," which was fine by him. He was out here to get away from it all, not meet strangers.

While Wall gently pressed the jerky between his molars in an almost fanatical devotion to dried beef, he massaged his swollen arm a few fingers below his right shoulder, the spot where a 7.76 round from an AK-47 paused his military career for a few months. It hadn't bothered him in nearly a decade. Groaning, he mashed the heel of his calloused left palm into the spot where the Army surgeons screwed steel to bone. Fortunately, his sleeve covered the engorged spot, which had been discolored in deep purples and putrid greens almost from the beginning of his trip. Wall, with his emergency first responder training, was pretty sure that it wasn't infected, but he planned on visiting urgent care in the morning all the same.

This was the first time he touched electronics since his GPS died two days into the wilderness, the batteries having corroded with that white powdery growth that happened so often. While navigation was harder, it added an element of Lewis and Clark style to the adventure. He stuck to his self-imposed vow not to sync with the outside world until the end, and it was well worth it. After all, electronics would have ruined the whole point of the trip, to clear his mind so he could reset and forge forward with his five-year plan. With the pullout point so close, Wall waited for the device to bleep a few more times.

With a quick glance at the time in the top right corner of the display, he said, "4:47." After losing his watch about ten days ago, the imposition of a diurnal pattern had imprinted a peaceful stamp on his vacation which was now ruined. "4:47. That gives me...half an hour." At a steady pace, he could cover the half kilometer in seven or eight minutes, so he leaned back against the stump and sucked the joyous sweet smoke from the second-to-last needle of his jerky supply.

As he feared, his first brush with electronics brought back the weight of his work. He needed to update his syllabus and review his class notes, then record a few videos for his introduction to biochemistry course. More important to

Wall, he needed to get back into the lab and print a series of new genetic experiments. In order to keep his competitive edge, he couldn't take off any more time. Thorsten Towning, one of the most impactful people in modern bioengineering, was correct that Wall needed a mental break. But now he had to return to his passion, fixing the world one bacteria at a time.

Attuned to nature, he listened to the westerly breeze and felt the cooling afternoon air on his two-week-old beard. Wall could almost ignore the acrid smoke in the air, preferring to focus on the late summer's earthy forest scent. He listened to his steady heartbeat as it gently tapped like a flawless metronome. A squirrel chittered somewhere nearby.

Gradually, his mind returned to balancing all the facets of his research and cajoling complex concepts into organized theoretical and laboratory experiments. His groundbreaking work into microorganisms that rusted various types of metals was going to be a game changer for the environment. With his latest modification to the Chilean bacteria, *leptospirillum ferrodiazotrophum*, he could rust through the exposed rebar of an abandoned building within a day or eat away the hull of a beached ship within a week. Or at least that was what his models and lab work predicted.

The millions of tons of metal waste flooding the world's dumps, rivers, and oceans every day was a serious problem, and Wall wanted to be part of the solution, one that couldn't be solved by recycling alone. Recycling could only do so much, was expensive, and couldn't handle the millions of discarded household or industrial items made by combining plastic and metal or different types of metal. The goal of re-claiming ground for the natural world was why he received the inaugural Thorsten Towning Award for Environmental Scholars, which came with a research award of two million dollars. While most of his colleagues would have gone out and spent the unrestricted money like mad, taking sizable incomes for themselves, Wall was more reserved and strategic. He had only hired a single researcher, Marius, a peculiar French man with a propensity for grumpiness and disappearing whenever Wall needed him.

The man on the trail yelled as he fell to his knees with his suitcase's handle in his hand while the case remained stuck on a root.

Wall shook his head. "Who brings a suitcase into the backwoods?"

Putting them out of his mind, he closed his eyes, but that only invited in thoughts of work. As a second-year professor, his first two graduate students would arrive in a few days, a prospect he anticipated with dread and excitement. He worried that he might be one of those professors who ignored their mentees in favor of doing their own research, a very real possibility given his inability to focus on much else besides his experiments. At the same time, he looked forward to guiding these two exceedingly bright, like-minded students into a new and important career path.

The fat man in the field cursed from his butt in the middle of the trail. "It wasn't my fault, Helen! It just broke. Stupid piece of..."

"Dammit, John! Just get up. We need to keep going."

Wall pressed his eyes tighter and sucked on his jerky.

Unfortunately, the Towning award's prestige, something that the University of Oregon loved to tout, was almost more hassle than help. Wall wanted to continue his research without distraction, but ever since Towning's foundation announced the award, the provost kept calling on him to talk to wealthy donors or, worse, reporters, all of whom attempted to spin the truth for a better story. He understood why he needed to attend functions when Towning came around, but the rest of it was a bunch of nonsense.

Once again, he considered what he might do with the sizable monetary grant from Towning's foundation, but failed to see what he could do with it. In truth, the two-million-dollar award was overkill. His research wouldn't become expensive until he tried to deploy the microbes on a large-scale scrap yard, and that wasn't going to happen for at least another couple of years. The problem wasn't whether the microbes would do what he wanted. The trick was to contain his corrosive bacteria, to keep them from contaminating things people didn't want to rust, like buildings, cars, batteries, belt buckles, and every other modern convenience that humankind relied on every minute of every day.

"Ah!" the woman yelped as she nearly fell over.

Wall watched a new couple dressed in heavy camping gear, the man carrying a baby in a sling on his torso, quickly walk around the older couple at a pace that would soon tire them out. The out-of-shape couple and the well-equipped campers gave each other a wide berth, pulling off the trail on opposite sides. His distracted mind didn't pay enough attention to notice the worried looks on their faces or the fearful glances they gave each other. Instead, his thoughts circled inward, to past, present, and future.

He wondered when Towning would invite him to his "summer cabin" again. As far as he was concerned, a nine-bedroom mansion didn't count as a cabin, no matter how much you disguised it with giant logs and a slate roof. When the old man showed him the fourteen thousand square foot fully automated gleaming-white lab in the basement, the scale of the house no longer mattered. The first weekend, he jumped at the opportunity to spend time with the old man, literally jumping into the helicopter like a giddy fanboy.

While Towning's butler, Paris, took care of every convenience, from fantastic meals to evening drinks, the two of them geeked out on the future of environmentalism, continued during walks through the gorgeous old-growth forest, on the porch with Scotch, in the subterranean lab over microscopes, and at the dinner table. That first weekend accelerated Wall's research by at least a year, redoubling his lead over other bioengineers pursuing the same goals. It was the best weekend of his adult life, like sex for the mind.

"Finally." The tubby couple reached the opposite end of the field, giving Wall a moment longer to ease from his pre-industrial vacation into his technology-driven life. In the back of his mind along the long hikes and early mornings, he had unwittingly connected his advantages so far and how he would extend his studies into the future.

When Wall returned from Towning's cabin that first time, techs had already installed next-generation equipment in his lab, stuff that not even the largest biotech companies could get yet. The gray-haired genius upgraded his computers and installed copies of the latest industry software as a gift. Wall wanted to believe that he would somehow repay the elderly philanthropist one day but knew better. What could he do for a man who could afford and accomplish anything?

"Do your part in repairing the environment," the genius said on Wall's third visit to the mansion cabin. "That's all that I ask. Restore the balance. Work toward the environmental singularity." Towning coined the term, "environmental singularity" to describe the point in time when technology would heal the planet more than scar it.

Breaking him from deep thoughts, the *thwup-thwup* sound of a helicopter swelled from barely audible down the gorge to thunderous as it screamed overhead, flying low enough to batter the treetops this way and that. It was an Air National Guard chopper, probably an HH-60 Pave Hawk, the upgraded version of the famous Black Hawk. When Wall was shot in Ethiopia, a Pave Hawk had finished off the ambushers that killed his fellow soldiers. The National Guard sometimes ran exercises up and down the Columbia River and occasionally aided in rescue and recovery efforts, saving the dumb and ignorant, like so many of the fools he'd increasingly passed. It wasn't a surprise that they were out here to rescue one of these idiots.

Switching his nearly drained jerky to the other side, he whispered, "I hope everyone's okay."

With the fly-over, the last illusion of existing in a pre-industrial world flaked away and vanished as if into the wind. He could no longer avoid everyone by skirting campgrounds and lodges and jogging past roads with too many parked cars. The fact that he hadn't seen a plane or even a single contrail in the past weeks had kept his illusion of yesteryear alive.

Standing, he stretched out to his full height, nearly two fists taller than the average man. Wall extended his unusually long arms and cracked his knuckles, elbows, and back in one smooth motion. After shaking out his lean muscles, he picked up his carbon-fiber backpack with a grunt that would have done his father proud. Reciting his dad, Wall said, "Real men grunt. Getting things done requires hard work." He said the same about women, stating that Missus Mathison could grunt with the best of them.

After shimmying his pack into place and adjusting its straps, Wall patted himself down to check that everything was in place: his synthetic composite multi-tool, lightweight binoculars, and the filtered water nozzle fastened to his shoulder strap. The pack fit perfectly, heavy in all the right ways, though far lighter than any set of equipment he'd ever seen. "Thanks again, Towning," he whispered. He'd have to express his gratitude to his benefactor for the gift as soon as he got back. The lightweight gear, made from synthetic composites and advanced fabrication techniques, almost felt unsportsmanlike to call what he did backpacking.

In the distance, the search and rescue helicopter looped around to the west.

With no further excuses to slow his progress toward the small town of Cascade Locks, nestled on the bank of the Columbia River, he took the first steps of the last leg of his trip. After two weeks on the trail, his feet moved almost as if they had a mind of their own, automatically adjusting to the uneven ground, which allowed Wall to look this way and that, appreciating the beautiful old firs for one last time before returning to the halls of research.

Four trail runners jogged around a curve from the west. "No, not trail runners," he whispered. Fully decked-out soldiers, with everything from beige combat boots and camo uniforms to M4 carbines, sidearms, and body armor, stormed toward him. These weren't kids playing airsoft or paintball games. In fact, one of them was almost as tall as Wall but much broader in all the Greek god sorts of ways.

As they approached, Wall stepped off the trail and stood at attention, honoring his fellow servicemen. While he hadn't been in the army for about a decade, he respected the hell out of the men and women who served the greater good and felt a deep camaraderie with them. After a single tour of duty, he decided to serve in a different way, one less likely to end at the pointy end of supersonic brass.

He respected the institution all the more because, without the G.I. Bill he never would have ended up with a bachelor's degree in bioengineering, not to mention a Ph.D. and professorship in a top-tier biochemistry department. He now served humankind by making advancements to one of the most important subjects in environmental science, restoring waste to natural materials. Having goofed off in high school, he owed the Army for the do-over it granted him. Without it, who knows where he would have ended up?

Wall's gut twisted uncomfortably as the soldiers spread out around him, forming a wide semi-circle. Still standing at attention, he realized that these weren't simple grunts. Their tactical gear wasn't standard issue. Everything from their modified helmets and desert scarfs to their custom-coated assault rifles and unique body armor screamed special forces of some sort.

While he didn't know what they could possibly want, this wasn't a simple search and rescue mission. He knew he didn't have anything to fear, but the way they held their rifles at ready sat about as easy as a bundle of magnets in his gut.

The woman—or at least that was what he suspected from her mostly obscured physique—at the center of their flanking formation stepped a pace closer and tapped her black-gloved index finger in a one-two, one-two pattern above the trigger. Her intelligent dark-brown eyes, tinted behind yellow shooting glasses, told a story of danger and consequence.

Wall stood perfectly still, confident that things would go bad if he moved wrong. He was strangely glad that his beige Glock 20, a bear and wolf deterrent, jammed up about a week ago, so he'd stowed it away in a baggy at the bottom of his pack rather than wear it on his thigh. Having served, he was comfortable with the firearm in a way that few civilians were, particularly rare among academics. He didn't collect firearms like some of his Army buddies, but he owned a few and practiced with them every month or two. His pistols served a specific purpose: protection in a town with increasing drug use, particularly meth and fentanyl. Out here it was supposed to be a deterrent for dangerous predators like mountain lions. Firearms were tools, not toys or collector's pieces for him, utilitarian and practical.

"Are you Lieutenant Terrance Mathison?

CHAPTER TWO

"Are you Lieutenant Mathison?" she said louder from behind her desert shemagh, not so subtly tapping her finger above the trigger again, tap-tap, tap-tap. Under the helmet, shooting glasses, body armor, and Army uniform, there was little he could tell about her, but from the tone of her voice, he got the sense that she wasn't asking, merely insisting that he confirm his identity.

While she stared him down, her giant companion, who could have dominated as a defensive lineman in the Superbowl, kept watch, eyes swiping smoothly left and right and up into the trees. Most people didn't look up, a fatal oversight in the wrong situation, a mistake that a serious warrior wouldn't make. The other two men were nondescript under all the gear, emanating nervousness, but the woman and the bull held themselves with confidence and ease.

Green Berets? Wall wondered. Regular grunts weren't allowed to modify their gear with custom sites, specialized handrails, and suppressors. And if he wasn't mistaken, everything was covered in a dull greenish-black layer that Wall couldn't identify. They were spec ops of one kind or another. Their lack of name tags or ranks added to this impression.

Despite the big guy's size advantage, Wall suspected that the woman was the more dangerous of the two. He wasn't sure why, but he was confident about his intuition. As would anyone who was threatened by superior forces both in number and skill, he slowly raised his palms in the standard "I surrender" gesture.

"Yes, sir," he said, surprising himself with how steady his voice was, bolstered by the formality ingrained by the military. For clarification, he added, "But I'm not in the Army anymore. You–"

"Listen up, Terrance," she interrupted, "lest we have an allergic reaction that undoes what nature so graciously gave you." Her voice, rich and a little breathy, had a subtle Hispanic accent. More importantly, her words carried command as easily as she carried her firearm. "Now, Wall, take off that pack and set it on the ground." When he didn't immediately respond, she subtly tilted her modified M4 in his direction, not at him but closer than he or any sane person would encourage.

"Okay!" he said, bending subtly at the knees and waist, an evolutionary imperative to form a smaller target. Slow and steady–because fast and jittery got you shot–he unstrapped the pack and set it down. "Do you mind telling me what this is about?"

She jutted her chin outward and said, "Step back one pace, good looking. Good. Now strip down."

"What the?" To be detained by the Army on US soil was unheard of. The Posse-Something-Or-Other Act outlawed federal troops from interfering in civilian affairs. To be forced to strip down at the dangerous end of a military rifle was as unconstitutional as it came. If they were FBI, it might make sense, but this... "This isn't–"

"Mathison," the big guy interrupted, his voice deep and easy, making him only marginally less terrifying. "Make this easier on all of us. Shut your mouth and do as she says."

As a tall man in the best shape of his life, Wall had little to be ashamed of, yet he turned sideways as he stripped off his shirt, planning to hide his junk when it came time.

"Aught!" she barked, bringing Wall to an abrupt halt with his long-sleeve shirt pulled over his face, blocking his sight. "Turn back toward me. That-a-boy."

He continued undressing in the chilly afternoon breeze, or maybe it was the unsettling state of things that raised his goosebumps. All sorts of thoughts knocked around in his brain, with notions ranging from idiotic to defiant to that of a conspiracy nut. One instant, he wondered if they sent the Army after him for filing his taxes wrong. That year was the first time he ever filed several of the forms, and he wasn't sure if he'd filled them all out correctly. The next second, he worried that a military coup had overthrown the country while he was camping, and they now lived in a dictatorship. He considered running into the forest for the briefest of moments before he got his boots off, but then his opportunity passed, not that he would have made it more than a step before she turned him into a pasta strainer.

He pondered if this might be an uprising against the rich, which they erroneously thought he was because of the Towning award. *Or maybe,* he thought. *Maybe it's a hostage thing, an abduction to coerce Towning into unloading a safe of untraceable bills.*

"All the way," she said once he was down to his boxers. When he hesitated, she tapped at her carbine. "Do I look like a delicate flower, Wall? You're wasting time. Don't make me pull out the hourglass." So, he dropped trou right there on the trailside, hands covering his manhood, face turning rust red.

"Well done, Wall. Now, take two steps to your right. No. Your other right. No, not little steps. Big ones like you mean it." She demonstrated as if he was an idiot.

The twigs on the forest floor dug into his calloused arches as he sidestepped, but he forced himself not to wince. He might not be able to retain much dignity after disrobing in front of a woman at gunpoint, yet saved what little he could.

"Paulson, Anders, disinfect the asset."

The two men at the extremities of their semi-circle rotated their single-point slings to vertical positions behind their shoulders and walked forward with spray bottles that contained transparent cobalt-blue liquid.

"What the hell is this?" Wall asked, thrusting his right hand out in a useless straight-armed defense while the other hand still cupped his junk.

"Put your hand down, Lieutenant Mathison," the woman said in a neutral tone. She didn't need to add a threat while holding her finger near the trigger. "Let these fine men do their job."

Wall closed his eyes and lowered his hand, allowing them to douse him from hair to toenails. The cold liquid clung to his skin, raising every goosebump in the cool breeze, filling his nostrils with the smell of bleach and pine-fresh floor cleaner. "Slowly raise your hands to the sky," one of the men said, then proceeded to spray the underside of his arms and a double dose for his armpits, which made him flinch despite every attempt to stifle it. When he blinked, the blue bleach dribbled into his left eye, and his face contorted as if he was stung by a scorpion.

"Piece of..." he cursed, then politely cursed again as his foot slipped and he caught himself on a particularly painful twig. The university's sensitivity training, a concept he thought enabled entitlement, instilled a strong resistance to swearing, a habit he picked up in the Army despite his strict Iowa upbringing.

"Language," the big guy said jovially. "Don't you know you're in the presence of a delicate flower?"

"Nice one, Rhino," she said happily. He imagined them fist-bumping. While Wall didn't appreciate the banter given the current circumstances, it was common in the military, even, and sometimes especially, in stressful situations. It served to relieve tension and keep cool heads. He'd rather jokes at his expense than nervous silence.

The spraying stopped, and the man to his right said, "Now scrub it in with this." A sponge touched his right fingertips and he grabbed ahold of it. Eyes closed and shaking, he turned the two-sided dish scrubber over in his hand, soft on one side and scratchy on the other.

"You heard Anders," the woman said, neither menacing nor demeaning. She didn't need to make him cower. Sopping wet and helpless, he was completely subjugated, fully under her command. "It'll go faster if you use the rough side. Really get in there and get the germs off."

Germs? That was the clue. They were worried about a bacteria or virus. Counter to how most people would react, Wall immediately relaxed. He understood diseases, being tangential to his work on environmental bacteria. Wall modeled his research on pathogens, relying on similar factors like reproduction rates and transmission statistics to estimate their efficacy at rusting a handful of metals.

As Wall scrubbed, he wondered if the pathogen was airborne or spread from person to person via physical contact. *Maybe both?* Their face coverings might suggest an airborne transmission vector. Then again, it might be a spec-ops thing like wearing yellow-tinted shooting glasses and carrying specialized firearms. They had yet to touch him and wore gloves, which could imply direct contact. While he sincerely hoped that he wasn't infected with whatever disease they thought he had, he–

The coarse side of the sponge swiped over his right arm just below the shoulder, and he bronzed over like a statue, physically frozen by a mental slug. *Is the swelling around my plate and screws related to a contagion? Possibly attacking scar tissue? Nah. If that was the case, then the scars from his knee surgery would have hurt too.*

"What's the problem, soldier?" the woman asked without even the slightest hint of anxiety. He noted that she used the word *soldier,* a designation that hadn't applied to him in a decade.

"It's nothing," he said and continued scrubbing himself down.

"Spit it out, professor."

He tried to blink his right eye open to see her but regretted it immediately as more blue bleach stung like hot peppers.

"Let me guess. You're worried about your injury from Ethiopia?"

"Yeah, how did you–"

"Never mind that, lieutenant. Get on with it."

"Use the spongy side on your armpits and schlong," the big man suggested, his voice friendly and calm. "No sense in harming the goods if you know what I mean."

Wall saw through the good cop and bad cop routine but followed the man's advice all the same. "Thanks." This whole strip-down precaution was probably a scare tactic for something that some bureaucrat blew out of proportion. The concept that someone believed he was infected with a mysterious disease was ridiculous. Couldn't they see that after fourteen full days of backpacking through rough terrain, he was in great shape, showing no symptoms of any sort? He was not sick.

"Tilt your head back. I'm gonna flush your eyes," said the man to his right, the voice belonging to a New Jerseyan. "Open your eyes while I pour." Wall wordlessly complied, completely at their whim. "That's good."

The guy stopped pouring water, then handed Wall an eyedropper with a medical label on it, ciprofloxacin, the last syllable, "cin," suggesting an antibiotic. Despite what the man said, none of this was *good*.

"Three drops in each eye," the guy, maybe Anders, said. Once complete, the soldier handed Wall a lintless towel and said, "Dry off." He felt like a grunt back in basic training, forced to play an uncomfortable game of Simon says. The thought that the tiny towel could dry a full-grown man was laughable, not to mention a man of his span, but he did his best.

"Step to your right another two paces," the woman commanded when he finished, her voice and posture relaxed but her gaze dangerously intense. Wall sidestepped to where Anders laid out undergarments, a camo uniform, non-latex gloves, a helmet, and boots. His gear matched theirs but without any of the various shrink-wrapped accouterments and weapons. "Cover up that sexy body of yours before I get all steamy."

His skin burned from too much cleaning residue as he donned the clothes, which fit his lean but long frame, a sign of detailed planning, not some fly-by-grunt mission. He didn't let his discomfort from the clothes on scrubbed-raw skin show because complainers weren't prone to receive a copious supply of sympathy among the armed forces.

Confronted with the thought of wearing Army fatigues again and the complete loss of freedom, his gut threatened to violate its one-way policy and make a scene that might result in another scrub-down. He was either enlisted or captive, neither option sitting profoundly well with him. As he fumbled with the desert shemagh, he tried to figure out what purpose he could serve or what crime he'd supposedly committed.

Then it hit him. "This is about the Anarchist Cookbook, isn't it?"

As a junior in high school, Wall's friend, Owen, found his uncle's updated copy of the delinquent's guide to blowing shit up. Like an idiot, Wall digitized the whole thing and sent copies to all of his buddies, who distributed it to their friends, and so on, until practically everyone at school had it. Wall was expelled, taking the whole blame for what he thought of as an expression of his first-amendment rights. That one transgression all but ruined his chances of getting a scholarship, which set his whole life on a completely different trajectory. Had it come back around to bite him in his bleached white ass fifteen-odd years later?

"Ha," the behemoth said. "That book's for fluffy kittens and nanna's doilies. They don't send serious people like us out to retrieve super-nerds like you for batting at balls of yarn." Wall pulled on the brain bucket, noting the thick coating over the whole thing and the plastic wrap layer on the inside.

"Mathison," the woman said, cool as mint-chip ice cream, the voice coming through small speakers in his helmet. "Am I correct that you are going to behave?"

He considered asking her what right she had to detain him. He was a US citizen on US soil and hadn't done anything wrong. However, seeing the steel in her eyes, he simply said, "Yes, sir."

"Good. Paulson and Anders, disinfect his belongings. Meet us back at the helo."

"Yes, sir."

"Rhino," she said to the big man. "Take point." Without hesitation, the buffed dude turned and jogged double time but with a unique style that made him nearly silent. "Fall in, Mathison." She jerked her head toward the massive soldier. Definitely spec ops. Sparing the quickest of glances at her non-standard M4, he set down the path, easily keeping pace.

From behind, she said, "Tell me a tale from your childhood, Mr. Mathison."

His helmet holder jammed for a moment. "What? Why?"

Slowly and deliberately, she repeated herself.

"Um, okay." He thought for a second. "Well, when I was sixteen, some friends and I made napalm out of gasoline and styrofoam. We got the recipe from–"

"The Anarchist Cookbook," she interrupted. "Got it. Next."

"Okay." He rifled through several more stories and landed on one. "When I was around twelve, my buddy and I were mountain biking in the woods. About five minutes away from where we put in, I jumped off a culvert that ran across the trail. The problem was that my front wheel–"

"Came loose, and you got that case of road rash along your left side. Next."

Being interrupted like that was going to piss him off, but he squelched his pride, reminding himself that she was holding an assault rifle and he had nothing to defend himself. "Why don't you tell me what you want to hear?"

"Fair enough," she said. He imagined her shrugging. "Tell me two truths and a lie."

"What?"

"You heard me, big boy," she said with a bit of Hispanic sassiness. "Pretend we're on our first date at a fancy tapas restaurant. Give me two truths and a lie."

He shook his head disbelievingly, his foot slipping because he hadn't gotten used to the new shoe fit of the combat boots. "Ah! Piece of..." After a few awkward steps, he said, "Don't I have Miranda rights or something?"

"Nope. Not today. Possibly never again." How could she be so carefree about a man's rights? Never again? Did she mean he was going to "disappear?" With an overly annoyed intonation, one that he suspected was for his benefit, not resulting from her emotions, she said, "I still haven't heard those truths and the lie, handsome."

"Fine. I'm a bioengineering professor, my favorite color is green, and I have a BB stuck under my right eyelid."

"Naughty, naughty," she said. "I wanted two truths and one lie, not two lies and one truth."

"But–"

"You are an *assistant* professor of biochemistry." She talked right over him, having placed emphasis on the word *assistant,* a designation that he hated. Wall was nobody's assistant. He was a pioneering bioengineer. "And the BB is under your left eyelid."

"How?" he asked. He never told anyone about the BB because it made him look like an idiot. At thirteen, Owen convinced him that the BB gun wasn't loaded and that the blast of air felt cool, blasting a puff of air into his own face to prove that it didn't hurt. Being a sadistic ass, the prick secretly slipped a BB in and fired, lodging it into the distal side of his left eye. Wall hid it from his folks, who would have taken away the air gun. The active bleeding stopped by the time he got home, whereupon he claimed that he ran into a corn stalk and that the stalk won the battle. Only a handful of people knew.

"It's her superpower," Rhino said over his shoulder. "Plink is damn near clairvoyant. She's in your head now, Wall. There's no–"

"So, Lieutenant Mathison," she interrupted without raising her voice or adding harshness. "Why did you do it?"

"Do what?" Wall asked, a bit more annoyance seeping out of his mouth than he intended and far testier than was wise. "I haven't done anything."

"Why did you let your bugs loose?"

CHAPTER THREE

"Wait, what?" Wall said, turning on the spot and falling on his butt. The devil that rode on his shoulder ever since he learned how to make a blowgun out of corn stalk, needles, and corn silk, had been right to fear his research. The worst had happened. They were here because he had fucked up, and not in a little way. "That can't be. My research isn't ready for field experiments. My strains could cause serious damage." He trailed off, which had less to do with the woman's fully loaded carbine and more to do with the precautions he took with his work. "Oh, no. This isn't good, as in really, really bad."

"Ha!" Rhino laughed. "Someone, call the university. The professor nailed the definition of *understatement*."

Standing back up, he pointed back and forth between the warriors and him. "That's why you're...Why I'm?"

"Yes, Lieutenant Mathison," she said, still the picture of calm. "Now, turn around and fall in."

Instead of obeying, he pleaded with her. "I would never. Nobody would. It's not safe. It could–"

"Mathison," she said, smooth as a well-greased ball bearing. "We wouldn't be here if somebody hadn't done something very, very wrong." She watched his eyes transform between a variety of emotions, the chief among them being dumb-struck confusion. "Now, turn around and keep jogging."

With his shoulders slumped and an unseen pallor spread across his slack-jawed face, Wall complied, strangely more tired than he had been at any point on his grueling camping trip. "How bad is it?"

"Lieutenant," she said, once again poking at his fear of being enlisted. Could they try him for war crimes without the need for due process? Send him to Guantanamo Bay? "It's bad enough that we're here."

Needing to know the scope of the damage, he asked, "How far did it get? Is the chemistry building okay?"

"The building?" she asked almost playfully.

"Yeah, the chemistry building. Did my bacteria damage it? The wiring? The air-conditioning? The steel structure?"

"You could say that," she said, frustratingly ambiguous.

His voice urgent, he said, "Please tell me that it didn't get outside the building."

"Why, lieutenant?" This repetition of his former designation was starting to get on his nerves. "What would your critters do if they got out?"

"It depends on which strands. Some could get into the groundwater, and if that happened..."

"Yes, lieutenant?" He almost snapped at her for using his old rank like some sort of psychological weapon.

"Well, the *leptospirillum ferrodiazotrophum-theta-nine* could reach the foundations of surrounding buildings on campus and eat at their rebar and structural beams." All of his strands corroded metals faster than those found in nature and spread very quickly.

"And the other germs?"

"Please tell me the *leptospirillum* didn't get out."

"Mathison, what about the other germs?"

He wanted to scream. Deciding that the best way to prove his innocence was to work with them, he pinned back his shoulders in regulation posture and said, "They'd all F—" he almost swore "—up the building and half could corrode parts of the surrounding buildings if they got into the groundwater. Not as fast as *leptospirillum*, but fast."

"Is that why your security was so lax?" she asked.

"What? No." He almost laughed. "Thorsten Towning's people upgrade the security. He had a connection with a local startup that installed sensors throughout the lab. Biometric readers on everything."

"That's an interesting relationship." She sounded conversational as if they were at a cocktail party. "Tell me, how well do you know Mister Towning?"

"A bit," he said nervously. "I guess well enough that he invites me to his summer cabin sometimes." If he were at a bar with her, wanting to impress, he would have played it up but thought better of it here. *Stick to the truth,* he told himself. "It's not like we're drinking buddies or anything."

"Huh? I thought I saw a picture of you drinking Scotch with the biotech guru."

Wall knew exactly which picture she was referring to. The school plastered that pic everywhere. Towning wasn't exactly the most photogenic old man, but he was in a great mood when he presented Wall with the award, which apparently made him more palatable to the university's marketing people. He explained all of this to her, but she cut him short.

"Lieutenant, why do you think Towning liked you so much?"

"It wasn't me that he liked. It was my research. My approach to healing some of the damage we're doing to our planet. And would you stop with the *lieutenant* thing? I'm not an enlisted man anymore."

"Sure thing, Wall. Mind if I call you Wall?"

"Fine," he said as they trotted into a field with the HH-60 at its center. The high-pitch whine of the twin engines filled the air as part of the pre-flight check. The sound brought back memories of Ethiopia. Not in the bad way that some of his buddies experienced, stemming from too much awfulness. His time on deployment changed him, but not for the worse. It hardened him, solidifying his goal of fixing the world in any way he could. His undergrad research project focused on using metal-eating bacteria to consume landmines safely to save soldiers' lives. The initial idea turned out to be ineffective but led to graduate research in environmental remediation, which was also a worthwhile cause.

Stopping short of the slowly spinning rotors, Rhino turned with a bottle of blue sanitizer. Shaking his head, Wall said, "Don't worry. My bacteria can't infect people. They're not contagious."

"It's not for our sake," the woman said, patting him on the shoulder. "It's for the helo. We're already infected."

"That's ridiculous." Wall laughed, suddenly relieved. "My bacteria can't infect people."

She turned on him and shrugged. "Then it isn't your bacteria, is it?" With a pitying look, she said. "Feel your arm."

"Yeah? And?" He couldn't pull the long-sleeve camo up but knew how engorged it was, something she couldn't have missed during the strip-down.

"We've been seeing a lot of this lately." She pulled up her pant leg to reveal a swollen purple and green shin that matched his arm in appearance, scar tissue and everything. "Everyone with metal hardware gets them." The big man sprayed him down, helmet to combat boots, then proceeded to douse himself.

Wall stood still as if his chin was rusted open. "You're telling me that someone actually turned a rusting bacteria into a contagious disease."

She tilted her head, eyes pitying. "That about sums it up, Wall."

"We're infected," he whispered to himself as he wiped in the sanitizer.

He would have liked to say he couldn't imagine why someone would combine rusting genes with a pathogen. While weaponizing it made no sense for a sane man, a guy who was off his rocker might do anything. Too many people were angry, pissed off about the system, alone, driven to desperate measures by seclusion or fear or mental illness. A biohacker, one of the many fringe people with labs in their basements who did things like growing a third nipple, might do anything just to see what would happen as an experiment. Hell, his Romanian postdoctoral researcher had a lab in his attic so he could experiment on himself outside the purview of the university.

"No," he mouthed. "Marius."

His evil side liked to imagine how reality could go sideways, which helped him see the weaknesses in his own work, a reason he took so many precautions to isolate his research from the outside world, both in terms of humans and accidental release. Of all the bacterial strains in circulation in academic and industrial research, his bacteria were the most effective and therefore dangerous. His manipulation of their genetic codes and massively parallelized survival of the fittest approach meant his metal-eaters were a hundred times faster than their natural equivalents. A communicable disease based on his research couldn't be contained. Once unleashed, it would spread indiscriminately.

Perhaps it was like from a basement lab or a military facility like COVID-19 from Wuhan's lax practices. Or maybe Marius had a cure or vaccine because he wanted to take over the world. With control over the disease and who was immune, giving himself and his friends insane amounts of power.

Wall scrunched his face up. *Did Marius have friends?*

Working backward, Wall tried to figure out when his shoulder first started hurting and discoloring. Was it on the second or third day of the trip? Had it been that long ago? Almost two weeks. If so, then he was infected even before he left for the mountains. Marius probably timed it to align with his vacation to keep him out of the way.

The knowledge that he was responsible for the damage to the chemistry building—no, more—was his fault set in. The scope could be unimaginable, and— "It's my fault."

Unemotional and cool, Plink said, "Are you admitting that you did it?"

"No. I wouldn't—You think I did it, don't you?"

She shook her head. "Well, Wall, until a few minutes ago, we thought so. You looked guilty as a gaggle of whores on Sunday."

"Of course." He disappeared before the symptoms started. And he was the preeminent expert on rusting microorganisms.

She confirmed his thoughts as she straightened his facemask for him, then said. "Plus, someone cleared out your lab."

"Cleared out?" He knew his priorities were out of order, but the loss of his equipment and samples struck his mind as hard as a horseshoe to the forehead. That fantastic equipment, miracles of modern engineering, momentarily overtook his fear of what the disease could do to humans, to our infrastructure, if spread widely.

She nudged him toward the helicopter. "Your lab was completely empty. Scrubbed down and everything. It happened in the middle of the night after you left." The draft from the rotors batted his clothing like a cleanroom blower.

There weren't any seats in the chopper's main compartment, having been stripped clean and coated in some form of black synthetic substance. *Holy crap,* he thought. *They aren't joking around.* They protected the whirlybird from contamination, even removing the doors to provide unparalleled ventilation.

The jumbo-sized dude patted the edge of the floor where the door wasn't. "Have a seat. Boots on the skids." Wall followed the instructions while Rhino strapped him into a harness that extended to the helicopter's ceiling. None of it was metal. "There we go. You won an all-expenses-paid trip with a window view."

The woman said, "He's not a popper, is he?"

"Nah, Plink," Rhino said as he clapped his hand on Wall's shoulder. "He wouldn't dare contaminate our fine machine with sick. Would you, Wall."

"Yeah–No," Wall stuttered, scooting for a better perch between Plink and Rhino. "No puking."

Twenty seconds later, Anders and Paulson strapped into the other side of the helo as the blades spun faster. They lurched up and forward as the wind thumped over him, instilling a fervent gratefulness for the harness. The late afternoon wind rocked the chopper, momentarily pitching him weightless but not long enough to send him flying.

Looking down at the webbing holding him in, he asked, "What is the harness hardware made of?"

"Carbon fiber," Rhino said, looking out at the lush forests of the Pacific Northwest. "Did you know that Thomas Edison created the first carbon fiber in 1879 when he baked cotton threads at high temperatures, which carbonized them? By 1958, high-performance carbon fibers were invented."

"Thanks for the history lesson," Plink said. "Rhino never stops spouting facts."

As they reached the height of the surrounding mountains, Wall saw how hazy the skies were to the west, so thick with smoke that they glowed an eerie orange. Moments later, the whole world looked like it was on fire, with raging forests, embers of towns, and blackened pastures. If he'd been out there another day or two, the fires would have swallowed him along with everything else. He'd been stupid to ignore the smoke for so long.

When the helo banked to the north, he got his first view of Portland, or rather the patches of Portland that still stood. Flames consumed suburban blocks. Ash and cinders filled the foundations of homes. Buildings lay toppled into cement piles. Awed, he asked, "How did this happen?"

"Most gas pipes are steel," Plink said, her face glowing against the orange and black backdrop of Armageddon. "Water mains are metal too. Fire engines are mostly aluminum and steel. With the severe drought, Portland stopped irrigating parks and lawns, making for a tinderbox situation. The chaotic winds cinched the deal. There's no way to stop it."

"No," he said, struggling to comprehend the extent of the damage. "Wait. Did you say aluminum *and* steel?"

She patted him on the knee while surveying the madness below. "Yeah."

"Not good!" As if iron wasn't bad enough. Aluminum too? "Did they say iron too? Or was that my assumption?"

Endless lines of cars sat abandoned in the middle of the roads and freeways. Most of those that weren't consumed in the fires had either a dull brownish-red tinge or sickly gray. *Rust and ash*, he realized.

"Where is everyone? Shouldn't people be fleeing?"

"Some are downriver," she said, amazingly unperturbable, consummately at ease with chaos. "But most didn't make it. Without power or cell phones, they didn't know the fires were headed their way."

As the helo descended toward the Portland airport, he saw people sleeping on the shores of the Columbia River. *Not sleeping,* he corrected himself. *Dead, probably from asphyxiation.* He had seen mass graves in Ethiopia, people shot or starved to death by their government, dead children and all, but this was the United States of America. Things like that couldn't happen in his backyard. It wasn't that he prioritized American's lives over others. It was that he couldn't imagine how something like this could happen inside the most powerful nation in the world.

The remains of an airliner occupied a long portion of PDX's main runway. The airport terminals weren't burnt, but multiple sections lay collapsed like the ramparts of sandcastles under a child's foot. The once-robust combination of cement and steel was reduced to chaotic rubble. A giant crater replaced the massive gas tanks that stored jet fuel. Two Boeing 737s were nothing more than burned piles of aluminum. Several airliners tilted with broken landing gear. An engine had fallen from the wing of another. Not a single airplane shined of polished aluminum.

"Two weeks," he said. "I was only gone two weeks."

"Hell waits for no man," Rhino responded.

Wall cocked his head. "If it's been going on for that long, why are you just getting started now?"

"Let's see if you can figure it out?" Plink said.

"I uh, I suppose you didn't know where I was until I turned on my sat phone."

"Yes, and..."

"Perhaps you didn't know it was a pathogen until recently."

"Why do you think that is?"

He stuck his tongue into his cheek, pondering for a moment. "I'd rather not say."

"Give it the old college try, lieutenant."

"Did the government suppress the rusting's underlying cause? Officials at the highest levels?"

"Three points for Wall. Who said professors were inept?"

To the west of the airport, they descended toward a dirt field where the army set up a minimalistic refugee camp. Several hundred civilians sat, stood, and milled about on the north side of the field while about as many army personnel busied themselves or lounged on the other, everyone wearing masks or clothing over their faces. A giant white tent with a red cross on the top divided the two sides.

"Where is the rest of the National Guard?" Wall asked.

"What you see is about half of what we have," Rhino answered solemnly. "There should be about eight thousand around the state, but most are cut off, abandoned ship, or died already."

"How many bases survived?" Wall asked.

"Almost none. Small outposts mostly. The entirety of the US armed forces ran on machines, technology, and steel. This helo is perhaps the last of its kind. NORAD. Fort Bragg. Campbell, Hood, Benning. The bigger the base, the harder they fell. Every type of communication is failing. Satellite feeds are almost all that's left. Even if the armories and warehouses weren't already wreckage and dust, there is no way to get fresh equipment to the people who need it. What's left of this base won't last long."

He almost asked why there weren't more tents for the refugees, then realized that most modern tents used aluminum posts, posts that would rust and collapse. There wasn't a single chair or cot among them, no hint of metal anywhere.

Plink hopped out of the helo as it landed, having already unstrapped herself. "Rhino, Wall, follow me." In contrast, Wall wiggled about like one of those flapping tube people outside car dealerships in order to unfasten himself. As soon as his feet hit the ground, Rhino nudged him into double time to catch up with Plink. "You're gonna have to learn how to use those straps, lieutenant."

A question ate its way out of his brain like a rat infestation escaping a sinking ship. "Portland isn't the only city like this, is it?"

"No," she said, factual yet kind, sympathetic yet unrelentingly truthful. "The bigger the city, the earlier it fell. Tokyo. Shanghai. Delhi. New York. Mexico City. LA. Beijing. But small towns aren't without their problems."

"Des Moines?" Those two words nearly consumed him whole. His folks lived on a farm outside Iowa's capital. His cousins. His high school friends.

"It fell a few days ago."

"What about–"

Rhino steered him toward a large green tent. "The answer is yes. Yes to all of them."

"It can't be."

In an almost reverent voice, the big man said, "Remember this moment, Wall. This is the time and place where your definition of *can't* changed."

CHAPTER FOUR

W
all followed Plink into an army-green tent supported by blow-up tubes. *Smart,* he thought. *No need for metal.* Before entering, Plink sprayed them down yet again, overly precautious. Or was it a perfectly appropriate safety measure? Definitely the latter.

Inside, a group of techs with surgical masks and blue non-latex gloves sat in bright-green plastic chairs, typing at laptops wrapped in clear plastic. They'd overheat without ventilation, which explained the pile of backups next to them. A man in a white biohazard suit with the creased eyes of an old and weary soldier stood facing a shrink-wrapped display that showed what looked like a satellite image of the heavily wooded grounds around a giant house. Moving red dots marked the locations of soldiers converging upon the mansion from all angles.

The wrapping distorted the image from above, and the live body cam video from the soldiers. With combat rifles held at the ready, they swept the surrounding forest for threats. The high canopy shared little light from the setting sun.

Plink stood at ease in the tent commander's periphery, gesturing for Wall to stand at her side. And so, he fell into old habits that he thought he had shrugged away long ago. Almost of their own free will, his feet spread to the regulation seventy-six centimeters stance and his hands clasped behind his back. He felt rather than saw Rhino's presence behind him.

"Alpha team in position," the team leader said, the sound muffled by the display's shrink-wrapped speakers. The soldiers at the front of the rustic manor stopped.

The group around back also halted, accompanied by another man saying, "Gamma team in position."

"Fish, are you shiny?" the Alpha team leader asked.

"Affirmative," another man said. "Power cut...now."

"Budget and Frost, approach access point C."

The radio clicked twice, and two dots on the sat view approached the house. They paused. "We're in." Their red dots continued inside, and their cams showed the interior of a rustic bedroom. While he had no idea what the mission was, Wall's heart thumped quicker and louder, picking up on the room's tension.

Two more dots followed Budget and Frost through the side entrance.

"Buffa and Nando, you're up."

Two clicks squelched through the speakers, and two dots from the rear moved toward what might have been the back of a garage. While the first pair pushed farther into a hallway, Buffa and Nando paused. "We're in." Two dots followed them.

"Sammy and–"

The satellite feed distorted, flaring white, and pixelated, accompanied by the rumble of an explosion from the body cams. When the overhead video refocused, the whole region had turned into a crater, gobbling up the house and surrounding grounds like a great meteorite impact. Some trees were burning while others leaned into the giant pit, and still others broke in half.

"Alpha leader, report," said the tent's commander, eyes fixed on the screen, looking as if someone plowed worry lines into his forehead. Static. "Gamma report."

"Here," said the Gamma leader.

Video from a helmet cam appeared on the screen, showing a crater with bits of burning house inside. "Beginning rescue and recovery."

"Redford here. Alpha leader KIA. Franky is injured. The status of others is unknown. Requesting medevac."

"Medevac denied," the white-suited man said with far more sturdiness than Wall could manage in his shoes. "See to your men, soldiers. Save those you can and report back. Give mercy and honor the rest. Colonel Raddick Out." The static of the audio went silent, but the satellite video remained on the wrinkly screen. A pair of legs stuck out from under a fallen tree.

Wall tried to put his thoughts in order but came up with a jumble of mental images related to his bacteria, to the burning city, to the refugees outside this tent, and to the men dying in an explosion as he watched. His imagination extrapolated the gore to the death toll in Portland to all the cities around the world.

Without turning, the stoic old man said, "Talk to me, major. Tell me some good news."

"It's a mixed bag," Plink said. "We acquired the asset, Professor Terrance Mathison."

The senior officer rocked his jaw back and forth as he turned to face her, Wall, and Rhino. "I presume from the lack of broken bones that he is not our man." The colonel stood in front of Wall, eyes assessing. Not harsh. Not angry. Simply appraising.

She said, "From the explosion, I take it that Thorsten Towning is guilty as rust."

Wall cocked his head in surprise, then mentally replayed the sat view and cam feeds of the house before it exploded. The proportions and style fit his recollections of Towning's getaway home, the one deep in the woods. If the subterranean lab collapsed, it could easily have formed the crater that swallowed the house. Tall fir trees surrounded Towning's cabin on all sides.

"Son," Raddick said, bringing Wall's attention forward as only a senior officer could. "Are you going to be part of the problem or part of the solution?"

"Um." Too many contradictory thoughts formed a log jam in his head. He blinked hard as if that would help clear things up. Towning had all the resources and knowledge he needed to pull off a global pandemic. But why would he? He wanted to heal the planet, not burn it down. He spent decades working on technologies to save lives. And why would Towning blow up his own house, his sanctuary?

Rhino leaned forward and whispered in Wall's ear. "The word you're looking for is *solution*."

"Solution," Wall echoed hollowly.

"Good," Raddick said, clapping him on the swollen arm. "It's your lucky day. As of now, you are once again part of the United States Army, Lieutenant Mathison. Your singular purpose is to fix this nightmare. We need super-nerds like you on our side."

Wall didn't mind being called a nerd. When he was a grunt, they called anyone with an overly technical job a nerd. However, he flinched at being conscripted. After an awkward silence, Wall saluted with perfect form as only an active or veteran soldier could. "Yes, sir."

Turning to Plink, he said, "Major Bradshaw, you have any and all remaining resources of the Army. Make use of Mathison. Promise me that you will fix this."

"I was already planning on it, Ben," she said casually, her smile practically visible through her face covering. "Anything else?" Without giving the colonel time to respond, she said, "Good. We're off." Plink hooked Wall by the elbow and pulled him outside with Rhino already in the lead. His thoughts spun so fast that if he had rotors, he would have taken off like the HH-60. Ideas formed, then washed away. Priorities shifted up and down in lists of their own.

Outside, the sky had turned a deeper shade of peachy orange as the sun sank closer to the horizon. Rhino led them around several rows of soldiers who laid on the ground in various states of attempted R&R. Wall had planned to get some rest, a good meal, and some beer that night before jumping into the normal frenzy of life as a pre-tenure professor. Now, his mind was too active to relax, wired far more than tired. He jumped as the rumble of a far-off explosion rolled through camp.

"What do you think that was, lieutenant?" Plink asked.

When Wall didn't respond, Rhino said, "She means you."

Right, he thought. *I'm a lieutenant again.* Conscripted. "Uh, I don't know. Maybe a gas station."

Rhino shook his oversized head. As if talking about the score of a Timbers game, he mused, "Nah. It sounded more like the collapse of a building."

"Sorry, Wall. I'm with Rhino on this one."

A voice sounded in Wall's earpiece. "Plink, Anders here."

"Go ahead, Anders."

"The nerd's kit checks out. It's some next-generation gear, ultra-light, mostly carbon fiber and Teflon. Really pricey stuff. No metal except the keys, a heavily coated sat phone, his rusted GPS, a dust-filled phone, one non-functional headlamp, and his jacked-up pistol." The headlamp stopped working on his third night out, which Wall now realized was because of rust. He hadn't checked his phone since he left, so he hadn't noticed.

"Interesting," Plink said. "Wall, tell me. Were those gifts from our favorite mad scientist, Towning?"

Looking over his shoulder, Wall asked, "Yeah, how did you know?"

By way of an answer, she said, "Piece it together, lieutenant."

"Deductive reasoning," he intoned, thinking out loud. "You believe Towning is the mastermind that brought this down on us. Therefore, he orchestrated my trip. Inductive reasoning: gear like mine is too expensive for a professor, and Towning is rich."

Rhino stopped next to Anders, who kneeled over Wall's camping gear. "Look at this stuff." He handed Rhino the tent, which weighed in at a single pound.

The big man tossed it in the air a couple of times. "That's pretty slick."

Plink whistled. "Tell me, professor. Whose idea was your camping trip?"

"It was–" He wanted to say "mine," but that wasn't right. "It was Towning's." The genius encouraged Wall to get away from the grind, to go off-grid. He even suggested that he clear his head right before classes started. Wall initially resisted the idea of an extended excursion, preferring several shorter weekend trips, but Towning insisted that it would invigorate him and spur his research to new levels. And it would have if...

"Let me guess," Plink said. "He helped you plan your trip, right?"

"No–yes."

"Jackpot," Anders said. His gloved fingers fiddled with the backpack's hip-belt pocket. Carefully, he withdrew a credit-card-sized baggy. Without delay, he handed it to Plink. "Looks hand-written."

She read it aloud.

Wall,

We did it. We achieved the singularity. You are a true hero. You may not appreciate it yet, but your research leveled the playing field between man and nature. Without your genius, not even I could have accomplished our goal. Thank you.

To honor your contribution, I leave you my summer cabin in the Cascades. I hope you live out the rest of your days warmed by the fact that you changed the world for the better.

Sincerely, Thorsten A. Towning

Wall leaned over, yanked his desert scarf down, and heaved a few strands of jerky and a bit of bile. Momentarily, he wondered if the foul taste would cut short his life-long love for dried meats. *No,* he decided, sure that his thoughts should be elsewhere. His bond with cured meats was too strong. As long as he breathed, he would never divorce jerky.

His mind snapped back to what mattered. There it was in writing, proof that he helped bring down Portland. Not just Portland. Every other city around the world. He braced himself with a hand on each knee, focusing on a piece of gravel to steady his mind.

"No," he said, as he struggled not to hyperventilate. "I didn't want–" He dry heaved. "This wasn't–" He wiped his two-week-old beard with the back of his wrist. "You have to believe me. I wasn't part of this."

"Ha!" she laughed and shook her head as if this was the funniest thing on this side of the apocalypse. "Lieutenant, you're the brightest idiot that ever wore the uniform." She showed him the sealed note. "This is your get-out-of-jail-free ticket."

He stared at the letter through watering eyes. The handwriting was most definitely Towning's, a distinct thin and tall italic combination of block and cursive letters. This note condemned Wall as an accomplice in bringing about countless deaths and unimaginable destruction. His culpability, the result of *his* purpose-driven work, and his naive collaboration with Towning were close to short-circuiting his mind.

He had idolized the man who wrote this note, the man who worked to heal people before turning his resources to the environment, the man who incongruously destroyed everything.

"No," he said, wanting to deny a molten idea rising to the surface of his feverish mind. Wall recalled a conversation after too much Bordeaux where Towning said that to restore the balance between humans and nature, we needed to remove humanity's technological advantages, a juxtaposition to the plan for the long-term environmental singularity that would be friendly to both nature and mankind. Without tech, humanity would nearly die off. "I agreed with him," Wall said weakly. He relayed the conversation to Plink, who took it all in. "It was a thought experiment. He was so..."

Plink looked up at him with downturned brows.

"I was such a fool. I can't believe I drank his Kool-Aid."

Rhino held up a finger and asked, "Do you know where that phrase comes from?" Without waiting for an answer, he continued. "It was coined after a delusional pseudo-guru named Jim Jones, who led his cult, the Peoples Temple, to mass suicide. Over 900 people, including 304 children, killed themselves by drinking from a vat full of grape-flavored juice laced with cyanide. Interestingly, it was not actually Kool-Aid that they drank. The–"

"The history lesson can wait," Plink interrupted, an act that few would dare in light of his large form and presumably deadly skills. "Our lieutenant is struggling to comprehend our new hell. Don't flood his swirling brain with irrelevant facts."

"The best way to understand the present and the future is through a solid grasp of history," Rhino countered.

"You gotta be kidding me," Wall said, his mouth moving faster than his gray matter. "Kool-Aid. Towning works with a startup called Pure Nature Drinks. They use plant-based, carbon-negative cans. With help, he could have contaminated the drinks."

"I told you," Rhino said, flicking Plink's shoulder. "All that crunchy granola-loving crap is marketing to take advantage of the rich and gullible. Cans made from plant matter? No good could come from that."

Wall shook his head. "Towning said Pure Nature Drinks was one of a thousand steps toward sustainability."

Plink tapped her helmet, "TOC, this is Bradshaw. Give me Raddick. Over." She said TOC like the last half of tick-tock, which took Wall a moment to remember was the abbreviation for Tactical Operations Center.

"Raddick is busy. Over. I can relay a message."

Her facemask bunched up, then she said, "Yeah. We have confirmation of Towning's guilt. Over."

"Acknowledged."

"Out." Plink tapped her helmet again, then turned to Anders. "Deliver this note to TOC. Once they copy it, bring it back to me. Don't open it. Don't let it out of sight. Don't let them breathe on it. That note belongs to me. If they try to mess with you, tell them that I'll shove my fist so far down their throats that I can pull their skid-marked tighty-whities up and out their mouths. Got it?"

"Yes, sir." He jogged off double time.

"Rhino," she said. "Tell me you memorized that note."

If shemaghs could smile, then his did. "You know it, boss lady."

"That giant noggin of yours may prove useful yet." Turning to Wall, Plink said, "So, Lieutenant, how do we unwind the end of the world?"

CHAPTER FIVE

"Unwind?" Wall asked, looking at Plink, dumbfounded. He knew he should be more respectful of a senior officer but couldn't be bothered to give half a shit. "This mess?" He pointed at the smoke overhead that painted the sky Martian orange. "I have no clue."

Plink stepped in front of Wall and pulled up his scarf. "Well, my gangly super-nerd. It's time for you to find a big-ass clue because you're all we've got." If she could see the befuddlement in his eyes, she didn't give any indication. "So fix it."

He laughed. "Like it's that simple?"

"It's your job to kill this sickness, and it's our job to help you."

Wall started giggling uncontrollably and couldn't stop. "Kill. It?" He couldn't speak more than one word at a time because his absurd laughter clamped down on his lungs like a tightening lasso around his chest. Ash-rimmed tears of frustration beaded in his eyelashes, stinging as he continued to laugh. His vision started to tunnel as he hunched over in the standard hyperventilator's triangle of support. Rhino's meaty hand gripped Wall's arm so he wouldn't fall. It took another twenty thumping heartbeats before he regained his composure, cheeks sore from smiling too vigorously.

"Got that out of your system, did ya?" Plink asked, neither concerned with his erratic behavior nor overly compassionate.

He nearly burst into another round of painful laughter but managed to hold it together this time by stretching his jaws. "Yeah, I think so."

"Break it down for us Barney style," she said.

With nothing better to say, he held up two fingers. "Two words. We're screwed."

Without the slightest bit of frustration leaking through her easy demeanor, she said, "Then pontificate, professor. What would you need in order to get a clue."

"I don't know. I suppose I'd need samples of the disease, of Towning's modified microbes."

She pulled up her sleeve by a couple of inches, drew a giant knife from her tactical belt, whirled it in her hand, then nicked the back of her forearm. Holding the pointy end up with a red bead gleaming at the tip, she said, "Yeah, and..."

"And a lab."

She handed him a pencil and a tiny notepad. "Jot down the equipment you need."

"It's not that simple. You can't just go out and buy this stuff at Labs-R-Us."

"Leave that to me and the US Army's finest. Write your list and do it fast before the world burns."

He stared at her, pencil in one hand, tiny pocketbook in the other. "I'm not the right person for this. You need a medical doctor, not the Ph.D. kind."

She shrugged. "Fine, Wall. Tell me the type of medical docs you need, and I'll find them."

He counted off his index finger. "An immunologist." He tapped his middle finger. "And an infectious disease expert. We'd need a CRISPR expert to print the right genes. A production engineer to mass-produce a cure. The list goes on."

"Paulson," she snapped. "Find us Portland's finest immunologists and disease experts and we'll go from there."

Paulson ran toward Raddick's tent, nearly falling in his rush.

Wall furrowed his brows and locked gazes with Plink. With Barney-style slowness, he said, "You realize how impossible this is, don't you? How will we find the right people in this mess?" He waved around for emphasis. "Even if we find a lab with the right equipment, won't it just burn down? And without electricity, we might as well have no lab at all."

She tapped him on the helmet and said, "Lieutenant, that's why they pay you the big bucks. Time to become a rainmaker. Write down that list for Labs-R-Us."

"Okay," he said, trying to convey as much doubt as he could in a single word. Even so, he sat on the hard-packed dirt and started jotting down equipment and supplies in Plink's palm-sized notebook. Not being an expert in the various areas they'd need, he erred on the side of too much equipment, adding a column to the side to indicate how mission-critical that item was. Having devoured plenty of journal articles on communicable diseases, many suggested by Towning, he found that the list flowed from his pencil far faster than he thought. Working on the wish list kept his mind busy so he didn't have to think about what he'd done, what Towning piggy-backed off his research. Constructing a mental submarine to hold back the deepening pressures, he held off his otherwise suffocating guilt.

Meanwhile, Rhino vanished and Plink talked to various people through radio comms on channels he wasn't privy to. From time to time, she looked over his shoulder and read off a high-priority item. Once Anders returned, he laid out shrink-wrapped solar-charging battery packs that wirelessly fed various devices–also sheathed with layers of plastic, including radios, night-vision goggles, mini drones, and more.

"Break it down Barney style," Wall reminded himself. He divided the list into discovery, experimentation, and preparation steps, ignoring mass production because he knew so little about it and that stage wouldn't come until much later. His mental submarine sprang leaks several times, but he quickly recovered, forcing himself to focus. When he finished, sure that he had forgotten plenty of items, he took to his feet and handed over the list.

"That wasn't so hard, now was it?" Plink said like a nurse with a needle-shy boy.

Rhino stopped his recitation of the finer points of waterproofing and its importance in the history of mankind, quoting sources from China in the Xia

Dynasty to Nordic boat-making. His knowledge of all things waterproofing impressed Wall, even if he wasn't paying much attention. The guy was a virtual Wikipedia.

"Paulson," Plink said as she tore pages from the notebook and held them out like a deva to a lowly assistant, but with enough exaggeration to come across as funny. Humor, the ultimate in defusing the stress of chaotic situations. "Find us a superman-level miracle." The soldier, who hadn't spoken in Wall's presence yet, jumped up and ran the wish list to the command tent. "God, I love him," she said with a triple click as she tucked the remainder of her palm-sized notebook back into her chest pocket. "Such a good boy."

With a ballerina's leap, she launched forward eloquently, which was made all the more amazing because of the load she carried. "Time to gear up. Anders, check in with the flyboys. Make sure they're ready to go. Oh. And Anders. Don't lick the helo."

"Loud and clear." He ran off, winding his way between clusters of men.

Wall followed Plink as she walked away, Rhino two paces behind. Cracking his neck, he said, "You guys are spec ops, right?"

In his low, rumbling voice, Rhino said, "I'm a SEAL and she's 1st SFOD-D."

Wall whistled. "Holy–that's...seriously legit." He'd never met either. A Navy F'n SEAL and a god-damned Delta Force operator. At one point, Wall considered going into the Rangers, but they were like panda cubs compared to these guys. With a bit of effort, he squelched his inner fanboy.

"Did you hear that, Plink?" Rhino said. "We're finally legit."

"Good to know, Rhino. I've always wondered."

"So," Wall said. "How did you guys end up here?"

"Plink and I were passing through PDX on the way back from Sudan when they grounded all flights." Wall recalled that his news app wouldn't stop showing airplane crashes before he took to the mountains. He imagined planes falling out of the sky as rust ate them from the inside like microscopic gremlins.

A touch sad, Rhino said, "Plink and I are cut off from our teams, so we're operating independently in joint ops with Raddick. I suppose we're Team Wall now."

"Nope," Plink said quickly, waving her index finger in the air. "We are *not* calling ourselves that."

"Then what? Team Plink? The Plinkertons? Los Plinkeros?"

Adding a playful sassiness and dialing up her Hispanic accent, she said, "Nope, nope, nope, and hell to the nope."

"The Plinkets?"

"Nope."

"Plinky and the Brain?"

"Lieutenant Commander Rhino, I can 'nope' all day long."

After an exaggerated sigh, he asked, "Then what do you propose, Major Nope?"

"Alpha Bravo," she said.

Rhino scratched his covered chin. "Alpha makes sense. We're the top dogs. Or at least I am. I don't know about the rest of you. But why *Bravo*?"

With a "duh" intonation, she said, "It's for *Biological* unit."

"Alpha Bravo, huh? I kinda like that. Simple. Easy. Alpha Bravo gonna rain down hellfire. Alpha Bravo gonna kick your ass. Alpha Bravo gonna haunt your nightmare's nightmares. I can work with that."

In a pause between their back and forth, Wall asked, "What about Anders and Paulson? Are they like you guys? Spec ops?"

"Nah," said Rhino, clearly disappointed. "They're National Guard. Solid fellas, though. Paulson doesn't say much, but he can shoot the tits off a gerbil from a hundred yards. Hunting is pretty much the only thing that gets his mouth moving. He's slow to set up a shot, but when he does, it's solid gold. Anders has a bit of a gambling problem, which is how he ended up with that stupid beard and no mustache." Wall hadn't seen the man without a mask, so he had no idea, but he imagined a white-trash version of an Amish beard. "He lost it when Plink beat him in an arm wrestling match."

A few paces later, Rhino added, "Raddick hand-picked them for us. I usually wouldn't take them into a hot zone, but...these aren't usual times."

Wall batted at a flake of ash that landed on his yellow shooting glasses, sparking the thought that people think about the heat of flames when they imagine hell. They rarely talk about unending suffocation by smoke. Microscopic ash particles burn the lungs, sting the eyes, and mercilessly aggravate whichever nerves are responsible for sneezes. He couldn't recall the numbers, but more people died from smoke inhalation than from flames.

"How could you do this?" he soundlessly asked Towning. The genius hadn't shown any signs of being crazy or sadistic. He led with compassion toward others. While Towning could have used his incredible mind to create weapons, he spent his days inventing medicine-related technologies that benefited billions of people. The old man that Wall thought he knew sought to repair the Earth, not quite literally burn it to the ground. Connecting the man to the actions required such a long bridge he couldn't see his way across. The optimism that Towning shared for the future ran in opposition to what he unleashed.

They walked into the W.D. Jackson Armory as if they owned the place, passing a line of men and women queued up, waiting for their turn to check out a firearm or some other piece of gear. "Supply Sergeant Miller," Plink said above the other conversations and walked past a woman with a plastic clipboard. "In a hurry."

"Not again," Miller groaned, adjusting her pristine white bio-suit and handing her clipboard to Rhino.

Plink pulled a next-gen black Kevlar vest from a hanger and thrust it at Wall, who barely pulled it over his broad shoulders in time to snatch an army-green backpack out of the air. Trying to keep up with the major, he opened the bag as they walked forward and loaded it with several knives, a vacuum-sealed pistol with an under-mounted light, half a dozen sealed 5.57 magazines, several types of med kits, and more. Plink called out each as she went, and Rhino followed behind, taking notes of their all-expense-paid shopping spree.

When the pack was fully loaded, Plink handed him a custom carbine with black-green heavy-duty coating from butt to tip and a clear cap covering the barrel, presumably to keep germs from getting in.

"Thanks, Miller," Plink said as they walked back out under the angry gazes of the soldiers who had to wait for their turns.

"Thanks," Rhino reiterated, handing the clipboard back.

As soon as they were back outside, under the orange of the smoke-filled sky, Plink said, "Double time." Despite the intervening years, Wall automatically sprang into the regulation cadence, flanked by the tier-one operators, matching them step for step. His poorly packed kit bounced and swayed awkwardly, hard corners poking him with every footfall. The army wasn't known for its fluffy pillows and soft edges, and now he was back in the middle of it.

Moments later, they met Paulson and Anders at the helicopter. A tech with a large container of hand-pumped spray drenched them from hood to sole in blue disinfectant. Wall found his spot at the doorless edge and fastened himself into the harness flanked by Plink and Rhino.

"Where to, Plink?" the pilot asked during the final stages of pre-launch.

"Marquam Hill. OHSU Campus," Plink answered. "The Vollum Institute." Wall visited them only a few months before for a workshop. Vollum was one of the premier research facilities in the region. Among the various labs, they would have everything a specialist needed for the impossible task of developing a vaccine or cure.

The pilot said, "Romeo 466 clear for takeoff north helipad, fly runway heading 31. And away." They soared into the air far too fast for a sane person to appreciate, then slowly spun as they climbed, which for a man who recently puked, didn't sit any too well. The dizzying view showcased the carnage from the fires, the devastation caused by his genetic manipulations. With so few trees surviving the fires, the decimation of Portland was all the clearer.

Clusters of people moved here and there among the desolate ashscape, largely close to waterways. Too many fires continued in pockets around the city and suburbs, each pushed eastward by the same Chinook winds that buffeted the helicopter. As they flew south over the Willamette river, people clung to the banks. Others waved for help from atop damaged bridges, looking woefully desperate and weak. Every fourth downtown building had slumped, collapsed, or burned. Wall watched a little girl wave at them through a broken window of a tall apartment building, a floppy stuffed bunny clutched in her other arm.

"Uh, Plink," the pilot said, coming to a hover and banking to the left so they could see the medical campus. What wasn't currently burning had already charred like overcooked toast. Any equipment in that ocean of fire was destroyed. Worse, anyone in there was already dead whether they knew it or not.

"Plan B," Plink said. "Find a spot on the south side of Oswego lake." She relayed the coordinates. In a few seconds, the aircraft turned and sped south, veering around a thick cloud of smoke that blocked out the nearly set sun. As the light faded, the embers and active fires grew more pronounced.

"Towning?" Wall mouthed. "What the hell did you do?"

CHAPTER SIX

Illuminated by the reflections of fire-lit clouds, the helo descended over Lake Oswego onto a well-manicured lawn of a stucco-sided home with a terracotta tile roof that had collapsed on the south side. In the last bits of light, he noted the missing giant front door and fully consumed handrail on the steps. Those were his doing. Both his success and his sickening failure.

"This is as close as we can get."

"It's perfect, Captain Bailey," Plink said, showing him the "okay" sign. "Rhino, you're on tail. Wall, stick to my ass like a manure-deprived horsefly."

Wall coughed, which had nothing to do with the smoke and everything to do with the unexpected mental image. He jogged after her, not in standard double time, but mimicking her smooth, toe-first footwork, a style that didn't feel natural. He assumed it was important for aim and or something that he didn't bother ask about while entering unknown territory. During the short flight, Rhino balanced and adjusted Wall's pack, so it fit snugly to his back, minimizing the rattle and discomfort.

In the dark, Plink whispered, "Wall, have you had the pleasure of meeting Doctor Magali Nellibi?"

His throat itched, dry and covered in soot. "She's the chair of immunology at–" his voice hitched on a slug of phlegm caught in his throat.

Before he could continue, she finished for him, "at the Vollum Institute, which is now up in smoke."

Imitating the operatives' stealthy jogging style, his bad knee clicked with each footfall. "Yeah. She's brilliant. Met her twice."

"Good," Plink said. "You're about to knock on her front door." They slowed to a walk at an iron gate barring the entrance to a stone-lined driveway. "Your mission is to convince her to come with us."

Plink ran at the head-height metal gate and leapt over it with nothing but the aid of her hands, flying sideways inches above the top and landing silently on the other side. She looked like a parkour nut, capable of inhuman feats.

Rhino kneeled at the foot of the gate and whispered, "Wall, you're next." Even with the lift from the Navy SEAL, he botched his attempt to emulate her. Without the powerful man's assistance, he never would have made it. On the far side, he fell on his ass and cursed as he scraped his elbow.

"Need a hand?" Rhino asked quietly, somehow already standing over him with his gloved hand offered. Feeling far more injured than the little scrapes could account for, Wall nearly batted the larger man's hand aside, but drowned his bruised ego and accepted the aid.

As they approached the large house, Plink clicked on her pistol light, illuminating the brick pathway, stylish shingle siding, and oversized oak front door. The once-fancy iron door handle now decorated the doormat with a combination of metal, rust chips, and dust. He stared at it for a moment, confronted with his first up-close evidence that Towning had released augmented forms of his bacteria. From the helicopter, he couldn't see the underlying cause of the devastation. Up close, the rusting was undeniable.

Plink prodded Wall forward and said, "Time to shine, Lieutenant."

Completely unprepared for what he was about to say, Wall pressed the doorbell to no effect. "Duh!" No metal, no electricity, no doorbell. He palmed his forehead, which only bumped his helmet. "Twice stupid," he mouthed. Knocking on the door, he called out, "Doctor Nellibi! It's Terrance Mathison. We–I need to speak with you."

"Movement inside," Rhino whispered through the earpiece. Wall looked over his shoulder to find that the big man had vanished, somehow seeing inside, probably through an infrared scope. He imagined crosshairs aimed over his shoulder. "Female adult. Walking down the stairs."

Wall shifted awkwardly, considering how strange it was to stand on a colleague's front porch dressed in full combat gear while the city burned. How would he react if their positions were reversed, and he was holed up at home? The submachine gun certainly wouldn't help ease the doctor's nerves. What could he say to convince her to leave with them? On that note, he turned to Plink and held out his hand to block the blinding pistol light. "Where are we going next?"

She clucked her tongue. "That, my new friend, is up to you."

He pointed at his chest, squinting at the bright light. "Me?"

He couldn't see into the darkness behind her shooting glasses but assumed she was closing her eyes in frustration. "Either we hunt down more super-nerds like you or we hunt down a lab. Raddick's team identified several of each that might be in fire-free zones. With OSHU burned down, Nellibi was at the top of his list. After that, you choose where we go."

"Okay, then." He hadn't thought about Nellibi specifically, but she had many of the skills they needed, with deep knowledge and experience in dealing with antibiotic-resistant bacterial infections. Wall turned back to the door and knocked again. "Doctor Nellibi. It's Terrance Mathison from the University of Oregon. We need to talk."

"She's coming to the door," Rhino whispered through the helmet. "Careful. She has a pistol. She'll be at the door in three, two, one."

"Doctor Nellibi? It's Terrance Mathison."

"Terrance?" said a muffled voice from behind the door, her husky mildly Indian accent easily identifiable. "What are you doing here?"

"She's watching you through the eye-hole."

He looked directly at the lens. "I need your expertise with a set of infectious diseases. There's an outbreak, and your skills are crucial."

There was a long pause. Wall nearly broke the silence, but she spoke half of a heartbeat before he caved. "Can't this wait until the morning? It isn't safe out there."

"We need you and the fires are coming. Your house won't last 'til morning." He didn't know if he was right, but it sounded true.

The deadbolt ground like sick metal, and Nellibi cracked the door open with an angry squeak.

Too quick to keep up, Plink dashed past him, and kicked the door in, snapping the door's chain latch and knocking the doctor off her feet. Without breaking her momentum, Plink stormed in with her carbine raised and scanned the interior, then kicked Nellibi's fallen pistol back toward Wall, and set her knee down on the doctor's upper back, pinning her face down. Before he could call out, "Plink, no!" Rhino shoved him aside to clear the room.

"Sorry, doc. You had a pistol. We couldn't take any chances." While Nellibi shrieked to the point of running out of air, Plink zip-tied her wrists with a single hand, the other still searching the foyer with her pistol. "Rhino, extract."

The oversized man picked the woman up smoothly, threw her over his shoulder, and jogged out, nearly knocking Wall over in his quick exfil.

"Wall," Plink barked, pushing him to the door, "Follow Rhino." The whole exchange took no more than a few heartbeats. Wall had fast reactions, but nothing like these tier-one operators. In the Army, he ran through drills but had never witnessed a show of speed and force like this before. The big man moved as smoothly with an extra buck-thirty load on his shoulders as he did unburdened.

"Sorry, Doctor Nellibi," Plink cooed while Rhino set her down behind an ash-covered Land Rover out of view from the house. Plink's light shined over their captive's shoulder, making her blink and squint, accentuating her wrinkles, a rag stuffed in her mouth. The harsh light accentuated a few new gray hairs and blemished skin that he didn't remember from their prior encounters, or perhaps he'd never seen her without a heavy dose of makeup. He had been sure she was about forty, but she now looked far older.

Wall took a knee in an attempt to emulate his frightening team. The situation went from talking to kidnapping stunningly fast. He realized that during the frenzy he was a detriment to Alpha Bravo, not an asset, getting in the way, an extra concern they didn't need. In an ideal world, Nellibi wouldn't have had a gun and everything would have gone smoothly, but if the world were ideal, Towning wouldn't have used Wall's research to throw flaming dog crap all over it.

"Ma'am." Plink snapped her gloved fingers several times in front of the woman's triangular nose, focusing her. "I'm going to pull the muffle from your mouth and you're going to remain calm, understood?"

Nellibi nodded slowly, moaning what could have been a yes.

"Good."

In an impressively even voice for someone who experienced the intensity of these elite soldiers, Nellibi said, "Terrance, what in the world is going on?"

"Sorry," he said, emphasizing his concern vocally, aware that his face was hidden by the desert scarf and his shooting glasses reflected light. "I didn't know they were gonna do that."

"Precautions, Doctor Nellibi," Plink said instead of apologizing. "You had a weapon."

Ignoring Plink, she searched Wall's yellowish-tinted glasses for human eyes. "This is insane, Terrance. Absolute insanity."

In way of contrition, he asked, "Can we untie her?"

Turning the question on the doctor, Plink said, "Stay put. No quick motions. Okay?" She reached around the doctor with a short knife that emerged from nowhere and quickly cut the ties.

"Ahhh," Nellibi moaned as she rubbed her wrists. "Now, what is this craziness all about?"

"Sorry, again," Wall said. Upon seeing the get-on-with-it expression pursed on her face, he cut to the heart of it. "Thorsten Towning released pathogens that are causing un-checked corrosion of metal. Our technological scaffolding is crumbling. Gas mains are failing. Electricity is out everywhere. Water pipes burst. He ran his gloved knuckle along the door handle of her rapidly aging Land Rover, coming away with reddish-brown flakes to accentuate his point. While Wall spritzed a heavy layer of sanitizer over his glove, her eyes jumped back and forth between his hand and the door.

He expected her to ask questions or demand to be released, but she sat there, eyes blinking over and over. "I know this is a lot to take in, but Towning weaponized rust. The smoke you smell is due to gas and electrical fires caused by the rusting disease. When we have you in the air, you'll see that a good portion of the greater Portland area is up in flames." As if to accentuate his point, a dime-sized chunk of ash landed on the tip of Plink's pistol, casting an eerie shadow over the light.

"Towning spread the diseases worldwide. We're assembling a team to cure it, but we know too little and have little time to act." He surprised himself with how confident he sounded, having not fully accepted their stupidly impossible mission yet. The very act of recruiting Nellibi somehow solidified his own role in what was most likely a futile effort. "We need to get the right people to the right places before everything rusts and it's too late."

"Okay," she said. "I'm in if we bring my family."

"No can do," Plink said. "We don't have room."

"Then I'm staying. I can't live without them."

"We'll get them to safety," Wall said before Plink could speak. He guessed that she was on the verge of kidnapping the woman again. "Then we go crank out a cure."

Nellibi held out her hand to shake. "Deal."

Wall started to reach for the proffered hand but pulled away. "Sorry, not without a glove."

"Go inside and get your family," Plink ordered, her commanding voice leaving no room for interpretation. "We leave in three minutes. Don't bring anything we can't douse with disinfectant. Shoes, warm clothes, and life-critical meds are all you need." When Nellibi didn't move, Plink tapped her wrist and said, "tick-tock."

With surprising speed, the older woman climbed to her feet and ran barefoot to the house.

"This'll work out just fine," Plink said, as calm as if they were out on a Sunday stroll. In contrast, Wall's muscles shook, his nostrils flared, and his heart pounded uncomfortably. She casually sprayed herself down with disinfectant. "I was born to scare the crap out of civvies."

Squelching her radio twice before speaking, she said, "Romeo 466, this is Plink. Prepare for outbound in twelve mikes with three additional passengers."

"Acknowledged. Twelve mikes with a total of two pilots and eight passengers."

She clicked the radio two times and turned to Wall. "With Nellibi on board, what's the plan? Drop off the family? Find a lab? Or more nerd hunting?"

Without hesitation, he used her vernacular. "Nerds first. Always life first."

She tossed something small into the air, pulled down her mask, and caught it in her mouth before her scarf sprang back into place. Chewing on whatever it was, she said, "I hope we don't live to regret those words." Withdrawing her tiny notepad, she flipped to a page and handed it to Wall. "We've got locations on four candidates who live in fire-free neighborhoods."

He scanned the messy scrawl.

9.1pts	Goldstein, Ari	– Geni4 Corp
8.3pts	Ueskev, Mika	– OHSU
7.6pts	Smith, Brenda	– OHSU
6.9pts	Konter, Jasper	– RNAY Inc

While Wall looked at the candidates, Plink stepped behind him and continued tugging on straps, repositioning his armor, and shifting his new gear into different pockets, starting where Rhino left off. "So," she said, "Are you cuddle buddies with any of those nerds?" He grunted as she yanked the shoulder strap tighter, digging into his armpits and nearly knocking him off balance.

He bobbed his head. "Yeah, I know Brenda Smith. She's a rockstar in the vaccine world, but she works with viruses, not bacteria."

"So, she's a no?"

"Yeah, we should–Whoa there!" He jumped and skipped forward when her hand pushed between his thighs.

"Calm down, Romeo." She was kneeling, waving him back. "Don't get your g-string in a bunch. I'm fixing your pistol harness."

Rhino's shoulders shook from half-stifled laughter as he scanned the darkness for possible threats.

"It's fine right where it is," he said and patted it for confirmation.

"It's all wrong. Either get it right or get dead, soldier. It's your choice." She beckoned him back and he assented to a little more groping.

After re-strapping the Velcro and slapping him on the ass, she asked, "Do you know anything about Goldstein at Geni4 Corp or Konter at RNAY Inc?"

He tested the holster, and to his surprise, it was at the perfect height and angle for a swift, smooth draw. "I read about RNAY a while back." He pronounced it as *Ren-ay*. "It's a startup that makes compact automation systems that streamline CRISPR integration with–"

"A 'yes' would suffice," Plink said. "All I need to know is, would RNAY make Konter useful to us?"

He reached for a bit of jerky, which wasn't there, and said, "Could do."

"Stop," she said mechanically. "You're filling me with confidence."

"Look, I have no clue what we're dealing with, so–"

"Shhh," Plink hushed him. "Nellibi is coming. Decide now. She needs confidence."

Sure enough, the doctor was locking her cringe-worthy deadbolt, toting a backpack, while a younger blond woman, maybe in her late thirties, carrying a boy in dinosaur pajamas. The little one may have been six years old plus or minus a year.

"Rhino," Plink said. "Take the lead. Wall, you're next. Eyes sharp." He mimicked the big man's silent walking style and fell in behind at a casual pace.

In that friendly adult way of talking to a child like he's a dog, the general said, "Hi, I'm Plink. What's your name?"

"It's okay," said the blond woman. "You can talk to the nice soldier."

"Lucas." His voice was quiet and sweet, too perfect for the chaos of Portland, marked by the orange glow of the sky.

"Tell me, Lucas. Have you ever ridden in a helicopter before?"

"No." He sounded cautiously excited.

"Would you like to?"

"Weeee!" The boy's shrill squeal made Wall jump. "Can we, Mimi?"

"Yes, Lucas," said the younger woman. "We can."

The boy squeaked again, shrill but happy. "Did you hear that, Momo? We're going on a helicopter."

Both moms? Wall thought. The fact that they were a couple didn't surprise him. The age difference did. *Go Nellibi.*

With false merriment, Nellibi said, "Sounds like a fun adventure."

At the electric gate, Rhino pulled a pin from the lever arm and the gate swung open under its own weight. Rubbing his scraped elbow, Wall suspected they didn't open the gate that way on their entrance as a test of Wall's agility, a physical exam that he failed. He would have to trust that Rhino and Plink had purposes for nearly everything they did. He was the grunt, the translator between tier-one operators and domain-specific geeks.

Nellibi sidled up to Wall and said, "Tell me what's going on."

Wall decided to collect more intel before answering, guessing that she knew more from two weeks in hell than he did in the last two hours. "What do you know already?"

"What you told me and the bits of news on satellite TV before the power went out."

As professionally as he could while placing his feet exactly where and how Rhino did, Wall said, "Please elaborate."

"Well, it all fits your rusting disease. The plane crashes started first because they received the most regular maintenance and represented the highest rate of common vectors. The House and Senate went into unscheduled recesses like the cowards they are. Then there were all the car accidents, again complex, often used, and regularly maintained metal machines. The Willis Tower fell. The Golden Gate Bridge collapsed. Should I keep going?"

"No. That's fine." Wall rolled his shoulders and felt how the net results of Rhino's and Plink's adjustments to the pack improved his posture.

Lucas and her Mimi were busy twirling their fingers while making helicopter sounds and laughing. The boy's ability to enjoy life while the world collapsed around him was inspiring. Wall had seen Ethiopian children play soccer with a plastic water bottle in the middle of a war-induced famine. Kids with joints that stuck out and distended bellies miraculously found ways to smile.

Even still, the young ones were the hardest to cope with. It wasn't just their suffering in the moment, it was their prospects if they lived through the ordeal. Mental health problems. If America went the way of war-torn regions, his growth would be stunted and he'd end up with any number of long-term illnesses.

Nellibi interrupted his thoughts with a whisper. "So, where are you taking us?"

Still lacking a plan, he diverted. "Do you know Ari Goldstein or Mika Ueskev?"

"Yeah," she said. "Ari is a…" She let several paces go by before continuing. "Interesting man." She clearly didn't mean the good kind of *interesting*. It was the type that meant, "I'm above bad-talking people but he's a complete asshole." The problem was that her distaste for Doctor Goldstein might mean that he enjoyed insensitive jokes or that he didn't work well with others. If he was mean like a cockroach, able to survive anything and everything, he might just be what they needed. Yet, cooperation would be a must for the team, and if the guy already grated on her, he couldn't be a bad choice.

Pressing, he said, "I need your opinion, can you collaborate with him?"

"In that case, he's the kind of man who would let the world crumble so he could take notes, including the number of times babies cried."

"Ha!" Plink laughed. With a sidewinder of sarcasm, she said, "Tell us how you really feel."

Not prone toward superstition or hocus pocus, Wall crossed his fingers and asked, "What about Mika Ueskev?"

"Oh, Mika is fantastic, unique, and egotistical, but fantastic. Is he on our team?" The hopefulness in her voice told Wall all he needed to know.

"We're on our way to Mika now."

Leaning in, she whispered, "Terrance, be honest with me. Am I the only doctor on your team?"

He let the time of a few paces drift past before answering. "Yes. It's the two of us and the Army's finest."

"Well, shhhhh...oot. Oh, no baby boy. Momo is just fine." Mimi passed the boy into Nellibi's hands. "We're going on a super-fun adventure, aren't we?" The rotor hadn't started to spin yet as they walked into the grandiose lawn of their neighbor. "Look at that?" Momo said. "That's a big helicopter, isn't it?"

While Wall decontaminated himself, Paulson and Anders saw to Nellibi and her family. Anders said, "Sorry, but this is gonna suck. You have to disrobe so we can disinfect you."

"Do we have to?" Mimi asked, looking nervously between Nellibi and her son.

"It's okay," Nellibi assured Anders and Mimi.

The little boy didn't protest to the nudity but began crying, squirming, and kicking as soon as Anders started spraying him down. It took both moms to keep the boy in place long enough to douse him in disinfectant. On the one side, he didn't want the little one to suffer. On the other, they were about to step into an incredibly well-balanced contraption that needed absolutely zero rusted parts. Between appeasing a child and opting for safety, he would choose safety every time. A cold and uncomfortable child will soon find a way to smile, a dead one won't. After they dressed in a layer of sterile army clothing, all of which looked hilarious on the women and even more so on the boy, the helicopter's rotors began to spin and Anders drowned them in another layer of the bleach concoction, eliciting even more screams.

While Anders lashed the ladies in at the back of the helicopter, the rest of them remained at the open doors. This time, Wall managed to fasten the harness with greater ease and as far as he could tell, Rhino and Plink didn't even check if he did it right. He wasn't sure if this meant they cared less about him now that Nellibi was onboard or if they trusted him and his animalistic imperative to avoid falling out of a helo.

While waiting for Anders to finish up, Wall's brain fuzzed over, so it took him a moment to realize what he was looking at. A pair of limp bodies lay at the edge of the lawn, one an elderly woman with a blood-streaked white blouse and the other an even older man with a similarly ruined sweater. They could have been anyone's grandparents.

"It's okay," Plink said, patting Wall's gloved hand, then leaned toward him and bonked her helmet on his shoulder. "They endangered the helicopter and therefore the mission. The mission is all."

"The mission is all," he parroted, pretty sure he didn't believe it. They shot an elderly couple in their own yard. In America. Absolutely insane. It wasn't the death itself that bothered him. What really got to him was that he was responsible for their deaths. So many deaths he couldn't fathom. He was at fault for the largest act of terror ever. These two deaths shouldn't have meant anything, but he couldn't take his eyes off them.

CHAPTER SEVEN

"Tell me, Terrance," Doctor Nellibi enunciated slowly and way too loud, overcompensating for the *whoop-whoop* of the rotors even though the helmet microphone and earpieces were top-notch. "What kind of lab do we have?"

"About that..." Wall grimaced, not bothering to twist so he could see her tucked deep in the cabin while his feet rested on the helicopter skid hundreds of feet above the ground. He sighed heavily. "My first two options are no-goes."

"Why? What were they?"

"Towning raided my lab in Eugene, then blew up his personal lab in the mountains."

As Lucas wailed loud enough to pick up on Nellibi's mic, she hiccupped. "So, it is only you and me with no lab?"

"We have more than we had half an hour ago," His voice was more reassuring than expected. "It's a start."

"Oh my giddy aunt," she said an octave lower than normal and hiccupped again. "I had no idea the fires were so bad." From downtown to the outlying suburbs, what wasn't burning was blacked out, either burned or devoid of electricity. The scale of it was difficult to comprehend. He watched the hellscape reflect off Plink's protective glasses, incapable of understanding the global scale of the ruins he helped bring about.

A little over a whisper, Nellibi said, "Thank you for saving us, Wall." He almost said that stopping off for her was Plink's idea but decided that the major would correct the misconception if she wanted. If she really could read people, she would want Nellibi indebted to him for a better working relationship. Bad cop. Good cop.

In awe, the doctor said, "This is…"

"I think the word you're looking for is *unimaginable*," Plink finished.

From her spot deep in the metal beast, Nellibi asked, "Who knew that a disease could do this?"

"Towning knew," Wall said silently. "I should have known. I should have seen it." If he'd been looking for the signs, he could have stopped this from ever happening. As they flew in silence, or rather in the intense noise of the open-sided helicopter with wind batting unnervingly at him, he tried to see the leaves for the trees, the details he'd missed. For a man who so often listened to the naughty angel on his shoulder, considering every way he could tweak things to fuck shit up, he'd been blind to the old man's intentions.

A few minutes later, Plink broke through the trance that had captured them all. "Doctor Nellibi, do you know how to operate a pistol?"

"Yes," she said confidently. "I fired it a few times. Some lady friends took me to the range after church." Wall choked over the image of a group of bible-thumpers in their Sunday best strolling into a stereotypical testosterone-heavy shooting range. Not exactly the usual patrons.

Kind and motherly, Plink said, "You were brave to answer the door. Foolish but brave. If things had been even slightly different, I could have hurt you. Don't be brave again. That's what we're for."

"Thank you," Nellibi said, her appreciation almost bottomless in her husky voice.

Plink wasn't nearly as delicate with Wall, but he took no insult at the discrepancy. Nellibi needed more bolstering. In contrast, Plink needed Wall to be harder, to be a go-between for warrior and nerd, not just a nerd. The combination of Wall's rusty Army training and Ph.D. set him apart from both and put him at the uncomfortable fulcrum of their mission. His skills and reactions needed to change fast if he was to help rather than hinder the elite warriors. He failed his first test of acquiring Nellibi and he needed to do better on their next outing–if they brought him on at all. It would probably be safer for the elite soldiers to go without him.

Wall spared a look at the doctor, who cradled Mimi, or whatever her real name was, and her son. A worry wedged into the crevices of his mind. *Did she join Alpha Bravo only to get her family to safety? Would she abandon the search for a cure or vaccine once out of Portland?* Her mission, her priorities, might be at odds with *the* mission. Then again, her family might provide the incentive he needed, a desire to fix things for her wife and child.

Watching the flames glide by outside their wiffleball of a helicopter, he asked, "Doctor Nellibi, why did you believe me about the diseases?"

"You showed up at *my* door with gun-toting soldiers. The news covered the mass rusting, but nobody ever came up with a reasonable explanation. Too many conspiracy theories. Misdirection. The government was obviously suppressing the flow of information." Wall had forgotten that Plink had confirmed their save-themselves mentality. There was too little time for so much information to sink in. But it made sense that Towning had help, maybe even people from both ends of the political spectrum. Religious fundamentalists and emphatic environmentalists. One man, even a genius, couldn't cause this flaming pile of chaos without help. *Was Marius part of it?* Towning had helped Wall find the eccentric bioengineer, a perfect plant. It only made sense.

Nellibi continued. "My sinks. My travel mug. My electronics. My car. It all started rusting two weeks ago. The only reason a bio-rusting researcher would come for *me* is if people are infected with his diseases." There was more than a pinch of accusation in her voice, adding to his sense of complicity. "As they say, the pieces fit."

"Fair enough, doc."

After a short pause, she said, "Hey. Why are you only starting now? Shouldn't you have formed a team weeks ago?"

"Towning tricked me," he said bitterly. "At his insistence, I was back-packing. I only found out hours ago." Talking about the old man's deceit struck a hanging burr that he only managed to contain by clenching his jaw and gnashing his eyes shut. "As you stated, there was an effective top-down program to suppress the flow of information."

She laughed with no mirth or humor in her voice, only condescension. "Welcome back to civilization–or what's left of it. You're lucky he didn't just off you."

"Yeah, Towning was a regular old sweetheart. He gave me his house and booby-trapped it. I was lucky I didn't die in the explosion." He mentally replayed the satellite and body-cam images of the flames and crater. Nothing and everything about Towning fit. It was all like too many mangled puzzle pieces.

"We're about to land," the pilot announced.

"Doctor Nellibi and Wall," Plink said. "You're coming with Rhino and me. Anders and Paulson, keep the mother and daughter company." They set down in a Safeway parking lot, ash flying into a blizzard around them, flames lighting the sky. The north side of the mini-mall had already burned like an unattended marshmallow while the southern half miraculously remained unscathed.

The fickleness of flames.

Plink barked, "Wall, you're on my fine posterior like shit on a pig. Nellibi, you're next. Rhino, you're on cleanup. Fall in." She spun on her toes and speed-walked to the narrow alleyway between a sandwich shop and a dry cleaner.

Plink quickly led the way up two steep blocks, followed by a right and a left. Along the way, Plink taught Wall a few hand signals she'd use if the need arose. Most were pretty simple. He already knew the basics from the Army. "Stop," "Look," and "There" were no-brainers. He'd forgotten things like "sniper" and two-digit numbers.

After winding this way and that on curved streets and cutting diagonally across a crisped park, Plink pointed at a 1970s beige ranch house with peeling dark trim. "That's it." The wood garage door panels were warped, and the windows looked like they hadn't been opened in decades. The front yard was filled with untrimmed bushes and random tufts of tall wild grass, a perfect fire starter.

"Here?" Wall asked. With boarded-up windows, the place might have been abandoned decades ago. She made several hand gestures to Rhino, who ran silently and leapt into a half-dead pine tree in the front yard like he was a giant camouflaged gorilla. Two mini drones flitted to life and flew out of Rhino's tree and over the dumpster of a house.

"Wall, you knock. Nellibi, stay behind and slightly to the right of Wall, your left hand on his right shoulder. I'll be behind both of you."

Feeling entirely too exposed, Wall pulled down his mask and led the way to the front door, which was behind a crumbling metal security grate. He knocked on the doorjamb and jumped back into Nellibi as the door handle fell and shattered on the stoop. Flakes of rust puffed into a cloud from the security grate, dusting the inner door and the front porch. Cursing, he nearly knocked the doctor over in his attempt to keep his boots from getting even more contaminated.

"Shhhh," Plink hissed.

"Jackrabbit," Rhino said, his deep voice easily distinguishable through the earpieces. The giant man flew from the tree overhead onto the ill-maintained house's roof like a long jumper and disappeared from view.

With equal grace, Plink darted around the right side of the house with her M4 held ready to fire, a smooth predator. Such was her speed that by the time Wall managed to raise his own M4, she had already rounded the corner of the house. As calm as a guest at a southern brunch, she said, "Wall, protect the doc. Nellibi, stand back-to-back with Wall as the two of you slowly rotate like backward dancers. Eyes sharp. Rhino, report."

The big man counted down from three. On one, the microphone picked up a frightened yelp and a short scuffle, followed by "jackrabbit acquired." Wall could only imagine what it would be like to have Rhino bear down on him with any amount of aggression. Normal humans weren't intended to take a fraction of the abuse that such a man could deliver, even by accident.

Plink said, "Identify the rabbit."

Like a pleasant telephone operator, he said, "Hold one." The mic picked up a stream of curses in a foreign language—maybe Russian or Serbian or something like that. "And, survey says...Mister Mika Ueskev."

"Rhino," Plink said as if reprimanding a toddler. "You didn't hurt the nerd, did you?"

"Nah. You're fine, aren't you, Mister Ueskev?" Wall imagined the big man lifting the foreign doctor by the collar and dusting him off like a dirty towel.

A few houses down, drapes shifted as a shadowed face popped up in a mostly glassless window, then vanished. He raised his combat rifle and swept over the spot with his vision magnified by the ACOG 6X48 scope on his assault rifle.

Rhino's mic picked up more curses that ended in "Damn Americans Power Rangers."

Plink said, "Back yard, secure. Wall, converge on us."

Feeling like an imposter, a boy in a soldier's costume among grownups, Wall held his carbine at the ready, scanning for threats, his finger nervously shivering above the trigger, the safety off. His scope jumped left and right nervously swinging like a branch in a chaotic storm. He jolted as the night sky lit up with an impressive flash, followed by the rumbling of an explosion somewhere nearby.

"Coming," he reported, sure that there was more professional verbiage used by special forces. Wall noted that he was woefully inept when it came to protecting Nellibi. He wasn't spec ops. He wasn't even a particularly great soldier. Like most people, Wall sometimes held the illusion that he was a badass, a natural-born killer, but at that moment, all such illusions vanished. The incident in Ethiopia and the medal he received made him seem far more dangerous than he really was.

Moments later, after partially knocking the side gate off its corroded hinges, Wall reunited with the tier-one operators. His heartbeat returned to normal, and his eyes stopped darting wildly from false threat to false threat.

"Nellibi," Plink said. "Pull down your mask so Ueskev can see you."

"Magali," Ueskev said in his thick accent, scrunching up his nose and squinting his eyes as if he had to sneeze. The weird shadows did little to make the round-faced and sunken-eyed man any more handsome, or rather less ugly. The golf-ball-sized growth at his left temple looked like it might gain sentience and crawl away. "What is meanings of this?" he asked in broken English. "We are the good times friends, no?"

"Yes, Mika," she said, her voice low and distant, her eyes bulging. She resided barely on the good side of fear-induced paralysis. "Yes. We're friends." She turned to Rhino. "Can uh, we take the cuffs off?"

The bull-chested man towered over the foreign doctor. "Don't run."

The portly doctor held out his bound hands and pumped a double-fisted thumbs up. "Famous Mika Ueskev not going to runs from big-time Captain America." Rhino wordlessly severed the zip tie with a frighteningly swift display of knifework. Harkening back to his middle school days, Wall thought, *if Rhino was a ninth-level fighter in a Dungeons & Dragons campaign, he would have rolled a natural twenty on his intimidation check.*

"Sorry," Nellibi said. "We need your help. We're building a team, uh, to stop the rusting."

With a puffed-out chest, the eccentric man said, "Of course, you need Ueskev's helps with diseases. I am tops expert."

"You knew about the disease?" she said.

"Of course, Ueskev knows of this diseases. I image thems in electron microscope before the crappy American equipment dies."

"Why did you use an electron microscope," Wall asked, having never needed one for his research on bacteria, microbes that could easily be identified under a high-magnification optical scope. The extra magnification was unnecessary and frankly a waste of time and resources.

Ueskev sniggered. "Oh, this is goods. You not knows that these diseases are viruses."

"What? No." Wall said. "Towning turned my bacteria into a pathogen."

"As usuals," Ueskev said. "American Army man is wrong. Precisely seven viruses I find. Not bacterias."

"Oh, crap." The snaggle-toothed demon in his psyche, the one that loved the beauty of flames even now, connected the pieces. "Towning spliced DNA from my rusting bacteria into viruses to make them more contagious and harder to cure."

"Towning?" Ueskev asked. "Stranger, what means you?"

Wall began introducing himself only to be cut off by Plink. "We exfil now. I'm in lead. Wall next. Nellibi and Ueskev follow. Rhino, you're on cleanup. Move out." Wall fell in and started telling Ueskev what he knew, which was far from a lot, especially now that the contagions were viruses. Yet, there was a lot to unpack in order to convey enough technical detail for the doctors.

Two blocks later, someone yelled, "Looters!"

A series of percussive *thwap-smacks* slapped his ears, one accompanying a flash from the dark shadows of a house across the street and a set of suppressed shots from Plink and Rhino. Wall raised his M4 as fast as he could, but by the time he aimed and let loose a short burst of suppressive fire, the enemy had fallen.

Enemy? Wall thought. A short, balding Asian man fell out of the shadows with at least four bullet holes in him. Answering the age-old question of bounce or splat, the man toppled and hit the pavement with his body sloshing and his head rebounding. It was one thing to combat the totalitarian army of a government attempting genocide through war and famine. It was entirely different to fire on and kill a US citizen, especially one whose crime was attempting to protect his neighborhood.

It shouldn't have happened here. He had a concealed carry permit for his pistols as a form of self-defense because of Eugene's growing drug culture and associated crime. Crime was almost a foregone conclusion. But the Army killing upstanding citizens? *This if fucking nuts.* While he shot nearly a second later than the elite soldiers and probably missed, there was a good chance that he dealt an equally fatal blow. He was now a murderer. Or, rather, he had been for the last two weeks. He just didn't know it yet. How many people already died as a result of his research? This poor man was another casualty among the many.

"He died with honor, protecting his own," Plink said, drawing attention back to her. "Move out. Tight together like a centipede." Wall reflexively followed her militaristic orders, glad that he wasn't in the driver's seat. He could only imagine the pressure building underneath her calm exterior. "Romeo 466, six minutes from wheels up," Plink said.

The comms squelched twice in confirmation.

Ueskev's heavy breathing worried Wall. He had to wonder how a man could get so unfit as to huff so badly from this short hike. Then he retracted his thought, considering that the guy could have any number of conditions, from allergies to emphysema. No matter the cause, if they ended up in a serious skirmish, the pot-bellied man wouldn't be able to keep up.

"You shot that man," Nellibi said loud enough to draw attention and even louder in his headphones.

Sympathetically, Rhino said, "Would you rather save the world or save one man? Plus, it was your life versus his. I would make the same decision every time."

Wall gulped at Rhino's heavily loaded statement. "Save the world." The magnitude of their mission was terrifying. They weren't only saving themselves, or Portland, or Oregon, or The United States. The success or failure of their mission would ripple across the planet.

"No, but..." Nellibi stammered.

After a thorough spray-down, with a double dose for Wall on account of the dust cloud at Ueskev's front door, they took their positions in the helicopter. Ueskev took the strip-down and dousing like a champ, boasting loudly, "Ueskev knows of Russian cold. This nothing to Ueskev."

They sausaged the Russian in the back with Nellibi and her family while Wall tried to pretend that hanging out of a helo didn't bother him. He was Army again. He needed to act like it.

With pity in his eyes, Rhino said, "There will be a great die-out no matter what we do. Cures don't happen overnight. Mass death is inevitable at this point. Fires, starvation, and every combination of conflict, from robberies to wars. The sooner you all digest what history tells us, the stronger you will be."

They hadn't given Wall much time to think about the implications of the downfall. Humankind's population explosion was enabled by ever-improving irrigation, high-yield crops, and mega-farms that fed the city-dwellers. With the majority of the population living in urban areas, most would starve.

Nellibi asked, "How many people did the world support in the stone age?"

With Wikipedic knowledge of world history, Rhino stated that "Experts estimate about one million people lived during the Paleolithic Era."

"No," Ueskev said. "You haves it wrong, my friend. Copper, bronze, and brass do nots be rusting. How many peoples lived in bronze ages?"

Rhino shrugged. "Bronze age? The global population was around six million at the beginning and around twenty million by the end. That's only three ancestors per thousand currently living."

"It won't be that bad," Wall corrected them. "There are about seventy million rural Chinese peasants and over five hundred million farms globally. The world can support far more people than it did back then. We know more. We have better crops. There are more irrigation ponds and artificial waterways."

Rhino shakes his head. "But you forget the nature of mankind, history's lesson. We fight, and we kill, and we destroy. Look around. Farms are burning. Plows will fail. Buckets will crumble. Shovels will break. We use almost no bronze anymore. The downfall will kill off more than you think."

"Da, but no because Ueskev has–how do you say? Oh yes. Ueskev has amazeballs and fixes problems."

"Ueskev has big-time amazeballs," Rhino agreed.

"Wheel's up," the pilot said over the group comms.

"Where to now, Wall?" Plink asked as they rose into the air. "Brenda Smith? Or our first choice of labs."

CHAPTER EIGHT

"We go for Smith," Wall said definitively while they gained altitude.

"Acknowledged," the co-pilot said without waiting for Plink to confirm.

As they took off, Wall mouthed, "I should have gone for Smith first." If he had known Towning used viruses, something that was obvious in retrospect, Smith would have been their highest priority. The fact that the old genius used hard-to-cure viruses, and seven sub-species no less, proved how sadistic he was and how much Wall had miscalculated. Towning's attack was thorough and made full use of what should have been Wall's beneficial legacy.

When the reckoning comes, he thought. *I'll have to pay for my crimes.*

"Heys now," said Ueskov. "I am first-most important member of A-Team. You watch that TV show? It was bestest show of all. I love it when a plan comes together."

"Wall," Plink said as she pulled out a bottle and squeezed a few drops of the blue disinfectant into her M4's barrel, then placed a new cap on the end to seal it shut. Their death sticks blew out any contagion when they fired at the old man, but if even a few cells of the steel-consuming virus reached the barrel, the gun would be toast. Before all of this, who would have considered leaving bleach in a firearm? It just wasn't done.

"We're on a private channel," Plink said. "I need to know something. If I have to decide between Nellibi and Ueskev, which do I save and which do I let die?"

"What the?"

She nudged her shoulder into his bicep and asked, "Which one of them is more mission-critical?"

"Both. Neither," he said, talking with his hands. "How can I make a decision like that?"

"It's in the job description," she said. "We take decisive actions based on the best knowledge at hand."

"Then, save Nellibi," he said, surprising himself. He swirled Plink's poisonous question in the wine glass of his mind, deciding that it was better to trust the person you know than the one you don't. She had more to lose than Ueskev if they couldn't find a cure. Therefore, she would be more motivated.

Plink added a few drops of cleaner to his barrel, then sealed it with another cap. "Great. Nellibi it is." She let the statement hang in a way that left it up for debate.

"No," he contradicted himself. "Save them both. Abandon me, then Ueskev."

Plink double-bumped her fist on his thigh. "That's a no-go, soldier."

"Why not?" It wasn't that he was trying to be brave. It was that when he looked at it logically, they were the smarter choices. If he had to pay for what he'd done in order to peel back any of the rust, he would.

She bumped him again. "We choose you first because you have the highest likelihood of seeing this through to the end."

He locked eyes with her. "Look, I only have a little training in viruses. I can't finish the job without them, but the reverse is possible."

"I'm good at reading people. You're in this no matter what. I knew it before you did. So, is it still Nellibi?"

He breathed deeply, then coughed due to the cumulative smoke. "Give me a sec." Stalling for time, he pulled his water bottle over his mask and took a swig. It surprised him when he said, "No. We need Ueskev." Nellibi may have been top-notch, but she specialized in bacterial infections, not viruses. In contrast, Ueskev specialized in viruses and had enough intuition and gumption to have imaged the contagions on his own. It had to be him. Wall relaxed. Bizarrely, the possible death of the family huddled in back didn't worry him as much. The choice was final, and he could put it in the past.

"Final answer?" she asked with her eyes locked on his.

"Yes. We need Ueskev." The words sat easy. The knowledge that he was Plink's first choice made a certain type of sense. Neither doctor was a good fit for the unstoppable chaos to come. They lacked the survival skills they needed for the new world. Ill-fit minds and bodies weren't going to survive long. Wall hoped that Plink's assessment of him would withstand exposure to the inevitable.

"Before we click off," she said. "I want you to think about the note Towning left for you. I think there's something there."

"What makes you say that?"

"It's just a feeling. It's my intuition. It's the same thing that told me you didn't unleash the disease even before I met you."

"Gotcha." From most people, he would have been skeptical of someone intoning a sixth sense, but he suspected that her gut feelings saved plenty of lives in her line of work. Exceptional people often attained success through intuition, an ability to piece together subtle clues, while the majority made mediocre decisions based on obvious indicators that were often wrong. Selection for Delta Force placed her in the exceptional category, especially as a woman. He had to trust her.

Then they squelched back onto the group comms. "–because Ueskev is the man. That is why–"

"Ueskev," Wall interrupted. "What subspecies of virus did you say he based his diseases on?"

"No," the Russian said adamantly. "Not sub-specieses of one virus. Not singulars type. Seven different specieses. HIV to the measles."

"Seven different species?" Wall rolled the three words on his tongue. That meant they needed seven very different kinds of cures, not one. Bacteria were easier to target, viruses not so much. This ratcheted up the complexity by a hundred-fold. What already felt daunting had just upgraded to practically hopeless. Even if they managed to find antivirals for one within a reasonable amount of time, the others could take years or never. No matter how successful they were, the diseases would spread further through humankind's building blocks of modern civilization.

Break it down Barney style, he told himself. Attack one problem at a time. "Ueskev, do you remember which viruses we're dealing with?"

"Of course, Ueskev remembers. What do you think? I am a hacks or something? I list them now. Pays attentions Army-scientist man. They are new variants of

Mumps,
West Nile,
Measles,
COVID-19,
Smallpox,
SARS,
And the HIV."

"Let me guess," Wall said. "Most of them are highly communicable airborne viruses."

"Da," Ueskev said, nodding emphatically. "Seven American football points for the Wally Man. Excepts for the HIV. I have no ideas how that works without the boingy-boingy in the doingy-doingy."

Wall stuck his tongue into his cheek, thinking for a moment while Ueskev started lecturing about stupid American football. He needed time to think from the old man's perspective. Towning was brilliant and excellent at strategy. Working the problem, or problems, backward from the current chaos to Towning's execution to the underlying strategy to motivation. Knowing how and why he did it might provide a hint at how to "unwind things" as Plink said at Raddick's depleted base.

Wall had ignored how egotistical the architect of this singularity was. He had shoved aside the public's criticism, dismissing such things as byproducts of jealousy and people's propensity to tear people down rather than build them up. Wall hadn't known many wealthy people prior to the generous donations, but attended several charity galas in the last year, meeting genuinely kind individuals. While a few were conceited, judgmental, or pompous, the majority wanted to help others, donating large sums of money toward good causes. When Towning spoke about his precious singularity at a single event, he managed to raise nearly a hundred million dollars for forwarding the science behind technological approaches to healing the environment. Those people weren't the bad people they were made out to be.

But the signs had been there. Later that night in a private conversation with Wall, the old man had called the donors "sheep, unable to understand the true purpose of scientific progress, incapable of really comprehending the good that the money would be used for." Wall had nodded, thinking he understood the future of the singularity. Oh, how wrong he had been.

On one walk through the woods, while Wall helped his mentor cross a stone path over the stream that ran through Towning's getaway vale, he complained that all he had achieved by advancing medical technology was to extend the lives of the weak and further dilute the human race with unhealthy breeders, promoting the lowest common denominator. At the time, Wall treated the discussion as a hypothetical scenario and suggested that someone could release a new disease to compromise the health of the masses. While absently looking out at Portland, he couldn't believe that he had actually said, "Through natural selection, the weak will die and only the strong would survive."

On their walk back to the cabin, Towning asked Wall how he would spread such a disease, to which he gave a wide range of ideas such as infecting straws—environmentally friendly plant-based ones, of course. That conversation ran late into the night with much of it fading into an increasingly drunk set of memories. Contaminated hairspray and lotions, again, sure to be environment-conscious products. The signs were there. He'd simply enjoyed pretending to be the devil while Towning actually was. But thoughts like that wouldn't help now. Wall needed to focus on the now and the future.

Ueskev hadn't stopped his complaints about American sports. "–rest of the worlds plays reals football, not–"

With memories of that night fueling his thoughts, Wall said, "Towning bred his viruses for maximum virility, minimum symptoms, prolonged contagious periods, and permanent infection."

"Why do you say that?" Nellibi asked, speaking up for the first time since the shooting.

"Because that's what I would do if I wanted to bring about the demise of mankind. Greater virility means an easy spread, which is a no-brainer. He wouldn't want many symptoms because he wouldn't want anyone to pick up on the fact that they are sick, so the CDC and others couldn't respond in time. Plus, asymptomatic people spread the viruses without ever realizing it."

It should have bothered him that he could think like Towning, predicting what a psychopath would do, but it didn't. His internal devil regularly asked what-ifs. In high school, he could usually predict what period the fire alarm would go off on what day. In Ethiopia, it proved useful because he could react quickly. As a researcher and professor, the devil helped him identify possible problems, realistic or far-fetched, in his research.

Continuing his reasoning, he said, "Prolonged contagious periods mean that a single man could infect others and metals for years or his whole lifetime, maximizing their spreading potential."

"Really? But that is..." Nellibi said, unable to step into Towning's ruthless perspective.

"Yeses," Ueskev said. "What Wally-boy didn't say is CDC bitches not bother to warn peoples because it is too late. The governments silenced all the peoples. No insult, big-man Captain American. US no better than Russia this way."

"The politicians were the first to abandon ship," Nellibi agreed. "The rat bastards."

Ueskev laughed, then said, "No doubts they had secret base to survive."

"Hold on to something," the pilot ordered with a sense of urgency in his voice. "This'll be bumpy." Every single one of Wall's muscles tensed as they practically flew into flames on the north end of Erwin Tucker Middle School.

"Wall, you're with me," Plink commanded as they set down. "Ueskev and Nellibi, stay with the helicopter. You'll be safer that way." Wall recognized the strategy. She wanted to keep one priority asset close to her and the others separate, thereby splitting her eggheads into different baskets.

"Da," said Ueskev. "I am too importants to die."

Inwardly, Wall said, *Keep telling yourself that, big guy.*

Plink extracted a bag from the tail and handed Wall a black respirator mask. "There is too much smoke here," she explained. That didn't bode well considering how much smoke he had already inhaled. Strapping one on herself, her words became muffled. "Wall, you're a Ken doll hot-glued to my Barbie ass. Got it?"

"Got it." He knew his eyes and mind should be focused elsewhere, but he couldn't stop from looking at her butt, which wasn't particularly well showcased in Army camo. But that didn't stop him from imagining what was underneath, both bendy and muscular. She jogged south, away from the worst of the flames with Wall in tow and Rhino close behind.

While it was worth not inhaling the thickening smoke, the mask was anything but comfortable. Hot. Humid. Sticky. Hard to breathe. Overall, it wasn't ergonomically geared for a casual run through a hellscape.

After two weeks of long days and an evening of short jogs, Wall's bad knee wobbled with each step but he pushed past the annoyance. "Moving targets are harder for citizens to shoot," he whispered to himself. That and the fear of burning alive were enough motivation to keep him moving.

In the back of his mind, Wall worried about his folks. He hoped their farm would escape the devastation that consumed Portland and all the big cities. His worry was that city folk would scatter like rats and swarm anything and everything, turning the Mathison corn farm outside Des Moines into prime eating grounds. The good news was that Iowa's corn and livestock industry could feed far more than the state's population.

Stay focused, he scolded himself, doubling his efforts to maintain situational awareness. If there were any onlookers, he wondered what they would think about a trio of camo-clad, gun-toting, and mask-wearing idiots running down the street in the middle of a chinook-fueled firestorm. Then again, only a crazy man like Ueskev would consider staying home to watch the world burn down around them.

"Abort," Plink shouted as they came to an intersection. On the far side, houses lay in ash and smoldering coals. By way of explanation, she added, "Smith's house is in that mess." She didn't need to say that the doctor was either dead or fleeing to who-knows-where. Either way, retrieving her wasn't any more likely than growing a third eye.

Wall wished he could mute himself and swear like Jimmy Twenty from basic training. That guy was always doing pushups for swearing in front of a superior. He never said a simple, "Yes, sir," or "No, sir." Swearing was like a nervous tic for him, completely impossible to stop no matter how many times the brass reprimanded him. Even when he told a story about his mom, she would be fuckin' doing this and shittin' out that. Wall nearly let loose with a litany that would have made Jimmy blush but pretended to be an elite operator and kept his shit under control.

Plink twirled her finger overhead. "About face. Rhino, take us back."

Wall's F'n knee twisted awkwardly as he turned, nearly toppling him in the middle of the road. "Gah!" he warbled as he recovered.

"Halt. What's your status, Wall?" Plink asked.

"Fine," he lied. "Just an old knee problem."

"Then giddy up." She slapped him on the ass. And they were off again. "And Wall."

"Yeah, Plink?"

"Warn me before fine turns to fucked."

He almost asked how this whole thing, everything Towning set into motion, wasn't already in the fucked category, but kept those thoughts to himself, instead opting in favor of a curt, "Will do."

As they returned to the helicopter, the wind shifted directions from westerly to northerly, fanning the flames in their direction, cutting off their retreat. The smoke stung his eyes and the heat felt like it might burn off his eyebrows. "Rhino, find us a way out," Plink barked. "Alpha Bravo isn't going down like this. I'm too pretty to burn like a bruja."

As if they weren't screwed enough, a car puffed into flames behind them cutting off both directions. They were completely surrounded.

"Push through," Plink ordered, firm but steady, fearless. Wall was pretty sure a giant helping of exploding barbeque-flavored fear was completely warranted. With his bad knee already aching, compounded by the weight of his gear, Wall wasn't sure if it would survive the coming full-out sprint.

"Hot on Rhino's rump roast, lieutenant."

The big man dashed into the fire and Wall took off after him, the rational fear of likely death urging him onward regardless of any protest from his knee. Smoke and flame blinded him. The roar of the omnidirectional inferno and his own yell deafened him to Rhino's nearly silent footsteps. With every stride, the heat intensified, at first like running your hand over a candle, but quickly growing painful, threatening to melt his gloves and singe the gap between his shooting glasses and helmet.

Then their path widened and he hadn't turned into a piece of fire starter. All of their camos smoked but hadn't burned. The hairs on his arms stuck to the thick long-sleeve shirt. Barely loud enough to hear through the earpiece, Plink yelled, "Double time." And they ran off, not giving Wall any time to stop and check himself for burns.

"Romeo 466, this is Plink." She sounded neither concerned nor out of breath, only muffled by the mask.

"Go ahead," said the pilot, through a considerable amount of static.

"We're cut off from you, headed south. Find us an evac point southward."

"Acknowledged. Wheels up in two."

Following the direction of the shifted wind, they raced for safe ground half as fast as he'd like and but at the limit of what his knee could handle without giving out. As it was, he had a slight hitch to his gate. His re-attached

ACL wouldn't last long like this. At first, the flames outpaced them, gaining ground, leaping from house to house with astonishing speed, embers jumping half a dozen yards at a time. Then the wind shifted to westerly again and they reached an already burned area that smoldered and smoked but didn't threaten to turn them into crispy kabobs.

Two hundred meters past the active flames, Wall's knee gave out and he fell, skidding like a land-surfer about to catch a wave.

"Halt," Plink ordered. "Stand up, lieutenant. This isn't nap time in pre-school."

"Sorry," he said with a nickel of embarrassment, a quarter of annoyance at her, and a silver dollar of frustration with his knee. He pushed himself up like a tripod, not trusting his right leg.

"Walk it off," she barked.

He tested it. It hurt but held.

"No time for nursing at the teat of pain, lieutenant. Follow Rhino."

He stuck his tongue into his cheek and forced his leg to obey, wishing he had that last strand of jerky from earlier. Jerky made everything better. To distract himself, he fantasized about a tantalizing pepper-forward strip of smoked meat, imagining the flavor and how it would excite the different areas of his tongue. The texture as it transitioned from firm to stringy, then soft and chewy.

"Wall," Plink said. "I told you to warn me before fine turned to fucked."

"Sorry, I–"

"Sorry is for the dead," she interrupted. "Are you dead yet? No? I didn't think so."

Up ahead, their helo waited for them in a scorched park. The blades spun slowly, thrusting ash away. As they approached, Wall's fight or flight response diminished, leaving him shaky and a bit numb. He sprayed himself down and rubbed the disinfectant into his clothes, not bothering to remove the ventilator. After clipping himself in, he leaned back and closed his stinging eyes.

"Ueskev says you guys being crazy Americans cowboys."

CHAPTER NINE

As the rotors sped up, Plink said, "Wall, we're on a private channel. We need to switch gears."

"Agreed," he said into the ventilator mask, propping himself up and opening his stinging eyes. "We need to find a lab."

She carefully placed her tiny notepad into his hand so that it wouldn't fly away. "I have a list of labs from TOC."

Moaning, he forced himself into a coherent state of mind, something he learned in the army, then mastered in grad school at the lab, which often required late nights that extended into the following day. A list of ten facilities with a rank number for each flapped on a page under the helo's blasting wind.

He wanted to pick the lab with the highest score and be done with it, assuming TOC ranked them according to the requested equipment and safety from fire. Securing an ideal lab for their needs was critical for any chance of success, which seemed farther away than ever. Seven viruses. Impossible. But if they found the right lab, they might synthesize one or two. The chaos of the firestorm rubbed arsenic into the wound. Nowhere would be safe.

"Wheels up," the pilot said.

Their attempt to find skilled professionals demonstrated how dangerous it would be to put their feet on the ground in search of a lab. They survived their flight from the inferno-ridden cityscape with what seemed like simple dumb luck but probably had more to do with Plink's and Rhino's calm under fire. If they had taken Ueskev or Nellibi with them, their chances of coming through alive would have dropped to zero.

No, Wall thought. *Plink would have left them behind.*

She tapped him on the knee. "We need a destination, Wall."

"Give me a sec."

Even if they found a safe lab, who said it wouldn't go up in flames the next day or week or year? They really needed the latter or even longer. They needed time. Lots and lots of time. Viruses–

"Oh no," Wall said as the extent of the fires came into view from a greater height.

"What?" Plink asked as mellow as vanilla ice cream, another luxury that would be lost to history if they didn't find a fix for Towning's pathogens.

Wall had to wonder if she was somewhere on the spectrum or perhaps some level of a psychopath, immune to emotion, honed as a morality-free weapon. He'd have to postpone that thought for later. "Vaccines for viruses have different requirements than bacteria. I listed the wrong lab equipment. TOC's choices aren't valid, and I don't know what we'll need anymore."

"Which of your colleagues do we bring into this conversation to identify the new equipment requisites?"

While he trusted Nellibi more, the Russian was more familiar with viruses, so he answered, "Both."

"Negative," she said instantly. "Ueskev will talk over Nellibi. He'll dig in if she tries to argue."

He couldn't disagree. For a woman who displayed such a narrow range of emotions, Plink was amazingly perceptive. *Isn't that a trait of most psychos?* He had to choose and choose fast because every second they hovered in place meant less fuel to reach their lab of choice. He had to decide whether to choose the decisive narcissist or the wiser doctor. His gut told him Nellibi, but his mouth said, "Go with Ueskev."

Plink tapped her arm pad and said, "Adding Ueskev."

"About time you responded," he said, having been ignored while they had their private discussion. "I was saying–"

"No time," she cut in. "Wall has a question for you."

Not giving the Russian time to interject, Wall asked, "Do you know what equipment we will need in order to create vaccines or antivirals for the diseases?"

"Of course, Ueskev knows. I always–"

Wall sighed in both relief and frustration. Ueskev was an invaluable resource as long as his ego could be trusted. "Good. Do you know where we will find all the equipment and supplies?"

"Yes. Ueskev knows all."

Ignoring the man's outward display of small-dick syndrome, Wall said, "Where are some places we can go?"

Entirely too quickly for Wall's brain to intake, the guy began listing labs, both private and public.

"Stop!" Plink interrupted. "I'm bringing in command com. Then, list them slowly. They'll rank the labs for us."

"No need," the arrogant man stated. "Ueskev knows tops number-one choice. Taffer Biogenics in Bend, Oregons."

"Why?"

"Simple," he said, taking a moment to enjoy his superiority. "Bend is farther from burnings of Portland but not too far for Americans helicopter." The Russian scientist may have been an ass, but Wall admitted that he could think through problems. He was a serious asset.

Tapping at the device on her wrist, Plink said, "TOC, this is Major Bradshaw aboard Romeo 466 with a request."

"Go ahead, Plink," a staticky voice said.

"Report on Bend, Oregon's fire status."

"Hold, please."

As heartbeats thumped at his growing headache, they hovered in place, wasting gas while waiting for a response. After reaching into his med pack, he pulled down his scarf and respirator mask, popped some painkillers, and drank a few gulps, swishing them around in his mouth before swallowing. He couldn't remember if it was Army training or wilderness first responder classes that taught him to always hydrate. Either way, thirst and headaches lead to a sluggish mind and sluggish minds lead to mistakes, ones that could have deadly consequences. They were already facing so many risk factors that they didn't need him adding another layer of idiot to the mix.

Discounting all the things that could go wrong with flying a helicopter in limited visibility while it sucks ash into its engines, the devil in his mind considered ways the others could get some or all of them killed. Accidentally unclipping a harness during a strong cross-breeze. Vomiting on the helicopter could spread germs too fast. He checked that his M4 was on safety so he couldn't shoot someone or the helo. The list went on. Too many failure modes.

Worse, poor decisions could prematurely end their mission. *Wait, what?* he thought. *When did the mission start to outrank my life?* He knew the answer. It happened the moment he grasped how many people would die no matter what they did, and how many more would die if they didn't fix this.

"Bradshaw, this is TOC."

"Go ahead."

"There are no fires in the vicinity of Bend, Oregon."

"Romeo 466 en route to Taffer Biogenics in Bend, Oregon. Out." The pilot immediately banked south by southeast and sped away.

Wall didn't know when or how he fell asleep, but he jolted to consciousness when a loud squelch sounded in his ear. He was lying on his back with his feet dangling over the lip of the floor. It took no time at all for his mind to catch up to where he was and what was going on. Plink, who had draped herself over his thighs, pinning him in place, said, "Go ahead TOC."

"Be advised. Fires began in Bend, Oregon. With current wind speeds, Taffer Biogenics may burn within two hours." The pilot brought the helicopter to a standstill.

"Thanks, TOC. Out." She righted herself and batted him on the knee. "Welcome back to the ever after, Snow White. We're on a private channel. Do you have any super-nerd ideas? I presume an hour isn't enough to get anything done."

"It could take months or even years," he answered when he considered the monumental scope of the task at hand. With a sharper mind after the spot of rest, he considered what that meant for the human race. The longer it took to find a way to "unwind" this mess as Plink put it, the worse the death count would be. Towning truly screwed them all. In a twisted way, his approach was beautiful. Don't just kill off humans. Permanently take away most of the tools that set humans apart so they could never return to such dominance over nature.

"Years? We won't have that sort of time. Can we speed it up?"

"Not likely. Sorry."

"Sorry is for the dead, lieutenant. Don't make me dead. You won't like me when I come back for revenge."

Wall bonked his helmeted forehead, trying to kick it into high gear. Mentally, he asked himself, *Why hadn't Ueskev or Nellibi mentioned how long it would take and how impossible their mission was?* Then it hit him.

Plink locked gazes with him. "Wall, what are you thinking?"

"I suspect Ueskev and Nellibi are withholding information. They know the process far better than I do. Curing bacterial infections is fast compared to developing vaccines or antivirals. Hell. HIV took decades to combat and still doesn't have a cure. Both of them would have said–or not said–anything to get away from Portland, Nellibi for her daughter and Ueskev for himself."

She nodded. "Agreed. As of now, we do not trust either of them for non-technical decisions."

The implications were clear. That responsibility belonged to him, the least informed of the trio. Without the necessary education, he would probably guide them astray. Deciding to go with the known over the unknown, he said, "We go to Eugene." If knowledge was power, then they had the best chances in Eugene. "There are several bio labs that sprang up around the university.

Come to think of it, a startup shut down a couple of months ago. If we're lucky, they haven't sold their equipment yet."

"Change of course," she said to the pilot. "Eugene, Oregon."

"Acknowledged."

She relayed their new destination to TOC, who reported that it was now raining in Eugene, which gave Wall a hint of hope. A wet town is less likely to burn to the ground. It wouldn't be safe, only safe-er.

Regardless of whether Nellibi or Ueskev withheld critical info, his doubt about them would corrode his ability to form an effective and collaborative team. If it weren't for Ueskev's invaluable knowledge and Nellibi's superior skillset, Wall might have thrown the Russian overboard for chiseling notches in his trust. Could he really blame either of them, though? Tough times brought out the worst and best in people. Alpha Bravo's success relied on disaster bringing out the best in all of them.

"I need to do better," he thought out loud.

"We all do," Plink responded.

Sometimes, Wall judged people based on the communities they chose and how closely they held to their bonds. Some people defined their communities as just their family or friends or fellow churchgoers. Nellibi's core group was undoubtedly her family. A self-centered man like Ueskev probably had a core community of one, himself. Wall belonged to the collective community of the US armed forces, about half a million strong in service of hundreds of millions. He considered the people in the biochemistry department part of his people. As an advocate for the environment, he worked for the global community.

He wondered how Towning viewed community. Did he consider himself the way Wall did, an environmentalist working in the name of all humanity? Or did he connect with the environment, including all flora and fauna, above all humans? Before today, he thought Towning worked for all of mankind, inventing medical devices and techniques for the masses and championing a cause for everyone. *What caused the shift?* Wall asked himself. No answer came to him.

Changing perspectives, Wall decided that the old genius must have planned this for years, if not decades. There was no way he could have achieved this cluster fuck without putting the pieces into place in a masterful long game. It wasn't just Wall that he tricked. It was everyone. He upheld an altruistic set of agendas so nobody would suspect him.

He couldn't help but wonder where the world-ender had holed up to wait out the downfall of man. A remote tropical island with all the amenities for living out his remaining days? Or would he have a high-mountain getaway, far from infected people?

Again, Wall awoke with a jolt, this time to high-pitched alarms blaring in his ear, ones that meant their craft was experiencing serious problems. Plink laid across his lap like before, an anchor, an extra safety belt for her primary asset. The helo shrieked and wobbled.

"–engine trouble," the pilot said. "Brace yourselves for–"

Wall's stomach lurched as the whirlybird dropped out from under him, throwing them up a foot, then dropping him on his tailbone with a non-trivial smack as Plink landed on top of him. Frightened screams accompanied the shrill sirens and grinding engine. A particularly piercing cry came from Ueskev.

Wall threw his long arm out and seized the co-pilot's seat as the helo leaned forward and the tail began swinging around the hull, a motion that threatened to pull his feet out the open doorway. He caught onto Plink's backpack, hauling her back into the cabin. The floor bucked as the pilot managed to slow their descent, but they spun faster, and the grinding grew louder.

A grotesque screech accompanied a whiplashing shutter through the aircraft and into Wall through his back and arms. Simultaneously, Plink's elbow dug into Wall's clenched abs, nearly knocking the wind out of him.

Then, they pulled back into the air again, threatening to break his grip on the major's pack with one hand and the co-pilot's seat with the other. Struggling to grasp which direction was up or down, Wall's body went weightless again. His words, "Don't die, don't die," blended into the numerous, discordant noises that waged war on his ears.

Then Plink was atop him again, her feet pressed into the ceiling and her back pinning him into the floor like a human vice clamp. He almost shoved her aside, but a metal-bending quake ran through the helo, rattling his hands and mashing Plink into him even harder. The good news was that the impact slowed their spin. The bad news was that hitting anything with a helicopter couldn't be called good news. It was like saying that you were lucky to be close to a hospital after a snake bite.

Then, they dove, in freefall, the worst-case scenario when inside a precariously honed metal beast. If not for Plink's hydraulic-like foot on the ceiling and her back smashing him down, Wall would have floated into the air, artificially weightless on their descent.

"Don't die," he said again.

Clamping his left hand onto the co-pilot's seat, and wrapping his other arm around Plink, he mentally prepared for ground fall. He sent out a prayer to all the gods at once, both past and present. Based on his complicity in bringing about the downfall of mankind, he doubted that any of them would listen. And if they didn't save him, he was pretty sure they wouldn't let him into heaven or Valhalla or the spirit world because of his hubris for thinking he could control the biosphere. He was the ultimate blasphemer. He tampered with nature's genetics with the intent of releasing engineered microbes into the world. In retrospect, who knew what consequences his bacteria would have had?

If Towning hadn't beaten him to the anvil, Wall might have achieved the same result by accident. Or someone else would have done it. An Amish or Mennonite extremist turned terrorist bringing everyone to a lower-tech existence, closer to god. An accidental outbreak by an over-excited biohacker playing in his basement for the fun of it. But it all came back to Wall and his lack of control over microorganisms.

Then, they crashed down, a cacophony swallowing them in a tumult too quick to reconcile with reality. Wall's arm buckled and his head struck something with a neck-popping blow.

CHAPTER TEN

A beautiful woman dressed in army garb hovered over Wall, illuminated by a tiny flashlight, haloed with a backdrop of clouds and stars. She could have passed for any number of ethnicities, but Wall suspected she was Hispanic. Her slender face, high cheekbones, thin lips, and pointy chin tickled his caveman claim a woman for himself instincts. She'd braided her hair in thin lines toward the back of her head like a UFC fighter, a method used to have longer hair for civilian life while keeping it controlled during combat.

"Hey there, big guy. Welcome back," said the woman with Plink's voice with a slight accent that matched his perception, possibly with a hint of Las Angeles thrown into the mix.

He ached everywhere, especially his neck, shoulders, and head. Raising his right hand to the base of his skull, intending to massage it, he only managed to catch his swollen middle fingers on his military collar. "Am I dead?"

She smiled sweetly and placed her hand on his cheek. "No, but you shouldn't have attacked the helicopter with your head. You have a serious case of whiplash and a concussion. Do you remember what happened?"

"The crash." Memories filled what little gummy gray matter survived the accident. He ate sheep's brain once, and it was gross and squishy like Jell-O. At the time, it didn't make sense how such a crucial body part could be so soft and delicate.

She leaned forward and shined her light in his eyes, checking for pupil dilation. "You don't remember the last two times you woke up?"

It took him a moment to digest her question. "No. I woke up?"

"Yeah," she said, concern worn plainly on her face. "You were a God-damned hero, lieutenant."

"Huh?" He squeezed his eyes together, willing himself to remember, but nothing came. Not a snapshot or a vague blur. Nothing.

"You patched everyone up before passing out the first time." Her worry transitioned into admiration. "It was like a one-person emergency room. Stitches here. Splints there. Injections and physicals."

"I can't remember." When he was ten, he earned a concussion by falling out of a tree and knocking his head on a branch mid-fall. But, that time fragments of dizzying awake time wove into a backdrop of blackouts like rapid-fire naps. After another long blink, he noticed her makeshift arm brace fashioned out of black webbing like the harnesses on the chopper, not fully immobilized but reinforced at the elbow. "Your arm?"

She smiled. "It'll be fine. You relocated my elbow and it barely hurts." She waggled it about. "See. And those pain meds are fantastic." He wondered how much of her nonchalance was bravado, how much stemmed from natural toughness, and how much came from lack of pain once it was set. If he remembered correctly, most of the pain dissipated immediately after relocation. "But you said to take it easy if I could, thus, whatever you call this monstrosity of an elbow restraint."

She cupped his face again. "You said that concussions can take days to heal, so I need to look after you. I knew you were a first responder, but where did you learn all of that?"

He got the sense that she already knew but answered anyway. "While my arm mended after the surgery, I volunteered at the VA hospital. A paramedic and I were the first line of triage, patching people up so they could wait until the docs eventually saw them." He blinked his eyes in an attempt to rid himself of a sudden onset of double vision. "I kept studying as a grunt, thinking it might come in handy someday."

"Good," she said. "Your long-term memory is working fine. How about after that?"

"In college, I took first-responder courses after school so I could take students into the wilderness. River rafting, rock climbing, camping. Stuff like that. The classes were fascinating, so I kept going. Lightning response. Hypothermia. Venom. You name it."

"You're a fascinating one, Wall," she said, patting him on the chest.

"F'n," he growled at the dull ache and stabbing pain that poked to the left of his sternum.

"Sorry, you think you have a broken rib or two beneath that armor. Not much to do about it." Holding out her good hand, she said, "Let's sit you up. Slow goes it. We don't want that concussed brain to pass out again. It's no surprise, though. Your tactical helmet cracked in two like a cleaved watermelon. Your damn skull practically took out the co-pilot's seat."

"Ha," he laughed, the sudden movement pinching his chest and stabbing his neck. "Mom always said I had a thick skull."

She smiled even though her brows knitted in genuine concern. "You said that last time too. At least you're consistent."

"How are the others?"

Reverently, she whispered, "Patton, Hawthorn, Anders, and Bree died."

It took a moment for his logic maker to click into place and figure out who all of them were. Patton and Hawthorn were the pilot and copilot. Bree must have been Nellibi's significant other, Lucas's Mimi. He sighed. "Ugh. How are the rest?"

She pulled her tiny notepad from his vest pocket and flipped through the pages. "Nellibi, possible internal bleeding in the abdomen, probably lower intestines. Broken clavicle. Triangular sling. Benzo, Vicodin, and a liter of saline."

He forced his mind to lodge the details into his brain. Benzodiazepine for shock and stress, Vicodin for pain, and saline for bleeding.

"Lucas: Eighteen stitches left calf. Nine on his left elbow. 400 mg ibuprofen. He'll recover nicely."

"Paulson: internal bleeding. Severed left ear. Coughing blood. Unconscious after pain meds."

Lost cause, Wall thought. *Hopefully, he'll die in his sleep.*

"Rhino: Suspected torn left ACL. Sprained left ankle. Concussion. Don't worry about him, though. The world will end with that guy eating the last cockroach."

"You didn't mention Ueskev."

"Coma. Pupils non-responsive. Pain: non-responsive. Apgar score: five. Probable broken neck." Ueskev's condition hit harder than all the deaths put together. He wanted to believe that it was because the man's inevitable death would be drawn out rather than quick and painless, but the cold truth was that the Russian was their best chance at finding a cure. He bunched up his nose in frustration and absently reached for some pocket jerky.

Looking around, he winced when his head pushed right against what felt like a makeshift neck collar. They were in the middle of a road behind a bright orange Jeep with a dilapidated and rusted roof. With a twist of his torso that sent spikes up his C-spine, he looked in the opposite direction where he could barely make out the silhouette of a road sign.

Plink filled in the words. "McKenzie River. Rhino filtered water and filled all of our bottles. As you said, 'hydration is a soldier's friend.'"

The helicopter's tail lay about thirty meters up the road and the crumpled fuselage rested at an angle near a crossroad, the name of which he thought he should be able to remember.

"How did anyone survive that?" he wondered out loud.

With a respectful fist tap to her chest, she said, "Patton was a superb pilot." The word, *was,* stuck out as the important part of that statement. Like so many others, he *was* no longer. Wall also tapped his chest out of respect for the man who saved their lives at the cost of his own.

Helping Wall to his feet with her good arm, she said, "The group is behind the helicopter. You and I came over here to discuss our options. Then you passed out, and here you are."

"What were the options?"

She tapped at her thigh, one-two, one-two. "Mostly. We agreed to help Ueskev die quickly. We were on the fence with Paulson. He probably won't recover. Internal bleeding will probably kill him."

That sounded about right. Ruthlessly humane. However, making the decision must have been uncomfortable. He was sort of glad that he couldn't remember. *Take the small wins,* he told himself. The world hadn't delivered copious amounts of luck today, so he clung to the micro-positives.

Careful to move his neck slowly, he looked up at the clouds and stars. "How long have we been here?" If he paid more attention during his astronomy course, he might have known the answer, but because he crammed last minute for that final exam, he forgot almost everything within days. If he could have smacked his younger self, he would have. Navigation by stars would become an important skill once all of the compasses rusted.

With a glance at her watch, which he now realized was a plastic My Little Pony piece of crap, she answered, "We've been here for about an hour and a half."

Ninety minutes of his life were gone, a crucial time that marked the boundary between pre-crash Wall and post-crash Wall. For all he knew, that was the last flight of any kind, ever. He might have made history. Regardless, he walked away from another near-death experience within hours. Perhaps there were more wins than he thought.

Trying to reign his distractable concussion brain toward the conversation, he asked, "When did we plan to leave?"

"Thirty minutes from six minutes ago. We'll split up. You and I go ahead while Rhino looks after Nellibi and her kiddo, which will give the swelling in his knee and ankle a little time to recover. The doc and Lucas need time to grieve. We need her to let go of the past so she can focus on the future. Hopefully, time will help."

"Sounds reasonable," he said with a shrug. They needed to get to the lab and secure it before something went wrong. The universe owed him that much. And they couldn't leave Nellibi and Lucas alone, unprotected. They needed the doctor. As sensical as splitting up was, it worried him to divide the special forces operators. He'd feel a hell of a lot safer with both of them at his flanks.

Wall tested his bum knee and took a few paces, trying to not limp. It wasn't entirely cooperative, but it held. Belatedly, he realized that smoke filled his nose and burned his nasal hairs. Before panicking, he sniffed himself to find that the smell came from his clothes.

"Don't worry," Plink said, placing her hand on his forearm, which also ached, though nowhere near as bad as his neck, head, and chest. "We all stink like a Romanian smokehouse from the Portland fires and the gas leak from the helo."

"I guess that's one less thing to worry about." Looking up and down the road, he asked. "How far are we from Eugene?"

As he paced back and forth a few times, he noted how many cars in various states of disrepair clogged up both lanes with outbound traffic from Eugene, none with inbound.

She patted a pad of paper, the top of which looked like a map, old-school and entirely appropriate for the new world. "About twelve kilometers to the outskirts of Eugene and thirteen and a half to Renegade Genomics." He was glad that one of them could remember the bioengineering startup's name. He shook his head to clear it but winced as his neck crackled and sparked like a billion molten nails.

"So, it will be a two-to-three-hour march," he guessed, uncertain if he did the math right.

"Slow your roll, Concussion Kangaroo. You have a limp and a propensity for passing out."

He slowly stretched his neck, gently pushing into the pain.

She tapped at the notebook and said, "BTW, there's a note here. Wall: 400 mg ibuprofen, hydrate." She pulled the bottle from his pack and handed it over.

He swished cold water around his mouth before swallowing then wiped his scruffy face with a little. Marginally refreshed, he said, "Let's check in with everyone."

"Lead the way, Romeo."

His trick knee threatened to lay him out, but with the right limp, it held. In the thirty paces around the helo, his cramped muscles loosened up by a rubber band or two. Three bodies lay in a row on the roadside. The pilot, co-pilot, and Anders, with their faces covered. They laid Ueskev and Paulson on their own. Bree's head rested in Nellibi's lap while Lucas had fallen asleep under her arm. He watched Nellibi pet her wife's hair.

Kneeling beside her, he scoured his mind for the right thing to say extending an awkward moment until his mouth decided on asking, "How are you holding up?"

"How do you think?" she sniped, her eyes squinting as if powered by death rays.

He hadn't known Bree, so he didn't mourn her passing directly but felt for Nellibi and Lucas, especially Lucas. He tried to think of something wise to say but came up with a completely empty cloud. Whether numbed by the last few hours of amnesia and chaos or altered by the concussion, he couldn't properly empathize. Rather than say something cliché, he kept his big dumb mouth shut and placed his hand on her shoulder, which she shrugged off, almost rousing the boy.

After what he hoped was a respectful amount of time, he said, "Plink and I have to find and secure the lab. I'm sorry, but we can't wait."

The slap came so fast that he didn't realize what happened until his face jerked to the side, sending shards of pain through his neck and knocking his brain hard enough to see double. If he wasn't already on his knees, he might have toppled like a drunk.

"I am *not* leaving her," said the double Nellibi. "And you're not going to abandon me."

When he managed to focus again, he pressed on. "Rhino will stay. He'll keep you safe."

She launched another slap, but he blocked her this time. Lucas stirred again. When he saw the disgusted downturn of Nellibi's mouth and eyes, he knew that she would never forgive him. "You should have left us at home."

He shoved his tongue into his cheek to keep from pointing out that Lucas would have died from smoke or fire if they remained behind, but that would have gone over like a tack at a balloon convention. With his knee aching in the kneeling position, he stood. "We'll stay for another fifteen minutes. Let me know if you need anything before then."

"Just go," she groused. "And take Rhino with you. We're done with your idiotic crusade. You're a fool. Everything is broken. Everything." She looked down at her younger wife and began sobbing, deepening the streaks down her ash-covered cheeks.

Wall almost took her at face value. He wanted Rhino to stay with Plink and him, to ruthlessly abandon her. But that was off the table. He–no, everyone–needed her skills. For some reason, possibly the distance caused by his concussed state, his emotional side didn't care whether she survived as a person. He wished Lucas every possible chance at a life, just like every child, but he couldn't deal with attaching emotions to the little boy. Besides, if he let such emotions creep into his mind, he might break down like her, too ruined to face up to what he brought about, and everyone deserved better. Rhino would stay and wait for her while she mourned and let the big man's leg heal for a day or so. Then they would come, the one remaining hope for a future.

The odds of finding someone with her skills in Eugene, someone who wasn't incapacitated or scattered to the wind, wasn't zero but darn close to it. He recalled a dinner party at the house of a guy named Roger Lockty, who would be a great fit, but couldn't remember where he lived. Wall always used GPS for guidance when driving, so he hadn't paid attention to the street or even the neighborhood.

"My condolences," he said and stood up to return to Plink, who knelt at Rhino's side on the upslope of the roadside. He got his first unshrouded glimpse of the muscular man, a tan, possibly Samoan, Hispanic, Arab, or mixed-race man with a crooked nose. Like Plink, he could blend in almost anywhere, other than his size that is. His neck was nearly as wide as his head. His ears awkwardly jutted and cauliflowered.

Wall looked to Plink. "Can you ask TOC where Doctor Roger Lockty lives? We could use his help."

"No can do, little Miss Forget-me-not." She tapped her temple to tell him it was another thing he forgot. "The radio died with the helo. My sat phone is busted. Anders sat phone is still working, but we can't get through to any of my contacts. So, we're on our own."

"What the ultimate Fuck," he growled. *How many times am I gonna have to re-learn everything only to forget it again?* Standing in front of Rhino and Plink, he felt like the weakest link, both mentally and physically. He'd have to work twice as hard to keep up, and doubly so if he conked out again.

"So, Rhino," he said, appraising the giant bear of a man. The bulge under his pants told of a makeshift field knee brace. As the SEAL stood up, his awkward balance and the way he favored his good leg suggested a lot more pain than his happy face conveyed. Wall guessed that the elite operator could make the hike faster than him even with a torn ACL and sprained ankle. The problem was that the hike to Renegade Genomix could do a lot more damage, reducing his effectiveness as a warrior. Rest would help–or so he hoped. Leaving him behind for a day or two was the right choice.

Even wounded the meaty man kept an eye on their surroundings, something Wall had forgotten since waking, and asked, "Are you good to watch Nellibi and Lucas? We can't afford to lose her all the more now that Ueskev is all but dead."

"No sweat, my man," Rhino responded in his usual rumbling voice with a friendly, almost jovial smile, his strength lending the confidence that Wall needed.

"So, it's you and me," Wall said to the alluring woman.

"Yup, buttercup. Let's spend the next few minutes wisely." With a tone of command that Plink and every leader in the armed forces mastered, she said, "Sit for a spell while I re-outfit your rucksack and gather equipment. You need all the downtime and the best gear we can scrounge."

"I will," he said. "But not 'til I see to Ueskev and Anders."

"Good call. Do it quick, then sit."

First, he kneeled over Anders, imperfectly detaching his emotions from what was right and wrong. Pre-rusting, they would have rushed him to a hospital, and the doctors would have saved him. Post rusting, the man would die directly from the injury or slowly from infection. Wall wished he had let/helped the man die during one of his amnesia time slips so he wouldn't have to remember what he was about to do.

"Get it over with," he told himself. "Don't shy away."

He drew the carbon fiber knife from his tactical belt, found the pterion bone, the softest access to the brain, and hammered his palm into the butt of his handle, shoving it into the man's skull with a crack and a slurpy sound. He breathed for a moment, then stood and saluted.

From over his shoulder, Rhino also saluted. "Private Anders, we honor your service."

After a moment to pay his respects, Wall moved on to Ueskev. Again, he did the morbid deed without words or complaint. He could have asked Rhino or Plink to carry out the inevitable but felt it was his responsibility. He was the one who helped Towning set these events in motion. All of their deaths were his fault.

"Go in peace," Rhino said this time. Both of them bowed their heads but neither saluted the civilian. A few seconds later, the SEAL said, "Wall, you need to rest for a minute."

The grunt in him, a part of him that he had worked hard to unwind over the last decade, knocked his noggin into compliance. He saluted the big man and said, "Yes, sir."

"Check yourself, Wall. In the field, we don't salute the living or show seniority. Out here, we speak in a familiar nature. It's a good way to point out your leader to the enemy and get them killed. I don't have an inclination toward dying any time soon. Hear me?"

"Yes, si–" He stopped himself. "Got it."

Ten minutes later, after watching Plink "appropriate" unsullied supplies from the dead, including a custom-built combat rifle with a longer barrel and an ACOG-6 scope, they moved out. Wall regretted that his carbine didn't survive the crash. As with all of their firearms, it was coated in that synthetic substance for which he never learned the chemical composition. Plink divvied up the extra 5.56 and 9mm ammo between the three surviving soldiers.

Wall, whose head pounded like a block of wood under a lumberjack's ax, resisted wearing Anders's helmet, but Plink's insistence won out. Safety over squeamishness. Likewise, he exchanged camo uniforms with Paulson's because Wall got blood all over his own, which would infect metal faster than anything on the planet. The problem was that the clothes were too small, not intended for a man as lanky or broad-shouldered as him.

And so it was that Wall walked away, following Plink, dressed in a dead man's clothes, weighed down by gear robbed from the deceased.

CHAPTER ELEVEN

After two weeks of backpacking about twenty kilometers a day, twelve kilometers should have been as easy as a waterslide for Wall, yet it most definitely wasn't. Every time his vision doubled and the spins began, they had to stop and sit for a spell, dragging out their short trip. He shivered as the dawn turned the high rain clouds into a colorful display of oranges and pinks.

"Hold up," he said from behind Plink as his right boot dragged over the wet ground, threatening to topple him, soaked clothes and all. "I need another damn break." Plink made Wall promise not to push himself too hard, so they already stopped three times, making this the fourth. It ate at him, but passing out again and possibly not remembering anything since the crash could seriously set them back and, more importantly, endanger the mission.

"Head or leg?" she asked from behind her mask.

"Both." Fighting off frustration, he whispered what Plink told him, "Slow zombies make easy targets. Keep your mind sharp and body nimble." Even when his mind cleared—or what counted for *clear* in his state—his body was anything but nimble. There was a reason the army removed wounded soldiers from action. You weren't only going to get yourself over the side of Dead Man's Curve, you could get your fellow soldiers killed.

Wall limped to the berm and laid down with a grunt that would have done his dad proud. Plink stood, constantly scanning their surroundings while he mimicked a lump of warm lead.

"More refugees at twelve o'clock," she said some minutes later, cutting through his congealed thoughts. They kept passing meek groups headed away from the "big city," refugees seeking "safer, more plentiful" grounds. Wall doubted that either was true. Hungry refugees could be as dangerous as anyone, and with the masses headed into the woods, they'd clear-harvest anything edible and scare off the fauna. As they learned from one group, lawlessness increasingly swept through Eugene over the last week or so. "To your feet, pretty boy. Stand casual but ready."

With the escape of a guttural "Guh," he rolled and propped himself up, intending to use a car's side mirror as a crutch but caught himself before he touched the post-rust vehicle. He would have to break many such simple behaviors in the coming days and weeks if he wanted to survive.

This new and particularly large group carried backpacks, dragged failing suitcases, or shouldered duffle bags. A large Latino pushed a wheelbarrow full of valuables, most of which Wall assumed were tokens that held sentimental value rather than practical worth. Public consensus told Americans to save family heirlooms in the face of disaster because everything else could be replaced. That wisdom might have applied to natural disasters such as floods, fires, or hurricanes, but without the safety net of insurance, federal aid, and local resources, practicality trumped sentiment every time. They now existed in a limited-resource world where food, water, and safety were the only three metrics that were worth a damn.

"Hello, officer," Plink said, taking on a Texan accent and pulling down her facemask as she had on previous "intelligence-gathering" interactions.

"Hi there," said a thick-bellied man in an unbuttoned police uniform with sweat stains under the armpits, his voice breathy and low, panting for air. "Thank God. Hey, guys, the National Guard arrived." The officer's shoulders slumped under his considerable weight, and his face slackened, giving him a braindead look.

His proclamation was met with everything from "Hell yeah!" to clapping.

"Sorry, sir," Plink said, with that southern affectation. "I lament that we ain't part of the National Guard. Wishin' we could help some, but we have orders."

The officer shook his head and wiped his sweaty brow. The pale band around his wrist told of a rusted watch. "Figures." His shoulders slumped even more. The poor guy practically aged a decade in a matter of seconds.

Sticking to character, she asked, "Sir, d'ya mind telling us what to expect in Eugene?"

"Not good," he said as he waved his group up the road. "We can't explain it. Everything is rusting. People turned to lawlessness. A lot of violence. Particularly among the homeless and gangs. I watched a soccer mom shoot a guy for stealing her pasta." It corroborated what they'd heard so far.

"Thanks, sir," Plink said. "It's pretty tame ahead of you for at least a few clicks. Lots of good folks like yourselves fleeing danger."

The cop wiped sweat from his eyes and plodded after his group. "Thanks."

She saluted and said, "Safe travels, sir. God bless you and yours."

The officer returned the salute with an abysmal form that would have earned pushups in the Army. "Same-same."

Plink nudged Wall to walk and pointedly remained between him and the group, the same pattern as their previous encounters. He did his best to walk without a limp. No sense in showing weakness in case anyone was watching. As soon as the group was behind them by fifty paces, she took point again.

"These clicks won't walk themselves, soldier."

After rounding the curve in the road, Wall asked, "How far have we come?" He was exhausted and wanted her to tell him they were almost there. The last time he had a full cycle of REM sleep was about twenty-four hours ago. The short naps aboard the helicopter and the concussion-induced bouts of amnesia didn't count for much.

"The last road marker put us at about ten kilometers, only a few to go," she said, taking a sip of water, then handing the bottle to him. They kept him on a regular hydration schedule to combat the effects of his concussion. She continued. "At our current pace, we'll arrive in about an hour."

"I can do that," he said, more optimistic than he'd been since leaving Rhino and Nellibi, which wasn't saying a lot because he started with as much confidence as a first-time skydiver. *Damn,* he thought. *A bucket list activity gone, taken by Towning. No planes and no parachutes.* In the grand scheme of things, an expensive activity wasn't a big loss, and it shouldn't have bothered him, but it did. It represented the thinnest line between technological humans and their interaction with gravity and air.

The brightening sky gave more form to dark clouds to the west that could hold a good amount of rain. The promise of more precipitation held its pros and cons. On the positive side, another soaking would help reduce the danger of fire. On the downside, Wall had just started to dry off from the drizzle a few clicks back.

"Keep it up," Plink said like a friendly high school coach. "Tortoise the hell out of this, Wall. Slow and steady."

After ten or more minutes, she interrupted his thoughts. "Big man, tell me a joke, won't ya?"

"Hey, Plink, what do you call an Army officer who goes to the bathroom a lot?"

"What?"

Overpronouncing each syllable, he said, "A Loo-tenant."

"Ha, Ha, Ha," she slow-laughed, with an overdose of sarcasm.

"Hey, Plink. What's a grunt's favorite day of the year?"

"I'm sure you're gonna tell me."

"March forth."

With playful distaste, she said, "Are all of your jokes dad-jokes?"

"Nah," he said. "A family is driving behind a garbage truck when a dildo flies out and thumps against the windshield." Wall slapped his hands together. "Embarrassed and trying to spare her young son's innocence, the mother turns around and says, 'Don't worry, dear. That was just an insect.'"

"'Wow,' the boy replies. "I'm surprised it could get off the ground with a cock like that!'"

This time she laughed in earnest, then asked, "Was that as good for you as it was for me?"

"Oh, yeah," he croaked instead of laughing due to the twinge in his ribs.

"Good," she said. "You're more alert. Keep those feet moving."

After a few more minutes, trees gave way to houses and farms. He usually drove with a lead brick of a foot through this area, ignoring these fields, which were small potatoes compared to his Dad's corn farm. He couldn't see anyone tending their crops, which could mean they didn't require much work this time of year or that the farmers were in hiding. *Then again,* Wall thought. *City folk could have killed them for their food stores.*

A bit later, farms transitioned into suburbs. They passed into Springfield, which Wall called East Eugene because the two blended seamlessly together. Here, more people walked the streets, perhaps drawn out by the light of day, which fought for dominance with the oncoming dark clouds. On a typical day, there might be a few joggers or people walking their dogs, but these men and women weren't there for exercise. Many of them gave the impression of being empty husks, milling around like pre-zombies.

Plink held her rifle in a way that said, "Don't look over here lest you earn a new piercing, a fat one that wasn't conducive to jewelry."

A long line, maybe a hundred people long, formed outside the Dari Mart. Several big guys dressed in black, armed with pistols, tasers, and clubs, walked up and down the line like lion tamers. The store's entry lacked a door, which had been metal and glass. The darkness inside meant that the power was out. *No surprise there.*

Wall didn't realize how tense he was until they were a few blocks away from the long line. In the span of half a day, his view of Americans transitioned from that of harmless sheeple to dangerous primates. The switch flipped fast.

A bit later, they passed a solar-powered speed limit sign, and he said, "We'll need lots of solar panels if we find a suitable lab, batteries too."

Passing Dutch Bros was a serious blow. He needed a double cappuccino like rust needs metal. Seeing the doorless entry, he asked, "Can we stop for a pick-me-up?"

"Not worth the risk," she said. "Fancy mochaccinos aren't mission critical. Slap yourself awake, princess."

Some of the houses and all of the businesses showed signs of rust. Broken windows opened easy access to most domiciles and buildings due to slumped or dissolved frames. Someone managed to board up the 7-Eleven with plywood, making him wonder who was defending it from the inside. It was smart to protect your food source.

The Shell station smelled of gasoline so bad that a match could blow the whole area. It occurred to Wall that Towning's rusting would pollute the air, soil, and sea with barrels of crude and the ashes of cities. The rusting didn't just infect people. It infected the land.

A while later, far after Plink's hour, they stopped short of an unassuming, gray cement block building with no distinguishing marks. Of all the times he passed it in his 4Runner, Wall never noticed it was there. The setback and empty parking lot made it completely unremarkable, flanked by tall firs and mildly obscured by a couple of trees out front.

"This is it," she said. "Are you ready to pop the top and see if Santa arrived early?"

Wall smiled. "The front door isn't rusted." A hint of hope sparked within him. For once, something was going right.

"We breach through the back," Plink said, pointing at the drive that curved around the east side of the building. She slapped her ass. "Spoon me like you mean it."

"Hold," Wall said. The top-tier soldier spun with her M4 raised, scanning for threats, deadly and smooth. He pumped his hand to calm her. "We gotta double down on decontamination before we go in."

"Acknowledged," she said, returning to at ready.

Around back, they sprayed themselves down, swapped out blue non-latex gloves, and strapped on their respirators. Then, they sprayed themselves again. When they were as good as they were going to get, Wall flourished his arm and exaggerated a bow, he said, "After you, m'lady."

With a curtsy where she lifted the sides of an imaginary dress, Plink said, "So chivalrous, you are." Her eyes sharpened and she double-checked her M4. Wall mirrored her.

At the back door, she stopped. The door handle had rusted away. It was one of those key-pad types that were supposed to add security but really dished out an oversized helping of annoyance. Either way, the thing was well and cooked.

He mouthed, "Someone already broke the seal."

Plink pulled a rugged plastic case from her pack and withdrew a tiny four-boomed black drone and its controls. Next, she tossed it into the air, and its rotors spun to life, almost silent. The control unit displayed a nearly three-sixty-degree view from the surveillance device's cameras. After testing its controls, she brought it to handle height and cracked the door open, the hinges of which squeaked like a champion 4-H pig.

"So much for stealth," he whispered as she steered it inside, letting the door close behind it. The view shifted to monochrome green with such detail and clarity that it could only be active-source infrared. Nothing moved.

Inside, dusty plastic sheets covered office furniture in an open floorplan that told of a well-funded high-tech startup. Nothing had fallen over or showed obvious signs of rusting. Nothing looked abnormal, decayed, or toppled, though he wouldn't really know until they were on the inside. He couldn't help but let optimism get the best of him. *At least the office is still good, so maybe the lab is too.*

The drone dove down and examined scuff marks from someone dragging their feet through the dust-covered floor into the dark interior. Having grown up hunting with his dad, Wall's tracking skills weren't bad, telling him that a single set of tracks led in and none out. They were old enough that they accumulated a thin sprinkling of dust.

Plink held up a single finger, then signed enemy, confirming his thoughts. On their way to Renegade Genomix, she distracted him from the trudge by continuing to teach him the various hand signals he might need if they found themselves in a less-than-agreeable situation. With his numb mind, he couldn't remember most of them, but several stuck, and those were two that seemed really important at the time.

"*Anti-bueno,*" he thought, intoning one of his dad's favorite word-play jokes. At best, an idiot found refuge inside. Between shiny and dull, a possible combatant lay in wait. Worst case scenario, someone trashed all of the lab's equipment and laid traps for them. If Towning had cleared out Wall's lab, then he could have cleaned out any number of other facilities, and the old man already proved he wasn't above blowing things up.

The drone passed into a conference room, which Plink cleared with swooping, smooth precision. The large digital display, fancy table, bookshelves, and chairs remained in pristine condition. The more he saw of the office space, the less agitated he became. Everything was in near perfect stasis as if the employees set down their pens and walked out without even bothering to retrieve personal items.

With the other rooms cleared, she followed the tracks to a shelf, where someone pulled back the plastic covering, revealing boxes of surgical gloves, masks, booties, and laboratory coveralls. Wall considered this good and bad news. At least whoever came here knew to think about biohazards. However, someone who knew only a little could do a whole lot of damage.

Plink's drone followed the footsteps to a door with a pristine handle, also the keypad type, and a small glass look-through panel. Someone piled a bunch of bags to the side of the door, of what, it was impossible to tell. In bold letters, a sign on the door read,

STOP!

CLEAN ROOM

STAGING AREA

"We're in business," Wall whispered. "The lab doesn't look like it was breached."

She flew past the door's cannon-ball-sized window, not presenting a static target to shoot or see. By setting the drone to hover in place and rewinding the video, they looked into the staging area, a bathroom-sized antechamber with benches and lockers and a shelf of everything one would need to decontaminate and protect oneself, or more importantly, protect the equipment inside.

The far door read,

STOP
CLEAN ROOM
ISO 5
CLASS 100

He winced. ISO 3 was the minimum he wanted for experimenting with some of Towning's airborne viruses, but they probably couldn't find a better space in Eugene. A colleague's lab might do the trick, but he suspected the university was a rust pile. Faculty, staff, and students coming and going in a complex web of progressively worsening contaminations.

He gave her a double thumbs up. This was as lucky as they were going to get. Both of the keypads were pristine and uninfected, meaning that whoever went inside had taken decent precautions.

She nodded and guided the surveillance drone back and stowed it away. The elite soldier signaled, "Ready?"

He nodded.

With simple gestures, she told him to draw his pistol with his left hand, his dominant side, then placed his right on her shoulder like he'd seen in videos of SWAT teams and Military training. Wall worried about the intelligence of wielding an unfamiliar pistol with a single hand, which was much harder to shoot than normal. But he didn't question her and gripped his Sig Sauer P17 down and ready.

She swept left and right with her carbine, giving him a feel for the range of motion he should expect. Next, she tilted her head and came in as if to kiss his ear and whispered, "Wall."

"Yeah?"

"If you see anyone threatening, remove your hand from my shoulder and use both hands to shoot. Otherwise, you are my new pair of undies. Understood?"

"Understood."

"And, Wall, no matter what you do, do *not* shoot me."

"Got it."

"I'm serious." She eyed him. "Don't shoot me."

"Don't shoot you. Got it."

As one, they stepped inside, knees and hips bent, stance slightly forward. She flipped on her rifle's spotlight, panning this way and that, and followed the scuff marks into the interior. He forced his creaking knee to obey but felt on the edge of collapse with every step. Despite her speed, she moved smoothly like she was part mercury and forced him into a flow that was unfamiliar.

They approached the door by sliding against the wall, not straight on like the tracks. She motioned for Wall to stay put, then tested the door handle. It didn't budge.

Yes, he inwardly celebrated. The lock was good from the inside. No rust. He hoped, but wouldn't let himself believe, that someone from Renegade Genomix was inside. One-way tracks. No sign of contamination or brute force. Still locked.

With deft hands, she slid a cylinder from her pack and shoved it into the lock with a quick scratching sound. The handle twisted open. She was about to open the door, but he squeezed her shoulder. After panning the room for trouble, she gestured, "What?"

He holstered his pistol and withdrew a spray bottle from his tactical vest, and doused the door handle, which had a narrow hole through the shaft, then soaked both of their gloved hands. Lastly, he pulled a rubber band off the end of his rifle, cut off a tiny chunk, spritzed it, and stuffed it into the hole she made in the handle. He was impressed with her patience, respecting the importance of preserving the lab. This was why she brought him along, to think from the nerd's perspective. Otherwise, she could have secured the building herself.

When they were sanitized, she proceeded into the staging room, clearing it with his hand on her shoulder. Their feet squeaked on a sticky mat customary for removing contaminants from one's feet. His face practically lit up upon seeing light shine through the window on the far door.

"Electricity," he whispered.

Plink swiped her head past the interior window and signaled one combatant. Wall barely stopped her before she punched a hole through the lab's door handle, then pointed at the coveralls and pantomimed getting dressed. Thankfully, she conceded, able to weigh super-nerd necessities with safety requirements.

With eyes darting back and forth between the entrance and the exit, they reluctantly set aside their backpacks and dressed in what were basically toe-to-face onesies. Even with extra-large coveralls, they fit uncomfortably over Wall's elongated frame, barely able to encompass the body armor. Plink was one notch shy of DEFCON 1 when she realized that their helmets wouldn't fit under the hoods.

She motioned for him to stay and drew her door-opener cylinder. Before she could breach the room, he motioned for her to stop and whispered, "No blood. It could contaminate the whole lab." Her eyes narrowed, but after a few seconds, she nodded. Coming close again, he whispered, "Don't kill him. He could be helpful." She tapped her fingers, one-two, one-two, and popped her neck.

Again, Plink bypassed their security with the push of her tool and the surprisingly quiet drill, then slipped through the door as silent as rust. Wall watched through the window as she sprinted at a figure obscured by a translucent plastic sheeting that dangled from the ceiling, held up by neon-yellow tape.

The scientist or tech didn't see Plink coming. Two fast heartbeats later, she slid like a softball player through the footing of the draped plastic, then bounced upright on the other side, landing on her victim. He couldn't see what happened behind the curtain, but whatever it was, they stopped moving almost instantly. For ten intense throbs in Wall's head, he waited for the ordeal to end as Plink let the scientist slide to the floor.

On the one hand, Plink quite effectively neutralized the target. On the other, she breached the ad hoc inner bubble, possibly exposing the inner lab's equipment to contagions. Somewhat assuaging his fears, she immediately sealed her entry point and looked to be spraying herself down.

As he entered the outer lab, she dragged a limp body out of a crudely constructed inner vestibule. By the time he reached her, she had hogtied her prisoner with a series of thick white zip-ties.

"That was amazing," Wall said, thoroughly impressed by her swift display of aggression.

"Shh," Plink said with her finger drawn to her mouth. "She's rousing." With a gentle push of Plink's foot, the hog-tied woman rolled onto her side.

The scientist looked up at them as if she'd entered a competition for widest eyes. There was little else he could tell about her under several layers of protective garments. "What—w-what, who are you?"

Plink kneeled at the woman's side. "Behave now, little one." Her words were all the more menacing because of the friendly voice she used. Plink tilted her head as if able to see into the woman's mind, quietly waiting. Behind her back, Plink counted down on her fingers from seven.

Within half a second of reaching one, the woman nodded vigorously, and asked, "What's going on? What happened? My lab?"

"I happened, silly," Plink replied as if talking to her best friend, her eyes by all appearances in line with her voice. "I'm Plink. What's your name?"

"K-Kayla," the woman stammered. "Kayla Williams."

CHAPTER TWELVE

P link's eyes conveyed a smile as if she and her prisoner were at a dinner party despite the latter being bound on the floor. "Nice to meet you, Kayla. Tell me. What do you do for a living?" The warrior's ability to act so normal in such a strange situation worried Wall. It begged the question, of whether she'd taken on a persona to get what she wanted out of him. How manipulative was she? How much inner thought was she hiding from him?

Scoring a nine out of ten on the worried scale, Kayla half-whispered, "I'm the Chief Technical Officer." Wall barely managed to keep himself from jumping up and whooping. As CTO, she would know their equipment and a fair bit of science. "My lab? You can't be in here. My equipment."

"Hmm," Plink intoned. She bobbed her head and nodded casually, completely disregarding Kayla's question. "Didn't I hear that Renegade Genomix shut down? So, what were you doing here?"

"You won't believe me," Kayla said as her lashes stopped stretching so wide.

"Try us," Plink said with a wink. "We've had some incredible adventures of late. Gullible folks like us might believe just about anything."

The woman pulled at her restraints. "Okay. I'll use simple terms. There is an ensemble of viruses with Hachimoji DNA sequences that oxidize and reduce seven distinct metals and metal alloys. Someone nearly ubiquitously infected humans with these virulent pathogens. I came here to investigate their DNA alterations. Now, can you let me go?"

Plink pulled a short black blade from under the elastic wrist of her coverall and reached behind their prisoner. "Move slowly lest I get the wrong impression," Plink said sweetly as she flicked the knife through the zip ties, then expertly closed it and slipped it back under her cuff.

Kayla rubbed her wrists and said, "Thank god."

"That was simple?" Plink asked. "Wall, translate."

"Sure. Someone modified the genes of the seven fast-spreading viruses about to corrode the seven metals. Basically, what we already knew."

In her affable intonation, the badass warrior said, "Tell me, Kayla. What did you find out about the diseases?"

"I doubt you'd understand."

"That's alright, dear. Pretend that we're your aunt and uncle at a family reunion."

She rubbed her wrists some more. "Fine. All seven of the samples exhibit elevated Ro, exhibit minute-but-measurable morphological variance from their parent unmodified sources and score zero on the symptom assessment scale within measurable uncertainties."

Plink turned to Wall, squinting her left eye. "Break that down for me Barney-style."

"Sure. She's saying that the seven viruses spread fast, look a little different from normal, and cause nearly zero symptoms."

Kayla winced several times as if Wall's words hurt her.

Plink shook her head and looked down on Kayla with happy eyes. "Why couldn't you have just said that?"

Taking her own pulse, she said, "His explanation lacked precision and was prone to misinterpretation."

Plink waved her hand dismissively, playing dumb. "Irregardless..." The nonword made Kayla flinch. "Why would someone make a virus like that?"

Kayla breathed heavily as if the question hurt her. Not because of the meaning, but because of the layman's terms. "The responsible party or parties sought to maximize the infection-to-detection ratio."

The astute operator rolled her finger for Wall.

"Towning wanted to spread the germs without anyone noticing."

Still probing her prisoner, Plink asked, "And why would someone do that?"

"Are you kidding me?" She breathed heavily, trying to reign in her frustration, which had fully replaced her fear by this point. Falling into a slow and ultra-condescending voice, she said. "They are psychopaths."

"Great," Plink said, dropping the dumb friendly routine. "Wall, corroborate each other's disease lists. Fill her in on Towning's involvement. I'm going outside to secure the perimeter."

Wall offered the former CTO a hand and pulled her to her feet. "Sure thing, boss-lady."

Kayla brushed off her bottom as if there was a spec of dust in the lab, sat on a stainless-steel stool, and checked her arterial pulse, keeping an eye on him the whole time.

"So, Kayla, which exact viruses did you discover?" He mentally checked off Ueskev's list as she relayed them, a perfectly matched set. Each was etched in his mind as if gouged by a Dremel with a diamond-carbide bit. He couldn't forget any of them even in his concussed state, "Where did you acquire your virus samples?"

"I identified the whole suite of viruses in samples of my blood."

"Shit," he whispered. The exact match in Ueskev's and Kayla's blood meant the ensemble spread as a complete package, and had across hundreds of kilometers, and thousands if cities around the world had already fallen. The matched count with his own research suggested that there weren't more diseases lingering out there, but he couldn't bet on it.

Over the next half hour, they exchanged information. She often said, "inane," "not rigorous," or things like "accurate but not precise." She treated him like two of the older professors in the biochemistry department back in Texas behaved toward grad students during qualifying exams, so he knew how to ignore her prickly personality, talk in her terms, and occasionally intentionally annoy her.

When he mentioned Towning again, she practically growled. "Towning and his side-along startup fund were Renegade Genomix's primary investors, owning fifty-one-percent stake and controlled three of five board seats." She squinted unevenly. "First, they forced us to move to this god-forsaken foggy town a year ago. Then they bought out Renegade and immediately shuttered the doors two months ago."

"Why would he do that?" He glanced around and it dawned on him that much of Renegade Genomix's equipment came from the same sources as his own and the gear buried in Towning's basement lab.

Her eyes brightened and her blue surgical mask rose at the sides in a genuine smile. "Towning augmented the HIV variant *I* developed." Her emphasis on "I" told him how much pride she took in her work even if it was used for such awful purposes.

He shrugged. "And why would he do that?"

"HIV-RG-912-A42 is superior."

Wall assumed the "RG" stood for Renegade Genomix and the "912-A42" corresponded to some form of test identification. "Superior how?"

Boastfully, she said, "*My* variant has the lowest symptom assessment score, lowest mutation potential, most efficacious delivery, highest virophage potential, and easiest kill switch. Most of all, it is the most rigorously tested strain."

Wall mentally translated so he could convey his findings to Plink later. Kayla's research centered around virophages, which means her version of symptomless HIV can kill other viruses. Once the target virus is dead, a simple medicine or gut-friendly bacteria can kill her HIV, leaving the patient completely healthy. It was a technique heavily tested and developed in Europe. As part of his bioengineering department's effort to catch up, they hired a Dutch scientist two years ago who was designing phages to cure the bubonic plague rampant in rats, groundhogs, and other rodents.

In other words, not only had they stumbled upon a working lab, they'd found Kayla, who could develop cures to the viruses. It was as if Towning left this lab in pristine order so she could eradicate his pathogens. While the biggest asshole in history cleaned out Wall's lab and tried to kill him, Towning gave her a chance to fix things–if she had long enough before everything rusted or burned down.

He rubbed the bump on his head and pleaded with his battered brain. *Please don't forget this.*

They discussed details of their respective research, with her frequently belittling his phrasing, and him often swallowing his pride. If he was more with it, he would have adjusted his communication but felt he was doing a great job for someone so mentally trashed.

When they'd conveyed most of the important details, Wall changed the subject. "How do you have electricity?"

"Ashton, our frustratingly bureaucratic COO, was converting Renegade Genomix to solar power so we could be eco-friendly. I thought it was a pointless waste of time, but now..."

He pointed at the inner lab. "What all do you have in there?"

She listed a surprisingly large array of equipment given the small footprint of the bubble, a benefit of Towning's gifted equipment. "It's the only spot with electricity," she explained. "And as it is, the batteries shut down about an hour after dark, making things frustratingly slow."

He pumped her for more information, like, "How long have you been here?" to which she stated, "six days and seven hours." She never left the lab and outer dressing room, surviving off of bottled soylent, a drinkable food-like substance, and catheters. "It's the ultimate in efficiency," she explained. The smell outside was from the bags of excrement she tossed into the office every two days.

Now, that's dedication, Wall thought. Repetitively opting for a catheter over stepping outside to pee was a prospect worse than a helicopter crash. Plus soylent? He tried it once and would never again. *Nasty stuff.* It had all the sustenance to keep you alive and all the flavor to make you wish you were dead. It turned out that Nature Fruit Drinks packaged soylent in biodegradable squeeze tubes, much of which was sent to refugees around the world through donations made to The Towning Foundation. But who was he to pass up a shine? Her dedication to efficiency was the universe's way of making up for the loss of Ueskev.

"Can I get back to work now?"

"Of course. Do you want help?"

"No!" The word flew out of her mouth so fast and fearful that he might as well have asked her to wipe his backside. "This is *my* lab. I can't risk you messing up, or worse, distracting me."

He bypassed taking insult. "Sure. I get it." She could be as prickly as she wanted as long as she worked on the cures. She was infinitely more suited for the job, and he understood the need for focus and lab precautions. He could be an asset, but he'd have to build trust first. *Start small,* he told himself.

"Well, I'll be outside if you need anything."

"I won't."

They both turned their respective ways.

After gearing up in the vestibule and walking outside, Plink relayed the numerous shortcomings of the building's defensibility, the most worrisome factor being that it was visible from the road. The advantages included its non-descript exterior, a tarred rooftop that allowed for an ideal lookout, and the property's abandoned appearance. Since Towning shut down the startup two months ago, weeds and shrubs managed to grow unchecked from cracks in the parking lot.

Plink had somehow reached and lowered the iron ladder with chipping paint that gave access to the roof. He climbed it slowly, spraying each rung with sanitizer to prolong its lifetime. Up top, someone had used a blue plastic milk crate as a seat while disposing of cigarettes in a soda bottle. A two-foot cinder-block wall ringed the roof, providing a cover if they ever needed to defend the place. From the crate, they could keep an eye on the road.

They walked the building's perimeter together, marking thickets and junk that Plink would clear out so "hostiles" couldn't find cover close to the building. While he thought that she took the possibility of threats too seriously, the rumors they heard from the refugees on the road told him to expect the unexpected. "After all, nobody expects the Spanish Inquisition."

"What?" Plink asked.

"Sorry. I didn't mean to say that out loud."

"You might consider working on that."

Wall was more concerned with preserving the building from Alpha Bravo's viruses than an attack. His hope was that by staying on the perfectly ventilated rooftop, they would minimize contamination and that UV radiation from sunlight would sterilize the rubberized roof. As long as they stayed clear of the solar panels and the defunct air ventilation units, they should be in good order.

Wall and Plink alternated between guard duty and rack time on a hundred-twenty-minute schedule, a duration that ensured a complete sleep cycle, timed by Plink's pink My Little Pony watch. Even though his clothes were wet and he had to sleep geared up in case anything happened, he found sleep in seconds, his head propped on his pack and "borrowed" helmet over his face.

When Plink woke him, he jolted, unable to remember his dream but sure it hadn't been a pleasant one. He managed to sleep through a fresh rain, so he was even colder than before. "Rise and shine, morning bear. My turn."

"Yeah. Uh." He was about to say something, but she already closed her eyes, by all appearances, asleep in record time. He whispered, "Play hard, sleep hard."

He checked the cellophaned sat phone charging on a small twelve-volt solar panel battery pack. The call history included nothing but "Call Failed" with times spanning from last night to only moments ago. He tried his mom's number, unable to remember his dad's, but was met with an immediate "Call Failed." If there was a time for phones to work, that was it. He spent his two-week backpacking trip without technology and desperately needed a return to civilization. Unlike everyone else, he didn't get to see the descent as planes fell out of the sky, as bridges collapsed and cars crumbled, as ships sank and supply chains broke. He missed the most profound news of all time. And now, he existed in a bubble without any possibility of news beyond the people he could see, not that he talked to any of the dreary men, women, and families walking by for fear of drawing attention to Renegade Genomix.

He wished he had a chance to say goodbye to his folks. If he hadn't been out escaping modern times, he might have gotten through to them before everything failed. "They're hardy people," he told himself. "They'll end up on top." He doubted a return to the bronze age would be kind to the elderly. Yet, if there was anyone gritty enough to survive the downfall it was Mister Mathison.

His mind bounced between his old friends from Iowa to Army buddies and pals from grad school in Texas. Except for undergrad, Wall collected friends wherever he went and kept track of most of them. He suspected it had to do with being an only child or maybe he was born that way. Here, in Eugene, he would stop in on Thomas, Alexus, and their daughter, Sarah when time permitted. If he could drive, he would be there now.

A *bang*, almost certainly a gunshot, sounded from the north. Without cars, music, or air-conditioners, the gunfire stood out against the backdrop of tranquility. He stood and began stretching, using yoga-ish poses he learned from his ex-girlfriend, Talia. He pushed through the various aches and pains he gained in the helo accident in an attempt to ease tight and strained muscles. He didn't buy into that namaste, incense, and aura crap, treating yoga like a set of pliers and screwdrivers that he could use to maintain his body.

He imagined his dad saying, "A strong body is the key to a strong mind."

To distract himself from his various aches and pains, Wall wondered how many other groups were working toward cures or vaccines. The CDC would have labs all around the country, possibly around the world. Other countries had similar organizations. Then again, Wall's shoulder devil argued that Towning and his co-conspirators would have targeted all capable labs before a broad strike or could have struck an initial blow to the members of the Infectious Diseases Society of America. Towning probably orchestrated buyouts of smaller labs like Renegade all over the world under a private equity fund or something. It was perfectly reasonable that very few capable people would have functional labs for long.

After stretching, he cleaned Anders's long-barreled M4, familiarizing himself with the weapon and sight and disinfecting every part as he went. He was pretty sure that the dielectric oil he found in his pack had antiviral properties and reduced its susceptibility to rust. Under normal conditions, it probably wasn't as ideal as his go-to Hoppe's No. 9, but Plink wouldn't have included it if she didn't think it was better for this new post-rusting reality.

For a while, he considered the suite of diseases and wondered which genetic strands of his seven rusting bacteria Towning spliced into which of the seven viruses. The old man had siphoned off of Kayla's HIV research as much as he had Walls bio-rusters, and probably combined the research of dozens of hard-working entrepreneurs and well-intentioned researchers.

Wall's inner devil put himself in Towning's shoes and asked how he would spread the disease. As he'd already considered, his environmentally friendly drink company was the easiest way to disseminate his viruses, especially with the major marketing campaign they launched last month. Over lunch at the cabin, the old man mentioned that he and a private equity firm bought a junk mail company. They were going to use exclusively sustainably sourced materials. By contaminating the envelopes, he could have infected almost every mailbox in America, and all funded by well-meaning companies that relied on junk mailers for business. Towning's investment people bought similar companies in Europe and Asia.

"Diabolical," Wall whispered as he replaced the cap on the end of his firearm. He rolled his neck slowly without the pinch he was growing to expect. "Oh, wait…" Towning boasted that a company he worked with was about to launch six new flavors of lip balm, which would have come out three or four weeks ago. All the profit would go toward environmental causes. A series of A-list celebrities promoted the glorified chapstick. What better way to infect people than tricking them into rubbing viruses on their lips?

Wall silently cursed after mindlessly reaching for an absent sliver of pocket jerky, a habit that none of his ex-girlfriends appreciated. Over the last two weeks, it had always been there, a friend ready to bring a smile to his face. So, he retrieved a meal ready to eat, or MRE, from his pack. Lemon Pepper Tuna.

"WTF? Who thought that combination was a good idea?"

While opening the package, he noticed a hint of rust on the once-shiny metallic wrapper. "Ha." MREs were supposed to last for years, if not decades.

Preppers, like his buddy Outhouse, stocked up on them for living out whatever end of days they thought was going to come. It's always the thing you don't see that gets you and leaves you unprepared. Countless stockpiled cans of food would corrode, uneaten. It was too tragic to laugh.

The absurd scale of Towning's ability to orchestrate the rusting pandemic chilled Wall as much from the inside as his still-wet uniform did from the outside. Nobody expected that an environmentalist would bring global-scale doom to humankind. Greenies were always thought to be "tree-hugging" weenies. Vegans. Kumbaya and all that crap. It all made a certain amount of sense. People from all political bents talked flippantly about a "reset" for one reason or other.

"Damn," he whispered as he remembered that wine-filled night on Towning's porch when they discussed a virulent downfall of society. Wall's internal devil, unhinged by booze, suggested that terrorists could weaponize toilet paper, an ideal way to infect the masses. He extended this concept to tissue paper, paper towels, surgical masks, and gloves. It seemed funny at the time, but now...

Needing to focus on something besides his own culpability, Wall turned his thoughts to all that would be lost. Wikipedia and all of the world's digital knowledge stored in server farms were a thing of the past. Any computer that anyone used would fail, even protected ones like they had at TOC. No answers at your fingertips. No weather forecasts. No streaming videos. All past tense.

"Physical libraries," he said, breathing a little easier. They would have old copies of Encyclopedia Brittanica, wouldn't they? Or, had they gone the way of so many things, replaced by the digital, even in libraries? "Oh, ffff..." The Towning Foundation led an annual effort to donate millions of environmentally friendly books in either content or sustainably sourced at the beginning of every school year, which started weeks ago for most K-12 schools. By contaminating them, he would have destroyed the future of metal in the name of supporting the next generation.

Wall came up with a dozen other ways that Towning could have poisoned the waters, both literally and figuratively. His next-gen water filter. The new non-aerosol spray bottles. The recyclable cold packs for shipping food. Over the last five decades, the genius moved the needle on dozens of environmental, humanitarian, and medical efforts. He might have leveraged any or all of them for his purposes.

The way all the pieces fit together suggested that Towning developed his end-of-days plan decades ago. Without a consistent spouse, distanced from his children and brothers, and having cut off most relations with friends, nobody would have been close enough to figure out his intentions. His shrewd business deals never would have brought about alarm. An inventor turned investor and philanthropist wouldn't strike anyone as threatening. It was like a multi-decade magic trick.

Even if the feds, whether FBI, HLS, FDA, CDC, or any other three-letter agency, sniffed something wonky, they would have been hard-pressed to see the scale of the master plan. Towning's many financial books were probably immaculate. He could have hidden his intentions in layers of complexity under blankets of obfuscation, where the plan coalesced as more than the sum of its parts.

"The why of it though?" Wall asked himself. Towning thrust the world toward his "environmental singularity," the point in the future where technology would heal the world more than damage it. He espoused technological solutions to better humankind and the environment.

"Why turn your back on humanity?"

He could have done it out of guilt, anger, or any number of emotions, but Wall guessed it had to do with hubris. Once, at a university gathering, the old man said that "rare people could be smart, but bloated societies are always stupid and made bad choices, which is why great individuals like us have to make the hard decisions and bring about change here and now." At the time, Wall swelled with pride, but on the rooftop, the memory churned in his gut like the tuna MRE. While the idealistic side of him wanted to believe that Towning was coerced into action, his more cynical side knew that the mother ruster did it because he could. The old man saw a way to bring about his precious environmental singularity within his lifetime, and he acted upon it.

CHAPTER THIRTEEN

Something sharp slid across Wall's throat just below his Adam's apple. He flinched and jumped to his feet only to find himself in a sleeper hold with someone riding his back. With a surprisingly clinical mind, he evaluated that he only had a few seconds before he passed out. It was entirely possible that he was already a dead man struggling, with his throat slit, only upright because he hadn't bled out and his startled neurons hadn't figured it out yet. His vision started to fuzz into a tunnel.

He leaned forward, then leapt up and back in an attempt to squash his assailant under him when he slammed down on the roof. While falling, his attacker let go and spun around him with smooth, quick motions like a human-sized house spider. He landed hard, rattling his pre-tenderized body, stunned, prone, and helpless.

"Not bad, soldier," Plink said from atop him, her knife at his throat, dressed in nothing but her sports bra and tight boxer briefs. She offered him a hand to pull him up.

He slapped it away and wheezed, "I'm fine down here." As he clutched his broken ribs, his eyes lingered over her, operating of their own will. His caveman brain appreciated her slender and muscular body, beautiful in a UFC sort of way. Various scars, including an unprofessional row of fresh red stitches above the left hip, gave her character. He suspected the threadwork was his own but couldn't remember.

"You need to maintain better situational awareness," she said casually. "It's at the core of any good offense or defense."

"And, you couldn't have told me instead of whatever you call this."

She shrugged unabashed about so much of her body showing or his inadvertently loitering eyes, pilfering every second they could get. "Some lessons are worth teaching the hard way. You'll remember this smackdown better than a lecture."

"In that case, can I opt out of future lessons?"

Thickening her Hispanic accent, she said, "I ain't got no plan to die any time soon. I'm counting on you to watch my smokin' hot ass. So, you need better situational awareness."

Wall closed his eyes. "Fine. I'm gonna lay here for a minute, okay?"

She smiled sweetly and said, "No, no, no, mi abuelita." He was pretty sure she called him little grandma. "You need to push through the pain. Show me resilience and fortitude."

"Sure," he said, pushing himself up with a dad-level grunt.

As she dressed in her dry white coveralls from the lab, he told her about his epiphanies, about all the ways Towning could have disseminated the rusting diseases as a complete package, proliferated internationally without anyone noticing. With each bullet of his mental Powerpoint presentation, he grew angrier, his muscles tightened, and his body temp rose. By the end, he paced back and forth, the abused state of his body forgotten.

When he ran himself dry of rants, Plink said, "It's not your fault, you know?"

"I know," he spat.

"Hey, look at me." She stood and faced him inside his personal bubble, looking up at him as most people did, her dark brown eyes drilling into him. "The National Security Agency didn't piece it together. Nobody did. So, how could you?"

"I know," he said again, this time calmer. Hearing his own words didn't change the fact that his research contributed to the global-scale shitstorm descending on them. With a heavy cleaver, he compartmentalized his rage at Towning and forced himself to use his complicity to drive him forward, not destroy him. "Don't worry and don't treat me like a wounded man. My head is where it needs to be. I'm pissed but focused."

"Good," she said with a smile. "We have an important task. Kayla needs more electricity, right? Do you know where we can get solar panels?"

"Yeah," he said, remembering the rough location of a solar panel shop. "There was a label on the electrical box. The shop is pretty close."

Plink fist-bumped him. "Excellent. Time to go shopping." She donned her helmet and walked to the ladder, swaying her ass the whole way. Without looking back, she said, "You're supposed to watch my six, not my ass. Get a move on, soldier." Wall couldn't help but smile. He hefted his pack and followed, spraying each rung as he climbed down.

A moment later, they walked westward down the road, passing snaggles of cars and a few people who ubiquitously stayed clear of them. His knee and head ached less after the short bit of rest and had even recovered from Plink's "teachable moment." His anger at Towning gave him the focus he needed to push through the various aches, pains, and fatigue. The stim tab he took after his tuna breakfast didn't hurt either.

As they soldiered on, Plink reviewed the hand signals Spec Ops used in combat situations. He always had a good memory except for names and dates, so her instructions stuck to the inside of his skull like burnt enchiladas to an old baking sheet.

They entered a deserted section of town with stores selling stuff like furniture and herbs. The roof of a dentist's building drooped dangerously. Plink pointed out a woman looking at them through an incense shop's window, and said, "Situational awareness."

He held up his fist, the "stop" signal, then pointed out the roof of a nondescript single-story building with a dozen or more mounted solar panels. A small sign in the window read "Solar City." She waved him to follow and jogged into the driveway, then leaped over the head-height chain-link gate like a pole vaulter, all the more impressive because of her heavy pack, body armor, and shorter stature. While in decent shape, Wall wobbled and huffed as he climbed and teetered all over again on his way down.

By the time he reached the other side, she had picked the gate's padlock. With his bucket of exasperation spilling over, he whispered, "Why didn't you do that in the first place?"

"And miss out on the blooper reel?" she scoffed. "Fat chance." More seriously, she added, "Learn to keep up or I'll have to leave you behind someday." With the grace of a mountain lion, which was Wall's high school mascot, she ran and leapt onto a pallet, maintaining momentum as she bounded onto a taller crate, then off a high storage rack, where she launched upward to catch onto the roof and pull herself up.

"C'mon," she whispered, leaning over the roof and waving him up. "I'll catch you."

Without her superhuman agility and cat-like jumping skills, there was no way he'd make it even halfway. Then he smiled. "Hold up." He pulled the tarp off the crate Plink used as her first high step. "Look at that." A pallet held a double stack of brand-new solar panels. "Twenty-four," he reported. Each read, "100 Watts."

While she leaped over to a lower part of the roof and swung down, he withdrew his carbon fiber knife and cut the tough bands that held the boxes in place. "Try to keep up," he whispered. They stood, admiring their precious treasure. Better than a dragon's hoard.

The *chk-chk* sound of a shotgun came from behind them. That sound, whether perfected by shotgun manufacturers to cause a human's inner animal to clench up or people learned to fear it from too many movies, performed its intended purpose of initiating his fight-or-flight response. Wall froze. A low throaty voice with a Boston accent said, "You and your short-and–harries might want to listen up. My shop is a crime-free zone. Capeesh? I have an itchy finger."

"Sorry, sir," Plink said, sounding far younger than she had a right to. "I need electricity for our grandma."

"Turn around," the man said. "Slowly, now."

Mid-turn, three quick sonic booms smacked their ears. *Bang, bang, bang.* Turning the rest of the way and drawing his pistol, Wall watched the man fall. Three holes, one in the heart, another below the Adam's apple, and the third between the eyes told of Plink's incredible aim. The surprisingly small man for such a deep voice crumpled like nothing more than a human-shaped sack of rice, thrice dead before he hit the ground.

When Wall's mind caught up to reality, his chest pounded and his breath caught mid-throat. She killed a man in the light of day, slain for protecting his property. She slayed him over solar panels. Like the guy they shot back in Portland, he didn't deserve it. When Wall's brain connected with his mouth again, he asked, "What the hell did you do that for?"

While he looked around, sure that someone else would emerge from the building or a police officer would roll up, she casually explained that "This guy pulled a shotgun on us, Wall. Never aim a weapon at someone unless you plan to pull the trigger immediately." She tapped him on the helmet. "Stick to that rule, and you may live through this." Turning back to the solar panels, she said, "Now, help me with these boxes."

One nut shocked and the other growing accustomed to chaos, he turned and set about the business of plundering. They strapped four boxed solar panels with inner bags onto each of their backpacks with lengths of DC wire. Once ready to head back, Plink said, "We'll come back for more on another run."

Pointing at the murdered man splayed out for anyone to see, Wall said, "Are we just gonna leave him lying there?" It wasn't a matter of seeing a dead body, having seen plenty of death in Ethiopia. It was the complete lawlessness here in America, not far from his home, a shoot and grab that he participated in. He considered himself a law-abiding citizen, not part of the rising crime in Eugene that grew over the last decade.

She bumped his arm. "We honor the man by giving his death a purpose. He'll deter others from taking our solar panels." Her nebulous logic didn't fit easily in his sense of morality. He knew he'd need to change long-engrained senses of wrong and right, some of which he could easily fit into his world-view, but her reasoning didn't sit well with him, or at least not yet. Seeing the tilt of his head, she added, "Remember, the mission is all."

A burr in his mind, nearly jammed up a mental gear, one that recalled talking to Towning on a private plane ride to Seattle for a bioengineering conference. Towning had used the same logic. While enjoying an aged tequila, he'd said, "Death is unavoidable in the name of true progress. It is necessary to protect all that matters." Wall had interpreted that comment as support for peace-keeping deployments and a nod to Wall's experiences abroad. Now, he looked at it from a different perspective. The bastard's plan was to kill in the name of environmental progress.

He followed Plink back to the lab, more aware of the people they passed. Any of them might try to steal their highly visible and cumbersome panels, stealing from the slow robbers that some might consider easy picking despite their arms and armor. About halfway back, he whispered, "The ends justify the means." A day ago, he might have said only evil men used that logic. Today, he had to change in order to be unerringly ruthless, to combat Towning no matter the cost, both to preserve his sanity and for any part of metal they might save.

"Wall, you're a smart guy. Don't let your overly bright mind confound what is moral and what is necessary. Warriors like us fight so others don't have to. We aren't civilized in order to save those who are."

"I'm not a warrior like you and Rhino. I'm a grunt at best."

"You are a sexy-ass combination of warrior and super-nerd," she said. "You'll see."

He followed in silence, unsure if she'd just called him sexy in earnest as a joke or implying the opposite. Unbidden, images of her in her sleek body in underwear popped into his mind as he trudged onward. He–

"And we're back," she said happily.

Wall grunted and nearly fell over his own feet as he came out of wherever his mind went when he couldn't remember. Straining his neck from left to right, he tried to take in everything, instantly afraid that something else had gone wrong. The quick motion sent his vision into a case of the spins. He wasn't sure what he found more disturbing, the fact that his brain was so injured that he kept blacking out or that he'd been unaware of his surroundings in an increasingly dangerous world.

They walked around back and climbed the ladder with the cumbersome solar panels on their backs, more than a little challenging for Wall in his post-crash state. Up top, he took a moment to hydrate, noting that they'd need to fill up on water soon.

Patting the stack of solar panels, she said, "Time to put that oversized brain of yours to use."

"Aren't you gonna help?" he asked.

"What? And break my pretty nails?" She spread out her gloved fingers as if to proudly display a perfect manicure. "Not a chance. I'll be back."

Over the next hour, Wall assembled and connected solar panels to the building's junction box, which had plenty of space for more. "Not bad," he said and stood back to appreciate his handiwork. The process went far slower than it would have if he didn't have to decontaminate himself and the hardware at each step.

"Slow is smooth, and smooth is fast," he said as he rested on the plastic crate and drank the last of his water, massaging his knee. Ever since Plink left on missions unknown, his peripheral awareness faltered plenty of times. He was glad that his Spidey senses kicked in when Plink returned. If they hadn't, she surely would have taught him another "lesson."

"Look what I bought," she said, pulling a half loaf of bread, a mostly full peanut butter tub, and dubious-looking red raspberry jam from a cloth grocery bag. He was pretty sure she used the word "bought" very liberally. As she smeared copious amounts of peanut butter on white bread, she asked, "How's my pretty-boy electrician?"

"He never showed up," Wall said and snapped his fingers as if exasperated. "So, you're stuck with this guy."

She slapped a piece of bread onto a mountain of jam, squishing it together. "You need all the calories you can get if you're gonna keep up."

He ate it slowly, sipping at a warm Doctor Pepper. The bread was stale, but he didn't give a turd's tail. The overly thick layers inside more than compensated. "Thanks," he said with a full mouth. "Fine dining at its best."

"I am a great cook, aren't I?"

"The best."

She checked the sat phone again and shook her head.

"No love?"

"It's like they aren't even there."

In the next hour, they repeated the solar panel snatch and grab, taking a different route this time in hopes of throwing off anyone interested in "collecting taxes." After connecting this set to the box, during which Plink went on some mission, they'd tripled their power. Next, they each carried a pair of thirty-two-kilogram lithium-ion batteries from the same shop. Plink, with her small frame, a head shorter, and much lighter, miraculously managed to keep pace with Wall. He supposed there was a reason she was part of the most elite unit in the US Army, general badassery.

"Break time," Plink said once Wall connected the last battery. She popped a warm, bio-plastic bottle of generic "cola," took a sip, and handed it over. "You know what?"

Wall slumped to the roof. "What?"

She smiled down at him. "You look like a soldier-shaped pile of crap."

He drank another sip, flopped onto his back, looked into the void of dimensionless clouds overhead, and said, "I feel like one."

"Do you know the cure for suffering?" she asked after laying down next to him, rolling onto her side to see him better.

He took off his helmet and wiped his sweaty brow on his sleeve. "I'm sure you're gonna tell me."

She nudged him in his rusting arm. "Death."

He slow clapped. "Funny." It would have been humorous if dying wasn't so likely and narrowly escaped of late. So far, they'd survived three close encounters with death, fire, crash, and shotgun. The question was, how many more close calls would he get? Nine lives like a cat?

They lay in quiet, and Wall's eyelids began to stick closed for longer and longer. Just as he started nodding off, Plink rolled over him as if prepared to do pushups and sniffed at him. "That's nasty. Time for a cold bath."

Begrudgingly, he followed her to the stream across the street. Plink stripped all the way down without any outward sign of modesty. When Wall turned away and stopped at his underwear, hesitant to openly display himself to the world, she said, "Off with them, farm boy. You can't scrub the nasties away like that."

Wall did everything he could to hide his swelling evolutionary imperative. Just the knowledge that she was naked was enough to get him going, so he tried to focus on scrubbing down with the scratchy side of a brillo pad while examining his bruises and scars. In the end, it was the freezing cold water that kept his buddy from standing at full salute.

Next, they scrubbed their clothes in the stream with some harsh powdered soap that Plink found while he was hooking up the electronics. Rather than dress in his camos, Plink brought a full set of clothes from one of her solo pilfering runs through the surrounding neighborhood. He dressed in the beige Maui long-sleeve shirt and overly loose gray hiking pants. At least they were tall, though not quite tall enough, so they didn't cover his ankles or wrists. They were better than his "borrowed" camos, and after cutting a length of cord to fashion a belt, they worked just fine.

"I could use a jacket," he said.

Taking on a barbarian's voice, she added, "Rest first. Then we pillage like Vikings."

All too happy to grant his body a respite, he loaded up and sprayed down his new clothes and his gear as he put it on. Heavily laden, she led the way back, him inadvertently glancing at her ass from time to time, which he was pretty sure she was encouraging with an amplified sway of her hips.

Up top, they laid out their clothes flat to bake in the first patches of afternoon sun. "Get some sleep," she said with a light bump to his shoulder.

"If you insist." He sat, sighed heavily, then leaned back, using his rucksack as a pillow. Most of his sore muscles slackened as he blinked heavily, his dry eyes clinging to their tired lids. With a second blink, he slipped into sleep.

Plink immediately nudged him, kneeling at his side. "Wake up, Wall."

He rolled to his side and groaned, "Leave me alone. I just got to sleep."

Nudging him softly, she said, "It's my turn, big boy. Your cycle is up."

He struggled to come out of it, sure that he hadn't been out for more than a few seconds. But then, the smell of coffee only inches from his nose roused him with the promise of liquid gold. He greedily accepted a dark-green ceramic mug that read, "World's Greatest Boss!" Then, his soul went from almost ascending to despairingly crushed when his fingertips touched the cup, depressingly cold.

"It's something similar to coffee," she said as she yawned and laid down for her turn to sleep. "Dreadful stuff but pound it back."

He cringed after sipping the gritty slurry. "This is an insult to coffee."

"I cold-brewed cappuccino grinds," she said. "Wait 'til you get to the sediment at the bottom. You'll want to gag but eat the chunks anyway. That's where the real caffeine is." She reached into her pack and withdrew a white-and-black bag of Wandering Goat Columbian beans, a local blend, and a chocolate bar. "If you munch on these together, it isn't too bad, and you'll get a good kick."

"Sure," he said. "I woke up hoping for a solid kicking."

Plink laid her head back, closed her eyes, and instantly began the steady breathing of a person in deep sleep, a skill that one learned in the armed forces, an ability he'd have to perfect again. Her face slackened as the stress washed away, leaving her more beautiful for it. In another life, Wall would have asked her out, but that world would have to undo Towning's blight. However, in that alternate future, their paths wouldn't have intertwined, and she'd be surrounded by hundreds of elite soldiers knocking at her door.

After gulping Plink's swill, Wall alternated between pacing and stretching slowly. He couldn't take on any pose that put his noggin below his heart because his head would thump, and he would verge on the edge of passing out.

"Noted," he whispered when he recovered. "Take it easy on the old thought maker."

While he was asleep, Plink had "purchased" a tool kit at the "five finger discount store" and plenty of other things, including two green plastic patio chairs, a variety of condiments, and water bottles. Everything smelled of bleach, a new normal he would have to get used to.

Torn between finding more rest and his urge to be useful, he considered if there was anything worthy of scavenging. Numerous options stood out as ideal assets. A jacket. A real belt. Better yet, new clothes. A pair of thick socks. Instant coffee. Yet, none of those furthered the mission. Once they got established, they could think of common comforts, or rather, vanishing comforts.

Kayla needed as much electricity as possible, and their panel-heavy setup was capped out because of too few batteries. "Batteries it is."

Moments later, after double-checking his compliment of decontaminated gear, he walked northwest in an unpredictable roundabout path to the solar panel shop. He practically vibrated with nervous energy, whether due to being rested, the coffee beans, or venturing into enemy territory without a tier-one operator.

On his circuitous route, Wall decided to drop into a TJ Maxx for a set of better-fitting threads, ones that didn't sluff off or chafe. Based on the numerous footprints through the rust-covered entryway, he surmised that he wasn't even close to the first person to raid the clothing store. That meant someone, or more worrisome, many someones, might still be inside. Every human interaction represented a potential threat, so he went in focused and ready, with his M4 drawn.

The early-bird shoppers had ransacked the store. Worse, most of the racks and stands corroded into piles intermixed with clothing that Wall had to avoid. The idea that he might not be alone itched at the nugget in his brain responsible for internally yelling, "Caution!" With his semi-automatic sweeping in an imitation of Plink's form, he cleared the store in a clockwise formation. About halfway around, a group of men and women ran for the exit with full shopping bags. In his overly amped state, he nearly shot them but held his trigger finger.

Once he finished his loop, he began shopping, starting in the men's section, which was far less dilapidated than the rest of the store, and the big and tall section was nearly pristine. He shoved two pairs of long green hiking pants and a long-sleeved shirt into his pack, keeping an eye on the door. Even better, he found bags of thick socks and boxer briefs. Best of all, he scored an ash-gray raincoat.

Next, he found drab beige equivalents in the women's section, guessing at Plink's size. His dad once told him, "Now, Wall. Never guess a woman's size. You either know it or you don't. If you overestimate her girth, you're telling her that she looks fat. If you underestimate her size, you're saying what size you want her to be, which means she's fat." Going against the fatherly advice, he plundered with his best mental gauge, aided by memories of their riverside cleansing. He silently cursed himself when he realized picturing her form had booted situational awareness to the curb.

Back outside, feeling better, he swung wide around the solar panel shop and approached it from the west, steering clear of men and women regardless of how helpless they seemed. A nagging feeling that someone was following him raised the tides of tension in his shoulders, so he circled back to spot his pursuer with his rifle twitch-level ready but found nobody there.

"It's just your nerves," he told himself and continued on his way.

The dead shop owner laid right where they left him in a dried stain of his own blood. He looked down at the body for a moment, regretting the avoidable death. There would be too much of that in the coming days and weeks as resources became more scarce. It was an inevitable truth.

"It's a shame, though."

As soon as he entered the building, he knew something was wrong, which was only confirmed by the grinding *chk-chk* of a shotgun. From an open doorway, a thin, short man pulled the trigger.

CHAPTER FOURTEEN

*B*ang!

The fact that the shotgun's buckshot hadn't laid Wall out and filled him with holes flooded him with a profound level of confusion and an even greater deluge of relief. When he regained his composure, he realized his assailant lay on the floor screaming in anguish. Whatever happened, Wall knew one thing; he had to end the would-be killer before the man recovered and shot again.

With each stride forward, he paused and let loose a single shot, not fancy or clean like Plink's immaculately placed bullets, merely good enough to hit the man close to his center of mass. The guy stopped yelling after the second thunderclap. It took five steps to close the distance. His target shook five times.

When he stood over his kill, Wall saw what had happened. Dumb luck saved his life. Where the butt of the shotgun should have been, only composite splinters remained. The right side of the guy's face looked like the world's scariest Halloween costume, ripped up and disgusting. Under his M4's light, Wall saw that the man's weapon belonged to the other dead guy outside, stained by blood, one of the most invasively corrosive substances to ever exist. It had backfired.

He quickly sprayed down his combat rifle and slid a new cap over the end, spurred on by his fear of a similar rust-induced accident. His hands shook and his mouth went dry. By all measures of luck and justice, he should have died, or at the very least, he should have flown off his feet with a number of new holes in him or his bulletproof vest. Instead, the other guy lay in his own blood, guilty of defending his shop and seeking revenge for the guy outside.

With the damage already done, he sidestepped around the corpse's fresh blood and did what he came to do: obtain more batteries. He tried to convince himself that if he didn't steal them, didn't give purpose to coming here, the man's death would have been for naught. While at it, he plundered a spool of DC wire, various connectors, and some mounting gear for the solar panels.

On his way back out, he awkwardly navigated around the growing pool of blood, noting how much this guy's diminutive corpse looked like the guy outside. The side of his face not destroyed by the backfire looked like a younger clone, marking this as a family-run business. The father and his progeny might have ended then and there as so many would.

By the time he wound south, then eastward, to Renegade Genomix, he arrived to find Plink awake and running around the building at him, all sorts of furious. Her nostrils flared. With fiery Hispanic anger, she yelled, "What the fuck, soldier! It's one thing for me to go out there alone, but you...You're not trained in urban warfare. If you take a risk like that again, I'll neuter you. Understood, soldier?"

"I'm a grown-ass man," he retorted.

"No, you're not," she said, a nut calmer. "You are an essential part of this operation. If you die, the mission is tanked."

In an attempt to de-escalate, he pumped his palms outward and stated, "Kayla has the science covered. I'm virtually useless when it comes to viruses, redundant and unskilled. You and Rhino are the warriors. I'm not."

"Have you heard the phrase, 'Two is one, and one is none?' We need redundancy and a backup plan."

"Of course," he said, "but, Nellibi is our number two."

"You are a survivor," she said, something other than professional concern on her face. "I can't say the same for them. You *are* the backup plan."

Relying on his sensitivity training as a professor, he said, "I respect your tactical perspective. Please respect my scientific viewpoint. It would take me a decade or more to replace either of them."

"Funny, Wall. You said it might take years for someone skilled anyway, so what's the difference? And what if they aren't resilient enough to survive the new world order? If they can't survive, then all we have is you."

"They're fine."

"For now."

"Then we agree to disagree."

She cracked her neck and sighed. "The damage is done. You might as well finish the job. Give her here." She took one of the batteries.

After connecting the new equipment, she gave him a thick strip of beef jerky as a peace offering.

"The jerky gods are bountiful this day!" he said reverently, kissing it and holding it to the sky. Then he lifted her in a spinning hug and bounced up and down on one leg as she laughed. When he let her down, he swayed side to side, dizzy but still smiling.

"Wall, regarding this jerky infatuation...the first step is admitting you have a problem."

He slid a sliver of salty heaven between his molars and gently mashed the gold standard of all food and moaned. "For some men, it's liquor. For others, it's gambling. Jerky is my vice of choice." For the next half hour, he regaled her with all things jerky. "The food of the gods. Ambrosia. Love in food form." He described how it was prepared, from cow to grocery store, and waxed on about his numerous experiences with making jerky in the backyard with his dad. He lamented that since he moved to Eugene, he had lived in a condo without a space to home smoke his own. "But," he said happily. "Without refrigerators, smoked meats will make a return."

"Hey!" someone yelled from somewhere behind the building.

With terrifying speed, Plink ran toward the voice, her M4 rising on the way.

"Hey, you up there!"

"What's up, Kayla?" Plink called down as she planted her foot on the short rim around the building, looking like a female Captain Morgan.

The scientist still wore white coveralls, goggles, and mask, her head barely sticking out the back door. "Stop stomping around. It's hard to concentrate."

"Come on up," Plink said. "We have peanut butter and jelly sandwiches."

"No," the scientist said. "I drink soylent."

Plink looked at Wall, who shrugged and said, "It's an efficiency thing."

"Coming down." Plink waved him to follow before sliding down the vertical supports like a fireman on a double pole, but with disinfectant-laden rags in each hand to buffer the friction against the old and crusty iron. He, on the other hand, took the slow way down, prepared to be the bureaucratic translator between Kayla the lead scientist/engineer, and Plink the lead of all things deadly. It wasn't a role he would have chosen, but it was the one he had to play.

Down below, the only thing he could see about Kayla, who only stuck her goggles and nose through the door, was that her eyes were even more sunken and rimmed with darker circles. Plink offered her a water bottle, but the scientist shook her head. "I have a drinking tube."

The ultimate in efficiency, he thought.

Plink held out a strip of jerky, only for Kayla to shudder. "I can't eat that."

"Why not?" Plink asked.

"I told you, 'I only eat soylent.'"

The Delta Force operator shrugged, "Nope. Not anymore, honey. You have a new diet. You eat what you can when you can."

"No," Kayla yelped as if Plink drew a knife, retreating by a couple of inches. "I have enough soylent for a month." He'd checked, and this wasn't even close to true. Their virus expert was rationing too much, but Wall needed to build trust, so he didn't press the issue. "Besides, my gut isn't used to other food."

Plink shrugged again. "Suit yourself. You'll run out eventually. Then your tune will change." When Plink took a healthy bite of the jerky, Wall practically slobbered, then cheered up when she handed the rest to him. The two ladies watched him descend into euphoria.

Plink turned back to Kayla and said, "So, Doc. What's the good news?"

"Good news?" she scoffed.

He rephrased the question. "What results have you observed through experimentation since this morning?"

Kayla's eyes reflected joy, almost as reverent as Wall with jerky. "Towning's work was impeccable, absolutely masterful."

Wall visualized the explosion that swallowed Towning's house and basement lab, a trap meant for him, and barely withheld an outburst filled with the sentiment of all the curses in all the languages that ever existed throughout time.

"Anything we don't know?" Plink asked.

Kayla squinted. "I presume you do not know–" She cut herself off.

With the joy of jerky in his mouth, he took a different tact. "What observations suggest Towning's level of skill?"

"He interwove sections of DNA from each virus into the others, thereby minimizing competitive interactions. Of note, he subtly altered *my* HIV's morphology for aerosol transmission." While such a feat must have been insanely challenging, Wall didn't like the admiration with which she spoke.

He swallowed his distaste and interpreted for Plink. "She says the diseases work together and he gave wings to the HIV variant."

Kayla's expression of adoration faded as she heard Wall's simplification. "A crude and insufficient interpretation."

"What else have you learned?" Plink asked.

As Kayla twisted her face as if physically wounded by Plink's words, Wall interjected. "Have you observed any other aberrant deviations from the samples?"

She whispered, "Towning removed my kill switch from his HIV strain. Further, he made the pathogens immune to my variant."

A series of curses flooded Wall's mind. After an awkward pause, he asked, "Are you saying you can't kill it?"

"*I* can achieve the desired outcome. However, *I* require silence to concentrate, and it will take time."

"Get some shut-eye, Kayla," Plink said. "You'll feel better with–"

The scientist drew her face back into the dark office, and the door closed behind her without so much as a wave.

"Back up top, old man," Plink said, shooing Wall to the ladder. He didn't point out that they were probably about the same age. "You damaged my sleep by going off base, so I need to start over."

While she conked out, breathing easily as soon as her head met the rucksack. He considered doing some yoga, which reminded him of his ex-girlfriend, Talia, the one who cheated on him with another instructor. Instead, he sat on the cement block crown around the rooftop for a beat, dangling his feet over the front of the building. "Living on the edge," he quietly sang in a bad approximation of Steven Tyler's unique vocals.

After his legs went numb, he leaned back on his backpack and watched the fog swirl, lift, then fall. It gave him time to ruminate on the past twenty-four hours. He didn't think he was traumatized yet, but there was plenty to unpack, and there would be an abundance of time for the downfall to change that. Therapists, a breed that might go extinct, would have a field day helping unload his "emotional wounds." The last twenty-four hours were like the worst stints in Ethiopia, a series of irrevocable consequences he needed to learn from. He regretted that some of his army buddies struggled with PTSD, and in most cases, strained themselves to adapt back to the "civilized" requirements of a peaceful society. Wall? Not so much. He considered himself lucky to transition back without suffering the way that all too many did. Things like starving kids and mass burial sites were enough to screw with anyone's head, and he wasn't immune to it, but he had a series of meaningful goals that saw him through. He could have given up after failing to adapt bacteria to consume landmines, but that mission transferred into a goal of healing the planet. Now, he had a different mission, to aid the healing of metal and man in any way he could.

For some reason, it pissed off his ex-girlfriends that he wasn't more damaged as if he needed to be broken so they could fix him. Shaking his head, he recalled Heather's complaint that "It hurts when you hide your true feelings from me." Such a load of BS. Some things were best left in the past, like today. He couldn't resurrect the dead, so why should he resurrect his memories of them? Ueskev wouldn't come back. The pilots sacrificed themselves, dead, irrevocably done and gone. The countless who burned in Portland wouldn't rise again.

"It's all about the future," he told himself. "About survival." The things to come weren't for the weak or those who couldn't adapt. They were headed toward a mass die-off. Alpha Bravo couldn't stop the downfall. Instead, they could only protect Kayla and Nellibi and fight for the eventual rebound of humankind.

"So we must improvise, adapt, and overcome." The phrase belonged to the Marines, not the Army, but who could care about that distinction anymore? Without firearms, fighter planes, and warships, the oft-rivaling branches were all but toothless now. They would remain so until they learned to forge bronze armor and swords. He wondered if the Delta Force and Navy SEALs used another phrase in place of, "Improvise, adapt, and overcome."

"Spec ops," he whispered. He needed to adopt the tier-one operators' skills and hone his instincts. Luck, like at the solar panel shop, would only carry him so far. He could learn and learn fast. One didn't get to be a professor without a sharp mind. The problem was that learning after the world went to shit wasn't ideal. Wall had to live through the short term to assimilate skills for the long run.

So, he turned to what he knew best; He would assimilate observations and practice techniques until they were part of him. In that vein, he drew, aimed, and dry-fired his custom M4 and Sig Sauer P17 pistol over a hundred times each. He couldn't fire precious rounds and didn't want to wake Plink with gunfire, so he had no idea if he was improving, but he doubted it could hurt. He also practiced loading and unloading magazines. Given enough time to set up, his aim was plenty good.

"I need to cut down on my fire time," he told himself. Any delay could end his life but rushing a shot and missing might be just as bad, so a few repetitions turned into a hundred, with frequent cleaning steps in between. By the end, he may not have improved, but he gained some level of fluidity with each weapon. He also practiced with his carbon-fiber knife, drawing quickly and reviewing the few attacks he knew, repeating them over and over. With no illusions about his skills, he said, "Bring a gun to a knife fight and a knife to a fist fight."

The loudest guy in his squad, Outhouse, named for the amount of BS that came from his mouth, said that "if you train during the apocalypse, you're already too late." Only through advanced preparation could you live through a mass culling event. He carried on and on about the bomb shelter behind his dad's New England fishing cabin, where they buried two shipping containers and reinforced the sides. They stocked it with guns and loads of canned food. His pops spared no expense. Having drawn the glitchy circuit on the brain-board, he didn't convince anyone to his extreme on the prepper spectrum.

"Outhouse," he whispered as he drew his pistol again. "You were right about the apocalypse. Just not which one." All that canned food wouldn't last long. Normal guns rusted and backfired. Steel shipping containers corroded and caved in. Even fishing hooks would rust.

He drew and aimed his M4 while walking the way Plink and Rhino did with bent knees and nimble feet. His knee clicked, and he fell over, nearly smacking into a solar panel, then shook his head in frustration.

"How did I not see this coming?" he asked himself. "The signs were there. He just ignored them."

Rolling onto his back, he considered where the greatest asshole to ever live might be, what paradise he chose for living out the remainder of his days. Wall would choose a tropical island, far from the threats of desperate people. The devil on his shoulder would have hidden a back door for a cure and taken his family into isolation, then waited until humanity found its equilibrium before returning to conquer humankind with steel and technology.

CHAPTER FIFTEEN

Wall nearly fell off the edge of Renegade Genomix when his head lulled, jolting him awake in the near darkness of dusk, nearly shrouded by mist and clouds. His dangling legs stung with pins and needles because the roof's crown had cut off his circulation. After a few heavy heartbeats, he slouched back onto the roof away from the danger zone, looking up at the darkening fog. The whole reason he sat on the ledge was so he would be too afraid to fall asleep.

"A lot of good that did."

Laying face up, waiting for his legs to return to normal, his senses flared. He couldn't tell what, but something was wrong. As nimble as possible, he rolled and rotated so he could poke his head above the short wall that ringed the roof.

Then he heard it. Somebody scuffed the pavement on the road to the west. Nothing stood out in the misty dullness of the parking lot or street. Wall let out a sigh when a scrawny coyote skittered down the road and the constricting nugget in his chest let up. Of course, it was an animal. Who on the sane side of the asylum would come out in that gloom? It was an excellent way to earn an express-delivered trip to a cheese grater situation.

Wall relaxed, thinking aloud. "Of course, we're safe. Nobody knows we're here."

While lying on his belly, hoping to see the coyote again, the sky grew darker still, a welcome gift from nature that would hide their set-back building. Then he heard it again. Excited about seeing the critter this time. What he would have given to have his phone's camera, but such technology was a thing of the past.

Then he saw them.

Six silhouettes strutted toward Renegade Genomix, sporting an array of guns. Two men carried hunting rifles. Another two held AR-15s. One shouldered a long-barreled shotgun. The guy in the center of their line gripped two pistols. Wall was amazed when the pistol guy swung the dangerous end of his firearms past his buddies, all of whom were short and squat, two of them particularly chubby. Each wore dark pants, bright white tops and shoes, and flat-billed black caps.

"A fucking gang," he whispered. So much tolerance toward methamphetamine was bound to bite Eugene in the ass, and here it was, come to extract its toll. With no illusion about being able to handle these guys on his own, he threw his plastic bottle of dielectric oil at Plink, not waiting to see if it hit home.

"Carlos and Mateo," said the handgun guy, no-shit pointing at them with his barrels. "Go around back." The guy with the shotgun and a rifle-toting guy split off, unaware they walked in front of their buddy's AR-15.

"Good," Wall whispered to himself. "No safety or training."

"Correct," Plink said in his ear, nearly scaring a curse out of him. "We have the high ground. They're out in the open." Wall still didn't like the six-on-two odds.

Their leader held up his fist in the well-known command for stop and redundantly called out, "Halt," nullifying the point of the silent hand sign. Wall smiled, recognizing the guy was racking up ineptitude points, which boded well if things came to exchanging bullets. The thugs stopped, meaning that there was some discipline among them, at least showing a hierarchy. This was even better. A stupid leader was a unit's most life-threatening attribute.

The central guy yelled, "Come out! This is your reckoning day."

"He's an idiot," Plink whispered before she crawled like a giant spider on hands and toes to the back side of the building, gone to take care of Carlos and Mateo. Announcing himself was a strategic error, a great way to win the state championship contest for the Kazinski Award. The two roly-poly guys with the ARs backed up a pace, probably aware of their leader's blunder.

"They're the smarter ones." Watch out for them.

Four quick pops, which carried the *clack-thud* of suppressed rounds, announced Carlos's and Mateo's ill-matched encounter with Plink. No yells or return fire ensued, a testament to Plink's marksmanship. Kill shots.

Out front, their leader reacted by pulling the triggers of his pistols with impacts climbing from the ground, up the building, and into the sky. Successive recoil in the hands of an untrained fool tended to raise each shot higher than the last. The guy would have been better served by holding one pistol with both hands and slowing himself down. All the same, Wall ducked behind the short ledge as a bullet whizzed just overhead, the classic high-pitch to low-pitch *zeeoow* caused by doppler shift as it passed.

Shot at twice in one day and three times in twenty-four hours exceeded Wall's quota by precisely three times. He had to wonder if there was something about him that attracted gunfire.

When the pistol fire stopped, Wall pumped up his confidence by saying, "Now," then propped himself on the short rampart and aimed his suppressed M4 at the leader. With as much self-control as he could muster, he let off two shots. The first bullet landed with that low *thunk* of a bullet on flesh. The second ricocheted off the pavement with a crack, a miss. He switched targets before seeing what happened to his first pin cushion and released another two rounds, forcing himself to pause longer between shots to recover from the recoil. The first shot battered the new target. A secondary boom synchronized with his follow-up shot, accompanied by a very close impact on the cinder blocks less than a meter away.

With the speed of a groundhog, he retreated behind the safety of the roof's crown. Someone shouted, "Run!" More rounds clapped, impacting randomly and flying wildly overhead, suppressive fire. The shots stopped, replaced by the patter of running feet. Wall popped back up with his rifle at the ready.

Both of his previous targets laid on the ground, the leader rasping and writhing, holding his chest with shallow breaths. The other was still and silent. The last two men ran for the road. Wall aimed at the slow, portly guy, followed him with the scope's red dot, and shot.

The rotund thug stumbled as his shoulder lurched forward and screamed, "Puta!"

Wall aimed at the fallen man, placing the crosshairs on his back, relaxed into the shot, and fired as he'd done so many times while hunting and practicing, earning the desired effect; the attacker stopped moving.

The remaining runner vanished down the road behind the trees before Wall could take aim. "Gah!" he whisper-yelled, angry that he let one get away. No good could come of the guy escaping. He could come back after regrouping with a larger cohort of his gang and attack with overwhelming numbers, and if they went up in the chain of command, they might have intelligence and strategy on their side.

Contrary to how people say time slows with hyper-focus in high-stress situations, this encounter sped by so quickly that Wall barely had time to register what happened, most of his response and thoughts coming as a result of training and instincts. The proof of the quick skirmish splayed out on the ground in the parking lot in the form of two men, one gasping for air, soon to die.

He was strangely upbeat about the outcome. Any conflict you came out of alive was a good one. Not better than no fight at all, but a win nonetheless. At the front of the building, three down, two of which were kills, the last of which would die soon. He imagined Plink's donations to the Grim Reaper out back. Five out of six dead, and no casualties on the side of Alpha Bravo.

After the fact, he contemplated the deed of shooting a fleeing man in the back. Honorable men didn't do such things, considered completely immoral by Americans. But, in the moment, he hadn't cared a spark's ass. These guys weren't civilized men who came to engage in a lengthy and polite discourse about the finer details of dick size. They chose to walk into his domain, guns blazing, and threaten his lab. "Screw 'em." They no longer lived in a moral world. Anyone who judged him wouldn't be worth their weight in rust during or after the fall.

Rather than guilt, a jumble of what-ifs plowed through his mind. What if he hadn't roused when he did and retreated behind the crown of the roof? Would they have shot him while dozing? If he and Plink hadn't owned the high ground, the enemy could have killed him. If those guys had more discipline and strategy, things could have gone very differently. Yet he remained unscathed–or, no more scathed than after the crash. Once again, luck was on their side.

He kissed his fingers, then tapped the cinder block, then cursed himself, winced at his own stupidity, and immediately began sterilizing his hand, then the M4. "Sometime, luck will smite me." Or had it already smote everyone pre-emptively through Towning?

"Come on down," Plink said, cracked two green glowsticks, tossed one to Wall, then slid down the ladder like a fireman's pole. He followed at a sane pace.

The two men in the back had holes in the tops of their heads, each one within an inch of the crown. There was good shooting, and then there was Plink shooting. In the Army, rumors spread that in some elite special forces circles, operators would fire upward of a thousand rounds a week so they could end a combatant's life before the enemy had time to pull a trigger on a bomb or gun. They also said that women typically make the best shooters because fewer of them learned bad habits before they joined the armed forces.

Before yesterday, he participated in exactly two gunfights, both in Ethiopia, the first of which ended with surgeons reconnecting the broken pieces of his right humerus. In the last twenty-four hours, bullets flew on four separate occasions, the other guys dying for the exchanges. Alpha Bravo was definitely doing its fair share of hastening Towning's great culling of man. They were the tip of the spear, the deadliest component of lawlessness. In each instance, the opponents threatened Wall and Alpha Bravo first. The mission outweighed the cost of their lives.

"Help me get rid of these men," Plink said, hefting one of their hands. "Stay clear of the blood. No sense in ruining your pretty-boy clothes."

Not relishing the job, he stepped forward and took the corpse's feet. "Where to?"

She jutted her chin. "About twenty meters past the trees, the dead Nissan Versa should have a plastic gas tank. Good fire starter." On their way into town, they passed plenty of high-end cars with rusted underbellies that smelled of spilled gasoline, whereas the cheaper cars held their fuel. As they went about the dirty business of carrying bodies to the budget car, complete darkness closed in, making the glowsticks absolutely necessary. The two fatties proved annoyingly difficult to carry, like a big FU from the not-so-great beyond.

After they loaded the last of the five bodies on the car, he re-sanitized and said, "This is the universal law of man: blood spilled cries out for more."

Solemnly, Plink asked, "Who said that?"

"My dad, but I have no idea where he got it from."

She tapped at her pants in that one-two, one-two pattern of hers. "They'll come back for blood."

Re-sanitizing himself after porting the bodies to the car, he said, "You're probably right."

Sliding halfway under the little sedan with a length of hose, she tapped the underside of the tank with a screwdriver, then retreated quickly, bringing the smell of gasoline with her. The highly flammable liquid collected in a bowl she had found in the neighbor's house.

"Ridding the world of bodies is nasty business."

While preparing the funeral pyre, she asked, "Did you notice the matching tattoos? No. Look here, there's a 541 on each of them." She folded back the collar. Sure enough, a fancy graffiti-style "541" marked his neck.

She splashed gas on the man. "What does it mean?"

"That's the Eugene area code. They must be a local gang. Probably meth."

"I hear it's a growth market," she said. "Or at least it was. No labs means no meth."

She splashed gas on the back tire. "The 541s won't let this stand. We killed five of their henchmen. They'll assume we're a rival gang and come for us with greater numbers."

"Some things never change," Wall said. "Assholes never stay at home to spare the rest of us."

Dumping gasoline on the front tire, she said, "It's a biological imperative, you know? Their alpha dog *needs* to emerge from this chaos as the lord of his kingdom. By killing his men, we challenged his alpha-ness."

Most men wouldn't want to eat anything while disposing of bodies, but Wall was no ordinary man, so he popped a sliver of jerky into his mouth. "The F'ing world is falling apart."

"Astute observation. How ever did you figure that out?" She lit a match and tossed it into the gasoline-soaked pavement. Within a few seconds, flames engulfed the car and consumed the bodies piled on top.

CHAPTER SIXTEEN

While Plink bowed her head for a couple of heartbeats in honor of the five gang members, Wall walked away, saying, "No respite for the righteous. Defenses won't prepare themselves."

The flames had already reached their peak and began to dwindle. His usual paranoia about spreading fire, compounded by his recent glancing blow with death in Portland, lacked weight in the heavy mist that clung to everything. At the fire's current rate of fizzling out, the flames wouldn't even be able to consume the thugs' bones, though he supposed it might be better that way. It would act to warn people away from Renegade Genomix.

She followed a few paces behind, smacking the sat phone as if that would fix it.

The 541s would come for them, and they'd probably come tonight with greater numbers and better strategies. If Alpha Bravo could replace Renegade Genomix's lab, he would have advocated leaving, not risking a head-to-head battle with what would surely be superior numbers. But they weren't likely to find anything better. They had to hold their ground, even if it came at the cost of his life.

Deferring to Plink, he asked, "What's the plan?"

She didn't say anything for a few seconds, then stopped in the middle of the parking lot. He may have proven his worth by killing three of the gang members, but she was the urban combat expert. With thousands of hours of training and team leadership, she was their indisputable leader here. In the gloomy light of the green glowsticks, he watched her face turn sour. She pointed at the stack of weapons they took from the dead and said, "I hate to say it, but we need to contaminate those firearms."

"Got it." He nodded, understanding her plan immediately.

"Good. You did say that brass doesn't rust, right?

"Yeah."

"Then, collect and clean their 9mm and 5.56 rounds and magazines."

Without question, he emptied the magazines, spat his rusting agent—aka saliva—into all of the gang's barrels, and returned a single infected bullet into each firearm. "This is criminal," he said as he waited for more germs to collect in his mouth. It went against everything his dad instilled in him about firearms. Maintenance of high-performance weapons was even more important now that nobody could manufacture replacements. Regretfully, he walked a hundred yards west, the direction from which the 541s came last time, and deposited them across the road so that oncomers would have to trip over them on their way to Renegade Genomix.

With the trap set, he began the finger-draining process of emptying the spare magazines, cleaning the bullets, then loading them again. "Mo' ammo is mo' better," he said as his mind started to drift. Too many factors were out of their control with regard to the 541s. They couldn't influence when the gang would attack. Would they prefer the misty darkness that night or wait for the fog to break? Or, come at the gray hours near dawn? The enemy could strike with overwhelming force, and no matter how well-prepared he and Plink might make themselves, a sufficient swarm would be impossible to stop. Or, a single badass sniper could take them down with ease. Wall wished he had paid more attention to his high school history teacher when he talked about the percentage of casualties that would all but guarantee a route. Rhino would've known with his wicked memory.

When Plink returned with a bucket of gasoline, she took on a sleazy voice and said, "How you doin'?" The green glowstick uplit her face, transforming her usually pretty daytime smile into that of a ghoulish grin.

"Everything's shiny," he said with false happiness. "What's up, buttercup?"

She crouched in front of him and winked. "You acquitted yourself well. You might even survive the storms to come."

"That's the hope."

She playfully batted his helmet. "Hope is for dead soldiers. Living takes hard work and discipline."

Wall intoned his drill sergeant. "Rest is for wusses and washouts."

"Truer words," Plink said, kissed two fingers, and tapped his helmet. "See ya later, lover boy." She popped to her feet and jogged westward.

"Where are you going?" he called after her.

"Shopping." She covered her glowstick and vanished into the black before he could tell her that leaving Renegade Genomix under the protection of a grunt was more than a bit foolhardy. Then he rescinded his thought. If they came now, it was probably a lost cause either way.

When Wall finished loading the last of the bullets, he dug into an MRE of beef strips in tomato sauce, a food-like substance that was confused about whether it was chili, pasta, or sweet gazpacho. He couldn't figure out why someone would intentionally combine those flavors and textures. The saving grace was juice, crackers, and cookies, which mostly erased the foul aftertaste. Then he burped and the foul taste came back, so he did what any sane man would, slip a dime-sized piece of Jerky between his molars.

Full, albeit with an untrustworthy digestive system, he said, "Time to check on Kayla." He figured she had to be freaked out.

Before entering the building, he rinsed off in the stream, an endeavor made all the worse by the mist and nighttime chill. Like last time, he washed his clothes with Plink's abrasive detergent. Uplit by the eerie light of his glowstick, he suited up in the tight white onesie, armored up, strapped his M17 to his thigh, and slung his M4 over his shoulder. Returning to the rear of the building, he sprayed himself down, always decontaminating, always vigilant. He shook the small bottle as it ran dry. There would come a day when they ran out of the good stuff, unable to refill disinfectant. That day would bring an end to any and all efforts to find or manufacture a cure.

Only lit by the dim green glowstick, he mostly felt his way to the lab's vestibule and cringed when the outer door stuck in place. His "this can not be happening indicator" dialed up to infinity. "Please don't be rusted." The downfall of Renegade Genomix would be a serious sausage punch. He quickly examined the handle and the hinges. No sign of rust. Likewise, the floor lacked the dusting that would have fallen from corroded hardware.

He pushed again. Still nothing, so he pushed harder.

"What now?" Kayla said as her sickly illuminated head popped into the other side of the door's viewport.

He recoiled and nearly fell over backward. "Ahhh!" Quickly recovering, he asked, "Why? Just why?"

"Is there any way you guys can be more annoying? I can't think with all your noise. What the hell are you doing out there?"

Patiently, he described the attack and defense using precise and concise language so she wouldn't interrupt with a condescending comment.

When he finished, she said, "You let him leave? That's...I wouldn't have–"

Flashing forge-hot, he interrupted her. "How about you come out here and do my job? I'll head inside and do your job. Sound like a deal?"

"Don't be absurd."

Wall rolled his kinked neck slowly and counted to three before speaking. "I was being facetious. Perhaps–" He cut himself off again. They were both tired. Lobbing verbal grenades across the battlefield wouldn't do anyone any good. "Sorry."

Her shoulders slumped and her sunken eyes grew even wearier, if that was possible. "How confident are you that they will return?"

"They *will* come back. Gangs aren't prone to forgive and forget. The unknown variables are the timing and size of the attack."

With her eyes drooping, she asked, "Is there anything I can do?" The offer seemed genuine, despite how tired she looked.

"Nah," he said, waving his hand. "We have it covered out here. You focus on the lab, alright?"

She breathed heavily. "Deal."

They stood in the dark for a moment, neither of them saying anything, Wall too aware of his own fatigue, which he saw mirrored back at him through hers. The longer they stood, the more awkward the silence became. But when her eyes closed and didn't open again, swaying on her feet, he said, "Whoa there. Don't fall over."

She jolted and looked around in surprise as if waking from an upright position.

"Before I go and you get some rest, tell me how the research is progressing. And, is there anything we can do to help?"

Under the dimmest of green light, her eyes refocused. "It is a slow process, even for someone like me. You must have learned the pace of true research in graduate school. Or perhaps you didn't at wherever you studied?" She didn't give him time to respond. "Exceptional work takes time."

"I'm well aware," he said in an overly calm voice, one that he used when dealing with irate ex-girlfriends or mad-drunk buddies. He scratched at his itchy beard through the surgical mask. Reiterating his latter question, he said, "Is there anything we can do to help?"

"Maybe if you hooked up more panels and batteries. More electricity means faster results."

He wanted to yell, "For fuck's sake, woman!" They'd already risked their lives several times to add to the lab's electrical grid. What did she want? They weren't an army.

Instead, he closed his eyes and stuck his tongue into his cheek. "So, nothing new to report and no requests?"

She sniffed–or rather snorted a loud wet one worthy of an allergic cocaine addict–and said, "I don't know. Maybe if I had vaccine samples for normal measles and mumps, I could tweak them for Towning's versions. It wouldn't be a cure, but it would be something. If I can't develop a cure with my RG-91A, it would be a backup. Beyond that, it's weak science like the stuff you academics do."

Every muscle in both of his hands clenched. Inwardly, he told himself that she was under combustion-engine-level pressure and couldn't be expected to maintain social niceties, though he bet she was usually like that. A subset of society practically exhaled verbal bitch-slaps after breakfast, lunch, and dinner. She reminded him of a thrice-divorced engineering professor who also loved to nitpick details and was a burr in everyone's side. Wall somehow "overlooked" inviting the guy to his Ph.D. defense. The difference was that he couldn't not deal with Kayla. She was the mission.

So he rubbed at his neck, forcing down the spike-tailed anger demon, and asked, "Is there anything else I can do to help?"

She stood silent for a moment. "Do you know which of your DNA sequences Towning spliced into the viruses?"

"Yes and no. It's–"

"Then, find me samples of your rusting bacteria," she interrupted.

"No can do. Remember. Towning emptied my lab. There aren't any samples left. I mean–" Wall cocked his head and pondered for a moment. Two weeks before the camping trip, he carried samples to MIT to see if a professor of environmental science, Bing Striver, wanted to collaborate on Wall's National Science Foundation proposal. Wall had meant to leave samples for Striver, but the partnership fizzled before it even started, a wasted trip aside from the fish and chips and clam chowder.

"Hey, you," she said, snapping her fingers. "Are you going to share or make me guess what you're thinking? I'm tired and don't need your interference."

"I left samples at home. They're in my gun safe."

She began to say, "Taking samples home is–" Then she closed her mouth, and they stared at each other for a moment. He gave her time to compose herself. In a caring tone, she said, "What's done is done. It's a lucky gaffe."

He swallowed his pride and said, "Agreed." As his Ph.D. advisor used to say, "Admitting mistakes is the mark of a good scientist, one prepared to make progress."

She looked at his M4. "By the way, you should know gun owners are more likely to shoot themselves than others. It's not safe."

Despite knowing that her words came from a place of kindness, his WTF-o-meter spiked into the red. Inwardly seething but outwardly calm, he said, "Without firearms, you wouldn't have a third of your electricity. Without firearms, those meth dealers out there would have come in, contaminated your lab, and done whatever the 541s do to helpless women. Respect the gun."

She shook her head. "You and your guns drew the 541s to my lab. As slow as my research was, those brigands didn't come when I was alone. I was safer without you. My research would have taken longer, but I'd be safer and less distracted."

Unable to contain his exasperation, he said, "Would you rather that Plink and I have died?"

She closed her eyes and popped her knuckles. "Maybe. Your deaths are insignificant compared to those I can save."

Shaking his head, he turned and walked away, loudly saying, "We're in the crap house now, darlin', so you best hope our guns save your ass." At least she didn't respond, or maybe he didn't hear because, one more word might have caused a rare allergic reaction where all of his muscles would constrict and contract in a manner that might break the door down so he could unleash a set of profanities that would make Jimmy Twenty say, "Oh, no he didn't."

Outside, Wall stumbled on something in the dark but caught himself before falling. "Of all the fucks in the world!" Thankfully, the condescending lab rat didn't see his gaff, not wanting to grant her another reason to look down on him. Three large-diameter PVC pipes spilled from a pile against the building onto the back driveway, which he kicked at out of frustration, only resulting in more falling pipes. "Piece of..."

While stacking them back up, an idea connected like magnets in his mind. With a smile, he said, "Potato guns." Back in high school, before he was expelled, he and Owen stupidly built close-range bazookas from oversized PVC pipes. He checked off all the things he'd need, almost all of which he could find in the pile.

"Who said a delinquent youth wouldn't pay off?"

After rifling through a box of PVC fittings, fluids, and a cutter, he strapped pipes to his backpack and climbed to the roof, excited by the potential of the chaos his creation would incite. Up top, under the pretense of watching for trouble, he kept himself busy and awake by cutting the pipes to length. Wall built a bazooka's combustion chamber from a half-meter section of head-width pipe with a reducer couple on one end and a threaded cap couple at the back. Next, he fit a two-meter section of fist-width barrel into the end of the combustion chamber. Last, he created a hole for a match powder and string wick.

About an hour later, he sat and admired his work, three functional "potato" launchers perfect for crowd dispersal. The challenge would be scrounging for the right shrapnel to replace the potato and an ideal propellant, both of which he was sure he could find downstairs.

Feeling accomplished, he sat in the green chair and considered making a PB&J sandwich but thought better of it. While Wall, with his large frame, couldn't sustain himself on minimal rations for long, at their current rate, they would run out of provisions in a few days. They had to think long-term. What he really wanted was a large supply of jerky so he could ignore his gurgling belly.

Speaking of..., he thought. Quickly savoring a nub of jerky, magnificence in food form, he listened to the strengthening breeze that had drawn dew across his right side, almost soaking his pants through. The jacket from T.J. Maxx did a great job of keeping his upper body warm, but he couldn't stop shaking. He had been able to ignore the cold while assembling his improvised explosive devices, or IEDs, but without that distraction, his shivering was growing intolerable. Wall stood and paced the length of the building to get his heart pumping. If his knee was behaving, he would have jogged, but that wasn't an option.

If the 541s returned, could he rely on his Spidey senses–or rather, luck–to save him? In another branch of the multi-verse, those dipshits didn't spook the fox, and Wall died in his sleep. Soon, the universe would bind Lady Luck's hands, and he'd end up head down in a deep hole. He needed to approach Plink-level skill soon, or they might not survive the night. And, if the 541s arrived while she was away, a risky gamble on her part, Alpha Bravo's mission would fail, so he practiced quickly aiming his M17 pistol and M4 assault rifle over and over. The dry repetition wouldn't count for much, but it couldn't hurt to try.

If only Kayla could fight. Then again, she would probably shoot him by accident or on purpose to showcase her point of how dangerous guns were. Even if she decided to contribute to their survival, she would quickly shoot off all her ammo like most amateurs and miss her targets every time. Either way, she would be a detriment, not a boon. Their odds were better with the lab rat glued to the lab. Otherwise–

"Lab rat. Hmm."

He ran-limped to the back of the building and descended at a safe but quick pace, then rushed through decontamination, regretting that all the layers of bleach stung his nose and burned his skin. Seconds later, he entered the building and knocked on the vestibule door, hoping she hadn't gone back into the lab yet. For that matter, he wasn't sure she'd answer the door even if she heard.

After knocking twice more, she yelled, "I'm sleeping. Leave me alone!"

"We need to talk."

"No matter how many of your neurons misfire, there is zero chance you could say anything more important than my sleep." As much as the door filtered her voice, her tired anger could not be missed.

He ignored her and articulated, "Can you make an explosive gas that is stable at room temperature and will combust in the presence of a spark?"

"Of course, I can," she snapped. "I'm not a hack."

"Get cooking," he said with a smile growing on his face.

"Why would I use my skills like that?"

With frustration building, he pressed his tongue into his cheek. "Kayla, if we don't fend off the 541s, there won't be a lab or "a Kayla" left, so please just make the explosive."

"Fine," she groused. "I'll create your exothermic compounds."

"Thanks." To stoke her ego, he added, "We owe you," to which she didn't respond. If nothing else, they would have another tool to combat the 541s.

Over the next half hour, Wall came to terms with his probable death. It was what he signed up for, to spend the rest of his life undoing his part in the downfall, no matter how short his life might be. If the bag of snippiness in the lab below was the best chance for the world to recover technology, so be it. Waiting for the enemy to attack required a different kind of resilience, one where he had time to ponder all the things that could go wrong when they showed up. Every skirmish he'd been in, whether abroad or lately, began with too little warning to ponder the meaning of his forthcoming death.

In true overthinking stupidity, he asked, "Have I survived so far because I had no time to process fear? Will the slow build-up of edginess get me KIA?"

CHAPTER SEVENTEEN

Wall's attention spiked like a prickly pear when the sound of a car rumbled up the road. He had only heard one car since they arrived, though several might have passed during his two naps. Plunged into the full darkness of the foggy night when he pocketed the dimming glowstick, he willed his eyes to adjust as he aimed his M4 eastward to lay in wait for an oncoming attack.

He had little allusion that he could fend off a gang on his own. All he could do was run or die. As was so often the case in combat, the outcome would depend on the circumstances and a series of snap decisions. The difference between grunts and apex operators was the extent of training that could hasten those decisions and improve their odds of success. While he gained more than average experience from "live training" in Ethiopia and trained harder than most infantry because of those experiences, he couldn't rely on decade-old habits to come naturally.

"This is gonna suck."

The rumble of the approaching car couldn't be farther from the quiet wine of an electric vehicle. The squeal of tires told of a speeding, erratic driver, arriving barely visible without headlights. Unable to see the driver or any passengers within the dark cab, he followed what looked like an old muscle car with his scope as it fishtailed into the parking lot and skidded to a halt on the east side of the building, out of sight.

With longer and quicker strides than was advisable for a guy with a concussion, an injured chest, and a bum knee, he bolted to the side of the building and peered over the edge. In the moment before spying the car, he imagined a handful of thugs piling out as the first wave of the attack.

"What do you think of my ride?" Plink called up, having already turned off the beastly engine, and popped out of the classic vehicle with a glowstick illuminating her shoulder as a warning not to shoot. Her smile, upbeat voice, and bouncing steps spoke of pure joy. She wore a visor that looked like skiing goggles but was fully immersive next-gen night-vision displays.

He whistled a catcall as he appreciated the vintage piece of automobile art. "She's a beaut. Where'd you find her?"

"A few blocks north on my shopping trip. Betty sat patiently in the garage under a tarp waiting for someone to end her boredom. The poor girl hadn't been touched in too long, which means she's rust-free. The owner left the keys by the kitchen door, practically begging me to take her."

He laughed. "Betty?"

She shed light on a sticker of Betty Boop on the back bumper, a scar on an otherwise pristine Mustang. "I don't know. The old-timer's name fits." She laughed like a girl with her first crush. After admiring Betty for a moment, she popped the trunk and said, "Look what I *bought*."

A jumbled pile of gear filled the back, none of which promised food, but he smiled all the same. While a less devious mind might have seen nonsensical items like styrofoam, one-inch diameter copper pipes, and ammonia, he saw a deviant's building blocks for war. Styrofoam for napalm. Pipes for bombs. Nails for bomb shrapnel. Ammonia and bleach to form poisonous chlorine gas. Bottles and cloth for Molotov cocktails.

"I like the way you think," he said, excited to make IEDs.

She laughed. "I like a man who appreciates the simple pleasures in life. Be a peach, won't you? Help me schlep these goodies to the roof."

A cargo net and rope simplified moving the gear that she, quote, "appropriated on behalf of the US Army."

Over what Wall presumed was hours, they assembled IEDs, aided by Kayla's explosive concoctions. They taped a thick layer of nails to each pipe bomb and stuffed the bazooka-shotguns with the rest, which would be pushed by cloth wadding. He sealed the potato shooters' combustion chambers with spoonfuls of Kayla's explosive liquid inside, which gave off fumes perfect for propellant.

Down below, Plink concocted napalm and set up her various traps, which fit into a master plan, one that involved driving their enemy into a kill box, not formed from conventional walls but carefully constructed deterrents. She hummed from time to time, enjoying their "hobby projects."

Plink had pilfered two bags of beef jerky, each containing four fun-sized pouches. He rewarded himself with a tiny strip every time he completed a task, an incentive strong enough to energize him no matter how fatigued he was. He wouldn't ever admit that anything was better than sex, but if there was, it would be smoked beef. At his current rate of consumption, these packs wouldn't last five days.

Plink came topside after some number of hours, a brilliant smile so wide it almost split her face in two. Kneeling next to him, she tapped his helmet and said, "Is your head screwed on tight? Any rust up there?"

He shrugged. "I still have a concussion if that's what you mean." He withheld the fact that on no less than four occasions, time slipped between tasks. Not for the first time, he noted how stupid it was for someone with an altered state of mind to handle explosives. The intermittent espresso beans kept him upright at the cost of shaky hands, again, not great for assembling IEDs. His worsening knee gave out more and more as they pressed on into the night.

Marshaling a smile, he said, "I'm fine, though."

She cocked her head. "Wall, you really need to work on your poker face. A gal wants reassurance from her knight in shining armor. I mean, not this gal, but there must be some pretty lass out there looking for some grade-A, jerky-fed country boy to come home and protect her."

"Not at the moment," he said, massaging his bad knee. Wall was the serial monogamist kind of guy who rarely had long stints of single life. He couldn't pass as a model or anything, but he did alright in that area. However, increasingly the gals he met were getting more and more eccentric or damaged, which encouraged him to cut off their relationships faster and engage in them for shorter stints. From the hoarder to the cheating yogi to the insanely sensitive wallflower, cray-cray. All of them hated sharing a man who was "married to his work," a term that every single one of them used as if they'd all been trained at the same school of armchair couple's therapy.

Over half of his ladyfriends wanted to fix him in one way or another. His latest gal insisted that he confront his trauma from battle-induced PTSD. She insisted that he needed to cry and mourn for the loss of his previous self. Ultimately, she left him with the explanation, "You're hiding your true inner self from me. It hurts."

Plink bumped his shoulder with a "buck up" sort of chin jut. "Are you single by design, or are you the toad waiting for your princess?"

Wall shrugged. "Probably a little of column A, a little of column B. And you?"

"Me? Oh, I'm like a 50-cal machine gun, three thousand soldiers per second trying to get into my chamber, if you know what I mean. Are you trying to get in there, soldier?"

"No," he said defensively. "I uh–"

Her head pulled back, and her finger waggled in his direction. "Oh, what? Am I not good enough for you? Not brainy enough?"

"No, I mean–"

She laughed. "Relax, soldier. I don't date old men like you."

He mimicked being struck by an arrow through the heart. "Old, huh? You're about my age."

"Wr-ong. Ladies are twenty-five years old unless otherwise specified. You're begging for a never-ending nag-fest."

"Then it's a good thing you aren't a lady."

She flicked the back of his helmet playfully, her smile broad and genuinely happy. "On that note, get some beauty sleep. You'll know when I need you."

Wall returned her smile with a villainous grin of his own, then turned to his sleep spot, double-checking his gear on the way. Constant vigilance didn't guarantee success in battle, but lack thereof can ruin the day. He tried to ignore the "Call Failed" message from the phone as he fitted his pack under his head.

His attempt to sleep was just that, a futile endeavor that only served to amp up the hypothetical scenarios that spun inside his hair stand. At one point, he thought the 541s wouldn't attack at all, deterred by their first smackdown. More probable, it would take them time to regroup, possibly days, which could give Alpha Bravo time to strengthen their defenses. He knew how to create any number of IEDs, from landmines to trebuchets to rockets. Conversely, the longer they waited, the more the 541s could amass weapons of their own. Then again, the longer they took, the more time rust could ruin the enemy's tools of war.

He reminded himself that they were prepared and that "Success is where preparation and opportunity meet." His mustached training officer repeated that motto so often in boot camp that they made a drinking game out of it. Now, Plink and Wall were prepared, or at least as much as they could be on such short notice. Their chances of survival would rely on their ability to spot opportunities when they presented themselves.

"Yet," he whispered, "no plan survives contact with the enemy." Preparations were critical, plans not so much. The night might have passed with sleep and peace if not for that insidious phrase. No matter how well they designed their defenses, their best-laid plans would run up against the unforeseen whims of the universe. In the fires of Portland, Plink planned to return north to the helo and the fires nearly swallowed them. The fires in Bend stymied their first plan to find a lab. Their trip to reach Eugene went down in grinding metal that killed five of ten. Two scavenger trips ended in murder and near death. Those trips drew the attention of the 541s. That feeling of being followed on his solo mission might not have been so far off.

In Ethiopia, plans often went sideways, particularly for whatever group Wall was in. Their actions shanked and shanked hard. Six months in, they found themselves in the mess where his right arm shattered under the 7.76 round from an AK-47. That monkey storm was a cluster from the beginning.

They left base to check on a convoy that, quote, "had radio trouble" with less than half of their platoon because of dysentery from a spoiled water filter.

The radio trouble turned out to be the kind where nobody could respond because they were dead or dying. Noogie drove them up to the other convoy without noticing that the passengers and vehicles had more holes than a hornet's nest on extermination day. When Noogie stopped, in the middle of a central square, backing up the convoy, the Ethiopian National Defense Force let loose with their Soviet-era AK-47s. Supersonic bullets pummeled Wall's half-platoon from all sides. Thumper—so named because he fornicated more than a bunny on testosterone—laid down 50 cal fire from his turret on the rear Humvee, but not before Noogie's head exploded and Wall's right arm transformed into a flap. While Johnson, whose real name was Deion, field-dressed Wall's arm, Wall heaved Noogie into the back seat and shimmied into the driver's seat. Wall screamed into the radio, "Reverse! Reverse!" then kicked the accelerator to the floor, pushing the next Humvee back the way they came.

When an IED blew up several buildings to block their egress, Wall yelled, "Follow me," and improvised by driving straight through a mud hut like a cartoon, creating his own road, a route that the rest of his half-platoon followed to safety. From then on, half of his army buddies called him Kool-Aid, after the red pitcher mascot that always ran through walls for some reason. The rest kept calling him Wall because he smashed through three mud-hut walls that day.

Supposedly, Wall drove the half-hour back to base, but he didn't remember due to blood loss. Wall felt better when he heard that a Pave Hawk turned their saboteurs into shrapnel, and another convoy recovered the dead American soldiers.

"That driving was the craziest thing I ever saw," Thumper said in his Texas accent every time the incident came up. He'd raise a beer and proclaim, "The one-armed road warrior! I never saw anything like it."

Whereas that incident messed Dumpster up something fierce, it was a positive pivot in Wall's life. The idea of using bacteria to eat landmines spawned while he was on medical leave. If not for that spark, he might have majored in something else in college, then skipped grad school, which–

"Damn," he whispered. His research was why they were on this rooftop, Towning's repurposing of his bacteria. Maybe in a parallel universe, Wall was a career army man, and society wasn't falling apart. What he always thought of as his lucky bullet, the bullet that changed to course of his life, turned out to be the unluckiest bullet in the history of man.

"No," he said, low but firm. "If it wasn't me, it would have been someone else." Towning would have used whoever filled the research void, perhaps not so soon, but soon enough. He may have accelerated Towning's plan, but that old man would have found a way. Only half believing it, he said, "It was all Towning, not me."

Wall stood and walked to where Plink sat in the green lawn chairs. "I can't sleep. You might as well catch some z's."

"Yeah, I noticed." She laid down and breathed evenly within seconds. Normally, he could do that. The Army instilled that ability. Back then, he found sleep whenever he found time and woke whenever ordered. He should have been able to do it still.

"*Should* is a long way from *do*," his father used to say.

Wall scooted to the front of the building and cycled through a round of stretches. The air was even colder now, flowing through his clothes. From the cobra position, he looked east to where the subtle glow of the moon faintly lit the sky, providing a hint of illumination in the swirling fog. The benefit of a foggy night was that your enemy couldn't see your defenses. The counterpoint was that you could see your enemy's approach.

Even after limbering up and taking a comfortable position, an otherness nagged at him like an improperly threaded lid jammed together with too little brain and too much brawn. It had something to do with best-laid plans, but whatever it was, he couldn't make the thought coalesce. The more he attempted to capture the wispy thread of tension, the more elusive it became.

In hopes of coaxing the idea out of its hollow, he popped a shred of Carolina's good stuff into his mouth and sucked on it like that weird kid who savored his candy for way too long. The sweet and salty flavors balanced the rich spices and sweet perfection, drawing out an appreciative moan. Fiona, the smoking-hot but absolutely crazy ex-girlfriend from a few years back, claimed that if he loved her as much as he loved jerky, she wouldn't have run over his bike with her Prius. The next day she acted like nothing happened and invited him to brunch with her parents.

"Crazy."

Wanting to end his contact with feminine insanity, he told her, "Sorry, doll. I'll never love you like I do jerky." She tried to spray mace at him, but he managed to slam his door just in time. He owed the next-door neighbor a set of terracotta pots and new flowers after her tantrum, but it was so worth it. A few days later, she threw a brick through the back sliding glass door and–

"Oh, crap!"

CHAPTER EIGHTEEN

Wall pushed to his feet and limp-ran to the back of the building, heart thumping within the confines of his pressure-wrapped ribs and iron-tight grip on his head. He stumbled in his hurry to reach the rear and nearly tripped over the short crown around the roof.

Something gleamed below, and he backpedaled, falling on his ass.

The *tddddddd* sound of fully automatic gunfire hit the building below and whizzed overhead with that too-close-for-comfort pressure wave past his left ear. The machine gun stopped with the telltale click of an empty magazine. The guy below blew his whole wad in a single string of shots, the tendency of the undisciplined.

Wall took advantage of the lull in gunfire and repositioned himself to peek over the ledge like a prairie dog. Four shadowy men were in various stages of climbing over the back fence, the ingress he and Plink failed to prepare. A fifth guy behind the fence released another round of wildly aimed suppressive fire with a pistol, his hand held sideways, which looked cool but provided absolutely no chance of hitting anything on purpose.

Not daring to expose his head again, Wall lit a pipe bomb, waited for the wick to take, and threw it. The explosion and ensuing cries told him what he needed to hear. Following in what he thought might be his only opportunity, he popped his M4 over the ledge, took aim at a flailing man illuminated in the flames of the burning back fence, and sent two rounds. He aimed at three more men and double-tapped each time in a tap-tap, pause, tap-tap pattern.

In twelve rapid heartbeats, he spent eight invaluable rounds, killing four out of five of the IED-wounded men.

The last guy, the sideways-holding idiot, held his pistol over a shortened and burning panel of wood fencing and fired without any concept of aim. Wall suspected that in Eugene, many of the local gang members hadn't fired a gun before, relying on what looked dangerous to dissuade any of the other gangs from stepping on their toes. Wall, strangely cold-hearted and logical, processed the mental math, the minuscule odds of the guy hitting home, so he acted upon the opportunity and lost two more bullets at three thousand feet per second through the fence. The squishy thud of the second impact told him that one struck home. The guy shot two more rounds as Wall prepared to send two more through the fence. Wall flinched as his left ear reported an explosion and his head jerked painfully to that side. Panicked, Wall felt his face and helmet. His brain bucket sported a notch, a grazing blow, one that rang in his ear but didn't reach his skin.

"You lucky–" He shot the asshole. Squishy thud. "–Bastard."

Something exploded behind him, at the front of the building. *Please be Plink's doing,* he thought as he imagined a 541 throwing an explosive her way.

Taking another calculated risk Wall abandoned the back of the building and scuttled to the front, where napalm lit the parking lot in waving oranges and yellows. A half dozen men sullied the parking lot's center, ringed by a wide circle of cement on fire, Plink's kill box. On the road, a cluster of choking men told of Plink's ammonia and bleach trap. Chloramine was nasty stuff.

Something big streaked through the night sky, hitting the building's east corner, the impact flashing like a thousand torches and shaking the roof and smacking his ears. The blasted section fell in on itself. The yell he barely heard was his own, certain that he would die as the structure collapsed, but the crumbling limited itself to the corner.

Then a dozen more 541s emerged on the road to the west, slow but chaotic, aiming pistols, rifles, and AR-15s in all directions, with no sense of tactical strategy. Even the Tigray refugees of northern Ethiopia had more sense than these guys.

"We might live yet."

Wall army crawled away from the crumbling section of the building only to have one of his homemade bazookas block his path. Gunfire popped, the sound distant and muffled, drowned out by an annoying high-pitched ringing. He lit the PVC shotgun's fuse, but his lighter wouldn't spark. "Work, damn it!" After running the steel roller along his pants, he tried again. This time it lit but blew out before it touched the wick. He sighed as it caught on the third try.

Someone yelled, "Charge!" This was exactly what Wall feared. A fast defeat in the face of overwhelming forces.

As he popped his head over the short ledge with his homemade launcher, he spied a group running toward Renegade Genomix, illuminated by the toxic napalm flames. Unlike the men from earlier, most of these men and women were sunken like strung-out addicts, their eyes hollow even in the flickering light of the surrounding fire. They were running a mob of expendable zombies, probably with the promise of meth after the attack.

The improvised mega-shotgun banged in his right ear, sending a wide spread of high-velocity nails into the oncoming crowd. He had no idea if he hit any of them because the combustion knocked him back and to his side.

"Gah!" he screamed as he smacked down on the roof, and his ribs went code red.

He thought he heard gunfire and a bunch of it too, but it sounded like dull pops. When he recovered from his own blow, he rolled to the next bazooka and fought with the lighter again. Way too many heartbeats passed before the wick caught. As his ears started to recover, he raised the thing over his shoulder and rose to the building's crown level. The group from before had stopped, including a cohort of men and women lying on the ground and another cohort stumbling over the downed ones.

Boom!

The improvised weapon sent its nails into the slow-moving mob. Again, the explosion within the chamber wrecked his hearing and knocked him onto his back, sending the world into chaotic spins of uplit mist and the reverse imprint of fire stamped on his retina. Forcing himself onto his knees, he watched the men and women flail in a tangle of bodies, falling over themselves, nails protruding from nearly all of them.

The trailing-most attackers still ran into the forward ranks, stumbling over the fallen.

Wall didn't waste time and switched to his M4. His world spun, but slow enough for him to roughly aim at the group without regard to hitting any one of them. He had no time or mental capacity to recognize fear or bother with the ethics of shooting trapped humans, so, round after round, he pointed at the mass of oncoming combatants and pulled the trigger fast enough to be useful but slow enough to keep his rifle trained on the stumbling and writhing mass.

Something hammered his chest like a knight with a lance, ramming him backward, nearly knocking him down, and aggravating his ribs all over again. He kept firing until his clip ran out. Rather than switch magazines, he spent valuable seconds leaning over his reluctant lighter to ignite a pipe bomb. Once lit, he righted himself, wound his throwing arm, and threw it. Or, rather, that was what he meant to do. Mid-swing, he fell back with another wrecking ball to the chest, this one pounding him onto his back.

Having lacked copious amounts of confidence in his prospects from the beginning, he thought, *This is how I die.* He had failed to defend the only thing that mattered, the lab that preserved the only known chance for humanity to survive.

He felt the ensuing explosion as much as heard it. A shockwave beat through him. A bright flash lit up the fog, telling him everything he needed to know.

Yet, he didn't die.

He patted his piercingly painful chest and came away with no blood, saved by the holy saint of protection, his next-gen bulletproof vest. He would have laughed if his lungs hadn't seized up from the bullet impact.

Then, a great rumble shook the building, and the world flew up around him. Momentarily, the laws of gravity lost their hold on reality. Or rather, he slid on his back, feet down toward the parking lot as if the falling roof was the world's worst water slide. On his descent into the mines of hell, men surged forward. Upon touchdown, he didn't bother to stand. His immediate reaction came in the form of ejecting his magazine and clumsily loading the next. Surrounded by flames on his left and right and facing a recovering mob, he pulled the charging handle and wildly fired, *tap, tap, tap,* not in automatic, but too fast to take aim at anything within the spinning mass of meth heads.

His left leg spasmed, nearly hyperextending, as his thigh smacked against the base of the slanted roof. A part of him knew that the kick to his leg resembled that fateful impact to his arm, which meant that he'd been hit. The other part didn't care. If he didn't keep shooting, he would die and his leg would be the least of his worries. Even if his life was forfeit, he would take down as many as he could.

Reminiscent of the men he slayed behind the building, Wall failed to maintain fire control, sending shots flying indiscriminately through the mob at nearly point blank, unable to miss. The wild masses, with their faces reflecting the orange and yellow flames, flailed and clambered for footing and escape.

Wall's right foot knocked sideways like in a low blow in football and knocked his shot left leg with it, which flung his upper body to the right, landing him hard on the uneven cement rubble of Renegade Genomix's front entry. He hissed through clenched teeth as his leg, chest, neck, and arm set fire to so many neurons that they confused his mind into a semi-numb state.

The good thing about his sudden landing was that he looked dead or close to it and nobody paid him any heed. Instead, those that weren't fleeing ran toward him where they could gain entry through the fallen piles caused by his hapless throw of a pipe bomb. With a full dose of the spins and an unhealthy measure of double vision, Wall drew his pistol, not even attempting to brace himself in his stupidly prone position, and fired at the oncoming men, unsure which of the overlapping double-headed assailants to aim at. In a four-four beat, he fired, pop-recoil on repeat.

One of his targets fell on him, belly-to-belly. As the guy pushed up, Wall dropped his gun, pulled his K-bar from his vest, the easily retrievable position that Plink insisted on, and sliced at where he thought the man's dual-headed neck might be. A red streak slit across the guy's face, eye to eye. Not waiting for retaliation, he reversed the direction and thrust as hard as he could. The man flopped down like the world's largest bone-in Kansas strip.

A blurry gray tunnel replaced the spins as the remainder of the raiding party turned and fled. One by one, they fell until the last one stood like a single untouched tower among a rusted cityscape. Then, the last man fell too. Plink emerged from the far side of the battlefield, pistol in hand, occasionally shooting the fallen as she approached. *No,* Wall realized gradually. *That isn't Plink. Too large. It's Rhino.* His massive form was unique among men, or at least among men Wall knew.

Plink–the real Plink–kneeled over Wall. "You did well, soldier." She hefted the dead man from atop Wall's belly. "You're like a giant rabbit's foot. I thought you were dead five times over." She quickly looked up, lifted her pistol, and shot into the dark interior of the building.

"No!" he said, too slow and too quiet. "Don't contaminate...the building."

Plink cupped his face. "Can you tell me where it hurts?"

"No."

She smiled. "You took a big fall there, fella."

He weakly smiled back, saying something that sounded like, "Grahhhh-blub." He blinked and his lashes stuck closed.

"No, you don't," she said, patting his face. "No passing out, rabbit." Her hands ran over his body, momentarily stopping at his chest. "You took two rounds to the body armor. You'll be fine." She ran her hands down his arms, then his legs, where she stopped again. "This is gonna hurt. I'm applying a tourniquet."

When the pain registered, he tried to push her away with poorly aimed, clumsy, and shaking hands. "Gah!"

She fiddled with something and said, "Count down from five."

"Five, four–" Before he was ready for whatever was to come, she mashed something into his bullet wound. Like a primal animal, trapped and wounded, he struck out with a fist. She simply tilted her helmet toward the blow, and he struck hard composite with his bare knuckles. "It's coagulant," she said, still pressing on his leg. "I may not know much about first aid, but we have to stop the bleeding. You're making a mess all over this artistic cement pile you masterfully built."

He blinked heavily, only to encounter a sharp smack to the cheek. He couldn't focus. Slow and loud, Plink said, "No falling asleep, lieutenant." She handed him two pills and a bottle of water. "Swallow these." With the flavor of cement dust on his tongue, he couldn't taste the tablets. His breath came shallowly, bringing the pills up with a cough on his first attempt, and barely managed on his second try.

Plink poked around his boots and his right calf. He registered that it hurt when she pulled the pant leg up, but it was the least of his concerns. She hissed. "Shrapnel. Nothin' serious. Your boot took the brunt." After patting him down head to toe in case she missed something, she said, "Wall, next time, try not to hurt yourself, okay?"

He smiled halfway, all that he could manage. "I can't promise anything."

As Wall's vision converged into one universe, Rhino stood over him. "You look like Cole Younger."

"Who?" Wall was pretty sure he wouldn't have recognized the name even if he wasn't so ganked.

Rhino shot another man with his pistol. A mercy shot. "Cole Younger was an outlaw who died at seventy-two years old, having carried eleven bullets inside him for decades. He was an awful man, but you have to respect his resilience."

Plink cleaned and applied antibiotics to Wall's shrapnel-battered lower leg inciting mild pain compared with the others. She looked up at Rhino and said, "You timed that perfectly."

He smiled. "I do everything perfectly. You should know that by now. I mean–"

Time slipped, and Rhino set him down against the back side of Renegade Genomix. He blinked forward again, and Wall drank water from a bottle that mysteriously appeared in his hand. He leapt through reality again to dawn. Sitting with his back against the building, the dim but slowly brightening fog clung to a new set of civilian clothes, suggesting that either he'd dressed himself or, more probably, had help.

While pushing his dry tongue into his cheek, he checked himself over. His left quadricep was pissed at him under a bulky ring under his pants. He screwed up his face as he slid his backpack under his bum knee. It may have burned to move his knee and thigh, but nothing was broken or torn. He already knew how both of those felt, and this wasn't it.

"No amputation," he told himself.

Wall holstered his P17 above the thigh wound, which chafed, but its deadly potential fostered a sense of control over his domain, even if that sway over reality lacked reliability.

"I'm not dead yet," he said, imagining the black knight from Monty Python. He would never gain acceptance among a traveling band of troubadours for his English accent, but without anyone to hear, he continued. "It's just a flesh wound." His laugh ended with a cough and wheeze in his battered chest. His bulletproof vest got in the way of investigating his ribs, which was just as well. He really didn't want to see it. He poked at the next-gen bulletproof vest and was amazed that he couldn't feel the spots where his chest told him he should find dents or scratches.

"Nothing," he marveled.

His helmet, on the other hand, sat at his side with a gouge at ear level. He vaguely remembered the impact that jerked his head while defending the back of the building.

"Damn, that was close," he said, slipping jerky between his molars, moaning in bliss. "And the world is right again."

The smell of acrid smoke mixed with barbeque wafted under his nose, beckoning him to rise. Before taking on the challenge of standing, he slung his flawlessly cleaned M4 over his shoulder and checked the magazine and chamber, both of which were full. He questioned the logic of arming himself with another loaded weapon when he was prone to passing out. After a few back and forths, he opted to keep its protective embrace.

Someone left a carved branch with a "Y" at one end, fitted with foam at the crook, a crudely fashioned crutch. What it lacked in beauty, it made up for in function, taking the worst of the pressure off his thigh as he grunted to his feet. The groan reminded him of his mom and dad, who he hoped were faring better than him. Even if they weren't, they would persevere, tough as iron, so he limped around Renegade Genomix to the front without complaint.

The southeast corner laid in a pile of cement block rubble, the likes of which he had seen in Africa plenty of times. Pockmarks peppered the front of the building, with the largest concentration flanking the hole he blew open. That section of the roof leaned to the parking lot. Unfortunately, sliding down to the hoard wasn't simply a nightmare because if it were, he wouldn't feel so crappy.

"Excellent," Rhino said from the rooftop. "The hero lives. We must rejoice."

Wall half-smiled. "Next time, it's your turn to blow yourself up."

"What? And scratch my feminine figure?" He waved up and down his massive body, the look of fake shock comically displayed. "Can you see alright?"

"Yeah. Everything's shiny."

He smiled broadly. "Good. You have work to do."

"Huh?"

Rhino cocked his watermelon-sized head. "Didn't you see the pile of ammunition we left for you?"

"No." Then, he remembered that there were several sacks next to him when he woke up.

"Those bullets won't clean themselves, my man."

And so, he returned and set to cleaning their hard-won brass. "To the victors go the riches."

CHAPTER NINETEEN

It took Wall longer than it should have to decontaminate the painfully earned bullets. He wasn't concerned that a virus would consume them, but even if brass was immune to the rusting diseases, they might be able to infect other metals, namely their guns and spare magazines. Until he had time to run experiments, it wasn't worth the risk.

He felt like last night should have messed with his mind more than it did. Emotionally, that is. Physically, his noggin was plenty screwed up. Near-death experiences were supposed to be profound and life-altering. The thing was that he had already lived through one impossible situation after the next, in Africa, the Portland fires, and the helicopter crash.

"I'm lucky," he told himself. Like his grandma used to say, "Every day I wake up is a good day." She lived with debilitating arthritis for decades but remained the happiest person he knew. With a fond smile for that wonderful woman, he said, "I woke up."

Focusing on the past wouldn't fix the future. No amount of wishing could get him un-shot. Even if he wanted to, he couldn't un-kill the 541s. The only thing he could do was learn from his mistakes, and that was a lesson for a time when his body wasn't so wrecked. That which is done is done.

Tossing another shined 9mm into the clean bag, he murmured, "The key is to look forward."

The scale of the mission was daunting as hell, but he had to try, both for humanity and for himself. The goal would drive him forward. Otherwise, it would be too easy to let the world consume him, body and mind. With a worthy purpose, he would find a way to soldier on, to be part of the solution, not the problem.

Their victory over the 541s hadn't been a glorious or dignified battle, particularly for Wall. It was a bloody, one-sided slaughter, only won because of superior weapons and tactics. He vaguely remembered that during one of his recent stints awake, Rhino said something like, "Defending a castle is far easier than storming one." He and Plink's knowledge of IEDs, their high ground, and the rusted state of the 541 firearms favored the defenders. The bazooka shotguns proved to be more effective than he could have hoped for. The pipe bombs too.

It was only through random luck that Wall remembered crazy Fiona and the way she threw a brick through his back door. If not for that, he wouldn't have thought to protect their sixes. From now on, he would remember Fiona's insanity with fondness, his muse for defending their castle. He wondered if her mastery in the art of madness would serve her well in the great fall.

"How's it going, Wall?" Plink asked as she kneeled at his side. "Are you still with us?"

He winked. "Fantastic. Bright-eyed and hairy balled."

She winked right back at him as she ran her finger over the gouge on his helmet. "As I thought."

"So, you've been thinking about my balls, have you?"

"Keep dreaming, Rabbit." Her brown eyes turned empathetic, caring, and happy all at once. She cupped his face. Then the moment vanished, and the warrior was back.

"How's the lab?" he asked. "Have you checked on Kayla?"

She whistled. "I'm worried about that head of yours, soldier."

"Why?" He rubbed the offending lump.

"You blanked again. After *you* went in, *you* said neither Kayla nor the lab was harmed. The office took serious damage, but the important stuff is fine. Kayla remains as single-minded as before. But now she's even more adamant about not leaving the lab and its vestibule."

It unsettled him to be told what he said during a previous waking time in part because it didn't bode well for a speedy recovery and in part because he worried about what sort of damage he could cause in the lost time. "Is she getting rest?"

She tapped at her thigh. "According to you, not enough." Worry eked onto her face.

"What about Nellibi?" he asked, half-panicked. "Rhino didn't leave her behind, did he?"

"No, she's inside and won't come out. She's like a maraca."

He screwed up his face. "Huh?"

"Shaken," she explained. "She wouldn't even look at your leg. She's still in shock. According to Rhino she was starting to come around on the trek here but broke down even worse when he ran ahead to help us. I tried to appeal to her motherly instincts, to pull herself together for Lucas, but she hasn't vagged up yet."

He threw a pebble. While he wasn't indifferent to her loss, their priority had to be working on a vaccine or cure. But pushing her to mentally heal before she was ready might make things worse. The lab was as safe a place as she'd find, and a cure wouldn't happen overnight. "She's a good woman. She'll come through, if not for herself, then for Lucas."

"You're a good man, Wall. Caring despite it all." She kissed her fingertips and gently touched his forehead. "Don't let your goodness kill you, okay?" She stood with a neat spin and walked away.

"Don't worry," he called after her. "Death isn't part of my five-year plan." It sounded better in his head than out loud. He was pretty sure he was trying to flirt. While his tall, muscular bod appealed to plenty of women, his charm didn't belong to what one might call a lady's man. He wasn't a complete dunce, though. As an elite soldier in a male-dominated role, she must have heard plenty of lines, so his flub wouldn't register as a blip in her radar.

She walked away laughing.

Concussion brain, he said inwardly, delusionally wanting to believe he wouldn't have said something similarly stupid under normal conditions.

Either way, it hardly seemed like the best time to distract his fucked-up head with clumsy attempts to appeal to her. He had to save all the spare energy for the mission. Once they secured Renegade Genomix, he might have the mental capacity for such thoughts.

He popped a twine of jerky and said, "I woke up, so it's a good day."

By the time he finished polishing the last bullet, he needed a nap like allergies need pollen on the wind. With shaky fingers and a worsening headache, he checked the pocketbook in his vest for the last time he'd taken meds.

"Good." It was time to re-fill the tank. He fumbled with an orange pill container, nearly spilling its precious contents all over the ground. These little tablets were insanely valuable now. Mass medical manufacturing of painkillers wouldn't come back unless Alpha Bravo found a way to reverse the downfall. In comparison, diamonds were scrap. While compressed carbon would last forever, pills were one-use wonders. Even while his painkiller clawed its way down his throat, he lamented its loss. At least Outhouse and his pops were right about hoarding the good stuff.

Spent, he slumped to the side, barely able to keep his head from knocking pavement on the way down, and drifted off.

Please remember this time.

When he roused, blinking until his eyes adjusted to the light, the meds still numbing the worst of his injuries, he rose with difficulty. Nearly every muscle and tendon clamped down while he slept. After a whole-body stretch and a few steps, he loosened up a bit.

Around the front of the building, Rhino leaned over the edge of the roof and said, "Hey, Wall." He looked like a Michelangelo statue, massive, muscular, and rugged beyond mortal limitations. The M4 looked tiny in his beef-stick hands. His deep, rumbling voice only added to that impression. The goliath jutted his chin out in a silent, eon-old sign of respect, a "well done" or "good-on-ya" that men learned as early homo-sapiens.

Wall jutted his chin in response. "Hey, Rhino." Both men knew that the simple gesture and two words each were the only exchange needed to acknowledge and move past what would have otherwise been an awkward conversation of mutual appreciation, which they might have already had for all he knew. Squinting up at the half-bear, Wall asked, "Where's Plink?"

With hand quotes, he answered, "Shopping."

That could mean looting any number of stores or homes for groceries or hardware or soap to replenish their supplies. Or would she raid the 541s crib now that most, if not all, of those shitheads were dead. Either way, he could only guess what she might come back with. Without realizing his mouth was moving, he said, "To the victors, go the spoils."

Rhino rolled a toothpick on his tongue. "True enough. Did you know that term was in use in politics as early as 1812? Senator William Marcy of New York made it famous when President Andrew Jackson ran for his second term as president." He continued talking about Andrew Jackson and his finer and not-so-spectacular traits.

At some point, Wall realized that the giant historian had stopped talking. "Hey, Rhino."

"Yeah?"

"Did any of their guns backfire last night?"

"Ooh boy, did they?! Plink told me what you did. Those things split open like explosive bananas. You, my friend, have some seriously potent saliva."

Not brushing his teeth for two days might have had something to do with that. "At least I'm good for something..."

"Nah, you are a master of chaos, a magnet of madness, an instigator of pandemonium. How you survived that shit show will become the topic of conversation for decades to come."

They fell into an easy silence, the kind that men around the globe shared, the sort that many women thought told of a lousy relationship, one mashing jerky and the other flicking a toothpick.

Wall limped in circles around the stained parking lot. Back when he was recovering from his shattered arm, the docs and nurses taught him how important immediate physical therapy was to a quick and full recovery. Volunteering at the VA reinforced the crucial nature of prompt rehab.

"Hey, Rhino!" he called up after coming to a halt.

"Send it."

"Does Doctor Nellibi think we need to cauterize my thigh?"

After a pause during which Rhino's face transitioned from "holy crap" to "this is hilarious," the Navy SEAL whistled. "Oh, man. You don't remember?"

A sinking ingot of steel tumbled in his gut as he imagined what Doctor Nellibi might have done during his last time slip. It explained why his thigh burned as much as anything else. Forcing the concern out of his voice, Wall looked up and said, "You're not messing with me, are you?"

Rhino took on a solemn demeanor and lowered his already baritone voice. "Warrior to warrior. I ain't messin'."

Wall wobbled for a moment and Rhino allowed him plenty of time for the mental gymnastics needed to accept that not only had they branded him, but his head was also in bad enough condition that he forgot all about it. Cauterizing wounds wasn't exactly considered best practices anymore, made dangerous by a larger surface to get infected. However, the burn would bind his muscles quicker, giving him the mobility he'd need in the short term.

The urge to pull his pants down and rip off the bandage nearly won out over reason. He wasn't concerned with exposing himself to another man, particularly another warrior. The only thing keeping him from dropping trou and investigating was the imperative not to contaminate the wound. The possibility of dying or losing a leg from gangrene was a mighty powerful deterrent.

Looking up at the big guy, he asked, "Do chicks really dig scars?" None of them seemed to particularly like the line and dots on his shoulder or the three little slit on his knee.

Rhino facially shrugged. "Scars never slowed me down."

"Tell me that Nellibi did a good job."

"Ha!" His whole body shook. "She didn't touch you once. She's been inside since we got here. Still grieving and shocked." He shook his head. "Are you really telling me you don't remember?"

He got the sense he was lucky to have forgotten. "Remember what?"

"Wall, you're one crazy mother fucker. You did it yourself."

"Really?"

"Nothin' but truth. I've seen some tough bastards in my line of work, but you Iowa boys are some seriously durable stock."

Wall nodded dumbly. He poked his tongue into his cheek, trying to imagine branding himself. "Huh. I guess so." Or maybe he wasn't as tough. If his mind was compromised, he might not have been of sane mind, a scary-ass notion that he couldn't disprove. What other stupid things did he do that he couldn't remember? He decided that he didn't want to know.

Misreading his concerned face, Rhino said, "But don't worry, my man. This isn't World War I. You slathered it with triple antibiotics and took a few oral antibiotics that Plink found in a neighbor's stash. You'll be fine."

Wall paced back and forth for a moment. "We all want new experiences, right? I mean–"

"Car coming from the west," Rhino cut in. "Take cover."

Wall hobbled to the corner of the building and knelt behind the fallen cinder blocks, then aimed his M4 down the road, grateful that he geared up upon waking. "Always be prepared," he whispered.

"Sounds like a big one," Rhino said, professional ease in his voice, the consummate warrior.

As the rumbling of a deep, growling engine approached, Wall hazarded a guess that it was a struggling semi-truck pulling an unusually heavy trailer. He imagined the damage that a ten-ton truck could do if it rammed the building kamikaze style. If the gang was smart, they would have used that tactic last night, then taken cover behind it.

"Ha!" Rhino bellowed. "Would you look at that?"

A dull-red Mini Cooper slowly rumbled into the parking lot. With the way the engine ground, you'd think a hundred full-grown clowns contorted their way inside. The poor thing brayed and squeaked and hissed, then backfired a few times for good measure. When the POS reached the building, the engine shut down, and Plink jumped out.

"Hey, fellas."

Rhino convulsed in a full-belly laugh. "If only I had a camera..." He huffed. "I think you have a new nickname. Howling Mini."

"How dare you," she said with a laugh of her own. "Shouldn't it be Her Majesty, the princess of Howling Mini?"

Rhino looked down on the car-shaped mouse with a lion's roar. "Plink, did you steal that from a deaf gnome?"

"Funny!" She pointed to the sky with her middle finger.

"Hey, Wall," he said. Neither of them could take their eyes off the tiny rumbler. "What's even harder than getting a pregnant woman into a Mini?"

"What's that?"

Rhino started laughing and barely managed to finish his joke. "Getting a woman pregnant in a Mini."

"Hey, Rhino," Wall said, laughing. "Is she really far away? I can barely see her car from here." The two of them continued like this for a while. From time to time, Plink one-finger saluted. Sometimes she emphasized her sentiment with a double salute.

When they stopped laughing, Wall tried to help unload the Mini Cooper but mostly got in the way, so he sat down against the front of Renegade Genomix. Rhino kept his sentinel stance atop the building, not bothering to help, and Plink didn't seem to mind hauling a wide assortment of goodies around back. All the makings of a defensible fortress, from snares to propellant for rockets.

"Hey, Rhino," Wall hollered up without craning his neck.

"Yeah? What's up?"

With a bit more concern than he intended to show, Wall asked, "Did we get the bullet out?"

"You managed to pull a good portion, but you wouldn't let us help, so who knows? And you rooted around in there like a toddler with chopsticks, taking too long for a sane man. You're one crazy dude."

"Huh. Ain't that something."

CHAPTER TWENTY

Wall sat against the building and watched Plink haul canvas bags from the dead mini. Her score of real groceries–well, there was almost nothing better for morale than a good meal. MREs could go a long way toward easing hunger, but they left you wanting. More importantly, Alpha Bravo had a limited supply of lightweight MREs, so they were best reserved for longer excursions.

He offered to help several times, to which Plink said, "Don't work your leg too much, Rabbit. You'll need your strength later." She said this last bit with two cups of innuendo and one cup of sultriness, then tossed him a book with a slender brown-haired woman and a tall, handsome, bare-chested blond. Seeing his face of incredulity, she said, "You do know how to read, don't you?"

"Yeah, but..." He held it out with forefinger and thumb as if it might contaminate him.

She smiled down at him. "Don't knock 'em until you rock 'em, baby. They'll teach you the way to a woman's heart." She walked away with a little more swagger to her steps.

"Do ya mind reading aloud?" Rhino asked.

He flipped through the book, then turned to the beginning. Within the first page, longing looks and unrequited love between a nobleman and a slave elf told of what was to come. Wall decided that he might as well get into it, so he read with gusto.

His mind wandered while he read the words but ignored their meaning. Without millions of books available on his phone, he had to take what he could get. In the span of two weeks, an almost infinite supply of knowledge was reduced to this, the printed word stolen when and where you could. Physical libraries would soon crumble if they hadn't already as common gathering places with a broad spectrum of visitors to infect them. Their walls and reinforced roofs would buckle. Their bookshelves would collapse. Exposed to the elements, pages would warp, bleed, and glue together.

He could practically see Towning sitting alone in his favorite chair with an expensive Scotch in hand, thinking of yet another way in which he could "level the playing field between humankind and nature." If knowledge was power, then the aged man cut away humanity's power like a virtual two-handed sword might cleave an arm. Wall hoped that someone, somewhere, was fighting to protect knowledge like Alpha Bravo fought to minimize the damage of the rusting diseases.

He had stopped reading, his mind returning to a cracked piston of thought. Even if Alpha Bravo could cure everyone today, the diseases were out in the wild, in people's homes, their offices, and their community centers. In mines and factories. Tainted metal would infect untainted metal, which would spread the contagion back to people and more metal. No freshly smelted metal could touch the ground or any surface that was contaminated. Towning forever impeded progress.

Once again, he mentally cursed Towning, then himself for not seeing it. Once, while waiting for the CRISPR to print a batch of new genetic strains for *Acidithiobacillus Ferrooxidans*, the genius grumbled that "This damn equipment is too slow. We'll never reach the singularity at this rate."

Wall didn't point out that they were using the fastest equipment that not even money could buy, only clout. Instead, he said, "We can't solve everything now. Change doesn't happen that fast."

His mentor had slipped a pill for his heart condition under his mask and swallowed it dry. "If we don't change soon, it will be too late. And if men like us don't act, who will?"

He thought they were acting, pushing the boundaries of science and engineering toward that goal. For a man who prided himself on imagining worst-case scenarios, Wall sure missed that one. He had presumed Towning was talking about forging onward to a constructive singularity, not committing murder on the grandest scale ever. Now, it struck Wall that the old man towered over the likes of Hitler, Mao, and Stalin in their destructive reigns. All of them were charismatic men. Egomaniacs. Uncompromising. However, Towning had the ultimate in powerful weapons, genetic engineering.

"It's my fault," he whispered. "I could have stopped it."

No, said his internal voice. Even if he could have stopped Towning, someone else, another environmentalist biohacker turned terrorist, eventually would have. As biohacking advanced year over year, empowered by new open-source tools and techniques, the outcome, or one similar, was inevitable. It wasn't the technology's fault. It was that humans used their knowledge as weapons rather than bandages. The goal of technology was to improve people's lives, not end them. But he knew better. Rhino would tell him that war spurred on greater leaps in innovation than peace. Whoever had the best technology ruled. From clubs and spears to submarines and nukes.

Wall cursed himself for being too idealistic in his pursuit of reaching the environmental singularity. He surrounded himself with like-minded colleagues in their pursuit of probing the boundaries of knowledge. While everyone feared nuclear armageddon, ebola-like pandemics, cosmic doomsday, super-volcanoes, and religious smiting, it turned out to be an environmentalist that cut humans down.

Idealists often said that humans needed to die off in order for the planet to return to homeostasis, primarily men and women at the fringe of the bell curve. People said it flippantly on social media and over luxurious cocktails or holding fancy mugs of decadent caffeinated beverages at coffee houses. The hardest-core environmentalists, the vegans, the people that his dad called "crunchies" professed how much better the world would be if ninety-nine percent of the population died off. But those arguments were couched in theory and idealism, not true threats, and always with the caveat that they could choose who lived and who died. Most of those gun-phobic armchair philosophers likely changed their tunes days ago or would soon, realizing they were on the chopping block.

Wall spent his whole adult life in service of humankind, first in the army, then in hopes to disarm minefields, and more extensively working to fix metallic blights on the land, to help man and the environment. He worked for humanity, not against it, toiling to bring people and the planet closer to homeostasis. He mistakenly believed that all ships would rise. Only imbeciles and extremists wanted to sink one to benefit the other.

He scrunched his eyes and silently cursed.

"What's that?" Plink asked, her back leaning against the building at his side, so close and having arrived so silently that he jumped.

"Damn it, Plink!" He clutched his aching chest. If she could sneak up on him so easily, perhaps his Spidey senses weren't as good as he thought. She tossed a cashew into the air and caught it in her mouth, then crunched noisily.

He swallowed and replaced a sliver of jerky without realizing he'd done it. "I can't get my head around all this. The Towning I knew was an optimist. He preached that we'd reach the environmental singularity."

Crunching on another nut, she asked, "Isn't that what he did?"

"Yes, but..." He struggled to find the right words. "He...He loved humanity and fought for it. He saved countless lives with his medical inventions."

Dislodging a bit of nut stuck behind her canine, she said, "You never know what goes on behind someone's forehead."

"You seem to."

She sighed as she flicked the offending piece of nut back into her mouth. "Some people are easier to read than others. Rare individuals don't register, or they disguise themselves as something completely different." She tossed a peanut into her chomper.

He stammered, "I just didn't see it. He had the means, but..."

"Don't worry about Towning," she said, leaning into him and nudging him with her shoulder. She stayed leaned into him and held out a few nuts. "Want some?"

"Yeah, thanks." He nudged her back.

She stood and said, "If you're done doing whatever you were doing here, go try to talk with Kayla again. Hopefully, she's in the vestibule."

He closed his eyes and said, "If you can't bring the scared cat to water..."

"Then bring the water to her," Plink finished, pulling him to his feet.

Around back, he took plenty of precautions before entering the building. The inside was different than he remembered. Light cascaded through the corner and rays shined through the spot he slid down. More dust coated the furniture-covering tarps than before, a consequence of crumbling walls.

"Hey, guys," he said, waving to Nellibi, who sat vacantly on the modern chic couch with her son. While Lucas waved back, bouncing on and off the sofa, Nellibi didn't show any outward sign of recognition. Catatonic. Shell shocked. He stepped close, but not so close that he might alarm the little one with his size, crutching lopsidedness, and guns, he asked Lucas, "Are you hungry or thirsty?"

"No, thank you," Lucas said, bouncing up and down as he pointed at a glass candy bowl. Dozens of wrappers littered the couch, coffee table, and floor. Two cans of Coke lay on their sides. "We have lots." His eyes narrowed, and he scooped up the bowl as if Wall might take it away.

He smiled at the hyper kiddo, hoping the grin extended beyond the surgical mask and through his goggles. "If you don't need anything, I'm gonna go talk to Kayla."

"You mean *her*?" He pointed at the lab door. "She's not very nice, you know?"

He laughed to the detriment of his chest. "Yeah, she's a bit grouchy, isn't she?" Given the scientist's general disposition, he suspected she wasn't particularly adept at talking to kids. Children weren't efficient. They brought chaos with them, which he doubted she could tolerate. "Lucas, if you need anything, I'll be over there." With a friendly wave, he crutched over to the vestibule door and knocked at the viewing port.

As soon as he touched the door handle, Kayla's masked face immediately filled the window, wide-eyed. She yelled, "Do *not* come in!" The way she blinked told of terror. She was pushing her hands into the door to keep it closed.

He drowned a laugh that was caused by the preposterous idea that someone of her mass could keep someone of his size from coming in. The mental image of her flying through the air as he slammed the door open tickled his funny nerve almost enough to consider it an option. He raised his hands so she could see he wasn't resorting to brutish measures. "Do you mind if I sit so we can talk?"

With a fist full of relief, she said, "Sit. Yes. Sit."

He slumped with his back against the door. "Do you need anything? Food? Water? A blanket?"

"No, no, and no. The only thing you can provide is quiet. No more explosions. Go away so I can rest."

Ignoring her, he asked, "Have you observed anything new since we spoke last?"

"Well," she said, shifting against the door and letting loose a mucousy snort. "In simple terms, science is hard, science is slow, and most of all, science requires quiet."

"Have you made any discoveries about Towning's augmentation of *your* amazingly innovative HIV variant?" He hoped that piling it on thick would mellow her wasabi-up-the-nose tendencies.

"What part of slow do you not understand?" The "you idiot" was implied.

He sat, providing a moment of silence for her, reviewing what he knew about her research, hoping that a once-through would help him recall it if or when he blanked out again. She designed her HIV variant to target and kill specific types of other viruses. Once her HIV eradicated that other virus, she killed her variant with a non-toxic compound, a genetic backdoor engineered into its DNA. The chemical was like a kill switch, leaving the patient disease-free.

The concept of therapeutic viruses that infected and took over other virus cells emerged in the 1990s and progressed slowly but recently made incredible breakthroughs. Genetically altered viruses that blitzed specific cancer cells were the most prominent and successful examples. Their use expanded exponentially once genetic printing grew fast and affordable.

She had hoped to take advantage of her back door to kill Towning's sub-variant HIV, but that didn't work. The question was, did Towning hide other kill switches in his rusting diseases? And if so, could she find them? It was a big if. And the possible chemicals that might kill his variants counted in the millions.

Wall smudged his safety glasses in an unintentional attempt to bridge his nose in frustration and silently cursed himself for nearly contaminating his hands. The gear was there to hinder errors like that. After years of working in labs, he still hadn't broken the habit. The average person touched their face about twenty-three times an hour. He estimated that he was far above that count of late, particularly with his eyes and skin stinging from the bleach and the scruffiness of his thickening beard.

He needed to try a different tact with Kayla. "Can we acquire anything to accelerate your research?"

"I told you. More watts, more watts, more watts."

"Understood. Is there anything else?"

"You still haven't brought me your bacteria samples."

"Yeah. I've been a bit busy, if you haven't heard."

She snorted. "Busy blowing holes in my building."

A jibe about her oh-so-pleasant personality almost broke free of his mouth like an irate prisoner from a rusted holding cell. Switching tacts again, he said, "Tell me this. Do you know which viruses rust which metals?"

"Of course."

He retrieved the little notebook from his vest pocket, flipped it to the page where he already jotted down the viruses, and said, "Would you mind enlightening me?"

"Not that it will help you, but..." She listed them off.

Mumps   –   Aluminum
West Nile   –   Chrome
Measles   –   Lithium
COVID-19   –   Iron
Smallpox   –   Zinc
SARS   –   Stainless Steel
HIV   –   Steel

Each metal corresponded to one of his research bacteria, verifying what he already knew; Towning piggybacked his strike against humanity on Wall's genetically modified corrosion bugs. A small part of him had held out hope that Towning pillaged the works of other scientists, which would have assuaged some of Wall's guilt. But, no. It made sense. The old man accelerated Wall's research for his own purposes. His mentor had insisted on certain parameters that Wall didn't understand, which he now suspected made them easier to splice into viruses. So, why would the mad genius go through the effort of befriending and then stealing from other researchers when he could focus on just one, Wall?

Kayla banged something against the door, jolting him out of his thoughts. "Hey. I'm talking. Did I break your brain?"

"Nope." He hadn't mentioned his concussion to her yet and didn't want her to know he was compromised for fear that she might stop talking to him altogether. "Not broken. Just sprained."

They drifted into a silence, during which Wall drifted off for a moment. When his head bobbed, he startled awake, words coming out of his mouth on their own. "Okay, Kayla, let's simplify this Barney style. Would another set of viruses that killers, of virophages that target different pathogens help?" The idea followed a moment behind his words, a habit that used to annoy his fellow grad students back in Houston, particularly because such thoughts tended to be useful. He wasn't sure if it was intuition or a good amount of thinking in the background that surfaced when brought out by a clue.

"Those types of virophages only target a handful of viruses, and aside from me, only the Germans and Swedes do any quality research. Obviously, obtaining their samples would prove difficult."

"Ha," Wall said, knowing otherwise. "What about Professor Karl Quinten's research?"

She scoffed, "What? Are you going to fly to Munich?"

He smiled wryly. "Karl joined my department a month ago as part of the university's efforts to expand into bioengineering."

"Quinten is a hack."

Contrary to her opinion, Karl was one of the most intelligent people Wall knew, rivaling Towning. He had Rhino's encyclopedic memory and da Vinci's creativity. Instead of coming to his colleague's defense, he pressed on. "Even so, would his virophages help?"

Almost inaudible, she said, "I suppose."

Wall had what he needed. After swooping by his apartment for his bacteria samples, they'd pay a visit to Karl's lab. Maybe, just maybe, returning with both would transmute her rusty personality to gold.

Harnessing his patient professor voice, he said, "That wasn't so bad, now was it?"

Silence.

"See ya," he said after too long.

No response.

Wall attempted to stand with the help of his stick, but his good leg had fallen asleep, and he collapsed under his own weight. A million scorching brands punished his thigh, and his head pounded twice as hard. "Piece of...!"

Lucas laughed and pointed, bouncing up and down only a few paces away. Rather than reddening in the face, Wall took pleasure at hearing the boy's laughter. They'd lost too much already. At least Towning couldn't kill the joy of children.

With the aid of his crutch and the door handle, Wall managed to rise on his second attempt. Nellibi was asleep now, so he coaxed the boy outside for a bathroom break. Freed of the confines of the office, he ran around with arms spread like an airplane, making a motor sound that was better suited for the classic mustang outside.

While watching Lucas, he approached Plink, who hunched forward with her hands propped on her knees and her head on her arms. Recognizing that she needed downtime like everyone else, even if she could endure exhaustion better than most, he backed up.

Without moving her head, she extracted a hand and patted the cracked pavement at her side. "Find a perch, rabbit."

"Are you sure?"

"Do I have to make it an order, soldier?"

He crash-landed, butt down in a semi-controlled descent.

Still resting, she groggily asked, "What did you learn?"

He scratched his scraggly beard and summarized his discussion with Kayla the Abrasive, carefully balancing between too little and too much detail. She appeared asleep the whole time, all the while saying, "Mm Hmm" and "Gotcha" at all the right times, then asking astute questions.

"Okay," she said when he finished. "Use that oversized professorial brain of yours and estimate our odds of finding a cure."

"Mind if I skin the cat from butt to head?" he asked. He cringed at using his dad's expression. Sure, he loved his dad, but old people had a way of saying whatever they wanted that a young man in an academic setting couldn't afford to let slip.

In true military fashion, she chuckled. "Skin the kitty from tits to taco for all I care."

"You inadvertently asked a bunch of intermingling questions all at once."

"Okay. Barney it for me."

"The first question is, what are the odds that we find a way to combat a single disease? The second one is, how many diseases can we stop? The next is, how much time do we have? Then, do you mean a vaccine to protect future generations or a cure for those infected now?"

Without looking up, she twirled her index finger in circles. "And?"

"Given enough time, we will almost definitely find a vaccine for at least one disease, probably two. The chances drop toward zero when we talk about all of them. The odds drop scarily if the lab is damaged sooner than later, days versus years. Failure is inevitable no matter what kind of precautions we take. When the instruments rust, we're done."

When he paused to order his thoughts, she twirled her finger again. "It revs my engines when you talk science to me, so keep it up, big guy."

"To put this in technical terms, finding a cure rather than a vaccine is a rat's left nut from zero. We haven't found a cure for HIV after decades and a hundred billion dollars of research."

Without looking up, Plink rolled her neck with a series of loud pops and then proceeded with her knuckles, a sign of lost hope. It was like discovering Santa didn't exist. Up to that point, Alpha Bravo focused so heavily on survival and securing the lab that they hadn't explored many of their long-term needs.

Plink's only response was. "Acknowledged. Next."

"Kayla determined which viruses cause which types of rusting."

"And?"

The list was burned into his mind. He would never forget the mental map between his bacteria and Towning's viruses. With mechanical precision, he listed them.

"And the implications?" she asked, tapping her fingers.

He slipped jerky into his mouth. "We will probably find a vaccine for aluminum, nickel, or zinc. Existing vaccines could accelerate our research. Note that those vaccines aren't for us. They're for our children and our children's children."

Finally looking at him, she said, "So, iron, steel, and stainless steel belong to the past. No more hard metals."

CHAPTER TWENTY-ONE

Plink yawned with a cute little squeak, then said, "Don't worry. I rarely kill the messenger." The droop of her face conveyed how exhausted and disheartened she was. "So, super-nerd, how do these new findings change our priorities?"

He rolled his tongue over his cheek while thinking it through. The hard-to-access depths of his mind had figured out most of the answers without him being aware of it, like thoughts surfacing in the shower. "We should work to develop vaccines for the two easiest viruses. It gives us the best chance of limited success. If we have more time to develop more vaccines or cures, all the better."

She massaged her neck and asked, "Which two vaccines would you make first?"

"Smallpox-zinc first. Measles-aluminum second." Nanoseconds later, he realized that in six words, he may have changed the fate of humanity, a conjoined utterance with unimaginable consequences.

"Explain."

He stuck to a perfunctory, Barney-style answer. "Without a vaccine for zinc, deficiencies will weaken our immune system. Without it, the common flu could kill us all and drive those who survive into isolation, too fearful of sickness to intermingle."

She stomped her booted heel into the crumbling asphalt. "That fucker! How else can he screw us?" Wall fumed with her in silence. For too long, they sat, tempering their rage.

"Okay," she said, regaining her composure and bumping his good knee. "First, we collect samples of the smallpox vaccine. Then we retrieve the bacteria samples at your condo. Is that right?"

"Yeah, and third, and far less likely to help, we obtain samples from Quinten's virus lab."

Her lips curled up at the corners. "We have three missions." She jumped to her feet, exhaustion all but vanished. "Time to go. Where can we find vaccines?"

"Hospitals, particularly pediatrics, have tons of vaccines."

With a growing smile, she said, "Saddle up, soldier. We walk in five minutes."

"What?" Wall said and pointed at his thigh to clarify with a single-word protest. When she just looked at him with a *so what?* expression, he said, "I'm shot. Won't I get in the way? Slow you down?"

"Wall, don't be dense. I need a super-nerd. Nellibi and Kayla can't go out there into the growing chaos. You're our guy."

"But my leg..."

Unperturbed, she said, "No problem. I'll be back with a new ride in twenty minutes."

He tilted his head. "What's wrong with Betty?"

"The poor girl sucked up rust from the road. She's dying from the inside."

"Crap."

Practically taking to bird-like flight, Plink loped toward the back fence. "Going off base!" she yelled up to Rhino.

"Have fun," the low, muffled voice replied.

Seconds later, she bounced off a tree and jumped over the back fence to the north.

Five minutes early, she returned in a mint-condition, old-school, army-green Jeep. As was typical of early Jeeps, the front window hinged forward and lacked a roof or even doors. The thing was light and small compared to most modern cars. Its superb condition probably meant that she found it in a garage like the Mustang, untouched because of its owner's appreciation of the well-loved vehicle.

In pure joy, she howled madly. "Can I pick 'em? Or can I pick 'em?"

Rhino whistled. It was hard to deny the antique's beautiful simplicity. Or was it simple beauty? "A true classic!" his ogling eyes told of his appreciation for the machine's military history. "Let me guess. 1950s?"

With a spectacular smile, she said, "The registration says 1954."

"You couldn't get something with doors? Or armor?"

"This little guy has a purpose. You'll see." She patted the passenger's seat. "Hop in."

Wall did something he couldn't quite call a hop, but he managed to wedge his long legs in, which had the added benefit of securing him without a safety belt.

Plink popped the clutch, and they bucked in a circle, the wheels grinding on the napalm-burned asphalt. To say that Plink was a speed demon was a horrible understatement. Because cars blocked long sections of the road, often in both directions, she swerved like a mad woman, on and off the pavement. At no point on the way could her driving style be considered safe. When she bumped off the road and skirted through Nobel Peace Park, where maybe a hundred refugees camped, Wall yelled, "Where are you going? The bridge is over there!"

Her only response was a twinkling-eyed wink.

He grasped her insane plan when she drove up the curved bike ramp. "You're not..."

"Yup!" She drove onto the suspension bike bridge across the Willamette River with approximately ten centimeters to spare on either side, speeding just as fast as before. With the railings either rusted or actively doing so, they provided no reassurance. A pair of rusting bikes crunched under the Jeep and nearly launched them off the bridge.

"Fuhhh!" he yelled.

Her manic smile did nothing to ease his very reasonable fear of a watery death down below. The only benefit of driving so fast was reaching the far side in record time. Upon landfall, she swerved this way and that, bouncing down slopes and speeding through parking lots, then along back streets.

Two blocks from Sacred Heart Hospital, she stopped weaving through the densely packed rusting cars and drove over lawns, between trees, and through shrubs, all the while smiling like a dentist's favorite patient.

Crap, he thought when he remembered that his dentist was supposed to fill a cavity in his twelve-year molar. Dentistry went the way of everything else. It hit the fan.

The Jeep jerked to a stop with the driver's side on a curb. Like the happiest cab driver ever, she said, "Door-to-door service," and held out her palm. "I take tips in silver dollars and gold eagles."

"Gold eagles?"

"Don't ask Rhino. If you get him started on the subject of early-US money, he won't shut up." She straightened his bullet-proof vest, patted his magazines, and slapped him on the glancingly shot helmet.

He almost said, "Thanks, Mom," but tangled his tongue in time to avoid catastrophe. He had learned the hard way that calling any woman "Mom" was a mistake you never wanted to make, even during an ugly breakup.

Plink signaled "silent" and "eyes sharp," then hopped out of the doorless driver's seat and rounded the Jeep with her M4 raised before he could get his first foot on the ground. Her short, swift steps were those of a slinking predator. When he grabbed his crutch from the back, she shook her head and mouthed, "No."

"But..." he mouthed.

She shook her head again.

He gritted his teeth and stood, testing his leg whereupon she placed his hand on her shoulder the way they did to clear out Renegade Genomix. He drew his pistol and nodded. She moved, slow and smooth, careful not to outpace him. He endeavored to imitate her fluidity only to approximate a stumbling zombie.

Yellow caution tape and shattered glass laid across the doorless entrance. Scuffs from a stream of footsteps had nearly cleared a path through the shards.

With the lights out, the deserted building practically screamed *don't go in! Don't go in!* Hospitals were the first to fall, and the wear and tear on the building spoke of an extensive rusting worse than any he'd seen so far. The elevator doors had vanished. The ceiling slumped in some places and had fallen in others. The reception desks and seats had collapsed like giant Jenga piles. The metal detector crumpled on its side.

This is a death trap, he told himself.

He pushed his life-preserving instincts aside and trailed her into the darkness, pausing when she stopped and following when she pressed forward. They stuck to the walls, her M4 leading the way. Stopping at the directory for a sec, they spotted pediatrics, and she held up four fingers to confirm with Wall. She shot him a bad-dog look when he inadvertently groaned at the prospect of climbing four stories with his ganked leg.

Plink led him through the propped-open door to the even darker stairwell. The dimly lit stairs shook with each clumsy step and the handrails had mostly crumbled away. He followed as she treated every step like it might present a new threat. Every flight of stairs was that much harder on his bullet wound and bum knee. With a length of rope from her pack, they tied themselves together to leap over fallen steps with at least some pretense of safety. When a stair crumbled under Plink's foot, she caught herself on the next stair up, which cracked but held.

Wall sighed when they reached the fourth floor, where a dangling sign read "Pediatrics." Only one window remained in place, the rest having lost their frames. Half of the metal-legged chairs and couches leaned one way or another. The other half had collapsed under their own weight. Rust was everywhere, on everything.

They wound around holes in the floor toward the reception. Halfway there, the floor cracked and fell out from under Wall's considerable weight. He fell to his knees on the rapidly stretching lobby carpet and choked off a yell enough that it could be described as a dad-worthy grunt. Plink spun and pulled him away from the expanding hole, towing his much heavier weight like an ox with a plow. If they ever discussed that moment, he'd be sure to omit the part about comparing her to an ox. It was never a good idea to talk about women resembling animals in the bovine family.

After he recovered from the butt-puckering fall, they walked more carefully across the lobby, where Plink untied herself from the tether and motioned for him to crawl behind a bent and broken desk. Once he was settled, she motioned for him to stay and watch for danger. He held up the "okay" sign, and she disappeared into the dark recesses of the building.

"This was a stupid idea," he whispered. There had to be other places where they could find what they needed. There would be another way. The longer he waited, the more he wanted to leave.

She returned dragging a zip-tied woman dressed in pink scrubs and set the unconscious twenty-something prisoner under a leaning desk next to Wall. There was no outward display of wounds, so he assumed Plink took care of her like she had Kayla when they first entered Renegade Genomix, a quick and effective but non-lethal attack. He was glad the true warrior was on his side.

Seconds later, she walked back into the depths of the eerie corridors. Inaction ate at Wall like sweat on a zipper. After a longer wait than before, she came back around and whispered, "Clear. Locate the vaccines. We leave ASAP." As if to accentuate their need to go, a water-logged ceiling tile fell and splattered like wet papier-mâché on the carpeted floor.

Wall rolled to his feet as if his leg didn't bother him, flicked on his pistol-mounted light, and pressed into the doctors' side of the pediatric office. Doors laid on their sides. A gurney was reduced to pads and dust. He stuck close to the walls in hopes that the floor might be sturdier. The smell of rancid cabbage would have repelled a more sensitive man.

Illuminating door placard after door placard, the hunt for vaccines was slow. He nearly pulled the trigger when a human-shaped lump on the corridor floor came into view. The blob transformed into a rotund woman dressed in cartoon-covered scrubs half-fallen into a hole in the floor. He approached with his scope's crosshairs at her center of mass. The fact that she was still—as in the never move again kind of still—barely stayed his twitchy finger.

Footprints ran through the pool of dried blood around her, a preserved record of someone stepping over her a while back.

The woman was the main source of the foul smell that permeated pediatrics. Most pre-rusting people couldn't handle such smells, but Wall wasn't most people. He imagined rewarding himself with a triple-sized section of Kentucky-whiskey-flavored jerky. "Jerky, the cure-all." Headache: jerky. Sore throat: jerky. Upset stomach: jerky. Bullet wound: jerky.

"Jackpot."

Looters, particularly those who needed a fix with their usual supply cut off, would kill a nurse for any drugs they could find. The doorway behind her had to be what he was looking for. The question was, did they run off with the vaccines too, either by accident or on purpose?

Someone ransacked the pharmacy/storeroom. Drawers open. Boxes and packages thrown about. Bottles on the floor. The plastic and rust remains of a refrigerator.

"Crap. So much for ASAP."

He flipped his backpack to the front and sifted through the debris for small vials, coming away with entirely too few for his pleasure. He tossed aside ones with rusted lids and applied the five-finger discount to a box of pink surgical gloves, a roll of clear plastic bags, single-use masks, and six miniature bottles of disinfectant spray. He sanitized a box that read "Smallpox, Quantity: 8" and tucked it into his pack. His tension let up when he found several bottles of Measles, Mumps, and Rubella vaccines. Having scored what he needed, he kicked around the junk a little longer, coming up with bandages, sterile needles for sutures, Amoxicillin, compression wraps, and more.

On his way out, Wall spotted a set of crutches, a tantalizing prospect to replace his makeshift one. He practically danced a jig only to realize they were made of aluminum, rust magnets. In a strange turn of life, a single makeshift wooden crutch was far superior to its modern equivalent.

"It's Wall," he whisper-yelled into the reception area as he emerged from the dark.

She alternated between a thumbs up and thumbs down, the question of "Success?" evident in the gesture.

He nodded and held two thumbs up.

She nudged the woman in pink scrubs with her booted toe. When she didn't stir, Plink slit the plastic cuffs, leaving her to sleep off whatever the elite soldier did to subdue her, a sign that she was capable of kindness when the circumstances allowed.

The return trip tested his fortitude, straining his joints and muscles in all the wrong ways. Rather than leaning forward to hold onto her shoulder, he kept pace with her, sliding his hand along the outer wall. Each step came too quickly to give him any respite and too slowly for someone who valued his life.

On the second floor, male voices carried through the open doorway. Wall hopped on his good leg to span the landing quickly, which wasn't exactly quiet. Either the men inside didn't hear his awkward hops, or they chose not to investigate. Regardless, he breathed easier with each following stair.

Wall slipped on the last step and only remained upright with a dash of willpower and a truckload of pain-inducing floundering. "Umph!" If the guys upstairs hadn't heard him before, they couldn't miss him now. Plink chose a faster pace to cross the ground-floor lobby, which he could only keep up with by paying the price in pain, having earned his punishment for letting his focus slip on that last step.

At the exit, she shifted and shot four times in a one-two, one-two pattern that matched the cadence of her nervous tick. Two men slumped in the classic Army Jeep, dead for attempting to steal their ride. She closed the distance, scanning from side to side as she went, and yanked the dead guy out of the passenger's seat before jumping up and kicking the would-be driver out the other side.

Wall climbed in as she turned the key. Nothing happened. Not even a click. She cursed a string of hyper-speed syllables in Spanish when she looked under the steering column.

While she fiddled with wires, he stood up with his M4 raised and swept in a three-sixty for potential threats, all concerns for his leg lost in the moment. He almost fired at a length of caution tape as it fluttered in the gentle breeze.

Then, the starter *click-click-clicked*, and his guts turned back upright. He dropped into the seat just in time for Plink to pop the clutch and rocket backward with the wheel spun to the max like she was in a demolition derby. They smacked into an igloo-shaped economy car that leaned on two wheels, with the Jeep's steel tail winning the battle against the flimsy car's fiberglass shell. With a neck-popping lurch, they sped back the way they came, plowing through bushes and skidding over lawns.

The sound of gunfire pursued them. One bullet hit the Jeep with a brass-on-steel pang. Wall sprang up and flipped backward in one motion with his knees on the barely padded seat and his feet rammed into the dashboard. In a quick series of one-two, one-two pulls of his trigger, he shot back. He had little chance of hitting the man and woman firing at him from the hospital entrance, instead wanting to freak them out long enough for Plink to speed out of range. During a rare moment of calm between flowerbed and tree root, Wall placed his crosshairs on the woman and fired. He never saw whether he hit her because the Jeep bucked and nearly heaved him overboard.

"Those–" Plink said before a series of grinding noises drowned her out. "They contaminated my little lady!" She slowed to a less terrifying speed several blocks away. He looked around the old-school vehicle. The red of blood, the perfect ruster, speckled their Jeep.

"She already sucked up rust like a coke addict, don't you? And you've ground her belly across everything you could find."

"Poor girl," she said. "You're dead. You just don't know it yet."

CHAPTER TWENTY-TWO

Plink spun the powerless-steering wheel this way and that and somehow found the time and concentration to fish a granola bar from her pack and toss it at Wall. "Healing boys need plenty of calories, so eat up. Fair warning, though. The foil wrapper is rusty."

He greedily tore into the bar, sending bits spilling everywhere as Plink continued her weaving erratically onto curbsides and bouncing off a sedan. "Mmmm. Nothing like industrial flavoring to spice things up."

"That a boy," she said, swerving south around a corner, narrowly missing a flower delivery truck. "That's the sort of positivity that scores you the prom queen." They wound westward toward his condo. "Speaking of prom queens, we only have enough time for a quick in-and-out at your place. Otherwise, mom and dad might realize I snuck out with a boy."

It took him a moment to dislodge the mental image of her up on a stage in a pink skirt receiving a chintzy princess crown. As she converged on his condo, he said, "Hey. How do you know where I live?"

"Do you think I'm dumb or something?" She pretended to be wounded.

"Dumb? No. Crazy? Yes."

She looked at him entirely too long as she nearly ran the left tire into a missing manhole. "Don't you think we searched your crib for damning evidence?"

He palmed his helmet. A few blocks west and a couple south, after she plowed through an abandoned one-legged stroller, he asked, "Where the hell did you learn to drive?"

As if talking about her favorite pet, she said, "Lawnmower derbies. Being a small ten-year-old on a supercharged beast gave me an advantage over the heavy bubbas. Speed, baby, speed. If they can't catch you, they can't play rough, and when they did, they never expected a little girl to hit back so hard."

"That's the only thing that makes sense since this mess started."

She careened around a roofless Porsche. "I barely passed my driver's license test."

"That, I believe."

"On the third try," she added with the utmost joy.

He laughed nervously. "You're kidding, right?"

She cruised over an abandoned tire in the middle of the street. "Yeah. I lied. It was my fourth try."

After flinching when she nearly hit an old man on the sidewalk, Wall said, "You're not building my confidence."

A bullet shattered the forward-hinged window as Plink threaded the needle between a crumbling dumpster and a cement wall in a back ally. "Don't worry." Another bullet hit the concrete half a meter from him. "Moving targets are hard to hit." The third bullet hit the back before she rammed through a white picket gate.

"*Hard* to hit," he said, emphasizing *hard*. "Not impossible." With one new hole last night, he already exceeded the FDA's recommended daily consumption of vitamin brass. The bullets stopped chasing them as she swerved around the corner.

Several blocks later, they jerked to a stop on the dead grass lawn beside his stucco condominium. She faced Wall and pulled his helmet into hers, locking eyes only inches away. "Is your head on straight, soldier? We're headed into an unknown hot zone." The next thing he knew, she leaned her head to the left and kissed him, more than a little peck and less than a Frenchy, a pleasant surprise. She pulled away, smiled slyly, and asked, "Did that wake you up?"

"No," he said with a guileful smile of his own. "I think I need several more of those."

She went in for another one but pulled away just before their lips met, then slapped his helmet. "You're cute. But not that cute." She smiled all the same, patted him down, and straightened his bulletproof vest. "Move out."

"Don't break our hard-won vaccines," she whispered as they neared the side door, M4 at ready.

He patted his backpack nervously with the mental image of vials cracking during a swerve, bounce, or collision.

Like every commonly used door in Eugene, his building's side entrance had thoroughly corroded. Someone swept the bulk of the fallen rust and glass into a pile in the grass. Avoiding the bits of the door still hanging from their hinges, she led the way in. Being a much larger specimen of the human race, he found it harder to dodge through without brushing against the rusted remains.

This was the most memorable time he entered his building. More impactful than buying his first place. Crazier than talking a tweaker out of crapping in the hallway by throwing cue tips like they were darts. Many of the doors were busted open or hung loosely from the remains of weakened hinges.

When Missus Lopez poked her iron-and-silver-haired head into the hall, Plink barely reacted. In her motherly Hispanic accent, Lopez said, "Hola, Plink. I told you Wall was a good boy."

"Si, señora," Plink agreed. "El mejor."

"Are you together now?" his nosy neighbor asked, meaning together-together.

While Wall answered, "No," Plink playfully said, "Why, yes. Yes, we are."

Missus Lopez giggled sweetly. "She's a good one, Wall. Keep her if you can."

"Missus Lopez," he said, following his tongue to a thought. "Do you have a phone that works?"

"No," she said apologetically. "All of ours broke back at the beginning."

He nodded respectfully. "Thanks. Good to see you, but we're in a hurry, señora."

"Oh, I understand," the old woman said, bobbing her head with a knowing smile. "Have fun."

"Bye, Missus Lopez," they said together.

Wall's door was not only open. It lay in pieces on the floor in the entryway. He and Plink cleared his condo, scanning each room as Wall was growing accustomed. A tornado couldn't have done a better job of randomly redistributing his belongings. Drawers, clothes, pots, and utensils were everywhere. A rat fled the kitchen, where an assortment of dried foods covered the floor and counter. A sentient woodchipper might as well have eaten his couch pillows. Someone cut up sections of the carpet.

Even among the chaos, the apartment clearly belonged to a bachelor, despite how his ex, Penny, tried to spruce it up with a more "mature" decor. The deep couch, which was now upside down with slits through the bottom, belonged in front of the too-large TV, which was smashed up on the floor, leaning against the fireplace. The condoms on the bathroom floor and the lack of fragrant soaps were the real giveaways.

"Clear," Plink said. "Don't you like what we did with the place?" She sounded like one of those home makeover hosts. "We call this style rummage chic. It's sublime?"

"It must be an acquired taste," he replied.

"We looked through everything and didn't find your safe," she said. "No loose floorboards. Nothing in the vents. No false-backed mirrors or closets. So, where did you squirrel it away?"

"Watch and be amazed." He knocked the TV from in front of the cheesy gas fireplace, pressed a tile, and the unit swung out like a door. The thing was about six inches deep, leaving about a foot of room behind it. "The fire never worked, so I make use of it." Inside, the Sturdysafe remained corrosion-free, without an ounce of rust on the custom-reinforced steel exterior or the hundred-digit radial dial. He appreciated the master craftsmanship, the artistry that would soon be ruined along with everything else.

Plink whistled. "How paranoid are you?"

"The best safe is one that nobody knows about." Kneeling, he rotated the dial to his lucky number, then the age at which his grandma died, and the month of his mom's birthday. In the year that he owned the sucker, only four people knew it even existed: Kayla, Plink, the safe maker, and the delivery guy. And none knew where he hid it.

Before opening the reinforced door, he swapped out his gloves and doubled up on disinfectant. Everything was right where he had left it. The orange Pelican box with his samples. His Glock 19, the smaller Glock 26, plus his stash of 9mm rounds. He held his breath as he opened the tough box. Fourteen labeled Petrie dishes, two per strain, remained in the precise rows he'd left them in.

"Always have a backup," he told himself as he sealed it up.

"Give 'em here," Plink said. He wanted to carry the samples himself but recognized the need for splitting up the two most important assets for Kayla's research. Two eggs, two baskets.

He left the cash, his passport, birth certificate, the thumb drive, and all the other things he thought were valuable before the great rusting. If he had listened to Outhouse, he would have stowed away more survival gear. "It's too late when you're already nut-deep in the pile."

"Ready?" Plink asked.

"Ready." It surprised him how little he cared about leaving his condo and all his belongings behind. He wasn't attached to any of the furniture Penny picked out. He could care less about the rusting pots or pans. The dried foodstuffs would have come in handy if Plink's team hadn't dumped them out to co-mingle with shards of glass from the upper cabinets.

Lingering would only increase the risk of mission failure and Plink had already introduced a serious risk factor by bringing an untrained gimp into a *hostile environment*. He almost laughed. The things people at the university thought counted as hostile environments seemed ridiculous in the state of the new world. Inflammatory words. Negative criticism. Mistaken pronouns.

A minute later, a family jumped out of the way as Plink swerved the Jeep around an SUV. Wall couldn't tell what was scarier, Plink's driving, or the growing rust rings circling every speck of blood on the dashboard. Blood was the new acid. Whether from Plink's abuse or from rust, the previously pristine relic lurched, leaned, and skidded into the bed of a yellow pickup truck.

As soon as the Jeep came to a halt, Plink said, "The vaccines? Give me your pack."

"Sure," he said, unstrapping the thing and shimmying it off his shoulders. The accident hardly seemed worse than her usual driving, so he didn't understand why she was suddenly more worried than before. But he had to trust the tier-one operator if he wanted to survive.

"Look at me," she said, pulling his helmet to hers. "Stay alive. Got that?" Without giving him time to respond, she tilted her head and kissed him passionately, a tantalizing escape from the growing chaos. The next second, she jumped out of the driver's side and said, "The mission is all."

Looking into the back, he found that his crutch was gone, probably bounced out by Plink's rough driving. He gingerly crawled out of his seat and cursed its absence. His bullet hole had ripped open or the bandage had slipped during the crash, and the pain suddenly caught up, drawing all of his attention inward. "Gah!" When he focused outward again, she was gone, vanished. He turned on shaky legs. "Plink?" He cupped his hands around his mouth. "Plink!"

Three cracks from a rifle echoed through the streets to the west, the third one somehow wrong, dull and rumbling. A long-bearded man wearing nothing but his tidy whities strolled across the road a block south as if everything was normal.

"Crap." It wasn't a spectacular time to stand in the middle of the road with his head solidly embedded in his ass like a tourist at Apocalypse Park. Two bricks fell from the retro facade of the building on the other side of the street, exploding into dozens of pieces, adding to the chunks of building that covered the sidewalk. "Don't just stand here."

"I need shelter."

He made a snap decision and tottered through the front door of a fancy puzzle store, the place where he bought his mom a present for Christmas last year. As good a place to rest and take stock as he would find.

Wall cleared the shop, imitating Plink's technique without a dusting of her grace. Thousands of puzzle pieces covered the floor like an experiential mosaic that shifted and slid underfoot as he progressed toward the back. He couldn't figure out why someone would vandalize a puzzle store, but for whatever reason, they did a thorough job of bashing the displays and shelves. The giant spray-painted penis on the ceiling added a flare of panache to their craftsmanship. In the storage room, the aluminum shelving units had collapsed from a combination of rust and good old fashion smashing. The back office received the same treatment.

"Clear," he said as Plink would have. He found a spot on the floor behind the bashed-in counter and plopped down. "Take stock and regroup."

The blood stain on his pant leg meant that his thigh wound had ruptured and soaked through the bandages beneath. "Just what I needed." He reached for his backpack, where he stowed the bandages from pediatrics, only to come up empty. "Piece of!"

Rationally, he understood that what Plink did was best for the mission. The imperative was to acquire and return with the vaccines and samples at all costs. Wall was the cost in this case. "So much for 'leave no man behind.'" In the post-rust world, she couldn't afford the luxury of calling for backup to aid in his recovery.

The other part of him, the animalistic side, wanted to throttle her, to shoot her in the leg and see how well she fared. He slipped pocket jerky into his mouth in an attempt to soothe his inner beast.

"What in the sweaty crotch of hell am I supposed to do now?"

No plan miraculously came to mind, so he turned his focus inward. His bloody thigh required immediate attention. He couldn't afford to lose too much blood for fear of worsening his physical and mental state. Further, the spilt blood might contaminate his gear, including his firearms, and they'd seen how fatal that was.

He retrieved a stack of brown paper towels from the bathroom along with a small red first-aid kit from under the junky cabinet sink and the foaming sanitizer dispenser next to the door. By rummaging through the lost and found, he came up with a pair of purple spandex biker shorts that were about four sizes too small.

"Improvise, adapt, and overcome."

When he returned to his spot behind the counter, he set aside and decontaminated his gear. "Keep it safe. Keep it clean." Cutting away his pants proved to be a crappy endeavor. He acknowledged the luxury of possessing the carbon fiber knife that Plink unceremoniously raided from the National Guard armory. It might be more brittle than a metal counterpart, but it wouldn't dull from blood contamination. He could rely on it in a way that he couldn't rely on people. Nellibi was a mess, though he hoped she might recover. Ueskev only looked out for number one. Kayla was becoming more and more agoraphobic, ready to flip out if she left her lab. Plink abandoned him. Rhino would have done the same in the name of the mission.

"The mission is all," he muttered.

Next, he slit the soaked bandage from his thigh, keeping well clear of his femoral artery. In a series of quick motions, he peeled away the sticky bandage, pumped the alcohol-based sanitizer into and around the wound, laid the largest band-aid he could find over the affected area, and pressed a dozen paper towels over the top. He barely had time to see the torn bullet hole and the angry red tissue from the cauterization that he couldn't remember doing to himself. Fortunately, the delay between actions and the accompanying sting kept him focused through the quick set of medical interventions. As it kicked in, he yelled uncontrollably, extending an invite to anyone interested in a wounded victim. His vision blurred, his head pounded, and his quadricep twitched.

When he recovered, he replaced the paper towels with a new bundle, then pulled a too-tight leg of the purple spandex over the whole thing. It was anything but ideal but would have to last until he found a better solution. Wall leaned back and wiggled his toes to check if the spandex was cutting off his circulation.

"So good so far," he said as his head numbed and throbbed at the same time, eyes drooping. He was pretty sure one of his blinks lasted entirely too long to be counted as safe. Sleep meant death in "enemy territory."

"Is this karma?" If he believed in a "what comes around goes around" universe, this would be the moment for it to smite him.

"Snap out of it." Plink wasn't there to kiss him into alertness. She'd taken off rather than put the mission at risk.

"What are my options?" He gently rolled his head to the random percussion jazz of a ganked neck. The quick pinch at the base of his skull focused his thoughts.

"Option one. Trek back home." With better clothes, his own first-aid kit, and a defensible shelter, he could recuperate before returning to active duty. Plink's abandonment proved how little use he was in the current state of things.

"Two. Walk back to base." It was farther away than home. Selfishly the idea of returning to Plink and Rhino and the promise of safety appealed to him. Could he hide behind the warriors and rely on Kayla to fix everything? A backup to the backup?

"No."

He sat for a while, looking up at the water-stained ceiling. Aimlessness nearly claimed him.

"Three?" he asked, leaning his head forward, away from the stubborn knot at the C1 spinal disk. Bricks fell from the building across the street, a clear sign of man's downfall and the need for him to find a safe place to rest.

"The mission is all."

After some unknown amount of time, he remembered that they had a third task: acquire Karl Quinten's viruses. Without him, Plink would be hard-pressed to find what they needed. With option three, he had purpose and hope.

CHAPTER TWENTY-THREE

"No time like the present," he said as he patted himself down and checked his firearms. The idea of walking across southern Eugene in the middle of the day without the ability to run required a sizable activation energy. The call to wait for the darkness of night beckoned him to stay and rest for a few hours. He couldn't stay, though. The puzzle store offered no food or water, and as much as he valued his pocket jerky, it wasn't much and wouldn't replace enough energy to keep going after losing blood. Besides, every hour he delayed was another hour that Karl Quinten's lab could collapse into ruin.

Before leaving the store, a group of eight men and women slowly plodded by with failing suitcases, backpacks, and duffle bags. They scurried faster when another brick fell across the street and burst into bits. Days ago, the idea of frightened, underfed refugees in America seemed impossible.

He tried to squeeze the pounding out of his head by clenching his eyelids together. "I need a new definition of *impossible.*"

Wall's first steps mashed at his thigh as the bandages shifted into place. The compression spandex helped stabilize his leg, granting him steadier and quicker strides—slower than he wanted and faster than he feared.

He headed south with the goal of stopping by his buddy's house along the way, followed by Professor Emeritus Knox's. He met Thomas through Fiona, who was a high school friend of his wife, Alexus. They gladly dumped the increasingly psycho Fiona in favor of him, treating him like family, like an adopted uncle to their four-year-old daughter, Sarah. Thomas, who was becoming a fast friend, would take him in for a short stint. It would be good to see them, to make sure they were alive, to help out in any way he could, to be part of their solution.

After that, he had to check in on Professor Emeritus Knox, his departmental mentor who was old enough to make walking with a cane look good. The white-haired man was one of the kindest people Wall knew, a bottomless source of positivity for everyone, supportive and helpful, an example of what a good man should be. Passing by without stopping in would be negligence. Both waypoints provided incentives and would break the limping journey into less daunting stints.

Wall crossed the street when a group of coed college-aged kids walked his way. These young men and women had transformed from kids that he would have helped pre-rusting into serious threats in the post-rust world. His new evolving values superseded those of his pre-rust luxuries.

Up ahead, he recognized a possible pinch point caused by an accident between a defunct SUV and a permanently stopped southbound bus. The funnel was perfect for rooftop sniping or up-close mugging. He weighed the pros of walking through a possible trap against limping the long way around. In Ethiopia, he never would have gone for it, but in Eugene, his leg won the argument.

"Here goes everything."

He hop-skipped through the narrow with his finger hovering near the trigger of his M4, ready to shoot any threat that presented itself. Two contradictory thoughts nucleated between his ears; *shoot anyone who so much as blinks at me*, and *please don't let there be a kid on the other side*. He sighed in relief when he came through without incident. American civvies hadn't yet reached the tactical sophistication that Ethiopian rebels used and loved.

Wall marveled at the stupidity of the situation. The idea that he, an injured vet who was only a grunt in his heyday, could influence the fate of humanity was ridiculous. Plink and Rhino were great whites among fish, ready and able to chew up anyone who threatened the mission. Kayla had all the skills they needed to counter the rusting diseases. He was a lesser Alpha Bravo member.

Regardless, he needed to be part of the solution for himself, if for nothing else.

A Viking's blow hit Wall in the back like Thor's hammer with the thunderclap and everything. He found himself falling face down on the sidewalk in a less-than-graceful dive, both bouncing and splatting upon landing, momentarily stunned and unable to figure out what happened.

"Ha! I–I–I killed you," a man stammered, only a meter or two away.

Buying time, Wall kept still, playing dead. He didn't know when the universe decided he should be a bullet magnet, but the decision clearly had been made. Swallowing his fear, he thought, *Screw you, universe.*

The robber stood over Wall and yanked at his M4 sling, somehow oblivious to the fact that it wound around his torso. The guy tugged at it again and yelled, "Y-y-you're dead. I killed you. G-g-give it to me." He sounded amped and hollow at the same time, not right in the head. Wall suspected that the stuttering had to do with an altered state of mind or an addict's need for another fix. When the guy pulled the strap a third time, Wall rolled to his side, drew his pistol, and shot three times, only stopping when the yellow-toothed, emaciated man collapsed, falling toward him.

Wall's newly amplified fear of blood snatched control of him and rolled him out of the way. With too much speed for his leg to handle, he pushed to his feet and began to skip-hop-run south. He swung his pistol wildly, looking for any other threats. Nobody came forward, so he plopped down between a set of dilapidated cars.

"Gah!" he yelled with a bestial rage into the empty street. Wall threw his cracked shooting glasses at the closest rust-mobile. It took him a moment to catch his breath, during which he sanitized himself. Dark speckles stained his pants and boots. He ran out of fluid mid-cleaning and pelted the bottle at the nearest building, a half-collapsed modern office, one of those co-working spaces with an industrial feel that exposed metal beams and duct work everywhere, a design that was particularly susceptible to disease.

"Keep moving," he said with a dry mouth and throat, wishing Plink hadn't stolen his water bottle. "She really screwed me good." If he could retrieve the virus samples, he wondered if he could face her again.

Wall headed westbound in the opposite direction from the university for two blocks on the way to Thomas's where he could rest and regroup. Upon reaching their blue and white cottage-style house, he almost pressed the doorbell but remembered from Nellibi's house that with no electricity, there would be no doorbell. So, he knocked with the brushed-bronze lion-head knocker, glad to see a matching door handle. The solid sound of the door boded well, suggesting bronze hinges. They'd be safe longer if all the other hardware in their house was also rust-proof. He knocked again and announced that "It's Wall. Thomas, Alexus, let me in."

"Hey, Wall," his friend said without opening the door, his voice muffled. "What's up?"

"Hey bud, can you let me in? I'm shot. I gotta rest."

"Sorry," he said, his guilty conscience as clear as a bell. "That's a no-go."

Wall removed his helmet and ran his hand through his sweat-soaked hair, then silently cursed that stupid motion, which contaminated his glove as effectively as blood. "Thomas, I only need a few minutes."

"I can't, bud. Hank stole a bunch of food."

Wall pressed his tongue into his cheek in frustration, having always thought Hank was a self-serving dick. Wall never understood why Thomas hung out with the douchebag but accepted it because he wasn't the kind of guy that drove wedges between people. It was stupid of Thomas to let Hank in.

"I have to think about Alexus and Sarah...I..."

Wall put his helmet back on. "I get it, bud. Say no more."

"Thanks for understanding."

Wall spent a few minutes telling his friend about the rusting diseases and insisted on the need to sanitize anything and everything. It sounded crazy, and he wasn't sure if he would have believed it if he hadn't seen the evidence. If Thomas was reluctant to let him in before, he would be doubly so now.

"I'm going to leave you my Glock 19 and a clip full of bullets, alright? It's the one we practiced on." Thomas was one of the few people in Eugene that knew he owned firearms. He'd taken his friend to the gun range several times. They never told Alexus because she wouldn't understand, and it would have caused a rust storm of an argument. "Do you remember what I taught you?"

"Yeah, thanks. I owe you."

"Mind if I take a moment to rest my leg on your porch?"

"Sure thing, Wall. Sorry I can't do more."

"Nothin' to it. Bye, bud. Stay safe."

"Bye."

He swapped his gloves for his last clean pair and laid down behind a large shrub. Facing the new world didn't feel so daunting when he chewed on the soothing comfort of another jerky sliver while lying on his side, eyes closed. His thoughts meandered down random paths as he rested. *Smoked meat,* he thought. *Will quickly become a mainstay of everybody's diet.* Without refrigerators, salting and heavy smoke were the only options for preserving high-protein meals.

The loss of flavor from his latest strand told him that ten to fifteen minutes had passed while he laid prostrate. A lesser man couldn't have resisted swallowing after a few seconds, but Wall was weird that way and decided that jerky would be his new measure of time.

"Gotta keep moving."

So, he regained his feet and headed south, content that his friends had survived this long. There was hope for them. Not much, but hope all the same. Another block down, he turned east on Thirteenth Street, which would lead him to campus in one straight shot.

Wall slid into an alley when a young-twenties couple with the CrossFit and rock-climbing kind of toned bodies sprinted by with a matching pair of heavily-laden red backpacks. Wall held his breath as they passed. Only seconds later, a guttural scream of pain and a high-pitch screech came from the direction the couple was headed. "Damn." Not even quick feet could keep you safe.

He reached his mentor's beautiful historic home with antique pane glass windows and slate tiles, relieved to have avoided any further incidents. He kicked the rusted metal gate off the entry path and passed under the perfectly manicured arch of flowering vines to their front porch. The house remained in better shape than any he'd seen to date.

Knocking on the doorjamb with blue-gloved knuckles, he called out, "Professor Knox, it's Terrance Mathison." Nobody moved inside, and the memorably noisy floorboards didn't creak. Noting that hearing aids would have failed fast, he guessed the Knoxes would have a hard time hearing his yelling, not to mention understanding it.

"Professor Knox. Please let me in." He rapped his knuckles hard enough to hurt. Still, nothing stirred from within. "Knox! It's important. This is Terrance."

He ducked when something moved in his periphery, stirring his lizard brain, whereupon he hunched low and spun on his good leg, then fell to his butt. Luck would have it that the white porch railing and the lush garden hid him from the view of the street. With his heart pounding in his head, he army crawled to the corner of the stoop to spy on the road through the foliage, which reminded him of his dad's hunting blind back in Iowa.

Two men and a woman dressed in black leather jackets rounded a house a few doors down, one with a wood bat resting on his shoulder, the woman carrying a shotgun, and the third shit-you-not twirling a replica Roman sword of shiny bronze.

"Come on out," one of them hollered when they stopped in the street a few car lengths down, his voice full of bravado and grit. The guy swung his sword some more. "Did you hear me, son? There's no need to die." Wall pursed his lips. "Look, son. I'm gonna count down. If you don't come out by then..." The guy counted down slowly. "Three." The woman pumped her shotgun, and the intimidating sound tingled Wall's spine.

"The mission is all," Wall mouthed.

"Two."

Wall set the woman in his crosshairs because she was the most dangerous at a distance and pulled the trigger, center of mass, hit, knocking her down. He refocused on the Roman wannabe who froze mid-swing. An on-target bullet later, the guy with the bat turned and ran. For a hot second, Wall paused to debate whether to shoot him. Deciding that the thug was a loose end, he fired but missed his moving target.

"Never bring a sword to a gunfight."

He considered knocking on Knox's door again but decided any chance of coaxing them out vanished with the gunfire. Then again, the elderly couple was probably dead, which might have been a mercy in the new world. So, he set off eastward past the fresh kills, the new addition to what he considered Towning's death count.

He turned the phrase "The mission is all" into a mantra as his limp progressively worsened and his mind grew fuzzier. His knee and thigh began to give out when he reached Little's Market, where he drooped under the covered entryway. The sirens of jerky and rest nearly drew him in, but whispers from inside broke his feverish trance.

Bribing himself onward with the very last string of Kentucky-bourbon-flavored goodness, he made it another block and nearly knocked down the boarded-up door of Noodle Head because the smell of cooking ramen ignited a riot in his belly. He hopped one-legged past the shop to put distance between him and the owners–new or old–who might have an aggressive approach to protecting their food stores. Stains on the road told him that others hadn't shown such restraint.

He nearly collapsed in relief when he reached the university. The comfort of his second home eased his shaky edges. This was the place where his mind could excel and play, a place dedicated to knowledge, so unlike the outside world.

CHAPTER TWENTY-FOUR

What should have been lush grasses were, in fact, unwatered and uneven fields. What should have been a comfortable bed of nature was a dried poky disappointment. The idea of the sleeping bag and camping pad that he kept in his office took shape in his mind. Ever since his first week as a grad student, he kept gear in his office so that when late-night research approached early-morning classes, he had a quick place to conk out. His mentor and all of his past girlfriends used to chide him about how unhealthy it was. Now, his "bad habit" would come in handy.

Well before he reached the Lewis Integrative Science Building, he realized how wrong he had been. The university wasn't an ivory tower. It was falling apart worse than anything he'd seen. The Ducks Store collapsed. The bike racks and bikes mostly blew away, leaving tires, seats, and handle grips behind. The lamp posts leaned or completely fell. All the stair railings vanished. Where a fire hydrant used to be, water trickled out. Few doors and windows remained whole.

"Hey, Grandpa," someone said from behind.

Wall half raised his M4 while he spun precariously. A group of what must have been undergrads dressed in trendy and highly impractical clothes approached menacingly. Maybe twelve or more boys and girls, like some form of privileged-kid gang with hand-made weapons like wood desk legs and cloth-handled ceramic blades. One held a plastic blowgun near his lips.

He didn't even try to count how many students there were because he wasn't fully coherent, and he'd lose focus if he did. As soon as his rifle pointed below their feet, they stopped mid-step.

"He's bluffing," said a handsome kid with perfectly combed black hair as he walked at Wall with a wooden scimitar full of swagger. "That's only an airsoft."

Bang.

He put a hole through the kid's shoe. As the students screamed, the loudest of which was the guy hopping up and down on one leg, Wall yelled, "Think I'm bluffing now?" All but one of the undergrads ran away before he could finish his question. The biggest guy, possibly a football player, rushed Wall.

"Shit!" He brought his rifle up and pulled the trigger. At this distance, missing was an impossibility. The M4 recoiled, and a hole appeared in the guy's gut. The bull of a young man still came at him, legs pumping like the giant haunches of a buffalo. *Fucking momentum!* A second bullet, then the third kicked, stomach and shoulder, and still the guy kept pushing. The fourth one, an uncontrolled shot as he rocked back on his heels, hit the football player's face.

As the athlete collapsed at his feet, Wall recognized him from Chemistry 1 in the spring. The athlete's busy schedule had required numerous accommodations, but his study habits were impressive. He earned mostly A's on his assignments and tests. All this went through his head as the last of the gang fled south.

"Fucker!" he yelled at Towning for putting him in that position, angry that he couldn't have recognized the young man earlier and reasoned with him, furious that the universe pitted students against teachers. Covered from boot to head with gear except for the eyes, the football player couldn't have recognized him. This kill stung more than all the rest put together.

He knelt at his former student's side, tears of frustration forming in his eyes. With too much effort and not enough leg strength, he pulled the big guy into a lifeless flowerbed. Unable to give him a proper burial and unsure if the gang would see to it, he covered the boy with a thick layer of dark mulch. It took all of his strength to tear a small branch from the closest tree, drive it into the ground with the dropped scimitar, and then lay the fake sword on top.

The words his dad said at his grandpa's funeral came to mind. "All gave some. Some gave all. We pity the prior and remember the latter." Having spent too much time honoring the foolhardy young man, Wall turned and limped away.

Time slipped, and he appeared at the entrance to the Lewis Integrative Science Building. The crackle of glass under his boots woke him from his daze as he looked up at the empty windows and doors, all signs of metal vanished.

Animals chittered in hyena-like laughter from the darkness within.

With a dry throat, he rasped, "The rebalancing of man and nature."

The smell of raccoons, the dumpster-diving champions that they were, permeated the central atrium. Their quick chirpy voices turned into growls and hisses as he climbed the stairs toward his office. Six sets of eyes reflected the outside light. If he could have afforded to waste ammo, the furry trash robbers would be no more. Instead, he clapped, yelled, and stepped forward, intimidating them into a slow and angry retreat.

Then he was past the pack of disgusting scavengers. Like all railings everywhere, the ones in his building had gone the way of the wind. The far side had collapsed. The floors were sticky and the whole place smelled moldy. Wall found out that the stairs had rust-rotted by putting a foot through one.

En route to his office, he stopped at the department kitchen, which smelled like spoiled milk and burnt hair. While the refrigerator, cabinets, and sink had transformed into a mess of dust and debris, someone had meticulously organized dishes, plastic utensils, cleaners, and rancid food on the floor. "Excellent," he said as he grabbed a full sprayer of bleach cleaner. "The good stuff." He began dousing himself even before he left the kitchen.

His door down the hall was no different from any other, meaning the handle disintegrated. He pushed the door, but it didn't budge. A bump with his shoulder produced nothing. He leaned into it. It held fast. He backed up.

"Here goes stupid."

With an awkward jump skip, he rammed the door. Pre-rust, the ensuing comedy of a guy dressed in one-legged pants, purple spandex around his thigh, and tactical gear flying into the office would have been internet gold. Feeling like an idiot, he quickly righted himself and leaned the door against the wall.

"Oh, so graceful."

The state of his office matched that of his apartment. The shelves, chairs, and desk collapsed. The contents of the drawers and filing cabinet covered the floor. Exams and homework assignments fluttered in the breeze that streamed through the mostly missing window. The computer screens he loved, the giant ones Towning donated, laid in piles on the floor. Bird crap adorned his desk, a gift from whoever created the nest in the corner.

He kicked books and journal articles aside, plucking goodies out of the ruins, each of which he tossed into the hall as he went. His sleeping bag and camping mat. A head-sized box of assorted candies. His backup clothes.

"Yes!" he yelled at the top of his lungs as he pulled a large package of jerky snacks from the wreckage. "I am man! Hear me roar!" He ripped the package open with quavering hands and tore into a small pack of Cajun spice, ignoring how undisciplined he was being with the meat gold. "Glorious."

Wall rolled up his orange blow-up sleeping pad, wondering how long he had nodded off in his soon-to-be colleague's office, a blank slate prepared in anticipation of a newly hired faculty member. He didn't remember changing into his spare jeans and Indian Motorcycle T-shirt or settling down for a nap. Another worrying time slippage. He wasn't sure if they were getting worse, but they sure weren't getting better.

His nap was long enough for the pain meds to wear off and short enough that it was still daytime. He dry-swallowed a hydrocodone tablet, which scratched down his dry throat like a sea urchin.

To get the taste out of his mouth, he chewed into a mini-Snickers bar and said, "They have nuts, so they must be healthy." Besides, the milk chocolate shell had milk, a great source of vitamin B, so eating it was the responsible thing to do. Even better, it made him smile, and scientists had proven that smiling was important for mental and physical health, so he practically had to.

After packing his sleeping gear into a backpack he didn't recognize, he opened the mostly empty toiletry bag he kept for late nights/early mornings. Inside, a razor with a pack of sealed blades, wet wipes, a toothbrush, and toothpaste promised a level of refreshment he hadn't found for weeks. Dry shaving in the reflection of a large shard of the fallen window might not have been the most pleasant experience, but the extra time he spent brushing away the disgusting tooth gunk made up for it.

Feeling a little less rabid now, he focused on his highest priority. He couldn't afford to get any more dehydrated. Pain and fatigue already attacked his mental clarity, and adding dehydration to the mix would compound his inability to respond in the face of danger. If he was going to handle Karl's pathogens, he needed as much lucidity as possible.

With his supplies tucked away, he rolled his neck with a crackling noise reminiscent of a static-filled analog radio signal. He patted himself down to double-check his tactical gear and lamented the loss of his shooting glasses and the small spritzer bottle that fit perfectly into his tactical vest.

"Time to go. There's—"

"Hello?" a muffled female voice said from the other side of the door. Wall reacted swiftly by bringing his M4 to bear, ready to extinguish whoever belonged to the voice. "Who's there?" He recognized the prissy London accent of Emma Stenning, the professor of exo-planetary life.

"Emma, it's Terrance Mathison," he said as he opened the door.

"Oh, thank the—" She jumped back and froze with wide eyes upon seeing Wall's lowered rifle. She looked like chrome crusted over. Her pale face was smudged, eyes sunken in, and gauntness exacerbated by the past two weeks.

"It's okay," he said, spinning the slung weapon behind his arm. "Remember that I was in the Army? I'm embedded with them again." It surprised him that the words rang true and didn't bother him. Maybe all the times that Plink called him lieutenant or soldier imprinted on his psyche, or maybe it was all the shooting and threat assessment. Either way, he was an Army man again.

Emma's eyes almost returned to their normal shape.

"How long have you been here?" he asked.

She didn't take her eyes off his M4, her chin quivering.

Wall never talked about his firearms or going to the range with anyone on campus. Almost every academic viewed guns as one of the greatest evils of society and espoused that view to their students. He suspected that there were a few professors or students like him that hid their views for fear of losing friends or their jobs. They couldn't directly fire or kick anyone out for talking positively about weapons, but they could find other excuses to banish a second amendment defender.

Sounding hollowed out, she said, "I've been here for a week, no, more, no, well, thereabout."

He wondered how she survived for that long, then remembered that someone lined up the cleaners in the kitchen. She sustained herself by indexing and consuming everything in the building. She hadn't been able to raid his office because her stick-thin body lacked the mass and strength to knock the door down.

"Why didn't you go home?"

She chewed at her cheek, dragging her hawk nose to the side. "My car broke down, and I live up north. It's too far to walk alone." She lived in farm country outside Eugene because her bees–no butterflies–were "happier" in the country.

"Are you hungry?" he asked, holding some precious pocket jerky.

She looked somewhere between mortified and grossed out. "I do *not* eat meat. It is a disgusting habit."

Recalling Plink and Kayla from earlier, he burst into laughter, the whole-body kind, a break in tension that he desperately needed even though it punished his broken ribs. The prissy look on her face only added to the hilarity. "You–" he tried and failed to speak for a moment. "You've got to be kidding."

"No," she said with a level of prudishness that certain women spent their whole lives honing. "It's a perfectly valid choice. Meat is murder."

"Emma, have you seen what's going on out there?"

If anything, her indignation amplified. "Of course. Others may descend to baser proclivities, but I shall not abandon my principles."

Still laughing, he shook his head in disbelief. "Suit yourself, Emma." He pocketed his jerky, then rummaged through his pack for the box of candies. Her eyes widened, and her stiff righteousness vanished. She swiped it from his hands with a scary smile, stuck it under her arm, and plunged her hand in, coming up with a Reese's Peanut Butter Cup. Like a greedy little Oompa Loompa hater, she unwrapped it and shoved it into her mouth, chewing as if her jaws were on hydraulics.

"Do you have a clean water supply?" Wall asked, feeling that an exchange of food for water was more than a fair deal.

All decorum vanished in the face of hunger as she shoved a Twix bar into her mouth and mumbled, "Yes."

"Emma, please lead this horse to water."

As she tore a Kit Kat bar open with her teeth, all decorum lost, she moaned and walked down the hall, avoiding the fallen-in sections that he hadn't noticed on the way in. Even with so much focus on the candies, she walked a good pace faster than him. Downstairs, she stopped, opened several candies, and made an *eee-eee-eee* sound that might have been a bad imitation of a dolphin. The raccoons ran from the darkness across the atrium like angry fat cats. He watched in horror as she threw four candies to them. The trash ninjas descended on the bars with excited chitters and more than a few swipes at each other.

"What the!"

He hopped down four stairs, yelling and swinging his arms at the oversized maggots. The biggest raccoon stood on its back feet like a bear with its front claws held out as if it might swipe at him. Turning on Emma, he said, "That's food! You can't just throw it away!"

She tossed another candy bar to them. "They are hungry. Yes, you are, my babies."

Unbelieving that anyone could be so stupid, he snatched the candy box from her and shook it. "Human food." He shook it again. "Not for animals." He rattled the bars around a third time. "Do you understand?"

The raccoon growled and hissed.

She pouted like a little girl who had her favorite doll stolen. "But–"

"Not for raccoons. Understood?" He held the candies just out of reach.

"Fine." He wasn't aware that a woman in her fifties could sulk so effectively. She relaxed when he handed it back, half expecting her to dole out more sweets, but she resisted her trademarked variety of stupidity.

"Now, please. I need water."

She wordlessly walked down another flight of stairs into the dark of the basement, so he flipped on his M4's light. At the bottom, five inches of standing water covered the floor and his heart sank. "You don't drink this, do you?"

"Absolutely not," she said as if he was a barbarian at his majesty's court. She held her head higher and thinned her lips.

He nearly mentioned that vegetarianism in the face of starvation made as much sense as drinking stagnant water from the basement. Instead, he tried to view it from her stance. Pre-rusting, he chose options that weren't necessarily the cheapest or most practical for the betterment of the environment while opting to eat meat, which was neither environmentally friendly nor ethical. If he was forced to go vegetarian, he would have found it hard to do, especially going without jerky. Morality didn't always mesh well with one's circumstances.

In reality, he worried about her inability to adapt to their new world, to change habits that fit the post-rusting times. Most citizens from rich countries like the USA didn't need to develop a strong survival instinct beyond looking both ways before crossing a street. And the university buffered a lot of

academics like Emma from the harshness outside to the point of policing what
words you could and couldn't say.

Recognizing that she was out of her element, he apologized. "Sorry. No
insult intended."

"Very well." She didn't look pleased but led the way again, splashing
through the water in her impractical flats. As he followed in waterproof boots,
his limp on the "slippery when wet" floor nearly toppled him several times.

A hint of bluish light swirled from a few doorways ahead, and she walked
in, clutching her candy box greedily. Inside, nearly a hundred bioluminescent
jellyfish glowed in a mesmerizing dance. He covered his M4's light to see the
blue mushroom-shaped swimmers, beautiful and peaceful, so different from
the reality outside.

"Magnificent creatures, aren't they?" Emma said with a dazed awe on her
face.

"This is salt water, isn't it?" he asked, glad that the darkness and his mask
hid his judgmental face.

"Yes," she said with a distant voice as she poured a finger of jellyfish
smoothie into the tanks. She stood back and watched the jellyfish as if he
wasn't there.

"Emma," he said as patiently as possible.

She didn't respond.

He waved his hand in front of her face. "Emma."

No response.

He set his hand on her shoulder and repeated her name.

This time she came out of her trance and shook her head.

"Please, lead me to water."

"Yes," she said absently. "Over here." She shuffled through the layer of
water on the floor, walking into the corner where a giant white plastic tank
was labeled "Purified Water" in large red lettering.

He sighed in relief. "Thank you." Swiping a coffee mug from the counter
that read, "Congratulations," he greedily filled it to the brim. A few swishes
around his mouth and a gargle prepped his throat to swallow a small helping,

then repeated larger and larger gulps until he emptied the mug. His belly sloshed uncomfortably after the third brimming cup.

While Emma stood still in a hypnotized state, he pillaged the rows of supplies Emma lined up on collapsed shelves, organized by shape rather than function. His lips curled up when he found a mostly full box of blue lab gloves, then slid on a set of lab glasses and pocketed a backup pair. He half expected Emma to protest his pillaging of her belongings, but she only had eyes for the jellyfish.

"Two is one. One is none."

He continued down the line, scanning for goodies.

"Score." He stuffed two fist-sized containers of fish antibiotics into his pack. Outhouse used to tell anyone who would listen that fish antibiotics were the perfect topical and oral substance to fight infections, potent and rarely plundered.

Once he scrounged all the supplies he wanted, he waved his hands in front of Emma's face again. Nada. "Earth to Emma." Nada.

Something large broke in the building with enough force to shake the saltwater tanks. Wall raised his voice and shook her shoulder. "Emma!"

She didn't take her eyes off the tank. "Yes?"

"Have you been to Karl Quinten's lab? Is it still safe?"

Her face grew grave, drawn all the thinner by the rippling blue light. "No. Some primitive thugs ransacked it, so dangerous. Pure insanity if you ask me."

Wall's shoulders and head slumped, disheartened and defeated. Finding a useful set of virus killers in Karl's lab had been a long shot, but without them, cures for the rusting diseases would be nearly impossible. Now, if Kayla couldn't pull a rabbit out of her HIV-RG91 variant, then their only real hope was to develop vaccines for future generations, not current ones.

"I need to see it," he said. With the barest filament of optimism, he ascended the two flights to Karl's lab with Emma following absently. Fortunately, the garbage goblins didn't approach this time because if they had, his frustration might have pushed him to waste valuable ammo.

Wall stopped down the hall when he saw the holes in the lab's window. More disturbingly, someone had thrown samples and supplies into the corridor and smashed them to bits, releasing any number of airborne pathogens Karl might have brought with him from Munich. Even at this distance, he worried that he may have already contracted something.

"Did you go near Karl's lab?" he asked.

More awake now, she said, "Not since they ransacked it. It isn't safe."

"Do you know who did it?"

"No. They created an awful ruckus one night. The next morning it was like this."

He imagined stupid teens taking bats to the windows and shelves for the fun of it. *No*, he thought. *Towning probably sent private mercenaries to bust it up.* If worker bees emptied Wall's lab, it was all too likely that he had people ruin useful facilities around the world.

"I failed."

The words sank deep into his psyche.

CHAPTER TWENTY-FIVE

Wall leaned back on an orange legless couch in the central atrium of the Chemistry Department, mourning the loss of Karl's lab. The failing springs made for a lumpy place to rest, scarcely ranking above his thin camping pad. His aches and pains had almost vanished now that the Hydrocodone he stole from Lianne's stash, a well-known pill popper, set in. He saved most of her harder pain meds for some later time when he could afford to let his brain fuzz over.

"Be part of the solution," he told himself. If he didn't have that thought playing on repeat, he would have given up, aimless and susceptible to the whims of the downfall. Instead, he would return to Alpha Bravo and do what he could to further the mission.

He was ready, having plundered the department of useful supplies like a Teflon water bottle and a bundle of zip ties. Something cracked loudly down the hall, heightening his need to leave ASAP. The building might be only hours away from failing. He'd been stupid to sleep there.

"Can we please go to my house?" Emma asked for the tenth time. "It will be safe there." He didn't bother to re-explain that nowhere was safe anymore and that someone had probably plundered her abandoned home by now. It wasn't worth the effort to go round and round again. The fifteen-ish kilometers would take hours for a healthy person. In his state, it could take days.

After he dragged out the silence long enough, she said, "Fine. I'll go with you."

He clapped his hands together and stood. He had convinced himself that the world needed wickedly smart people even if they weren't yet adapted to their new environment. In truth, protecting her gave him a small, achievable purpose. "As I said, if you're coming, you do what I say, when I say, and how I say. No debate or hesitation. Understood?"

"How do you yanks say it? Hurrah?"

"Just say acknowledged, okay?"

When she didn't repeat after him, he rolled his hand to prompt her.

"Acknowledged."

He checked to see that the green running shoes stolen from Diane's office were double-knotted. She had protested wearing them, claiming that they weren't as comfortable as her wet flats, and only assented when he threatened to leave without her.

Outside, he said, "We walk in single file. I'm in the lead unless I tell you otherwise. Fall in." While they walked northwest off campus, he taught her a few rudimentary hand signals and tested her on them. She was a quick learner like nearly every professor around the world. The question was, could she use what she learned under extreme stress?

In this area of town, normal people walked around without being mugged or killed, looking to be law-abiding citizens, albeit skittish ones. Wall kept clear of them, and they shied away as well. He was the most dangerous-looking one among them, though he tried not to make such assumptions. He'd seen firsthand what happened to soldiers who didn't respect refugees for what they were, desperate.

"Can I have a gun?" Emma asked.

"Absolutely not. You aren't trained."

"Yes, I am. I shot a BB gun once at—"

"Ha! That's a toy." He harnessed what patience he could manage now that they were entering unknown terrain and said, "Firearms require practiced handling. You wouldn't even know how to load the chamber. And, if you managed to, you would likely shoot yourself or, worse, me."

"So teach me."

"Not gonna happen, Emma. Learning in a hot zone isn't safe."

"But–"

"This isn't a debate."

"What if we get separated? I'll need one."

"Then you best glue yourself to my hairy ass."

"But–"

"Emma, I'm tempted to take you back to the department and leave you." He was surprised that he wasn't bluffing. They had been colleagues. She was a proponent of hiring him right out of grad school and went out of her way to welcome him into the department when he first arrived. He should have felt more compassion, but...

Her face blanched so much that he could practically hear it. "What? No."

"The deal was that you do what I say, when I say, and how I say. And what are you doing?" Her heavy huff took the place of a retort. He didn't want to be harsh, but he couldn't allow her to keep distracting him.

Someone boarded up all the windows of The Original House of Pancakes and painted an upside-down peace symbol on each of the boards. "Gang sign," he whispered and crossed the street in case they viewed him as a threat. The purple and yellow Manala's Thai Cuisine and the aquamarine Chula's were also boarded up with the same sign, a symbol of the law and order that let these people walk safely around this neighborhood. He wondered how much they charged for their "protection."

At Whole Foods, hundreds of people stood in a line that wrapped around the block. A pair of burly bouncers dressed in body armor and armed with pistols, mace, and tasers blocked the entrance. Another two walked up and down the line. The meek people who had cued up were corralled by a line of corpses, a sign of what would happen if anyone caused trouble. He wondered how long their law and authority would last. At some point, the crowd would grow too hungry to stop, they'd rush the bouncers, and there wouldn't be enough bullets to cow them.

"Stay close," Wall hissed when Emma lagged behind, staring at the bodies. As aware of his surroundings as he could be on the hydrocodone, he looked this way and that for trouble, but in this part of town, nobody bothered them.

Coming out of another time slip, Wall snapped to awareness in the middle of a road. This part of town was marked by bodies hanging out of windows, slumped at doorways, and collapsed on sidewalks.

Half a block to the north, a triple layer of corpses blocked the road with a blue "W" marking a boundary with a new gang. Spotting a possible border guard pacing beyond the morbid barrier, Wall backtracked and wound west under the overpass. He no longer had to warn Emma to stay close because she was practically a barnacle on his hull.

At code red, he moved westward, scanning left and right with his M4 raised, ready to shoot anything that moved. A block over, a hollow-eyed man with a blue band on his arm sprinted at him from a small warehouse, yelling and wielding a rusted machete. Wall put him down before realizing he'd pulled the trigger twice. Emma shrieked, shrill and echoing down the dead silent street.

Cursing through clenched teeth, he hop-skipped west, trying to put distance between him and his latest kill, then turned north toward the walking bridge again. "Shit on a stick." A mound of bodies provided a deterrent to anyone who favored living over dying. Yet again, he retreated, pushing his leg and pounding head as fast as he could.

Falling behind, Emma kept repeating, "Oh my god, oh my god."

A few blocks south, where the bodies thinned out, he darted into a designer clothing store, where all the delicate attire was completely impractical for the descent into the great culling. The center of the shop had collapsed, letting rain in. Most of the clothes had fallen into the rusted remains of their displays. In the dark storage area in the back, he plunked down to give his leg some rest and take some time to regroup.

"Well, ain't that a kick in the crotch?"

Spraying them down, he tried to come up with a new plan. The footbridge wouldn't–

Wall jumped through time and space, roused by the beautiful scent of barbeque meat. To the best of his reasoning, he had followed the aroma to its source while he was out of it. A line of hopeful customers waited outside a hamburger joint for their turn to trade whatever they had for sustenance. No matter how many horses stampeded in his stomach, he had no intention of waiting for the veneer of order to shatter, an inevitability as far as he was concerned.

"Stay close," Wall whispered to Emma.

He crossed the street, keeping an eye on the would-be burger eaters and the trio of guards at the burger shop's entrance. At first glance, the three looked like they belonged to a biker gang, but under the facade, they resembled hippies posing as tough guys. Wall cursed himself for getting close enough to tell.

"Hey, dude," one of the leathery-skinned guards called out and jogged across the street in a muppet-like impersonation of running. He was nearly as tall as Wall and skinnier than a fire pole with a long gray ponytail that fit well with the Grateful Dead t-shirt he wore under his leather vest. Marijuana painted his eyes glossy red, and the thick smell-aura of skunk spoke affirmed Wall's suspicion that the guy was a "free spirit."

Wall tensed, shifted in front of Emma, and palmed the handle of his M4, angling it so he could draw quickly if things went tits up. He eased up on his grip upon spotting the rust on the guy's revolver.

"Whoa, man," the guy said as he stopped and bobbed his head with a vacant smile. He held up the peace sign. "Like, I come in peace."

Wall couldn't see what good could come from sticking around for a chat. He nervously checked his periphery and rocked onto his toes, knees bent, so he could quickly spin and react if danger presented itself. There were entirely too many people around here watching him. All clear for the moment, he said, "State your peace, and I'll be on my merry."

"Peace, man," the hippy said, bobbing his head a few more times. "I come to barter, dude."

Cautiously hopeful, Wall sensed a bad deal coming his way. "Trade what?"

"Yeah, like, we have meat. And you have bullets, right?" When Wall didn't respond, the guy continued. "Trade, you know? This for that. Commerce. Mutual love, man."

Hyper-conscious of his surroundings and the eyeballs on them, he kept his eyes in constant motion. "And the terms of trade?"

"Oh, man, you're in for a killer treat. The last guy traded four bullets for a steak patty. Four for one, dude. He was *not* disappointed. You know what I mean?"

Wall's mouth watered, and his stomach swooned at the thought of a hearty meal, almost making the deal worth it. Yet, bullets were too precious to give up. Food could be grown. Bullets were finite. "No deal."

"Okay, man. I see. Hard bargain. Two for one, two bullets per patty."

Wall lowered his M4 a hint, considering the offer for a moment. "The answer is still no. Have a good day."

"Wow, man. Like, you're good. But one patty per bullet is the max I can do, you know? Bosses orders."

"Deal." His stomach made the agreement rather than his mind, and he was pretty sure he'd regret it. The question was which side of the grave he would regret it from.

"Righteous, man. So, how many d'you want? They're like peace on Earth."

Wall nodded and eased his stance but didn't stop looking around for trouble. His trigger finger stayed put, but the tension ebbed. "Six 9mm rounds for six patties."

"Sweet beans. Six of Bessy's best coming up." As he moseyed back to the restaurant, his head bounced back and forth like he was listening to a jam band.

With one hand on his M4, Wall fished out a clip and carefully removed six rounds, all the while panning for trouble.

From behind, Emma said, "Meat is murder."

Wall didn't bother to respond. She'd learn in time.

Just when he thought the dude might not return, he emerged from the burger joint with a plastic bag in hand, cool and casual. Wall salivated like a saint bernard at the smell of fresh-cooked meat. He loved his jerky, enjoyed candy bars, and didn't mind MREs, but he missed having a real prepared meal, or at least something approximating one.

Nervously, he held out his free hand and gave the guy the precious brass. The hippy-bouncer brought the bullets in closer for a better look. Wall tensed and nearly raised his M4 when he realized his focus was on the man and not paying attention to his surroundings.

"Woah, man," the meat trader said. "Everything's like copacetic, okay?" He handed over the burger bag, which was warm and promising. "May the rust be with you."

Wall laughed despite himself until he realized that Star Wars and all other movies belonged to the pre-rusting earth. The survivors would have to return to fireside storytelling and plays for entertainment. He nodded. "You too."

The man ambled back to the burger store, lazily tossing and catching one of his newly acquired bullets. Once the man was at a safe distance, Wall turned west, waved Emma to follow, and channeled Plink. "On my ass like a fish on a hook." As quick as he could walk, not that it was particularly fast, he put distance between himself and the burger joint before checking his grocery bag. He sighed. The dude delivered on his promise.

"Terrance," Emma said curtly, a sharp anxiety in her voice that grabbed ahold of his amygdala.

He spun to see two men dressed in Winterhawks jerseys and full sets of hockey gear, everything except for the skates and gloves. Dried blood stained the tape on the puck end of their hockey sticks. Both were stocky and about average height with matching brown beards and kindly blue eyes similar enough to tell anyone they were brothers.

Upon completing his turn, Wall raised his M4, not exactly at them but close enough to shrivel their raisins. "Emma, get behind me. Now." Without argument or debate, she followed his orders with remarkable speed. Fear could be a strong motivator, and if she clung to that life-preserving inclination, she might just survive.

With as much swagger as he could marshal, Wall said, "Now, boys. I'd rather not add you to my naughty list." He hoped his outward display of cockiness would dissuade them from acting stupidly. And if that didn't work, there was always the M4. One of them whispered and they split up to flank him, pulling his attention in opposite directions.

"Gents, if you don't stop where you are, I'll have to put you down." These siblings might have been fun to drink with under other circumstances, but these weren't other circumstances. Drinking with strangers would be a stupidly dangerous error in the new world, a quick route to making yourself an easy target. "You really don't want to bring sticks to a gunfight."

The robber to his right said, "If you give us the patties, we won't kill the lady."

With a dead-even voice, Wall said, "Gents, let's talk about–" Rather than finish his sentence, he shifted to the right, barely aimed, and fired center of mass once, then swiveled to the left and fired again. The second guy was remarkably fast, reminiscent of the football player on campus. Not fast enough, though. He was so close that Wall didn't even have to aim.

"Terrance!" Emma screamed.

Driven by instinct, he pivoted, aimed, and nearly fired at a third hockey player who shielded himself behind Emma, which was sort of silly since she was a fraction of his size. The guy held a rusty knife at her throat. Steadying his aim, he almost shot. A gentle pull of his index finger would have ended the man, another life closer to Towning's equilibrium. The problem was that the guy was gripping Emma tight and shifting the knife back and forth threateningly.

"Drop it, or she dies." His deep voice held just the right amount of command and intimidation to be taken seriously. Not many people would have disobeyed this man before the rusting, and even fewer since. His face was contorted with rage and grief. He had a similar stocky build and face as the other two. Another brother.

Wall spared a quick eye dart over his shoulders to see if the other two had risen. Neither did, though the first guy cursed with a gurgling rasp. He exhaled and said, "Okay. Let's find a deal."

"Put the gun down," the hockey player ordered.

"Okay," he said, keeping his aim steady. "On the count of three, you let her go, and I put my gun down. Alright?" Wall counted slowly, conjuring a shell of calm over his half-cooked nerves. "One. Two." He fired.

The man's head slammed back, pulling his screaming hostage with him. Sure that the third brother would never stand again, Wall turned in a circle in case any other brothers, or cousins, or uncles, or friends of their step sisters uncle were bearing in on him. Emma rolled away from her deceased captor and curled up, yelling in strange short bursts as she hyperventilated.

With nobody approaching and those within eyesight having disappeared, he knelt next to the rasping brother and pressed his knife between the guy's ribs. It punctured the man's lungs and heart with surprising ease, a quicker, more merciful death, or so he hoped.

Aware that more relatives could arrive at any moment, he mechanically wiped his knife on the man's jersey and sprayed it down, followed by a quick cleaning for his M4. Three enemies, three bullets, no friendly fire. While avoiding the exchange altogether would have been preferable, any encounter he could walk away from counted as a win.

"Never bring a hockey stick to a gunfight," he repeated.

He returned to Emma, who stopped yelling but was still hyperventilating, then examined her forehead, where blood dripped into her hair. "It's just a scratch," he told her as he sliced a scrap from the third brother's jersey and pressed it onto her forehead. She transitioned from hyperventilating to whimpering. "It'll be fine."

Out in the open, they stood out like gold on iron, so he collected the bag of patties and prepared to leave, offering a hand to help her up. "Keep pressure on it. We have to go."

She sobbed, still in the fetal position.

"I'm leaving with or without you." Again, he realized he wasn't bluffing. He wondered what that said about him. Abandoning a helpless woman felt wrong, but so did dying for her. Turning in another three-sixty, he pointed at just about anything, entirely too twitchy to be safe.

She stopped crying and looked up at him as if he'd grown antennae. "You wouldn't."

"If you can't move, you're as good as dead anyway. I'd rather not, but..." He let the threat hang.

While he looked around for any inbound threats, she resumed weeping. Two heads poked around a building to his southwest. His trigger finger nearly pulled on its own. Someone spied on him from a second-floor apartment and ducked down when he brought his M4 to bear. The tantalizing smell of burgers was drawing people out. It wasn't their fault. Hungry people would do anything, as the brothers just proved. They'd force him to kill yet again.

"Here," he said and reached into the bag of patties. The least he could do was leave her with some food. "Take this."

Emma looked back and forth between Wall and the burger as if he grew squid tentacles and offered her poison. She shoved his arm away. "Get that away from me. I told you. Meat is murder."

He plopped it on her knee. "Not anymore. Eat or starve. Goodbye."

She knocked the meat off her knee onto the sidewalk.

He ground his teeth together, unbelieving. "Fine, Emma. You chose this." He picked up the soiled burger and walked away, heading north.

CHAPTER TWENTY-SIX

Did he feel guilty for abandoning Emma? *A little,* Wall admitted as he limped north toward Skinner Butte Park, where he could hide among the trees for a break. He might not have abandoned her if she had taken a burger. The exo-planetary biologist lacked two characteristics needed for the days, months, and years to come, the ability to adapt and the resilience to recover quickly. He couldn't quite justify leaving her behind, but she didn't give him much choice.

"She was bound to die soon anyway," he told himself.

He desperately missed his crutch, concerned that he was the slow zebra that would die first.

With a few blocks between him and the shooting, Wall pulled out the patty Emma dropped, blew on it as if that would clean it, and bit off a good-sized chunk. The burger didn't taste at all like it smelled. As hungry as he was, he didn't care about the chalky flavor. They must have padded the meat with something that stuck to the tongue and ground between the teeth, something like cement.

"Gross," he said and bit off another mouthful.

He slid through another time warp as he hit the ground and rolled sideways down a steep driveway toward a brown house that must have belonged to a hippy owner. Halfway down, he came to a stop looking up at treetops and the gray sky above. The day's abuse had left Wall weak and shaking. After a moment of deep breathing through clenched teeth to ward off the various aches and pains, he said, "I gotta stop blanking out."

He sat up slowly and patted himself down to see if the fall wounded anything else. Nothing hurt more than before. He belatedly checked his surroundings, finding himself north of where Lincoln Street entered the park. A sunburned man without a shirt walked north into the park without noticing Wall or purposefully avoiding eye contact.

Safe for the moment, he checked his gear. The fall scratched various bits, the most important of which was his M4, which had multiple contusions through the outer protective layer, which would expose it to infection.

"Piece of..."

While sanitizing his gear, he noticed that the house's wood garage door was open by about a foot. He smiled weakly and limped down the rest of the driveway, then got stuck while trying to shimmy under the door, exposing him to dangers inside and out. For entirely too long, he laid with his feet sticking out until he slowly realized he could push it up, which seemed obvious in hindsight. It was evident that his mind had suffered too much in too little time to think clearly. Inside, he stayed on the floor and closed his eyes.

Sometime later, he woke up in the dark, stiff and in pain, meaning it had been several hours since he took hydrocodone before he left the biology department. He vaguely remembered crawling into the garage. After swishing water in his mouth, he downed another pill. In the dark, he couldn't tell which one, but at the moment, he didn't care. He just wanted the pain to go away.

Rolling on his side, Wall couldn't believe his turn of luck. He was practically underneath a classic VW bus covered by a canvas tarp. The orange and white siding was barely visible in the dark. He awkwardly gained his feet, turned on the M4's light, and pulled the car cover off. Working out the kinks in his body, he walked around the old-school minibus. If not for the state of his leg and head, he would have done his happy dance. It hadn't been infected yet.

"Thank you, universe."

Adding to his excitement, he didn't have to learn how to pick the lock. The door swung open with a loud creak, but then the nasty smell inside made him wince. Someone tried to mask the scent of rot with incense, patchouli, and the skunk-like stench of marijuana. He flipped the driver's side visor down in hopes of finding a key.

"Nobody's that lucky."

Having no idea what he was doing, he hopped out and looked under the driver's column, wishing he'd watched an instructional video on how to hotwire a car. "It can't be that hard, can it?" he asked, craning his neck.

"Holy!"

Someone already hotwired it. Holding his breath, he connected the two red wires that hung loose, and the little bus chugged to life with an extra few clicks and a whine from a dying alternator or battery. At full blast, Willy Nelson sang "On the Road Again," which nearly scared the piss out of him. Wall cranked the volume dial to no avail. Willy belted out in his uniquely chill voice. "Goin' places that I've never been..." He tried to eject the tape cassette. No good. "...get on the road again..."

"Damn."

Sure that he drew attention, either from the owners of the house or someone outside, he sprang out of the VW, hopped to the old garage door, and heaved it open. Just as quickly, he hopped back into the driver's seat and slammed it into gear.

In junior high and high school, he hated the manual transmission tractors on his dad's farm. He used to wish that Mister Mathison floated the cost of a new automatic transmission, to which his dad always said, "If it ain't dead, why put it out to pasture?" Now, he appreciated the dying skill. The old thing stuttered forward with a dozen putts and gasps, then bucked and revved its way up the steep driveway.

"On the road again!" he belted out with Willy. It was like the VW had called to him in his time of need.

The road was completely blocked to the south, so he turned north. A few seconds later, the old gal bobbed down the road through the park. Afraid to abuse her too much and preserve the nearly empty fuel tank, he kept it in first and second gear. Without Plink's ability to drag race a vintage vehicle, winding around abandoned cars was slow going, nearly flipping him down the slope on his left.

When he reached the larger road of Cheshire Avenue, having driven on the walkway for the last hundred meters, Wall cursed. The way to the west was completely blocked off. On the other side of the road, all varieties of tents and lean-tos filled the dead-grass field. Hundreds of homeless, some new and some old, counted this area as their new landing pad. The orange slug drew all of their attention as one, reminiscent of a zombie hoard, hungry and slow-moving. Panicked, he hit the gas and weaved east between abandoned cars in his best approximation of Plink. In a game of one-sided chicken, he nearly hit a desperate soccer mom with three little ones following her. A man in a business suit managed to chase him down but misjudged the speed and bounced off like a rubber ball.

As Wall jumped the curb, something or someone shrieked behind him. Drawn to the sound, he looked into the rear-view mirror. Completely distracted, he ground the right side of the bus against a rock retaining wall, which bumped the orange machine into a glancing blow with an SUV, knocking the left-side mirror off.

A shrill noise from the back pierced his ears with every bump.

Having outpaced the hoard, he slowed up, worried that the antique bus might fall apart. Then, he cursed as he drove into another clearing with an even larger crowd of rust zombies. Gunning it into third gear, he sped down the walking path, running over the corner of a tent and glancingly hitting a twenty-something runner who attempted to block his way.

"Get out of the way!" he screamed a second too late. "Damn. Never bring a body to a car fight."

With so many cars clogging the road and desperate masses blocking his way along the path, he set off through the grass field on the south side, weaving between tents and all sorts of trash. He knocked off the passenger's side mirror on a big yellow Bronco, an SUV that he secretly loved despite its horrible gas milage, an environmental nightmare.

He bounced off the curb into a parking lot that dumped him onto a road, and that road let out into the street next to the Goburg Road Bridge. He'd come full circle when he nearly hit the mound of corpses next to the blue "W" he saw with Emma. Preferring the mostly empty bike paths to the backed-up roads, he swerved left downhill. The brakes protested as he pulled the wheel east under the main bridge with the fastest of the rust zombies still chasing him.

Then, the entrance to the walking bridge came into view overhead. He cranked the wheel hard while keeping up the leaning bus's speed and sputtered uphill to the entrance of the footbridge. The bus started to wobble as it rounded the last curve before lining up for a clear shot over the Willamette.

Ahead, a pair of shotgun-wielding guys dressed in black blocked the on-ramp. Wall leaned down toward the passenger's seat while one of them shot, shattering his windshield. The terrified wailing from the back seat took on a new pitch. The bridge keeper on the left bounced off the rounded corner of the bus.

Then Wall was past them, flinching as he scraped the bus on the bridge's corroded handrail, unable to control the wobbling wheels. The VW crashed into the right suspension cables, where it slid into a precarious tilt with the front right corner hanging over the edge. Sure that he would fall off the side of the bridge, his breath caught as if the air in his lungs would tip the scales toward death.

A cable twanged like a giant guitar string when it snapped.

Two counteracting thoughts battled each other like UFC fighters in his mind. The first let loose a one-two combo of *get the hell out of the bus* while the other landed an illegal knee kick to the groin, arguing to *find out who is in back?*

The decision was taken out of his hands as the lump under a blanket turned into a black-haired girl with wide eyes.

"C'mon," he said, waving her to get out. Just then, the VW ground sickeningly sideways. He opened the driver's side door and yelled, "Move. Now!"

To his surprise, she leapt into the front passenger's seat as easily as a frightened monkey, then dove over him like Wonder Woman, a quick set of motions that left him thinking he imagined it. As the bridge clanged and the bus ground further toward the promise of death, he jumped out, yelling.

The girl, maybe twelve or so, yelled, "Idiot!" She howled when she punched him in the belly, or rather the body armor covering his stomach. She proceeded to pound his shoulder with surprising force for someone so small. "You ruined my hideout!"

"Hideout?" He looked around, especially toward the shotgun duo, one of whom aimed at him but decided better of it and backed away as the bridge twanged and shook again.

"That van." She hit him again. "Was all I had!"

Wall half-hopped, half-limped to the bridge's north end with all the grace of a newborn panda. The girl easily ran at his side as she cursed him for wrecking her orange palace, pummeling him the whole time. He could care less what she was yelling, especially when another massive clang shook the bridge, accompanied by a rumble and a sickening wobble, which propelled him into a higher gear, one immune to the pain in his leg. The girl kept yelling, oblivious to the scary mudslide of a situation that transpired behind them.

He passed the halfway point and kept the speed up, hoping that the suspension wires on this side of the bridge might keep it from crumbling without regard to Wall's desire to live. The screeches of bending metal and a cacophonous crunch followed by an impressive splash announced the collapse of the southern end. The northern side swayed like a cracking cement snake. Finally noticing the peril they were in, the indignant young lady sprinted like an Olympic track star, leaving him behind to die alone. With every step toward the northern bank, the bridge grew steadier. When he reached the red metal towers, beyond which the cement remained uncracked, he turned around. His mouth hung open, awed at the destruction that followed in his wake. The southern half of the footbridge was gone, descended into the Willamette.

The girl, dressed in purple and black, started pounding on Wall again, screaming incoherently.

"Stop," he said. The hits didn't hurt, but when she kicked his shin, he cringed. "Please." He caught her arm. "Stop." He caught her other arm. "That."

"Don't," she yelled, pulling down on his grip, somehow flipping upside down, and propelling herself upward, ramming her feet into his chin. "Touch me!"

Wall involuntarily let go and stumbled back, shaken by the intensity of the young lady's blow. For a second, he worried that he had dropped her on her head. Somehow, she landed on her hands and rolled out like a tire, then bounced up and ran at him again. This time when he grabbed her, he immobilized her in a wrestling move he learned from Dingo, one of his Army bunkmates, called the "barbed wire," where he drew both of her arms tight across her chest, pinning her back to him.

Writhing like an eel but unable to do anything against his superior mass and strength, she yelled, "Get off me!"

"Calm down, little one." He was impressed with how strong she was. Nothing to match a healthy adult male advantage, but strong all the same, probably stronger than he was at her age. She continued to pull and twist and buck and thrash. He calmly held on, careful not to hurt her. She tried to hit and scratch and bite and kick. He simply held on. She cursed at him. He held on.

After maybe thirty heartbeats, she slowed down, losing some of the fiery spice of unrequited anger.

"Where are your parents?"

"Let me go, and I'll tell you."

"Are you going to attack me again?"

She paused before answering. "No."

Wall released her and immediately took a defensive stance, prepared for her to spring at him regardless of what she said. She dashed a couple of meters away before turning. Slowly, Wall said, "So, where are your parents?"

Backstepping another pace, she said, "Gone."

"Gone where? Can I help you find them?"

"They died years ago. Duh! Old people are getting dumber and dumber these days."

He wanted to argue that he wasn't old but didn't take the bait. She was looking for holes in his mental armor. "I'm sorry for your loss."

She crossed her arms while walking backward. "Don't be. They weren't good people."

Wall looked around nervously, aware that the bridge collapse would draw a ton of attention. "Is there anyone else I can help you find?"

She turned and walked down the ramp while raising a single finger for his benefit.

He double-timed his limp in an attempt to keep up and said, "Do you want a hamburger patty?"

She spun so fast that she practically drilled a hole through the bridge's offramp. Those were the eyes of a starving kid, both hopeful and skeptical. He reached into his pack and pulled out a patty. When he offered it to her, she stepped barely close enough to snatch it, nearly tearing it in half. Upon retreating, she shoved it into her mouth, nearly fitting it all in with one large bite.

"Whoa, there, tiger. Breathe a little."

She completely ignored him, swallowing chunks large enough to bulge her throat as they went down. He tossed her his water bottle. Without wasting time on niceties, she pulled the nozzle and drank like a water buffalo at a river.

"Slow is better," he said.

She kept drinking.

"Sorry I ruined your hideout."

She flipped him off again.

He laughed. "Do you have anywhere to go? Can I get you there?"

She stopped drinking, belched, and patted her belly. "No thanks, grandpa. I don't need saving."

"Of that, I am sure."

She waved. "Well, it's been...awful. So, I'll be off." She turned and burped again with the water bottle still in her hand.

"Where will you go?" he called after her.

She single-finger saluted him yet again.

Not sure why, he wanted to help this girl, who probably hated him. Without logic or reason, he hollered, "I have more patties." The first curious and hungry refugees in the park reached them, and he wished he hadn't announced his supply of food.

A smile brightened her face. "Those are the magic words, mister."

"Stick with me for a while, and you can have more."

She gave him the side eye. "Why?"

He guessed that she wouldn't take pity or sympathy. She was too skeptical to think he wanted to be a good guy. So, there weren't many angles he could play that wouldn't end in her walking away.

"Well, I feel bad about ruining your hideout."

"Good," she said. "But you do see the optics here, don't you?"

"Huh?"

"You're a man," she poked one index finger into the okay gesture on the other hand. "In a park. Bribing a girl."

"Eww! No." He paused, then laughed. "Fair enough." He set two hamburgers on a large maple leaf, then backed away. A couple eyed them until Wall pointed his M4 in their direction. "Take those for your trouble."

"You're an odd one, mister."

"As odd as they come," he agreed. "You should know that if I was that kind of evil, I could have–" He cut himself off. "I'm not the bad guy here."

After retrieving the patties, she said, "That's what monsters say before they disembowel you, play with your guts, and eat them like kielbasa."

"That's quite the visual. Thanks."

Backing away, she said, "All sorts of monsters dress up in human skin."

He couldn't argue with her. Too many awful people walked in plain sight, pretending they were just like everyone else. He suspected she saw plenty of them in her time in and/or out of foster care. And the worst ones were probably thriving all the more during the downfall as the masses grew more desperate.

Wall walked down the path after her, fearful of the group of refugees coming up the ramp to see what had happened to the bridge. A few eyed the girl's burgers, several only dissuaded by the fact that he held his M4 ready for trouble.

From behind, he said, "It was good knowing you. I have things to do, so you might as well run off and do whatever it is that you do."

"Nice try," she said, slowing down to walk beside him. "Do you think this is the first time someone tried reverse psychology on me?"

"You know," he said, the pain in his leg returning after the adrenaline wore off. "Right now, I couldn't give fewer shits. As you said, I'm not a good man. I've killed dozens of people in the last few days, three in the last hour. I abandoned a colleague who I worked with for a year. I ran over a woman with a bus." He laughed at the fact that everything he said was true. "To top it all off, I helped create the diseases responsible for the rusting. Get the hell away from me before I ruin your life."

"You're crazy," she said. "You know that, don't you?"

His lips upturned. "I suppose I am at that. Best be off and gone before I get you killed."

She smiled. "I can work with crazy. I know crazy. Where are we going?"

"I'm serious," he said, surprised that he wasn't using reverse psychology anymore. "You'll end up dead at the ripe old age of whatever you are. I'm a chaos magnet. You saw the bridge back there, didn't you?"

She walked backward while he limped forward. "Yeah. Believe me. I saw, heard, and felt it. But it's better to have chaos on your side, right?"

He stopped. "I'm serious. I was in a helicopter accident two days ago. The pilots, a woman, and two army guys died. I had to mercy kill a fellow scientist. You don't want to be near me."

Her eyes widened, not in fear but in excitement. "I hear ya." She kept pace backward. Her eyes darted this way and that as she talked, keeping a constant lookout.

"Girl. I was a gnat's hair from dying in a fire before the helicopter fiasco."

She nodded and said, "Gotcha. Fire."

"I blew people up with pipe bombs and homemade bazookas." He made an imaginary explosion with his free hand.

"Shway. Can you teach me how to do that?"

He blinked, annoyed that she wasn't getting the hint. "Nope. Not gonna happen. We're splitting ways. Run off now."

"C'mon. What else have you done?"

"So many things not appropriate for a twelve-year-old."

"I'm thirteen," she spat. Her face bunched up, and her body tensed as if she might leap on him and try to pummel him again.

He shooed her away. "Now git. Go on. I don't need a girl to look after."

She tilted her head quizzically. "Your commitment to reverse psychology is impressive. I like that in my crazies."

He massaged his neck and groaned. "Fine. But if you're coming with, you'll keep your burger chewer shut and eyes wide."

"Deal. I mean. It's easy to be quiet. Once, I didn't say anything for about a month. CPS took me out of that home when they found out. It was–"

He held out his fist for a fist bump. "I'm Wall."

"Shway. I'm Aspen."

CHAPTER TWENTY-SEVEN

As Wall and Aspen walked down the bridge's ramp into Nobel Peace Park, once a lovely tree-speckled green that now became a squatting ground for the destitute, he kept a lookout for anyone who might get the impression that they were worth robbing. Both of them stood out too much. While she bounced around with far too much energy, so different from the rust zombies that counted the park as their new home, he carried a cornucopia of deadly riches with his M4, Army helmet, bulletproof vest, and full backpack. To make matters worse, they smelled of recently cooked meat. He could defend against one or two rusters, maybe even three or four if he was lucky or they were the slower ones, but he couldn't do anything if the horde rushed him, a throng of starving mouths in search of food at all costs, unafraid of death because they were on the edge of starvation.

Pretending to be casual, he said, "So, Aspen, what the hell is shway?"

"Ancient men like you used to say, *cool* or *groovy* or stuff like that."

Faking affront while enjoying her spunk, he said, "So, I'm ancient, huh?"

"If you don't know what's shway and what's way not shway..." She easily matched his speed while bouncing or jumping every few steps, kicking a rusted lamp post here, spinning like a skater there.

As they reached the bottom of the ramp, another gaggle of refugees pushed past them to see what happened to the bridge, drawn by Wall's trail of destruction. For a moment, the mob swept Aspen into their rush, but then she appeared on a cement wall, balancing like a two-legged cat.

More branch-fortified tents and refugees occupied the park than in the morning, a sign of how fast the world was falling, faster and faster with every passing hour. Many of the remaining park residents watched vacantly as Wall and Aspen walked toward the lab. The weaker, more sparkless zombies couldn't be bothered to investigate the noise behind them.

His short-term goal of returning to Alpha Bravo doubled now that he had another soul to look out for, one he thought might survive the downfall with or without him. Despite having just met Aspen, he bonded with her in a way that he never could have with Nellibi and Emma, both of whom taught him a valuable lesson. The new Darwinian order meant that resilient survivors might have to leave the rest behind, and Aspen was on the right side of that inequality.

When they reached the far corner of the park, Wall mentally cursed as his Spidey senses pulled him out of a short blackout walking mummy state and pummeled his brain into overdrive, suddenly aware of five wasting men and women about eight meters behind. "Stay on my six," he barked to Aspen as he pivoted on his good leg, M4 rising with the intent of firing a warning shot over the center one's head. As was common among average soldiers, he led the shot by a fraction of a second, which didn't give him time to reach the desired height or full spin. *Crack!* The gal just left of center spun backward and left, hit in her left cheek.

"Oh, crap."

Two men charged, screaming wildly as the other woman dropped at his victim's side, already sobbing. Before her knees hit the pavement, he shifted and aimed at the guy at their group's center, who held a meter-long branch in both hands, swinging it back like a club, his twisted torso slowing his progress. Like a good but not great marksman, Wall led the shot again and missed. The second bullet found its new home a few centimeters below his Adam's apple, a lucky shot if there ever was one. Either the guy would die of asphyxiation or hit the ground with a fatal spinal wound, a quick and clean death, better than slowly starving.

Shifting to the other bum-rusher, who had fashioned a poor substitute of a sword out of PVC piping, trailed a second behind his compatriot, a second that Wall was determined to take advantage of. This time, he overcompensated and swung past his target before firing, a rooky mistake that he'd have to rectify soon. His fourth and fifth shots found the unfortunate man's left lung and shoulder only two meters away. Wall ducked and dodged to the left as the man's weight and still-pumping heart kept him aloft, narrowly missing him as he stumbled by and fell.

"Go time," he said to Aspen with urgency but surprisingly little fear. The one-sided skirmish drew even more eyes to him than his conspicuous gear had only moments before, unwanted attention to be sure. While the refugees couldn't take their eyes off the train wreck of a situation the five men and women blundered into, he doubted any would choose to place their lives at risk, having seen what would happen to them.

"Never bring clubs to a gunfight," Wall said as he turned and limped diagonally across the intersection, confident that none would follow.

"You are a chaos magnet," she said as she twirled and danced forward. He wondered if her indifference to the short conflict was a facade, an acceptance of the ruthlessness that had become part of life, or some kind of resilience learned from the foster system.

With a shrug, he said, "I told you. Now, keep your eyes sharp."

"Always do," she said, skipping a circle around him.

Wall led them through a fallen metal gate into a BMW dealership. Most of the cars were missing, either stolen or lacking replacements because the on-demand supply chain broke down. Most of the new cars suffered stage four rusting, but a few were pristine.

"Hey, Aspen. Wanna play grand theft auto?"

"Ooh," she said, bouncing like an extra-coiled spring, then ran over the hood of a dark blue sports car that would have cost twice his annual pre-rusting salary. "Yes!"

He suppressed a chuckle to save his chest from punishment. "Stick behind me when we enter the showroom, okay? I don't want to shoot you."

She laughed. "Old man, you couldn't hit me if you tried."

"Aspen, I'm serious. This is no joke. We're headed into a high-risk environment. You saw me put down those proto-zombies back there."

"Zombies?" she said as she ran over an SUV from front to back. "Are you crazy or something? Seeing things?"

"No–I mean." Exasperated, he lowered his voice and growled. "Behind me now, or we don't go in."

"Who shoved a can of grump up yours?" she asked while running back to Wall and taking the indicated spot.

He patted his shoulder and said, "Keep your hand here."

Now he understood how Plink felt with him in tow, responsible for an untrained monkey. Emma couldn't do what he needed because she was weak. He hoped that Aspen wouldn't get herself killed because she couldn't reign in her bouncy nature, then relaxed as she transformed, quiet, watchful, and prepared to act like a true survivor. "Do as I say, when I say, how I say."

"Sure, Mister Officer, sir," Despite her playfulness, her edgy whisper told him that she was committed to following his orders. "BTW, what type of poe-poe are you? SWAT? FBI? CIA?"

"Army." He almost added "retired," but "reinstated" was more like it. "Now, shush."

Barely audible, Aspen whispered, "Were you in World War I or II?"

Instead of falling into her trap, he soundlessly turned his head and held his finger to his lips. She fully silenced herself this time, so quiet that if her hand wasn't on his shoulder, he might have thought she wasn't there. As he emulated Plink and Rhino, she copied him minus the limp he was struggling to squelch. They walked through the collapsed back door, both of their shoes noisily crunching over the shattered glass, announcing their entry to anyone who might be inside. With his M4's light, Wall led the way past missing doors, making it easier to clear the building and search for key fobs.

At the second doorway, a fresh trail of blood led into the fourth room. Wall's more cautious side told him to backtrack and leave the dealership behind, but the demon stabbing his gunshot wound argued that he needed a car, without which his leg might give out before getting back to Renegade Genomix. The demon won out. Before he passed the red streak on the doorway, he spotted the source, a suited businessman in a pool of his own blood with a wood stake protruding from his chest, killed like a vampire. The story of the man's demise told itself. The dealer died defending his precious cars like the owner of the solar panel shop.

Once he cleared the room, avoiding the blood, he realized that exposing a teen to this level of brutality might scar her. However, she showed no signs of being disturbed by the corpse. With the damage done, he pointed two fingers at Aspen, then to his eyes, then to a scattered mess of fobs behind the demolished desk.

She nodded and ducked down to collect the keys in her shirt like a kangaroo with a pouch. After she'd scooped up several dozen, Aspen stood, smiling like it was Christmas day. Seconds later, she return to his back and they exfilled.

Outside, Wall said, "Time to get clicking." Her smile couldn't have been brighter as she tried the first fob, and a silver-and-rust-colored junker let out a slow, eerie *whoop-whoop* that could have belonged in a haunted house. She clicked fob after fob until she finally found a pristine SUV. Aspen jumped up and down and ran to it, bouncing off the hood.

He smiled at her exuberance. "We're in business now." Before she reached for the passenger-side handle, he yelled, "Stop!" To her credit, she froze and scanned for trouble. When she didn't see danger, her face cycled between annoyance, confusion, and excitement. "We have to disinfect ourselves before we get in."

"What-what?"

Explaining things in short, simple terms, he told her about the rusting disease and the need to sanitize, glove up, and strap on a mask.

She laughed. "Old man, you're as battered as pancake mix."

"Truth."

All the same, she sprayed herself down and said, "This is some serious conspiracy theory stuff. I dig it."

Once doused, he said, "Stand over there for a moment."

"Shit," she groaned, then started walking away.

"Aspen, hold up. It's not like that." She turned back to him, eyes squinted and arms crossed. "Just hang there for a sec. You'll see."

His joints practically squeaked as he slid into the fine leather driver's seat, a cushy mom-mobile that, while spacious, didn't quite have enough room for a man of Wall's size. He took a moment to appreciate the sturdy doors and firm seats that told of fine German engineering, the likes of which would decay into the past, to become stories that grandparents would tell to unbelieving children. He slid the car into drive and pulled forward by five car lengths, regretting what he was about to do.

While Aspen watched with her head tilted, he jumped out and opened all of the doors before returning to the driver's seat, then popped the beautiful machine into reverse, took a deep breath, and gunned it, doing his best with the rearview display to thread the parking space he just left. The gorgeous SUV launched backward with far more acceleration than he was prepared for, but the brick of a car practically drove itself.

He couldn't help but flinch as the four doors pried off their hinges, bashed off by the neighboring cars. Despite immediately slamming the brakes, the back end rammed a beautifully curved sports car that would have cost three years of his assistant professor's salary.

When his mind cleared, the dashboard lights flashed red and yellow and warning bells dinged in discordant tones, the angry protests of his new steed. Aspen was already seated beside him, laughing, happier than a blemish on chrome. "You ruin everything, you know?"

He shrugged. "Everyone has a talent. Now buckle up."

Without any of Plink's urgency or crazy weaving, he drove to the lab the long way around. Two blocks from the dealership, the car pinged, followed by the quick crack of a gun. He converted the delay between the two into distance: roughly two hundred meters. They were thrown into their seats as he kicked the accelerator, but before they could catch much speed, a quick follow-up round shattered the windshield, sending spiderwebs throughout his view. As he sped away and swerved, partially blind, several more shots sounded off, but none hit as he drove faster and steered erratically.

Wall skidded to a stop in a narrow alley between a ruined burger joint and the remains of an appliance store with a sign that had most of its letters missing, reading "appl e." He kicked the shattered windshield several times until it came loose, and he could peel it off, adding to the car's already custom-engineered ventilation.

He had been stupid to drive slowly, to present an easy target. Harnessing his namesake, the time when he bashed through walls when necessary, he opted for the danger of driving maniacally over giving the enemy a chance to pick them off. They would be in a hot zone until humanity came to its new equilibrium and they settled down somewhere. Then again, the new equilibrium might be a constant state of war between tribes or city-states, so the nuts variety of driving could be the new norm. So, they sped off with erratic swerves, skids, and too much speed to be considered safe in a pre-rust society. Snippets of memories from Ethiopia returned as they fled eastbound toward Renegade Genomix and the protection of Alpha Bravo.

"This is awesome!" Aspen yelled, sticking one hand out the door and the other through the sunroof. It was like she was born for the chaos of post-rust.

A few minutes later, they reached the lab, where Wall slowed and tapped the horn two times to announce their arrival. "Don't shoot! It's Wall! Friendly!"

"All clear!" Rhino boomed.

As he climbed out of the BMW, Plink jogged from around the ruined corner of their building with a giant smile across her face. "When you didn't come back, we thought you were dead."

He met her ear-to-ear grin with one of his own, all discomfort about her abandoning him gone. "Me too."

She ran into his personal bubble, pulled his head down to hers, and kissed him passionately and full with lust.

"Ew," Aspen said as if she had stepped in a smelly pile. "Old people kissing."

Wall did his best to ignore her and enjoy Plink's soft lips. When they came up for air, she said, "That, my friend, is for coming back to us." She slapped

Wall playfully on the helmet and stepped back, smiling once again. "That was for not coming back sooner."

Turning to Aspen, she asked, "And who is this young lady?"

"Hi. I'm Aspen." Now that the kiss was over, she sounded as cheerful as ever, bounced forward, and held out a fist to bump. "Wall, who's your girlfriend?"

She met the precocious teen's fist bump with a favorable snap judgment. "Major Bradshaw. Call me Plink." To Wall, she said, "Tell me, big man. What have you been up to?"

"I visited the biology department to get Karl Quinten's virus killers."

She nodded, and her demeanor returned to business. "Excellent, soldier. I was about to go myself. Report."

He shoved his tongue into his cheek, vying for a moment before telling her the bad news, the nervous habit conveying everything she needed to know. "It's a no-go. The lab was rampaged, most likely by one of Towning's henchmen. Nothing was recoverable."

She slapped him on the helmet again and said, "Good work, soldier."

"Are you kidding me?" Aspen said with her head jutted forward and eyes bulged in disbelief. "Those stories are true? Wall isn't crazy? Loco? Smack-brained? Cray-cray to the nay-nay."

Plink smiled. "Not crazy? I wouldn't exactly say that. But not prone to lying." Looking back and forth between Aspen and Wall, she said, "Let's get you off that leg. You look like the part of hell they reserve for the bureaucrats at the DMV."

"I like her," Aspen said joyfully.

After Wall rested for a moment behind their bunker, he relayed a full account of his "adventures" and a few side bars for Aspen's benefit.

She shook her head when he finished. "You're like a bull in a doll house. What didn't you destroy?"

Aspen answered for him. "Only things he couldn't see."

"Rest up," Plink said sympathetically. "You completed the mission. No finesse but successful all the same. We'll have another mission soon."

He closed his eyes and leaned back. "Rest. That sounds good. But, ladies, you may want to leave. I'm about to drop trou and check on my wound."

Aspen leapt up the ladder like a monkey. Plink stood over him and said, "Wall, we haven't even gone on a first date, and you're already pulling down your pants? A bit forward, don't you think?" They both laughed, in part because it was funny and another part because it struck a note of awkward truth. She retrieved the medical supplies that he stole from the hospital.

Before leaving him to examine his wounds, she kissed him on the forehead and said, "Aspen really likes you. Are you going to be able to abandon her when the time comes?"

"Uh, I don't know."

She smiled with a sense of approval and something else he couldn't figure out, impossible to identify, like spotting a long-since-rusted nail in the dirt.

Pulling his jeans low, he set about re-dressing his leg with proper medical supplies. Most of the makeshift layers had shifted down several inches, nearly exposing the wound to his pants. The inner layers were soaked in disgusting yellowish puss and blood, which he peeled away with a teeth-clenching hiss. The aggrieved cauterized area resembled a greasy pizza on its way to infection with a spot of bubbling tomato sauce at its center.

If Nellibi was anything but comatose, Wall would have asked her to tend to it, but she, like Emma, was dead weight, an anchor that could take them down. He hoped that time would prove him wrong. Having only practiced on lemon rinds, he prepared the needle and dissolvable stitching thread. "This is gonna suck." He inhaled and began looping wide knots deep into his muscle, a butchery that would hold up better than neat and tidy shallow stitches. By the time he was done, the overly bound surface rivaled Frankenstein's gruesome work. With the grisly part finished, he took a break before packing his burn with powdered fish antibiotics, then covered it with a large surgical bandage and a fresh wrap.

After pulling his jeans back up, he flopped on his side like an overcooked noodle and blinked a few times. During one of his blinks, the sky turned to dusk, and his backpack tucked itself under his head like a pillow.

"How can you sleep during the day?" Aspen said from a few paces away, hugging her knees as she tapped her feet. "Let's go on an adventure, old man. I want to see more destruction and mayhem."

"Give this old man a bit of peace, won't you?"

"Wall?"

He forced himself upright. "Yeah?"

"Is there really no cure?" she whispered, not looking at him, instead staring into the distance of some awful future.

He imagined the weeks, months, and years to come, as bleak as the dimming gray clouds. Sitting up and looking at her mournfully, Wall didn't shy away, viewing it best to confront her fears with certitude and resolve, presenting a strong pillar for her to lean on, not a liar with false promises. "Yes and no. With enough time, Kayla will make a vaccine and might develop a cure for one of the metals. But her lab probably won't last that long, so the chances are slim."

As serious as a sharp blade, she asked, "Then, things won't go back to normal?"

"Yeah. This is the end of normal."

She nodded. "Shway. Normal sucked."

CHAPTER TWENTY-EIGHT

Wall nibbled at half of a cold chalky patty, watching Aspen draw a detailed black-and-white eye, with wispy lashes and impressive shadowing, the pencil and paper coming from Renegade Genomix's supplies. Her early dinner burger vanished in a few impossibly large bites. Then the second. Then the other half of his.

"You never know if someone's going to take your food," she said when he told her to slow down.

"True." He shrugged. Accepting that food was already a scarce commodity, he wolfed down the rest of his ground beef substance, ignoring the unpleasant taste. They would resort to whatever they could hunt or gather when the store-bought foods ran out, so he appreciated the meat for what it was. Plenty of people were already at the point of starving, relying on their fat to carry them through the initial culling phase of the fall. They'd eat anything from mushrooms to tree bark in hopes of filling their stomach. Calories were calories. They had to feast when they could and fast the rest of the time.

Through repetitive bribes, he learned very little about Aspen, who tended to keep her story to herself. He didn't probe too deep into her history because he recognized the value of accepting the pains of the past and focusing on the future, less bottled up and more accepted as an immutable past. Still, he wanted to know more about her, so he asked, "What kind of name is Aspen?"

"Not telling."

"C'mon. Tell me and I'll give you the last bits of burger." He swung the baggy side to side.

"Fine. It's short for Aspen Swan."

He tried to hide a laugh behind his hand and choked on a morsel of rogue patty. When he passed it to her, he asked, "Aspen Swan? Were your parents hippies or something?"

Picking at the bottom of the bag, she said, "No. Chinook."

Wall tried out her vernacular. "Shway. Are you Chinook on both sides?"

She shook her head. "I don't talk about them. And don't say 'shway.' You can't pull it off."

He shrugged casually. "Understood. No shway and no talking about parents."

She playfully stuck out her tongue, then returned to drawing, bringing another eye to life. He gave her a moment to herself, but she filled the silence. "Do you have parents? I mean, are they still alive?"

His folks came to mind a lot over the last few days, hoping they were faring well in the fall from the age of technology, but didn't and couldn't know. They were resilient, but the universe would lay waste to anyone it saw fit, regardless of how sturdy they might be. Then he took her real meaning. "How old do you think I am?"

She shrugged. "I don't know. Fifty?"

He laughed, trying not to take it personally. "Try thirty-two."

She pulled her head back and screwed up her face. "Are you sick or something? You move like a grandpa."

"I feel like one. I don't recommend helicopter crashes or getting shot."

"Didn't you say you were a professor?"

"Yeah."

"Aren't professors old?"

"Some. Not all of them."

"Professor Xavier was. Professor Dumbledore too. Indiana Jones. Should I go on?"

"How much TV did you watch?"

"One of my foster parents let us watch all day, every day. It was très shway. That ended when the school called Child Protective Services. They ruined a lit sitch."

"Shame," he said snapping his fingers with unmistakable sarcasm.

"Hey!" she said. "We didn't only watch Silence of the Lambs and the It."

Eyes bulging, he asked, "How old were you? Those are seriously messed up."

"Don't judge. I made sure that we watched the history channel and even the news. And the real world is scarier than any movie. People actually did those things."

He couldn't argue with that, smiling at the fact that the news hounds, the dealers of fear, lost their audiences. *At least one good thing came from this mess.* Then again, they would find audiences wherever they went, telling stories of plague and famine, of rust fairies and corrosion demons, of new religions that would sway people to their will "for the collective good."

"Wall," Plink said from the rooftop. "Can I have a word?"

He stood with creaks and groans like the old man Aspen said he was and held out his palm to the young teen. "Stay here."

"Sure," she said, spinning to her feet as if levitating within a swirl. Before he knew it, she launched herself up the ladder as easily as a normal person could walk. As he climbed his second rung, she reached the top. "Are you sure you aren't fifty or sixty?"

He shook his head as he sprayed the metal down. "What part of 'stay here' did you not understand."

"I understood just fine, old man. It's your lack of leadership that fell short. You should really do something about that, maybe an online course or an app or something."

Plink and Rhino laughed.

More joking than serious, he said, "Don't encourage her guys."

At the top, he found Plink and Aspen practicing martial arts. While Plink out-skilled, out-reached, and out-weighed Aspen, the teen was impressive. As Wall approached, they bowed to each other.

The elite operator whispered something in her ear, then Aspen cartwheeled past Wall, saying, "Smell ya later," and slid down the ladder fireman style.

"She's impressive," Plink whispered into his ear, making him jump. "But you need some work." With a broad smile, she gestured at the green plastic patio chairs. "Come sit."

He sighed heavily and squinted into the late gasps of daylight. She took the other seat without her usual energy and grace, a sign of too much wear and tear. "Wall, you did well. You may be a blunt weapon, but you're *our* blunt weapon."

"Nice backhanded compliment," he said with a weak smile, exhausted from the day. "I'm swooning with pride."

"Don't worry. We'll grind some finesse into you."

"Sounds fun. But seriously, you wanted to chat?"

"Yeah. We need to find backup labs."

He lowered his head, pinched the bridge of his nose, and scratched his scalp. "Why? What's wrong now?"

"Nothing yet," she reassured him. "We need redundancy. Two is one. One is none. Standard operating procedure."

"And you think I can snap my fingers, and a lab will plop out of a genie's ass?" He snapped, then turned this way and that as if to see if it worked.

"Yup. That's what we're counting on."

He snapped his fingers again, "Nope. Didn't work."

"Think on it, Wall. We don't need it now, but we will need it."

He squinted, trying to see her eyes in the deepening dimness of dusk. "And there's nothing wrong?"

"Not yet, but hope don't float a boat in a hurricane."

He sat, watching her turn into a silhouette. "Have you been able to get through to Raddick?"

"No. Rhino even found an old HAM radio, but he hasn't raised anyone useful yet."

"Piece of..."

She stood and jumped onto his lap, her face inches from his. "Thanks for coming back."

He ran his hand around the back of her neck and gently pulled her into a passionate kiss. After a short reprieve from the outside world, a pleasure to distract them from the brutality of the day, she said, "Now, go down and keep that young-one company." Before he could argue, Plink rolled away, leaving him wanting.

With innuendo thick enough to rain, he said, "We'll continue our *conversation* later."

Down below, in the sickly light of a purple glowstick, he and Aspen chatted easily about this and that and mostly nothing at all. He didn't press her in any direction, letting her steer the conversation, which she seemed all too happy to do. One of her foster dads taught karate to all of his foster kids. She kept at it by watching how-to videos online, many of which taught practical defense techniques for smaller would-be victims. She even taught introductory martial arts classes for the other foster kids wherever she went. Every day began with a regimen of stretches, pushups, squats, jabs, kicks, and whatever else she wanted to add to the mix. Every night was a repeat plus or minus a few electives.

When her eyes began to droop and his various aches and pains worsened in the cold night wind, he said, "Time to rack out topside."

Instead of countering with a sardonic remark, she stood and climbed the ladder, not with as much speed as before, but far outpacing Wall, who double-doused the rungs, a final cleaning like brushing your teeth before bed, careful to get into the nooks and crannies so it wouldn't develop cavities.

By the time he reached the roof, she was following Plink through a series of exercises, economical, quick, and precise. If he weren't so destroyed, he might have joined them. Wall certainly could have used the training but in his state, he wasn't going to absorb anything. As a kid, he took ju-jitsu but stopped at the blue belt when the teacher moved away. In the intervening years, it faded away like so many things when you don't maintain them. It wasn't like riding a bike.

By the time they finished their nighttime ritual, Wall had unpacked his sleeping bag and blown up the pad for Aspen. Wall would take a thick blanket Plink or Rhino stumbled on during one of their outings. In about two minutes the teen conked out, looking like a slug-shaped blob in the insulated sleeping bag.

While Plink took the first watch, he crawled under the blanket and propped his head on his backpack. No matter how much he tried to clear his mind and catch some sleep, his thoughts wandered, mainly focusing on the people he cared about. His folks were at the core of his worries even though they had a ton of advantages. Their compound bows and crossbows were useless because of their metal components, but the old pair of synthetic long bows and fiberglass arrows would be perfect for hunting and long-term defense. The carbon-fiber chopping knives he bought for his mom's birthday were ideal for butchering animals and close combat fighting. If they could protect their chickens, their eggs would supply plenty of protein.

His army buddies might find themselves in any number of situations. Axe, who turned to booze and drugs after two stints in the sand, might have no choice but to flop onto the wagon with one of two outcomes, debilitating sobriety or a much-needed course correction. Robert, who never got a nickname, ballooned to twice his Army weight as a desk jockey in New York. While it might take longer for him to starve, in his condition, he'd struggle to take care of his wife and kids.

Most of Wall's academic friends wouldn't fair well, better suited for labs and computers than the increasingly harsh outside world. A few of the outdoorsy ones might have better chances, but if only two in a thousand were going to survive, the odds were that none of his friends or family would live through the downfall. Even armed with Wall's pristine Glock 19 and the knowledge to sanitize it against the rusting diseases, he'd only prolonged Thomas and his family's lives, not saved them.

"Always get back up," Wall whispered into the dark cloud-covered night.

His thoughts circled back to Towning, wondering where he was. Did he have getaway homes all over the world, each a masterpiece of sustainable living, completely off the grid? Solar powered. Geothermal heating and cooling. Were they like the giant cabin, with logs carefully sourced from his property to improve the health of the forest? No roads in or out, only self-contained trails like the ones he and Towning had walked while they talked. Did he maintain fuel-hungry helicopters to travel from one to another, summering in the north and wintering in the south?

"For fuck's sake, Towning. Why did you do it? We were men of progress, not destruction." Wall questioned how well he could have known the old man, the supposed mentor who bequeathed his mansion to Wall in an attempt to kill him. "Fucking sociopath."

"Wait!" he said loud enough to stir Aspen. Hadn't one of the breaching team members said that they cut Towning's power remotely? He was sure of it. The getaway was self-sufficient, which meant it was a second house, some other retreat that looked like the one he remembered. He wanted to yell into the wind. Instead, he mouthed, "Fuck you Towning. We're coming for you."

Too excited and agitated to sleep, the crankshaft of his mind spun other details into place, so he dropped any hope of catching some z's and joined Plink on her lookout. "Guess what?"

"What?" she asked mischievously. "Have you come to continue our *conversation?*"

He desperately wanted to say, "Yes," but regretfully, his thoughts were too all-consuming. He wouldn't be able to get Towning out of his mind. Plowing through her enticing offer, he said, "Sorry. Do you have the note from Towning?"

"Yeah. Why?"

"I need it."

She slipped the zip lock from a slit in her backpack that he hadn't noticed before, reminding him that the safest vault is one that nobody knows about. "It doesn't have an encoded message if that's what you're thinking. CENCAM tried to crack the cipher."

Impatient, he asked, "Can I have it anyway?"

She handed the baggy over. "Are you gonna tell me what this is about?"

"Listen. Towning had a second cabin similar to the one that exploded." Over the next few minutes, he described the subtle differences between the two mansions, recalling more, including how the sunlight was wrong for sunset and how some of the trees weren't in the right places or were too small. The path in front of the house was broader than it should have been.

"I was stupid. I missed it all. I didn't question my pre-conceived assumptions."

She cupped his face. "It's okay, Wall. That was thirty minutes after you learned about the rusting. It was a lot to take in." She searched his eyes in the purple glow and waited for him to recover his calm. "So, you think there's a clue on the note?"

"Yes."

He hoped to unravel the clue and find Towning at the getaway so he could punish him. How many holes could he put in the old man, starting at his hands and feet and gradually working his way inward? The psychopath deserved nothing less. As good as revenge would be, the true value of the property was the far larger lab, which included production equipment. In Towning's lab, Kayla could do wonders, particularly if the old man left notes of some kind. The inventor turned environmentalist turned bioterrorist did nothing without reason, and if he didn't intend to kill Wall, there must have been another purpose. Did he believe Wall was sympathetic to the anti-human approach to the environmental singularity? His note sounded that way.

Ignoring all the questions that came to mind, Wall said, "Hold the light. Good." Heedful of wrinkling the note more than it already was, he removed it from its baggy, then dabbed bleach onto the back with his white coveralls. Chlorine was an ideal base for reacting with thymolphthalein, better known as invisible ink. Plink huddled close to watch.

"Ha!" Wall yelled as the first letters materialized. "I told you." he read it aloud from start to finish.

"Choices made, whether bad or good,
follow you forever and
affect everyone in their path.

You have many miles
to go before you sleep."

44.883638, -122.021201"

Wall laughed. "That, right there, is our backup lab."

"How did our guys miss that?" Plink asked, close to losing her calm.

"Simple," Rhino answered from the dark, his deep voice making Wall jump in surprise. "They only transcribed the words, then gave the real note back per your request."

Plink's face pursed up scarily in the uplit darkness and she tapped her thigh, one-two, one-two. "That note is one oversized can of earthworms. The last part is a poem, right? What does it all mean?"

While Wall tried to recall the poem, Rhino walked up behind him and said, "In Robert Frost's work, written in 1922, he meant for sleep to represent death and miles to go as a metaphor for achievements to accomplish. So, Wall, you have plenty to do before you die."

"Ha," Wall laughed. "At this rate, that doesn't seem likely."

Plink continued tapping her fingers. "And the first part?"

"Spredemann refers to the first amendment and one's right to speak their mind but cautions that others will respond to your choices and words as they see fit. It could either refer to how society will view Towning or be a caution to Wall about the choices he'll have to make. In the context of the other quote, I'd say the latter."

"Wall," Plink said, drawing his attention. "What do you think Towning has in mind? Good or bad? Help or harm?"

He shrugged. "How in the devil's short and curlies am I supposed to know? I didn't notice that he was a genocidal maniac. I'm not a people reader like you."

She cupped his face again and her bunched features turned sad. "I suppose that simplifies things. Once Club Genomix goes out of style, we throw a party at Towning's cabin."

CHAPTER TWENTY-NINE

Aspen hopped into the circle of purple light, covered in her sleeping bag like a crossbreed between a kangaroo and a giant caterpillar.

"Evening," Wall said.

"Way to be indecisive," Aspen responded. "Is it a good evening? A bad evening? Are you telling me that it is evening, which I can clearly see? Or do you think it should be evening, but aren't sure?"

Plink did a horrible job of hiding her laugh, even in the dark. Same with Rhino.

After a few seconds of paddling for a response, he said, "All of the above. A pinch of good, a half cup of bad, two tablespoons of telling, and a teaspoon of asking."

She snatched a chunk of Carolina-Heat Jerky that he hadn't realized he pulled out, and popped the whole thing in her mouth. Wall stood dumbfounded, in shock that someone would commit such sacrilege, ruining a talisman of the all-supreme jerky gods. Through her stuffed maw, she said, "Oddly specific. Have you been sitting on that one, waiting for the day you could whip it out?"

The elite operatives laughed outright at seeing Wall's face. Aspen looked entirely too pleased with herself.

"Young lady," Wall said. "You can insult me all you want, but you never steal a man's jerky."

"Do you want it back?" She opened her mouth.

"Oh, little one," Rhino said, placing his giant hand on her small shoulder. "Wall is like a religious fanatic. You just committed a major sin."

She pulled the wad out of her mouth. "Here, take it."

Wall shook his head. "No respect for the finer things."

Tossing the ball of half-masticated jerky back into her mouth, she said, "I knew you were weird, but not this strange. Crazy, sure, but a devout meat-lover?" She waved at him. "First, chalk burgers. Now, this stringy stuff?"

"Stuff?" Wall almost launched into a diatribe about the proper method for eating jerky but held his tongue. He wondered how someone so small could eat so much more than a full-grown man. He could practically hear his mother's voice in his head saying, "You could'a eaten a heifer whole at that age." Again, he thought of his folks and how they might be faring. *They are resourceful people,* he told himself.

"So," Aspen said. "What's this secret meeting about? You damaged my sleep, so the least you can do is spill the beans. Is Wall gonna annihilate another bridge? More cars? Ooh. How about we blow up one of those dorms at the university? That would be so shway."

"Rabbit," Plink said, facing Wall.

"Huh?"

Aspen giggled. "Is that like love-muffin or sweetums?"

The big man explained. "Wall is like a damn lucky rabbit's foot. How he survives despite his blundering destruction is a point of conversation between me and Plink."

Plink fist-bumped the Navy SEAL. "Truth. Aspen, you should hear how Wall got his nickname?"

Aspen laughed. "Tell me."

Plink launched into the retelling of the story, exaggerations compounded as are all legends. The teen laughed through it all and they joined her. Even with the poky ribs, it felt good. Once she finished, Plink changed the subject. "Since we're all awake anyway, Wall and I are going shopping."

Unsure if he wanted to be included in more mischief after so narrowly surviving the last dozen blunders, he asked, "What's on the grocery list tonight?"

"And ruin the surprise? What's the fun in that?"

Predictably, Aspen said, "I'm coming too."

"No," said all three adults in unison.

Wall got the sense that if Plink wasn't on his side, the teen would have argued endlessly and disregarded him. Instead, she simply crossed her arms and fake-pouted.

Plink shook her head. "Don't even try it, sister. The three of us have seen kids far more desperate than you."

"But I want to see Wall's destruction."

Plink winked at her. "Oh, don't worry. You're gonna prefer what we have planned for you."

Aspen looked dubious. "I don't think that's possible."

"Over here, little one," Rhino said, waving her toward the collapsed corner of the building. She bounced out of the sleeping bag in two hops and kept going at his side, her mouth moving faster than a woodchuck could chuck wood.

Seconds later, Plink slid down the ladder leaving Wall to climb the rungs the slow way, decontaminating, always decontaminating. At the bottom, she said, "Visual only," then waved for him to follow. She leapt over the charred remains of the back fence with ease. He, on the other hand, resembled a drunk giraffe. From the way her silhouette shook, he was pretty sure she had a few jokes that remained unsaid.

Then she jogged through the backyard of their neighbor's abandoned house. While his leg felt a lot better after a bit of rest, better was a far shot from good. She slowed the pace when they reached the other side of the neighbor's house, out of view of the building.

"So," he whispered. "What are we shopping for?"

She slapped his helmet and silently shushed him.

Barely keeping himself from pressing his luck, he almost said, "I'm an overachiever. You get both audio and visual from this model."

They walked for about five minutes, winding deep into the neighborhood, silent except for Wall's imprecise limp. In the darkness under a tree, she waved him in until they were cheek to cheek. For a flash, he thought she was going to kiss him, but no such luck. Instead, she whispered, "We're requisitioning dirt bikes from a private residence. The home is occupied by an older couple."

He signed, "Okay."

"We're going in quiet and leaving fast. Got it?"

He signaled affirmative again.

"Double time," she ordered, leading the way.

"Plink, I can't. My leg. It won't–"

She spun, kissed him into silence, then whispered, "Pain is for poets and philosophers. Are you either of those? I didn't think so. Keep up."

He almost commented that her statement was profoundly philosophical but held his tongue. Hop-skipping after her, he tried to tap into his Spidey senses, using all their recent catastrophes to spur him into an otherly dimensional watchfulness. As he approximated a run, the stabs of pain in his leg and chest became a metronome that pounded in his head.

She slowed, then stopped. With signals and whispers, she conveyed the plan, which was entirely too simple to be of much use. Open the side gate, walk into the side yard, start the motorbikes, and ride away. The contingency plan was to shoot the owners, then take the bikes.

Killing people in the name of the mission kept placing him on the asshole side of the spectrum, even if the mission was all, more important than one life. He'd like to be on the good side again, not the aggressor or stupid idiot sparking chaos wherever he went. Was that too much to ask for?

She grabbed him by the bulletproof vest and whispered, "Are you with me, soldier?"

"Affirmative."

Plink spun around and slinked to the side gate, then prodded the padlock with a stick and tapped the iron handle, both of which disintegrated. The gate swung inward with a screech worthy of the banshee's queen. They ducked inside, where two ill-used motocross bikes waited for them to abscond with.

Plink sashayed–or something close to it–around the first bike to the second and hopped on. Wall, with his troubled leg, stumbled on the uneven stonework and fell into the first motorcycle, nearly knocking it onto Plink. She held up three fingers and counted down. On one, she leapt up and came down hard on the kickstarter which cranked her bike to life with the distinctive rumble well known to outdoor enthusiasts on all seven continents. Wall, with his weight advantage, didn't need to jump. The problem was that his left leg gave out before he could kick the starter. Balanced better this time, he kicked. No-go.

"Faster!" Plink hissed.

Chk-chk. Boom!

Within half a second of when Wall had ducked low, his head jerked forward, Plink twisted and shot her P17 behind them. *Crack, crack, crack.* That was all the inspiration his leg needed to jump so he could come down harder, which finally started the engine. He revved and accidentally wheelied through the front gate, barely able to hold on. Plink's engine spun up a few octaves as she sped around him like the fricken ghost rider. The badass graphic novel, not the Nickolas Cage catastrophe. Wall might have thought he was good, but she trampled any such notion then and there.

Three blocks up and two blocks over, she stopped with an endo, her bike whirling all the way around. Wall skidded to a halt only narrowly missing her. She hopped off her bike, leaving it running, and dashed to his side. "Are you hit?" She patted him down like a concerned mother.

"I'm fine. Keep going."

She stuck her fingers through the back of his helmet and wiggled, scratching his scalp.

"What the..."

With steady hands, she unstrapped his helmet and yanked his head down for a quick look. "Well, Rabbit. You really are the luckiest unlucky SOB I've ever met." She kissed the top of his head and laughed, then shoved his helmet into his hands and jumped back on her bike.

Looking down at his helmet, he found two holes in the back and a couple of buckshot pellets rattling around on the inside. Then, he felt the top of his head for an injury. While it was pain and blood free, the centerline down the top felt funny.

She revved the engine, a goofy smile on her face. "Rabbit, put that pellet-catcher back on. Let's get you back to base before you attract more bullets." She giggled while he strapped his helmet on. In seconds, they revved and spun off, taking the long way around to Renegade Genomix. Minutes later, they rolled into their parking lot, waving at Rhino and Aspen who were barely visible with their glow sticks.

"I heard a shotgun," Rhino called down. "Everyone okay?"

Plink killed her motor and said, "Oh, Rhino, Aspen, you gotta see this." She walked over to Wall and pulled off his helmet, then shoved her finger through the hole. "Can you believe this guy?"

Rhino's deep laugh could have rumbled elephants off the plains of Batswana. Aspen's laughter bent her over.

Plink flourished her hands grandiosely to display Wall's head. "That's not the best part. Wall, look up at them." When he did, Rhino almost fell off the building and Aspen plopped to her butt, such was their hyperventilation.

"He looks like a–"

"He is a–"

Wall, not in on the joke, looked at them in confusion. "Like a what?"

Plink hunched over, hands on her knees, attempting to breathe. Above, Rhino took a knee and Aspen disappeared from view, presumably giggling from her back.

"It's so good...it hurts," Plink said, squeaking the words out between gasps. "You...gotta see...yourself."

He walked to the BMW and looked at his reflection in the driver's side mirror. The buckshot and helmet shrapnel had cut and melted his hair over the centerline of his scalp. The two longer sections on either side stood up like rabbit ears. Between his wide-eyed expression and the hair, the effect was complete. "Holy crap. I'm a..." The latter half of that sentence never came, replaced by an uncontrollable case of giggles.

"Here, bunny, bunny," Aspen said as if holding up a carrot, sending them all into painful laughter. It was fortunate that nobody came along just then because they were all incapacitated by the ridiculousness of it all.

After too long, they recovered, and Plink said, "You, my friend, are a magnet for chaos." She drew near, then whispered, "Please don't get shot again."

"I'll try."

"Good." She tippy-toed and kissed his cheek, then stepped back. "Do something with that hair. I can't take you seriously." She chuckled as she pushed her motocross bike behind the building.

Even though motorbikes were the ultimate in ventilated vehicles, Plink and Wall wiped them down for good measure. While cleaning, she said, "You know what the bikes are for, right?"

"Yeah, for when this place fails."

"You know, Wall. You're not as dumb as they say."

He gave her the side-eye. "They?"

She shrugged. "You know. People. People say things."

"Sure they do."

The meticulous nature of sterilizing the bikes was both annoying and strangely soothing. While cleaning would never rank among Wall's favorite activities, it served a purpose. It propelled their mission and didn't require too much concentration, so he could let his mind wander. Too much of too many ideas and recent memories rolled through his slow mind. After rounding a whirlpool of thought, he emerged with an odd notion, "Did you know that we're a criminal biker gang now?"

"Hey. You know. You're right. I've always wanted to be a biker babe."

"I can see that." He smiled. "You should get a ton of tats, and I'll grow mutton chops."

CHAPTER THIRTY

After shaving his scalp with the sealed razors that he had retrieved from his office in the reflection of the BMW's side mirror, a process that drew more than a few nicks, Wall stood on the rooftop looking back and forth between Rhino and Aspen, jaw hung low in disbelief. With accusation and dismay mingled in a bundle of distaste, he said, "You did what?"

Rhino, not perturbed in the slightest, responded, "Aspen needs to learn how to handle firearms." He used the time when Wall and Plink went on their motorcycle hunting "adventure" to teach Aspen gun safety 101 and gave her Wall's small Glock 26, which now sat snugly in a holster at her hip. The SEAL timed the lesson to curtail any discussion with Wall, which he must have known wouldn't have gone well. As the one who brought her into Alpha Bravo, he felt responsible for her.

"But, Rhino. She's only thirteen." He almost added, "What right do you have," only managing to avoid that can of words by a fraction of a second. Who was Wall to say what Aspen could or couldn't do? He wasn't her father, uncle, or even foster dad. He was some random dude who stole the VW bus she was living in. And that was only a few hours ago.

Rhino held his gaze, only a little shorter despite seeming taller because of his mass. "Wall, you grew up on a farm, didn't you?"

Wall could see where this was going. "Yes."

"Then you learned to shoot at a young age, right?"

Internally bucking against Rhino, Wall said, "This is–"

Interrupting, Rhino led Wall through the inevitable truth. "How old were you when you learned?"

"Eleven."

"How is this different?"

"There's a huge difference, Rhino. The way things are, she's bound to shoot people, not animals. That's not a hunting rifle. It's my Glock 26, designed to put down humans. It doesn't even have a safety. She could shoot someone by accident. Do you want that on her conscience?"

"Want? No." He rested his giant hand on Wall's shoulder as he seemed to do with everyone. "Among a set of bad options, I'd rather she live with a heavy heart than die with a hole in it."

Aspen yelled, "Stop! Don't talk about me like I'm not here. It's my choice."

And there it is, Wall said inwardly. Discussion over. "Whatever."

"Besides," she said. "He mostly taught me safety, only a little bit about shooting."

Rhino looked down on her, proud and approving. "She's a quick learner."

Keeping his voice conversational and curious rather than argumentative, Wall said, "Did you teach Lucas or Nellibi?"

"I offered to teach her and instruct the boy on knives, but Nellibi went from catatonic to bat-shit-crazy, yelling unintelligibly. Immediately after, she went still again. She's getting worse."

"Fucking hell. We need her."

"I know."

The contrast between Aspen and Nellibi, or Aspen and Kayla flipped a switch for Wall. Alpha Bravo would be as good as dead if they had to rely on either woman outside Renegade Genomix in the wild. Adaptation and perseverance were necessities in the new world, the notion doubled-downed by Emma's reaction, the difference being that they couldn't abandon the two downstairs. Both of society's best chances at developing a resistance to the rusting viruses weren't exactly stable. Everyone needed to transition quickly. He had argued the wrong side. Kids, both Aspen and Lucas, had to learn how to use any and all weapons they could. To think otherwise was willful denial.

The next question that he had prepared before jumping over to Aspen and Rhino's side. Kayla wouldn't leave her lab or let Rhino in to teach the basics. He didn't revel the day when she would have to leave her castle.

With hopes of extricating himself from the pile he walked into, Wall said, "Show me what you learned."

Aspen eyed him as if trying to figure out his angle, the reason for his about-face. Deciding to roll with it, she reviewed the four main rules of firearm safety, then talked her way through checking if the Glock was loaded. Her small hands had to stretch, but the undersized concealed-carry weapon was ideal for someone of her size. He hid his flinch when the pre-chambered round flew out. A full clip was one thing. An unsafed pistol with a round in the chamber was scary as shit in the hands of a novice. But she was learning from a tier-one warrior who knew she could draw faster and wouldn't forget to load the chamber when bullets started firing. And, this way, she would learn to treat every gun as if it was loaded and ready because hers always was.

He told himself that *if you're gonna go for it, go all the way.*

Rhino watched carefully, pointing out minor tweaks to her form as she spoke. Disassembling the pistol proved hard with her small hands, but with Rhino's adapted technique she managed. Next, she listed off every part of the pistol as comfortably as someone who traded firearms. As she reassembled, loaded, and holstered the Glock, she sprayed it down with an appropriate dose of isopropyl alcohol and dielectric oil, proving to be more responsible than most of his army buddies.

"You have skills," Wall said when it was strapped onto her hip. His father had taught him the strength in admitting he was wrong or didn't know something because it cleared up headspace to learn. "You and Rhino were right. You're more adept than most. I commend both teacher and student."

She beamed at the praise. "Rhino, when do I get the next lesson."

He nodded approvingly. "Soon enough. Take the time to review what I taught you. Repeat, repeat, repeat. Commit it to memory. It needs to be as easy as breathing."

"Acknowledged," she said like a mini warrior.

Rhino turned to Wall and said, "Your turn. You have some bad habits."

If Wall's ego had been weaker or stronger, he might have taken insult. Instead, he appreciated the opportunity to learn, reminding himself to *always be the dumbest person in the room.*

As dawn began painting the clouds with absolutely none of nature's glorious colors, gray and dismal, Plink pulled her chair next to Wall's, sat, and whispered, "How's your head, soldier?"

Wall watched Aspen sleep. In the middle of the night, the girl had spooned his backside, which he appreciated for the extra insulation but worried about its appropriateness. He was a grown-ass man, she was barely a teen, and they just met. It hardly seemed right. Yet, they shared an odd and frighteningly fast bond that could only be explained by going through the grinder together from moment zero. Sometimes it was the same with soldiers who fought side by side.

He returned his attention to Plink, with whom another type of connection was building. "My head? Still attached." In retrospect, he decided the statement wasn't funny. He broke one helmet in the helicopter crash and damaged the second with two more shots.

"Seriously," she said. "I want to know because...well..." The implication was full of fuzzy thoughts that would only serve to distract them. She continued. "And I need to know for operational security. Most people would crack under the stresses you found yourself in. Can I rely on you?"

He thought for a moment, trying to evaluate himself objectively–if such a thing was possible. "I'm certainly not at one hundred. My leg keeps slowing me down. Breathing hurts. The pain meds dull my mind. I keep losing chunks of time, and I could easily get us killed."

"And emotionally?"

He smiled. "Well, I keep thinking about kissing you and I'm pretty sure that's not healthy."

She gave him a courtesy laugh. "Seriously."

"It's a mind-fuck that Towning used my research for all of this. I keep dwelling on what I've done during my blank outs. I'm unreasonably worried about a teen I hardly know. You keep kissing me. By all reckoning, I should be dead. It's a matter of time before I am. Other than that, I'm the picture of sanity."

Plink patted his good knee and left her hand there. "The measure of a warrior isn't how often he gets knocked down, but how he fights for his team. Will you keep fighting for us?"

He poked his tongue into his cheek, then said, "My head ain't rusted yet."

She squeezed his knee. "You up for another mission?"

He grinned. "Why die tomorrow when you can do it today?"

"That's the go-get-'em attitude we need." She stood and pulled him to his feet.

Lifting his pack, he asked, "What's the target this time?"

She winked and smiled devilishly. "Food. We're blowing through our stocks. Especially with Aspen's stomach. She's like a camel with the hump on the front."

After dislodging a strand of jerky from the gap between his canine and first molar, he said, "Who are we stealing from this time?"

She nudged his arm. "Rhino's downstairs waiting for you."

"You won't even give me a hint?"

"What's the fun in that?" Her deviousness practically sang through her whisper.

Down below, as he wiped off the last rung, Rhino spoke into his left ear. "Situational awareness." Wall jumped and almost elbowed the big man, or rather, his instincts could have tried, but the SEAL surely would have blocked.

A moment later, they sped away in the BMW, not as maniacal as Plink under Rhino's control but necessarily reckless all the same. When he hit the accelerator, the silent beast practically took flight on a straight stretch. "You know how to pick 'em, Wall." In too short of a time for any safety-minded person, they arrived at the Eugene Country Club, where the big man drove onto the golf course, spun a few donuts, then stopped inches before hitting a large tree.

Admiring the ruts he dug into the golf course, he said, "I've always wanted to do that. Was it as good for you as it was for me?"

Wall winked. "You give good donut, big man."

After a solemn moment for knocking an item off Rhino's bucket list, he whispered, "Eyes only."

They hopped out, and the SEAL led the way, pointing out the cork-like goose droppings that covered the golf course's untamed grass. The uneven tufts were proof that nature had already begun to reclaim the human domain, returning the balance to equilibrium at the cost of human life.

Wall was starting to get used to imitating the warriors' smooth style of walking, halfway between the stalking of a predator and the powerful bent-kneed paces of a careful man, mingling the best parts of defensive and offensive stances. They crossed the unkempt grass to the other side of the pine forest that divided the fairways, then between the trees.

Rhino signaled to the opposite end of the putting green, where thirty or more geese waddled aimlessly, approximately two hundred meters away. He signed for Wall to shoot, so he began to kneel for stability, a hunter's best friend, but the SEAL stopped him and shook his head.

Okay, he thought with a doubtful tilt of his head. *We're doing it the hard way.*

Wall removed the rubber cover from his ACOG-6 and aimed the long-barreled M4, a weapon that, in theory, was good out to four hundred meters but wasn't exactly the Prince Charming of hunting rifles, made worse by shooting from a standing position and doubly so after the abuse it endured on his misadventures. He was pleased with the scope's six-X magnification. With one bird zeroed in, accounting for the drop chart next to the crosshairs, he flipped the safety off. His finger gently pulled the trigger until he felt the point at which it would fire with a paperclip more pressure.

"Hold," the big man whispered. "Push your left toes back for better stability. Lean forward slightly to account for the kick. That's good. Stop dropping your left shoulder. It's a sloppy habit unbefitting a soldier. Right there. Hold your right hand farther up the handguard for better precision. Open both eyes for peripheral awareness."

He almost commented that the geese wouldn't fight back, so there was no need to monitor his periphery, then remembered how mean they were. When he was about five, one attacked him, leaving him bloody from numerous scrapes and bites. Now, his finger practically pulled itself with the urge to exact revenge on their kind.

"Send it," Rhino said.

Wall slightly increased the pressure. The suppressed round popped, and half a second later, the bullet reported the distinct thwap of supersonic metal hitting flesh. The shot knocked the bird into a roll. Meanwhile, the other birds barely noticed. He smiled and mouthed, "Retribution." The M4's accuracy hadn't dropped despite the abuse he put it through.

"Again," the master marksman whispered.

Wall took aim, and Rhino nudged his right shoulder. "Both eyes open. This time don't blink. And...send it."

The second shot also hit home, stirring the gaggle but not enough for them to disperse or fly away. Despite his best effort, he blinked, and his shoulder dropped immediately after he pulled the trigger. This time he corrected his errors before Rhino did.

The tier-one operator poked his belly, and his stomach tensed reflexively. "Two shots this time, back-to-back on two targets. And...send it." As soon as the first round left the barrel, he knew the second shot would miss, but he found that by the time he aimed at the next bird, he barely had to reset.

"Again."

This one hit home while his target flapped its wings before taking flight.

"Again. Lead the flying bird." With the next in full motion, he sighted in front the way he would with a shotgun and let it fly into the crosshairs. With the final pull of his finger, this one fell while the others flew away.

The master whistled and said, "Six birds in six shots. I'll–Oh, there's another one. Aim and send it."

He brought the rifle up, aimed, and fired. The goose kept pecking at the ground like Darwin's loser, unperturbed by his fellows dropping dead.

Rhino tapped his arm. "Shoulder up. Two eyes. Tight core. Lean forward. Feel the ground through the soles of your boots. Send it."

He fired, and it dropped like the others.

"Lesson over," the SEAL said, slapping his ass like a football player.

As Wall sanitized the M4, Rhino lectured about how disciplined form was the basis of a competent marksman. "Seven birds in seven shots with good but not excellent technique. One miss out of one with farm-boy habits."

"Gotcha. Lesson learned."

Mid-sanitizing, the elite warrior barked, "Firing position."

After a second of confusion, he adopted the stance, which earned a hard smack on his shoulder and a quick kick to the shin. "Are you a soldier or a good-ol' boy?" While Rhino enjoyed a peanut M&M from Wall's office candies, he snapped to and shot the same bird over and over until the clip ran out.

"Not bad. Nineteen hits out of twenty-three. It needs work, but admitting you have a problem is the first step."

"Thanks," Wall said, impressed with the results of the quick lesson.

The big man smiled. "Let's collect *my* bounty."

"*Your* bounty?" he asked incredulously. "I shot them."

"Yeah. When you followed my instructions, we bagged them. When you did whatever you call shooting, that goose out there taunted you mercilessly. So, it's *my* bounty."

Wall paused roughly ten times on the two-hundred-meter walk to their prizes, practicing Rhino's form. The SEAL pointed out adjustments and judged attempts, never granting a score higher than seven out of ten. They left the bird that he used for continued target practice behind because it could hardly be called a bird anymore but took the rest back to the BMW. The FTX

5.56 NATO rounds did a serious amount of damage to the rest, but they'd still make good eating.

With twelve webbed feet loaded in the SUV's back, they sped off as Rhino whooped and spun more donuts through the golf course. "Don't tell Plink about this," he said mischievously. "She'll drag you back out here and tear up all eighteen fairways." Then they rocketed back to base.

A minute later, the BMW stopped inches from Renegade Genomix, and they hopped out. "We return victorious!"

Plink looked over the roof at them. "Did he run donuts through the golf course?"

"Nah," Wall said, sure that she could read the truth.

"I can die happy," Rhino said with a big fat grin.

Admiring their bounty, Plink asked Wall, "Do you know how to cook a goose?"

"Does a snake slither?"

She blew a kiss at him. "Excellent."

He carried several of the fat geese behind the building where Aspen sat drawing. "Give me a hand, won't you?"

Her flag of incredulity flew higher than any national symbol in history. "Uh, no thanks. That sounds like a Wall chore."

He threw the birds on the ground and looked at her like his father used to look at him, then internally swore at how easily he took on his old man's mannerisms. "Do you want breakfast or not?"

"How about I say 'no' now, then 'yes' after you cook them."

"It'll be good for you, put hair on your chest."

Hand to heart, she said, "That's a hard pass on the hair thing."

"Hop to. There are three more in the back of the car."

"Fine," she groused.

Over the next few hours, Wall instructed Aspen on the proper way to pluck, dress, and cook geese. He explained the difference between warm-weather and cold-weather aging, why freezing was preferable to cooking right away, and why you pluck the feathers as gently as possible. After the first goose, she got into it. Several years ago, Aspen lived with a foster mom who wouldn't watch anything but the cooking channel, so she already knew many of the basics.

They built fires in the neighbor's gas firepit, the shiny built-in stainless-steel grill, and the large Green Egg. The high-end hickory coals and bottle of fire-starter Aspen found under the grill were perfect for a slow cook. By the shine of the backyard amenities, the previous owners loved owning the finer things but never used them. They would probably be horrified by Wall's ugly modifications.

"Their loss is our gain."

He taught her everything he knew about quick cooking and, more importantly, slow cooking. Turning raw meat into disease-free food was a crucial lesson for post-rust survival. The primary difference was that you had to quickly cook small bits at high temps. Slow cooking, whether it was boar, dear, or bear, involved large cuts of meat at lower temps.

Wall taught her how to cook shish kabobs and the hot-rock method. Taking advantage of the Big Green Egg, a convenience that they wouldn't usually have, he cooked the finest bird at a perfectly managed temperature. He demonstrated how to slow-cook the last two geese underground on a thick layer of coal covered by rocks, then the birds, another layer of hot rocks, followed by wood poles and dirt.

He could hardly wait to turn some of it into various-flavored jerky.

CHAPTER THIRTY-ONE

Wall sat on the roof, waiting for the birds to slow-cook for a couple of hours, grateful for an uneventful morning without a single gunfight. Someone not too far away also lit a fire to barbeque, the smell of which blissfully mingled with his own artwork. It was enough to warm his chilled body.

After Aspen's cooking lesson, she repeated pistol safety with Rhino, then the ins and outs of firing. She practiced with at least fifty dry fires before shooting her Glock for the first time. Seeing her bounce up and down with exhilaration put a smile on his face. It made him think back to the first time his dad let him shoot the bronze-plated lever-action twenty-two. It took a bit of practice killing those beer cans, but after a while, he caught the hang of it and hit them nearly every time. The sense of control over the firearm was liberating.

While watching her, he whispered, "Why did you tribe up with us?" Earlier, when he asked, she told him that she wanted to watch Wall's tornado of destruction, but he suspected something else. It–

"She intuits that you connected with her," Plink whispered in his ear, then kissed his cheek. "You won't abandon her the way Rhino and I would if our hands were forced." Plink began stretching, her movements creating a tantalizing combination of curves.

Meanwhile, he poked his tongue into his cheek, contemplating her words and the challenges of being responsible for someone so young. It wasn't the same as the brotherhood of the Army or the comradery he was developing with the others. For her to live through Towning's crappy legacy, Wall needed to elevate to the top of the survival pyramid and learn how to be ready all the time. The question was, would the long-term stress of looking after her wear him down and crack him like a damaged boiler?

As if sensing his thoughts, she said, "Burnout isn't an option. The spoils go to the resilient. You can't just win once. You have to survive and keep rebounding to win every time. Diligence is the price we pay for living."

He saw that in some of his army buddies. Ethiopia, while called a peace-keeping mission and not a war, broke too many men and women. PTSD followed them wherever they went, which made reintegrating with civilization difficult. He worried about their frayed edges and heavy consciences even more now that they would have to battle for survival. Would a return to war, albeit without the Army, break them or thrust them into leadership roles? He suspected both.

He watched Plink stretch with incredible flexibility despite her surprising strength, like a grown-up gymnast. She contorted into a perfect left-facing split and said, "Simply focus on the mission and Aspen's survival. Nothing else matters. They will keep you motivated and sane." She reversed the direction of her splits, managing it but not with as much ease. "In the Army, you went back to combat rather than taking the desk job you could have. You returned to your unit because your friends relied on you and you on them, right?"

"Yeah. How do you know these things?"

She rolled backward, thrust her feet into the air, and propped upside down on her shoulders and elbows. "I understand people the way you understand biochemistry."

Most people assumed that you were either good at science or not and that it didn't require years of extreme dedication. Yet, Plink wasn't like most people. "So, you spent a decade learning?"

Impossibly rolling over her head into pushups, she said, "Yes, and like you, I had an aptitude that accompanied my interests. Innate talent, gumption, and purpose don't often align."

"True enough." Sore and stiff like a bent spoon, Wall lowered himself to the roof and demonstrated his general lack of bendiness and damaged state. As odious as the light exercise was, he knew it was the only way to keep from completely seizing up like a recently sickened padlock.

After a two-armed one-legged round of pushups, he said, "So, what insanity do you have planned for us now?"

"Rhino thinks you should stay behind with him." He sensed a joke coming. "But, with your propensity for destruction, I don't want you around Kayla's lab any more than necessary."

"Ha," he laughed weakly. "It's funny because it's true. But don't skim over the real reason. You want to split up the super nerds. One egg in Rhino's basket. The other egg in yours."

Plink smiled and said, "I keep telling the paparazzi that you aren't as dumb as they think, but they won't listen." She rolled to his side and placed her hand on his chest. "Lean back on your elbows, legs extended. Good." She mashed her palms into his thigh above his bandage, the sensation eliciting the quiet groan of a man who didn't want to look weak. The urge to push her away nearly won out over logic. "There we go." The soreness began to ease up.

"Roll over," she ordered. "I'm gonna do your hammies." Even though he knew how important PT was for recovery, he almost called her off.

"So, Wall," she said as she tortured him. "Have you ever wanted to rob a jewelry store?"

"Hasn't everyone?" he asked with a double scoop of no-duh.

"Then, you're in luck."

Between heavy breaths, as she drove her knuckles into his IT band, he said, "Are you pulling my chain?"

"Not a single link. It'll be a straight-up smash and grab."

He grinned. "We're like land pirates, stealing anything we want."

She began torturing his calf. "Arr, matey. Time for a plundering."

He smiled. "Let me guess. We want silver, gold, and diamonds for trading, like currencies of old."

"Yes, and?" she asked while digging into his calf.

"Platinum and diamond are hard. Useful in a world without iron or steel."

"And Wall for the win," she said, mimicking a football announcer.

Aspen walked toward them and asked, "Can I come? I wanna be rich."

"No," they said together.

Plink added, "It's bad enough that I'm bringing Wall. I'd leave him behind if I weren't counting on his ability to level everything in our path." She switched over to his good side and tore into his other IT band. "Besides, Aspen, you need more firearm training. Keep practicing with Rhino."

"Sure." Aspen shrugged and returned to the big man. Somehow, Plink had a way of getting her to comply without a round of smart-ass comments.

After a short stint of less painful PT on his good side, she returned to his wounded thigh. The phrase, "No pain, no gain," fit physical therapy better than any other activity conceived by humankind.

When he rolled onto his back, and she pulled him to his feet, he tested his leg and said, "Thanks. Much better."

She smiled deviously. "You know there are easier ways to convince a lady to touch you than getting shot, don't you?" She slapped his ass and walked to the ladder.

He waited until she reached the edge of the building before he said, "Then it's a good thing you're not a lady."

As she disappeared in a controlled slide, she said, "We leave in five."

Moments later, he waved to Aspen and Rhino from the passenger's seat of the sick-sounding BMW. "Good shooting."

The budding soldier stuck her tongue out and answered, "You too."

Wall hoped this excursion wouldn't come to a round of "assertive bartering." He was on a roll, having survived a whole twelve hours without someone trying to kill him. He stuck out his tongue and raised her a goofy clown face.

Then Plink screeched off. The way she sped around rusty junkers and threaded between abandoned cars reminded him of how the Millennium Falcon careened through the Death Star. "May the rust be with you," he whispered. Two minutes in Newtonian time and zero seconds in relativistic time, they skidded to a stop with the BMW's tail end turned facing a jewelry store. In addition to rusted doors and broken windows, thieves ransacked the place, leveling nearly every display case.

"There can't be anything left inside, can there? Look at it. Someone already looted the sucker."

Plink winked at him and said, "Sure there is," then threw the BMW into reverse and gunned it. They soared between the pillars, over the remains of the front doors, and bounced atop the demolished showcases. Instead of slowing, she kept speeding up and rammed into the far wall like a drunk driver through his ex's front door. Drywall and rusted steel studs flew in all directions as they plowed through the first wall, then into another, where they stopped like crash-test dummies.

Through the cloud of dust and rust, Wall looked around at Plink's work, glad for his poor excuse for a neck brace, facemask, and shooting glasses. "And you say I'm destructive?"

Stock full of glee, she said, "As your superior officer, I blame you for this mess." She pulled the car forward two paces, put it in park, and hopped out. She shoved a section of drywall aside and said, "Behold. I present to you the much-coveted safe."

The beige vault lay on its back, having fallen over when Plink bashed it with the heavy rear of the battery-laden SUV. The trailer hitch left an indentation in the safe's door but didn't break through to the interior. The impact pulled the floor-mount bolts from the cement base that was supposed to keep it in place.

"I love electric cars," she said, clearly impressed with her work. "They're so much heavier than the old ones. And that engine. Momentum and kinetic energy, baby."

Giddy about bringing his life-long dream of robbing a jewelry store to fruition, he asked, "Did you go to school for your level of crazy?"

Her eyes beamed brighter than jewels. "Self-taught." She tossed Wall a set of neon yellow towing straps. Going full pirate, she said. "Quit lazin' around, ye scallywag, and get yer plundering arse to work." She looped the tethers around the vault while he secured them to the D-rings on the side of the BMW's bent trailer hitch.

A moment later, they mounted up, and Plink drove out of the store, abandoning her usual demon driving in favor of gradually increasing the torque until the vault budged. The car jolted forward with cacophonous sounds trailing behind. The safe smashed through the chaos in the store, snapping, crushing, and crunching everything in its path. Then they were outside, and the unholy grind of metal dragging on the pavement announced their actions to the world.

"Wall!" Plink yelled, barely audible over the trailing caterwaul. "Stand up! Combatants at nine o'clock."

He was sure he didn't hear her right. "What?"

"Combatants now at our eight!" She pointed to the sunroof. "You're our turret."

Then, he saw it. A full-sized white rape van was on an intercept course with a heavily bearded guy aiming his rifle out the open side door. When the first shot flew overhead, Plink smacked him in the bad leg and yelled, "Get up there, now!"

For a tall man encumbered by combat gear to maneuver in a car was a contortionist's dream at best. To do so while Plink weaved in random directions presented an opportunity for great comedy. Yet, with the zing of another round flying nearby, he managed it in record time. While Plink swerved left as fast as she could without losing the trailing vault, he anchored himself into the back-right corner of the sunroof and aimed.

A third bullet rang out, this one hitting the BMW and Wall still hadn't retaliated. Based on the percussive wind and the distinctive sound of ammunition in flight, he could have sworn that the fourth bullet missed his ear by a bee's wing. Right when he fixed his crosshairs on the van's tire, Plink swerved again, throwing him off balance.

He yelled, "Stop swerving!"

Screeching right, she shouted, "Damn it, Wall. Nut up and shoot!"

Another bullet hit their car.

Better braced this time, he aimed with both eyes open, leaning forward, his shoulder held up, and shot. Then shot again, and again, and again until he lost count. He missed and hit the van some number of times before he hit the shooter, who fell from the open door, landing face first at speed. Next, he turned his attention to the driver. Now that their attackers were de-clawed, Plink stopped swerving long enough for him to take a set of steady shots, placing two holes in the windshield at chest height. The ungainly vehicle slowed and turned, nearly flopping on its side.

Plink skidded to a stop, facing back toward the van, sending the safe looping around in a semi-circle as she tore back to the combatants, where a lone man ran away at full sprint.

While Wall reloaded, she yelled, "I got this one!" so he aimed but held his trigger finger. She sped toward the guy as if she might drive over him and braced for impact, but she spun in a skidding slide. Wall didn't see it and wished he hadn't heard it, knowing she painted the beat-up vault in red, the perfect corrosive for eating its way through the metal exterior, starting the safe-cracking process.

"Come back down," Plink said, tugging on his pant leg before veering onto the road. "Don't you know you could get hurt up there? Are you a maniac or something?"

He slid into the passenger seat, easier on the way down than on the way up. "That was..."

"A little late, but good shooting. Who says you can't train an academic?"

"Crap, Plink. You're bleeding?" Red dripped from under her helmet and down her neck. An ear-level hole ran through the side of her headgear.

She smiled. "Meh. Ain't nothing to it. I always wanted a piercing."

It shouldn't have come as a surprise that she shrugged off the wound because the armed forces' selected tier-one operators for ruggedness, for the ability to push through adversity when others would keel over in pain. Among other things, Rhino and Plink embodied resilience. "But you got shot."

"Yeah. Either that or it was one big-ass bumblebee."

"Hop out. I'll drive."

She kicked the accelerator, but it ground like an industrial scrap shredder. "Not a chance, mon petit frere."

Accepting that she wouldn't give up the wheel, he pulled out his med kit and began tending to her wound, starting by pulling off her helmet. She barely flinched from the abrasive pain. The shot scraped her scalp and tore off the top of her ear. In a moving car, especially one operated by Plink, he could only manage to staunch the bleeding.

"Those rape-van dipshits shot up my fine European automobile," she said. He didn't bother pointing out that her priorities were way out of wack, as in not on the same continent as wack.

When they reached Renegade Genomix, she pealed out again, sending the reddened vault slingshotting into a tree with a thunderous impact that brought down a rain of Douglas fir needles.

"Bonnie and Clyde return victorious," Rhino boomed from above.

"Clyde," Plink said as she slowly stood like an arthritic hunchback. "Can I see a scratch about a medic?"

"Yeah," he said, with his worry-ometer spiking red. He rounded the BMW to find her rubbing the bulletproof jacket at kidney level. "Oh, shit," he mouthed. Kidney injuries are as dangerous as they are painful.

"Plink, you shoulda told me about your kidney."

"Yeah," She hissed. "You might be right on that account."

Aspen bounded up to them like an excited dear. "I can't believe it. You guys really stole a safe!" She looked back and forth between Wall and the vault. "This is way shway."

He half smiled, his eyes not leaving Plink. "Not as cool for her."

Only now did she notice the elite soldier's new walking style, resembling the waddle of a pregnant woman, not that Wall would ever vocalize that comparison.

Aspen asked, "Are you okay?"

Answering for the doddering operative, he said, "She's tougher than a diamond, kid." Wall skipped around the corner. He could have helped her walk if his knee and thigh were in better condition, but things as they were, all he could do was prepare their pathetic outdoor emergency room.

"Um, Wall," Aspen said from the corner as she looked back and forth between patient and medic. "What's all the red stuff on the safe?"

He squinted, trying not to think about it. "Don't ask."

"Is that..."

"Yeah," he said and gently rolled his head as he took off his backpack and knelt over his gear.

"Seriously gross!" While her voice was that of the prissiest girl on the continent, her bulging eyes told of humankind's primal need to watch a train wreck. When Aspen opened her mouth, he expected a serious question or a disgusting statement. Instead, she said, "You should know I only wear fourteen-karat gold and diamonds. No pearls."

With an awful attempt at old English, he said, "Of course, m'lady"

"Seriously," she said, jumping up and down. "Can we pop it open?"

"Yeah. After I take care of Plink. Now, let me concentrate." He was relieved when she did as ordered. Aspen might have been a smart-ass, but she knew when to mess around and when things were serious. He'd take an astute smart-ass over an ignorant dumbass any day.

Bandaging up Plink proved to be far easier than yesterday when he worked on himself. While the scalp wound bled a lot and required shaving a patch of hair and seven ugly stitches, her ear didn't bleed much, only requiring some antibiotics and a bandage. She insisted that he not cover more of her ear than absolutely necessary so she could hear when Wall inevitably drew chaos to them.

Now that the bleeding had stopped, he turned to her kidney injury. First, he helped her out of her bulletproof vest and handed Aspen the gear so she could disinfect it and throw out anything that was irrecoverably sickened.

The bruise was as nasty as any he'd seen, and the area had already started to swell. When he gently pressed on the puffiest spot, she arched her back, tensed every muscle, and screamed like a barbarian, then leaned forward onto hands and knees and puked. Kidney stones were said to hurt as much as childbirth, or in some cases worse, so he could only imagine the pain of a supersonic kidney strike.

"Here." Wall handed her a tiny tablet of ondansetron. "It'll dissolve in your mouth and reduce your nausea." She didn't move. "You need to take it." She opened her mouth but remained on her hands, moaning. Hoping he understood her meaning, he slipped the med into her mouth, thankful that he came away with his fingers.

While her pain worried him, his real concern was internal bleeding. The area had grown taught and clammy, which were signs he couldn't ignore. Her nausea was another symptom but not particularly diagnostic. Her heart rate was high for someone in such good shape. The other symptoms would take time to diagnose. Bloody or decreased urine. Drowsiness. Fever. He wished he had the stethoscope, thermometer, and pressure cuff from the helicopter, all of which began rusting when he tended to the wounded after the crash. So much for even the most basic of western medical practices.

He hated watching her reposition over and over in a futile attempt to get comfortable. About a strand of jerky later, after the nausea meds were in her system, he helped her take a tablet of hydromorphone, a step up from oxy, to ease the pain. She writhed through another jerky sliver until the opioid began to kick in. By the time her eyes were dilated, she had grown drowsy. He petted her head until she fell asleep.

Without much he could do for her, he rounded the corner to the safe, certain that their loot wasn't worth the cost.

Aspen was jumping up and down on a branch that poked through a crack in the back of the vault. As she treated the stick like a trampoline, he circled the vault, examining the infected outside.

"Cheap construction."

The back plate was weak in comparison to the front and sides. Even "top of the line" safes tended to use thinner metal on the backside to save on costs and reduce the weight for transport. He'd take the win, though. The half-assed American craftsmanship, so different from the useless safe at his condo, gave them an access point to the goods inside.

"Mind if I have a go?" he asked Aspen.

"Sure." She hopped down, still smiling.

With his considerable weight and leverage advantage, he managed to pry it open centimeter by centimeter. As the crack grew, it became easier to peel the thin sheet metal away, exposing the interior black velvet shelves, one after the next. Even as "easy" as it was to break in, copious sweat drenched his tired and sore body by the time he finished.

He stepped away and wiped his brow. "There you go, Aspen. Have at it."

She squealed and launched as if by a catapult at their bounty. "It's mine! All mine!"

"Careful about the sharp edges. They'll slice you open."

Bitter about the cost of securing the precious metals and jewels, he didn't even look inside, instead, turning his back on the treasure and silently walked back to check on Plink. While his cortex-driven mind wanted to be dispassionate about her injuries so he could be a better medic, his hypothalamus wouldn't let him disentangle his budding feelings for her.

When she slept through his examination, his fear for her bumped up to a new level. Her forehead was cold and clammy. She was sweating through her clothes and her heart rate was high.

"Fucking A."

CHAPTER THIRTY-TWO

A while before noon, Wall nibbled at a slice of Cajun-spiced goose, absolutely happy with the result. The thin strips that dangled on sticks above the coals needed time to absorb more smoke flavor, but they were coming along beautifully. He made good use of the neighbor's selection of spices, often ignored and lightweight treasures that could turn meals from awful to palatable. He and Aspen alternated between checking on the various cuts of meat and keeping Plink company.

The thicker cuts of breast meat resembled gamey steak, similar to bison and elk. Aspen ate an impossible amount of leg meat, preferring Wall's sweet teriyaki flavoring over the others. Her stomach stuck out comically as she walked around petting it. Rhino dove into a sizable helping of ginger-forward goose, espousing Wall's abilities in the way of slow-cooking. He fixed Plink a small helping of bland shredded meat, which she barely touched. He was just glad she was awake. Eating a few bites and steadily sipping water was the icing on the cinnamon bun.

Inside, Lucas dug into the brown sugar and maple syrup meal Wall prepared for him while Nellibi didn't even pick at a hickory-flavored shish kabob. She was barely responsive and had lost weight since the crash. If she didn't snap out of it soon, dehydration would incapacitate her and leave the kid orphaned. When the doctor fell asleep, which she was doing more and more, Aspen snuck Lucas out to run around and play tag. They disinfected him and got him back inside before he was missed.

After clearing paper plates, Wall cleaned up at the stream, careful to scrub all of the geese and ash out of the crevices. Cooking in the new world lacked the sanitary environment of stainless-steel countertops, ventilated ovens, and commercial-grade dishwashers, all of which had degraded inside their neighbor's kitchen. He could do without kitchen appliances. The household convenience he sorely regretted losing was the water heater. He'd have to get used to sitting in unsympathetically cold streams.

Once clean, he layered up and visited Kayla, staying outside the vestibule while she groused about his incessant interruptions from the other side of the door. Starting with his biggest concern, he asked, "How are you physically?"

"Ugh. I'm fine." Her voice came out as a mixture of grumpiness and fatigue.

"Are you getting enough to eat?"

"Of course." She sure hadn't looked like it when she showed her face through the viewport.

Wanting to shortcut what was bound to be an exercise in futility, he changed the subject. "I presume you haven't discovered anything new about the diseases or vaccines."

She yawned. "Your assumption is ill-informed and the sign of an unfit scientist."

"Okay, then," he said, letting her tired-induced snippiness flow over him like water across a pebble in a stream. There were far more important and painful things to think about. "What do you have to report?"

"I synthesized a protein that partially inhibits the growth of Towning's HIV variant."

"That's excellent," he said. "A possible vaccine?"

"No," she said, not bothering to explain.

After a moment in which he thought she might continue, he prompted her. "Do you care to elaborate?"

She didn't respond.

Aware that he needed to engage her before she completely tuned him out, he asked, "Have any of the viruses responded to the vaccines we brought you?"

"No reactions."

Over the next several minutes, he extracted a few tidbits about her research plan and challenges. The gist was that she agreed to balance her efforts between researching the HIV strain and investigating the other diseases. He couldn't pin her down on what that balance looked like. Fifty-fifty? Seventy-thirty? Ten-ninety? While he argued that she should spend more time with measles and mumps, he suspected she would focus primarily on HIV, her preferred virus.

After he gave up talking to her, he inspected the building from the inside. Lucas followed him around like a baby duck, asking him questions like "What's your favorite color?" and "Did you know that T-Rexes could grow up to twelve meters high?"

He silently swore when he saw rust around Nellibi's little nest. Not only did she sit, by all appearances unaware of his presence, but she also smelled of body odor, urine, blood, and feces. He pushed aside the coffee table and knelt in front of her. "Magali?"

No response.

"Doctor Nellibi?"

Nothing.

He snapped his fingers. "Magali, come on."

She didn't even blink.

He turned to Lucas. "Has she said anything recently."

The boy shook his head.

He eyed the full water bottle in front of her. "Has she been drinking?"

Another head shake.

He leaned in close to her ear and whispered, "Lucas needs you."

If he didn't feel her breath on his ear, he might have thought she was dead. With increased skill that must have come from durations that had slipped away, he ran through a full evaluation, or as close as he could without metal equipment like a pressure cuff and stethoscope. He almost swore but held back so he wouldn't scare Lucas.

"Is she gonna get better?" the six-or-seven-year-old asked.

"Yes," he said, pretty sure that it was a lie but hoping it was true. "This medicine should help," he lied again, mashing up a valium in a plastic spoon and filling the rest with water. He opened her mouth, leaned her head back, and dumped the liquid into the back near her uvula, then closed it up and rubbed her throat as he'd seen Thomas do with his dog, Rex. She didn't respond to the sour taste of the pill other than to choke on the medicine for a sec before swallowing.

While waiting for the chill pill to kick in, an act that he hoped wouldn't do more harm than good, he cleaned up the mess Lucas made with candy wrappers and rusting soda cans, sealing them in a bag along with Kayla's pre-sealed excrement. The boy followed him and drilled Wall with dozens of questions, from "are you a doctor?" to "how tall are you? I hope I can be that big when I grow up."

When Nellibi passed out, Wall threw her over his shoulder, all too aware of her stench, and carried her outside. He hadn't been sure if she'd go bat-shit-crazy if removed from her safe spot without the Valium. "Come on, Lucas. Let's get some air."

He ran outside at full throttle. "Weeee!"

"What happened?" Plink asked as soon as he stepped out with the doctor over his shoulder.

"Nellibi is starting to contaminate the building."

"Is that smell from her?" she turned away and put her palm over her already masked face.

"Unfortunately."

"Fuh–" She cut herself off as Lucas ran back toward them. "–udge." As soon as the boy ran off again, she asked, "What do you plan on doing with her?"

"For now, I'll move her into the neighbor's house. I saw a futon. No springs to rust. I have to clean her and start an IV." Mentally, he recited, "Three minutes without air, three days without water, three weeks without food."

"Good thinking. I'll bring water, soap, and rags."

"No," he said firmly, medical taking the lead over tactical when regrouping. "You need the rest."

She gave him a look that said she could say the same about him but didn't press the matter. Instead, she asked, "What about Kayla's research?"

Wall summed it up with brevity. "Worse than hoped, better than feared, and as slow as expected."

"Acknowledged."

When he returned from the nasty deed of relocating and cleaning Nellibi, he ran through a full evaluation of Plink. While he took notes, she said, "I need your unadulterated opinion."

Concern knitted his brows. "Uh, sure. What's up?"

She tapped at her thigh, her tell. "Will Nellibi recover?"

"No." The answer came so fast that he had to catch up with his one-word snap decision. But having heard his answer, he knew it was right. Harsh? For sure. Cold? Absolutely. Correct? Undeniably. Regrettable? Sickeningly to the point of raising bile in his throat. Plink watched him as if she could see the swift cascade of thoughts unfold within him.

With his stomach churning, he squinted his eyes as if that might block out his answer. She was a human being, maybe the last person he knew from before the fall that he would ever see. Further, it was a slap in the face. Grief, or fear, or whatever put Nellibi in that state took away Alpha Bravo's backup. Back to one is none.

"No," he repeated. "Nellibi won't recover. Or at least not for a long time."

"As I thought." She stopped tap-tap, tap-tapping her thigh. "We may have to leave her behind."

"I know." He sure didn't want to know.

"Are you okay with that?"

"No, but I'll have to be if or when the time comes."

With trepidation, she asked, "What about Aspen and Lucas?"

This time he delayed answering, fearing his response. Conflicting notions crashed together like high-energy particles in The Large Hadron Collider. They were drains on Alpha Bravo. Aspen ate too much. They would only serve to distract them. Protecting them might prove fatal. But he couldn't reject the undefinable. All he could say was, "I'm biased. Unfit to answer."

With compassion, she placed her hand on his chest. "I know."

He looked to the new clouds that were coming in, angling for more time. "They're both smart and resilient. Under different circumstances, with lesser consequences, I'd consider Aspen a resourceful team member worth protecting because she is the type of person we need in the new world. The boy is too young to tell." He braced himself for his own words. "But you and Rhino are busy protecting Kayla and me." The implication was that Nellibi was no longer a priority if they had to jet. "They'll add variables into the mix and increase the risk of our failure. The mission is all."

She cocked her head. "Yet..."

"I don't know if I can leave either of them. It's only been a day, and it doesn't make sense, but there's something about Aspen." Plink's face changed in a way he couldn't read. "The boy is so innocent. What are we striving to save if we lose our humanity?" The philosophical nature of the tier-one warriors was rubbing off on him, or maybe it was the depths of his mind trying to make sense of the last couple of days. Either way, he knew how he felt.

She hugged him, not sensual but needed all the same. Without pulling away, she looked up at him with searching eyes. "Humanity is not for the likes of us. We are the uncivilized instruments of a civilized society, not members of it. It has always been so for warriors."

Now it was his turn to say, "Yet..."

She smiled with tears on her lashes. "As the blade and bullet, we are responsible for safeguarding those who will herald tomorrow."

Even though it should have been her decision whether to bring along potential safety risks, he intuited that it was his choice. He nodded. "Aspen and the boy come with us. Their paths are ours."

"Oh, thank god," she said and kissed him, the salt of a tear on her lips. When they pulled apart, she recited Towning. "Choices made, whether bad or good, follow you forever and affect everyone in your path." She said it with hope, not anger as he would have. "Their paths are ours."

Her face hardened and transformed into that of a commanding officer's, reformed with undeniable strength. "We have chores to do and little time to waste."

"Time? Why? What's changed?"

"Nothing, really. We have three passengers and two small bikes. We need three larger bikes to be prepared in case we have to abandon Renegade Genomix on a moment's notice. Kayla will ride with Rhino. Aspen will ride with you. Kayla can wear Nellibi's body armor. However, we need armor for Aspen and the boy if we can find any that fit."

Wall sighed heavily in complete agreement about their need for both missions, new bikes and armor. The problem was that their injury-per-outing ratio couldn't be described as anything but abysmal. This was a clear test of their commitment to protecting the kids, risking adult lives for young ones. It was an emotional decision rather than a mission-critical one.

"Okay," he said. "I know where we can find body armor and off-road bikes." He had purchased the Glock 20 for camping at Federal Tactical only a couple of months ago. The gun store was southeast of Renegade Genomix, a shop owned by an ex-firefighter, as reliable a man as there was. It was the closest store he could think of and a solid choice.

Wall didn't know much about the outdoor sports store but always wanted an excuse to visit. Ultimately, the idea of wasting a boatload of money on an expensive toy that he didn't have time to enjoy kept him away. With such a temptation before him, he might not have been able to resist.

With a grimace, she patted herself down, readying herself to depart, but Wall stayed her hand. "You're not going anywhere. You need to rest. Rhino and I can do it."

The next thing Wall knew, he came out of a haze, mounting up on the red motocross bike, and kicking the starter. "Damn it," he whispered. The time slippages scared the shit out of him. Apparently, he was functional enough to not draw attention during his mental gaps, but that worried him just as much. What if he was only at eighty percent of optimal—or what counted as optimal in his physical condition? That missing twenty percent might get them killed.

The massive SEAL looked ridiculous on his highly maneuverable but small cycle. It almost looked like a toy that one might find under a clown at a monster truck rally. Wall's laughter couldn't be held back.

Rhino chuckled. "Go ahead and laugh. You look like a giraffe on a tricycle. Now, lead the way to Federal."

Wall rode the motorcycle the way they drove cars, wildly fast and randomly swerving to stay unpredictable in case someone was interested in target practice. He weaved eastward between and around the rusted husks of vehicles. They crossed the street whenever they passed families, couples, and singles migrating in one direction or another. Channeling his inner Plink, he cut across lawns or through parking lots, indiscriminately alternating between the road and sidewalks.

When a man jumped out of an alley and swung a baseball bat at him, Wall thought he was a goner. The bat came in at neck height, the typical head height for a normal man. Instinctively, he hunched forward and lowered his helmet just in time to earn a glancing blow off his helmet rather than a fatal blow to the Adam's apple. The impact sent a shock wave down his neck for the umpteenth time since the helo crash, nearly knocking him from his bike.

He reflexively clamped down on the brakes and skidded backward before coming to a stop.

Rhino swerved and rolled past as Wall drew his P17 and fired. Drawing on the SEAL's expert tutelage, both bullets hit home like a two-for-one deal. He didn't realize that he was seeing double until he holstered the pistol, spun his bike out, and rode after the big man.

When he caught up, Rhino said, "Soldier, you're the unluckiest farm-grown sack of meat I've ever met."

With a blink, Wall skipped through reality by ten blocks, where he slowed his roll, only a few doors down from the gun shop. Like so many other shops along the way, the front door went the way of the rust. Unlike most, this store owner managed to board up the entrance and its side display windows, telling of post-rusting wealth or a fast response to the downfall. The once-black Hummer out front sat on three wheels, the fourth having fallen under the thing's beastly weight.

"We're here," he said, pulling over.

"Slow and smooth," Rhino said calmly as they parked shy of the sidewalk.

Wall's Spidey senses hit max, possibly because of a subtle tension he hadn't noticed in the big man's voice or because his subconscious brain was piecing together details his forethoughts couldn't comprehend. His gut churned as they killed their engines.

Rhino raised his hands and Wall followed suit, assuming the SEAL saw something he hadn't.

When they stopped moving, the black lump on the shop's rooftop shifted, and a coarse voice said, "State your business." Wall recognized the voice of the proprietor. Upon closer examination, a beige rifle barrel stuck out of the mass, which turned out to be a net covering the retired fireman. The firearm wasn't directly aimed at them, the sign of a guy who knew his safety rules and was confident in his skills.

Wall's head throbbed harder all the same.

"What is that?" Rhino asked. "A desert-gray FN SCAR 17? Tell me, did you opt for the custom 6.5 Creedmoor barrel?" How he could tell the caliber of a rifle from that distance was beyond Wall. He knew of the legendary FN SCAR, a heavy beast of an assault rifle, but couldn't see enough of the weapon's unique form to identify it.

"Good eye," the shop owner said with a subtle shift that might have been a nod of appreciation. "Spec ops?"

"Yeah. ex-SEAL."

The man whistled in response.

Rhino pointed at Wall with his hands still raised. "This beanstalk is our embedded super nerd. He bought a Glock 20 here about two months ago."

Wall slowly pulled down his face mask.

"Yeah. You look familiar. Always nice to see repeat customers. What are you in the market for?"

Rhino nodded to Wall. "It's your show."

He gummed a piece of jerky he didn't remember popping. "We want body armor for a thirteen-year-old girl and a six-year-old boy. She's fifty kilograms fully loaded. I have no clue about his size."

"I don't have anything that small," he said. "Move–"

Boldly interrupting a man who could kill him with a shift and a trigger pull, he said, "What's the closest you have?"

"Depends. What are you trading? Money's no good."

Realizing he hadn't thought about what to exchange, his face went pale. Or rather, his pack was full. He just couldn't remember what he packed to barter. "Mind if I take my backpack off to show you?"

"Yeah, get on with it."

Before Wall lowered his hands, Rhino asked, "Your buddy with the sniper rifle back there won't shoot, will he?"

"Well spotted. Nah, he's a teddy bear."

Slow and purposeful, Wall unslung his pack and opened it, his ears hot from being downrange from forward and aft snipers, both of whom were undoubtedly excellent shots. Even before he unzipped the pack, he knew what was inside from the smell. Holding the pack up for the shop owner to see, he said, "Several flavors of goose meat. From top to bottom. Cooked it myself."

The netting bobbed. "Good trading material. But the closest I have is a woman's medium Class IV armor. I'll take the duck and your bikes."

Wall stripped a bite from the goose, popped it in his mouth, and moaned loud enough for the man to hear. "Sounds fair, but you should know my bike has the earliest signs of rust."

"You could have kept that to yourself," the man said. "You're good people."

"Less good than you might think," Wall said. "Times are what they are."

A pause accompanied what must have been deep thinking. "Deal. The armor for the goose and your bikes, regardless of their condition."

"Deal."

The FN SCAR's barrel tilted up, and the black webbing sluffed off the gray-haired man dressed in tactical gear with a gas mask. He stood slowly and took a moment to stretch out his aches and pains. After throwing a rope ladder over the front of the building's edge and climbing down, he picked up the bag that Wall had set down and backed away.

Before the firearms dealer retreated, he said, "One sec, sir. If you have any clothes for the girl or boy, they would appreciate it."

He knocked a pattern at the front door, and it swung open. Over his shoulder, he said, "I'll see what I can do."

Wall didn't mind the first minute of waiting, but the longer the shopkeeper took, the more he tensed up, imagining the sniper behind them blowing his head open like a watermelon with a .375 Swiss P bullet. A minute after he thought they'd been stiffed, the proprietor returned with Wall's stuffed backpack and set it down. "There you go, lieutenant."

"Thank you, sir."

The older gentleman grumbled something, then said, "Go before you draw attention."

He shouldered the bag and led Rhino west, both trying to hide their limps as they moved on to their next unannounced appointment.

CHAPTER THIRTY-THREE

Walking side-by-side toward Trak Powersports, Wall regretted the loss of their motorcycles. He and Rhino minimized their limps so an onlooker wouldn't think they were slow and easy prey. The best fight was one you didn't get into. Unfortunately, the easiest way to invite trouble in the post-rusting world was to present a weak target, which their slow progress made them.

As he walked, he noticed something mashing against his thigh above his wound. Reaching in, he felt a small velvety pouch with a bundle of shifting little peas inside. *Not peas,* he realized. *Diamonds. The new currency.* He almost pulled them out to see but thought better of showing off the jewels to anyone who might be watching.

He time-traveled for two blocks.

"Hey, soldier," Rhino said, nudging his shoulder. "Are you fit for action?"

Wall tried to pep up. "Like a hog on butchering day."

"Good. We're comin' up on a chokepoint."

The slanted tops of the Main Street Bridge stood out above the long-since-abandoned traffic jam. About six meters of light green trusses near the middle had collapsed into the Willamette River. Rhino stopped and signaled for silence.

The outbound sister bridge, which was packed with cars and trucks, re-mained mostly intact. The big man led the way across the small, overgrown park that separated the inbound and outbound bridges. On the near side of the bridge, several chunks had already collapsed. The rest was cracked and ready to fail at any time. If the bridge fell while they were on the other side of the Willamette, they'd be cut off from Renegade Genomix.

How long do we have? he thought. *Seconds? Minutes? Hours?*

Hunched low, a task made harder by their considerable heights, they approached the bridge and weaved between the cars in a snake-like path. Midway, as they passed over a narrow formed by two fallen sections, Wall thought, *If I was a bandit, this is where–*

Crack. The rear window next to him conjured a new hole with shatter lines radiating outward. He dropped to the concrete, bruising his oft-clicking knee and amplifying the pain in his broken ribs. As he scurried for the cover of a black SUV, Rhino rounded to the front of a rust and white sedan, then raised one finger and signaled that a "sniper" was about a hundred meters toward the far end of the other bridge. Next, he indicated another assailant twenty paces to the left with a pistol.

"Come on out," the nearer guy yelled. "You're pinned down. Either you give us your valuables, or we take your life and your gear. It makes no difference to us. Dump it and go."

"Okay," Rhino said. "I'm standing up. Don't shoot." He wordlessly told Wall to stay put. With one arm raised and the other angled down, he slowly exposed himself.

"Put both hands up," the guy ordered.

With the speed of a ninja, Rhino raised his P17 and shot twice with the characteristic thuds of bullets on flesh and dove to the side. The lack of a yell from the nearby bandit and the dull thump of a man falling to the ground implied well-placed headshots. Presumed dead.

The doppler sound of a bullet speeding by met its end in the tail of a hatchback, a miss from the sniper. Uncharacteristically, Rhino rolled up in a ball, breathing loudly, gripping his knee.

While Army crawling to the SEAL's side, he asked, "Are you okay?" Wall instantly knew how stupid the question was. A sprained ankle and various other serious injuries hadn't stopped Rhino yet, so whatever this was had to be bad. His steady string of whispered curses would have pleased Jimmy Twenty.

"Stay here," Wall said, then half-crawled half-slithered six cars down and two over, passing the would-be thief with unblinking eyes and two new head holes. His plan came together along the way.

He pulled two half-sized pipe bombs from his tactical vest and kissed each, then prepped his M4 for a shot, hyped himself up, struggled with the lighter, and ignited both wicks at once. He never excelled at baseball or football, but he could hold his own in pickup games, so he faced the other bridge and threw one incendiary device quickly followed by the next.

At the limit of his agility, he switched to his M4, forcing himself to follow Rhino's instructions. By the time he stood, the far bridge had exploded twice, sending shockwaves in all directions. With both eyes open, he spotted the sniper who had turned toward the explosions. Wall quickly took aim and pulled the trigger.

"Piece of..." He lost sight of his target because he blinked upon firing.

Wall scanned up and down the bridge with both eyes, hoping to see any combatants before they could spot him. Heartbeats passed. In the interim, his brain caught up to the present. His pipe bombs rendered the far bridge in even worse condition than before. A blackened swath of the trusses and more dangling cement were testaments to his destructive prowess.

Hunched such that he could still look over the cars, he moved down the bridge toward his Schrödinger's target. The sniper would be both dead and alive until he could be observed. Wall slumped to his knees once he saw the man lying face down, letting his head lull forward as it pounded.

Someone shook him. "Wall." It was Rhino. "Wall, come on, man. Come on back." The big man had kneeled beside him, pulling his eyes open. "There you go, soldier."

"I slipped again, didn't I?"

"Yeah. But not until the job was done. You came through."

He could barely remember the details of the skirmish. At that point, most of the exchanges bled into each other.

Rhino shook his oversized head. "For a bullet magnet, you're as lucky a guy as I've ever met. It's a sickness, you know."

"Yeah, I'll have the doc look me over at my next regularly scheduled physical exam."

Rhino stood on one leg. "You do that. Now, get up. We're too exposed."

As they limped westbound across what should have been an eastbound bridge, Rhino now the slower of the two, they found piles of "taxes." Roller bags, clothes, backpacks, food, shoes, and everything a troll could collect for passage over the bridge. If Wall had felt any guilt about killing the sniper, all such feelings turned to pride upon seeing a deceased family.

"The young ones are the hardest," Wall said

"Truer words..."

Wall blinked.

"Hey," Rhino said, leaning on a broken two-by-four that was acting as his cane. "Look alive. We're here." He couldn't remember the last several minutes, another slippage. There must have been more gaps he hadn't noticed, lost moments left unprotected, a danger to both of them. With worried eyes, the SEAL said, "You're getting worse, aren't you?"

"I think so. That bat back there."

"Keep it together, rabbit. We can't afford any more outages until we get back."

The rusting diseases damaged Trak Autosports worse than almost any building he'd seen in Eugene. The front of the one-story building collapsed into mounds, a disarray of wood, cement, and roofing material.

Wall cursed so quietly that not even he could hear himself over the growing breeze. The probability of finding a rust-free dirt bike inside ranked up there with pulling five aces in Texas Hold'em with no wilds. They traded away their two motorcycles and had no prospects for replacements.

Reading his thoughts, Rhino whispered, "We still have to go in."

"Stop," said a thick-bearded man who stood in a glassless window. His well-worn green cap and leathery look was reminiscent of a surly truck driver. He pumped his sawed-off shotgun. In addition to the classic *chk-chk* that everyone knew, a pepper grinder grit announced its state of decay. The stupid action told of ineptitude as an unused shell ejected from the chamber, reducing his armament by one. Nevertheless, Wall's inclination for testing the weapon's functionality or the trucker's skills failed to rise above pulled fingernails.

"State your business," the tough guy said with a "sit on it sideways" tone.

"Barter," Wall answered, harnessing Rhino's laid-back posture. With his body entirely covered, all he had to focus on was his voice and posture, which he hoped sounded and appeared lax. "We're a lookin' for motorcycles. I'm Wall. This big man, here, is Rhino. What can we call you?"

He scowled at them for a moment but relaxed the longer Wall and Rhino pretended to be casual. "I'm Tony."

"Nice to meet you, Tony." In actuality, it wasn't nice to meet him at all. Unlike the gun store owner, this man didn't seem like the kind of guy anyone would want to deal with. Wall's Spidey tingle practically itched.

"What do you have to trade?" His eyes lingered over their M4s and he licked his lips. "You aren't carrying much."

"We have diamonds." Wall dug into the pocket with the velvet baggy.

The idiot pumped his shotgun again, throwing away another shell. Dust puffed from the loading port, another point against the firearm's operability.

"Everyone needs 'em," Wall said casually. Trusting the SEAL to kill the man if things went tits up, he poured ten diamonds into his hands, an insane display of wealth before and after the fall. "Besides, your shotgun is rust-fucked."

His face twitched to concern before he masked it again.

"You should know," Wall continued. "Unsavory men might take advantage of you. Men like those *we* killed on the bridge." He emphasized the "we" to paint a picture of how dangerous the two of them were. The guy, who outwardly presented a tough-guy persona, blanched, looking back and forth between the would-be shoppers and the direction from which they'd come. The explosions on the bridge would have carried well past this dilapidated store.

Keeping his voice super friendly, he said, "Don't worry yourself. We're reasonable, law-abiding citizens." While spoken like sweet tea, undertones carried the warning label, "CAUTION: confrontation may cause bouts of death."

Tony nodded emphatically and said, "How-How can I help you?"

"Thanks for asking, friend. We want two rust-free bikes."

The man whistled. "That's a steep price, diamonds or no. And how do I know you won't stiff me?"

Wall smiled. "Tony, we're reasonable people. Let me demonstrate." After returning the diamonds to their black baggy, he tossed them over. The man nearly dropped his shotgun to catch it."

"See? Reasonable folks."

Rhino said, "Let me sweeten the deal." The SEAL pulled his P17 from its holster and quickly fired into the air twice. Wall's jaw nearly came off its hinges when he tossed it to the guy, who actually dropped his shotgun this time, bobbling Rhino's pistol like the world's worst wide receiver.

"Uh-uh," Tony stuttered. "Come in. Like I said, these may be worth a motorcycle, depending on what you're looking for." He waved the two of them inside. "After you."

Rhino walked in without a care in the world, though he had a serious limp to his step. The two of them gave off vibes that were a strange combination of deadly and wounded. The prior might provide a deterrent, but the latter would probably get them killed. Wall tried to watch Tony in his periphery without turning his head but couldn't keep him in view. He hoped like hell that the SEAL knew what he was doing by handing over his loaded pistol.

The showroom reeked of spilled gasoline, musky rust, and spoiled food. Most of the ceiling tiles laid on the floor, shattered and soaked. The row of motorbikes had fallen, all in decrepit states. *Shit on a stick,* he thought. *We handed over the diamonds and a loaded pistol for nothing. We've been–*

Click. It was the distinct sound of a dry fire, one that instilled both fear and intense anger within Wall. He turned with his M4 rising on autopilot and shot Tony from only a meter away. His 5.56 bullets operated as advertised, the first bullet expanding within the man's guts, the second through the stomach, and the third taking out the man's heart, the net result knocking him backward. As dear old Tony fell, Wall surprised himself by seizing Rhino's P17 before the guy hit the floor and more importantly, before blood coated it.

Without taking his eyes off Tony in case the rapidly dying man had any deadly tricks, Wall handed the pistol to Rhino. "Here."

Both immediately set about the task of cleaning their weapons. There would come a day when Alpha Bravo's guns would fail, either from too much cleaning with less-than-ideal cleaners or from specks of unseen blood. Wall just hoped that day would come long after everyone else's jammed up with rust.

Without tarnish or guilt over ending the man, Wall dug into the asshole's pocket and came away with his diamonds. He cleaned the bag and its contents before returning it to its "rightful place" next to his own bullet hole. For good measure, he spritzed himself down, adding to his essence of bleach cologne. In a matter of moments, he'd drained a good amount of his travel cleaner. On the one hand, over-cleaning was better than under-cleaning. On the other hand, they were plowing through disinfectant fast. If they planned on defending Renegade Genomix, they'd need to stockpile more cleaners.

"A clean kill," Rhino said, appraising the effectiveness of Wall shots. "But you gripped your trigger hand too tight in anticipation of the shot, so you fired a little early."

"Gotcha," Wall said, taking the criticism without complaint. Despite what should have been an adrenaline-filled moment, his heart rate had only spiked for a second and flattened out as soon as he pulled the trigger. "Hey, Rhino."

"Yeah?"

"Next time, it would be great if you didn't hand your gun over."

"Not to worry," the SEAL said in his deep voice. "The clip was empty. I wanted to test your response and give you more field practice."

"Field practice?" he said, squeezing his eyes shut. "Yeah, thanks for that. Good times."

With a closer look at the destroyed showroom, the only things that hadn't rusted through were clothes, plastic gas canisters, and other non-rustables. None of it was useful because everything was heavily contaminated or mildewy. Other than paying a high price for Aspen's dark purple body armor, their outing was a bust, or–

"What's wrong?" Rhino asked, sensing Wall's shift.

He slipped a piece of idea-forward jerky into his mouth with the firm belief that brains always worked better when fueled by cured meat. "That idiot wouldn't have stood his ground if he didn't have something worth the risk."

The big man nodded. "It tickles my undercarriage when you cognate."

Wall grinned. "Super-nerds are always overachievers when it comes to undercarriages."

"C'mon, rabbit, tickle your way to a conclusion sometime soon, won't you?"

He rolled out a spasm in his neck, then said, "This guy has a trailer out back. One prime for plundering."

"How in the devil's left nut could you possibly know that?"

"A hunch."

"Okay. Lead the way, Sherlock. I wanna see what you got."

Rather than expose themselves to more germs by walking through the smelly building, he backtracked and circled around, clearing each corner with Rhino's hand on his shoulder. Despite their shit-stick legs, they both moved smoothly, embracing the suck. Several times he found his shoulder slipping down but managed to pull it back up before the SEAL slapped it.

As they rounded the fourth corner into the back gravel yard, Wall signaled Rhino to look at the white two-story polyresin garage at its center. In contrast to the store, this synthetic enclosure showed zero outward signs of rust.

"An egghead is bound to be right once in a while," Rhino whispered, barely audible above the strengthening wind. "Don't let it go to your head." He nodded at the enclosure. "Show me how it's done."

In seconds, he cleared the outside with Rhino at his back, then proceeded to the entrance. The semi-transparent roof and siding let in plenty of light to see their reward. Nearly twenty offroad motorcycles of one variety or another were stacked in open-sided two-by-four crates that were sealed in plastic wrap.

"Clear," he announced.

"Papa likey-likey," Rhino said as he bound onto a double stack and cut the plastic wrap away. It was a bright white Honda XR 600R, a beast of a motorcycle that might have been big for almost anyone but him.

Finding a smaller but still overpowered yellow XR 400R at floor level, Wall shoved the upper bike off the top, momentarily forgetting how much his body ached. He bought a used 200 when he was twelve and wanted to upgrade to the 400 when he was seventeen but abandoned the idea when he went into the Army. It took the world going to rot to realize his dream of more power. After cutting the bike free of its plastic wrap and liberating it from its lumber encasement, he mounted up.

Rhino kickstarted his bike, and the massive engine roared like a white dragon, resonating inside the polyresin structure. The SEAL revved the motor and jumped off the upper box, landing with an awkward double bounce, nearly falling over on his trashed knee. He laughed maniacally.

"Let's ride, baby."

CHAPTER THIRTY-FOUR

After Rhino and Wall raced into Renegade Genomix's parking lot and killed their thunderous engines, Rhino yelled to the rooftop. "Where's the fire?"

On their way back, the unmistakable smell of smoke had grown stronger hand in hand with the rising winds. The fact that they had smelled it from over three kilometers away meant it wasn't a little thing. From her lookout atop Renegade Genomix, Plink said, "The fire started north by northwest about four clicks away. It's growing fast. Sustained winds at ten to fifteen kph with gusts in the thirties, all in our direction."

The quick blasts threatened to knock Wall off his bike half a dozen times between the bike shop and their bunker. With his large frame and lacking Rhino's mass, he was used to being a kite when it came to wind. In contrast, the SEAL was like an ICBM missile, plowing through the gusts like they weren't there.

"How long do we have?" Wall asked.

Even from twenty meters away, the pallor of Plink's face and the dark circles under her eyes told of a woman pushing through a hefty load of pain. "Could be half an hour. Could be several hours. Either way, we evac ASAP. Wall, you and Kayla grab anything you think is vital from the lab. If it doesn't fit in your pack, it doesn't come."

"Acknowledged," Wall said. He quickly sprayed down the motorcycle, relying more on a solid overdose of fluid and less on what barely counted as a wipe-down.

"Rhino, disinfect and pack up all our tactical gear. Yours, mine, and Walls."

In his characteristic, deep rumble, Rhino said, "Consider it done."

"What about me?" Aspen asked from up top.

In the short pause left by Plink, Wall said, "Keep watch. Expect panicking refugees to turn even more feral. And monitor the fire."

"Acknowledged." In the past day, the teen worked hard to assimilate into Alpha Bravo. While there was no substitute for the decades that the spec-ops badasses spent learning their trade or the technical training that he and Kayla had, she'd shown herself to be resilient and adaptable and, more importantly, a survivor.

"I gotta clean up and change," Wall thought aloud.

"Typical man," Plink said. "Getting dolled up for the ball."

Faking injury, he placed his hand on his chest. "Hey, now. Looking this delicate doesn't just happen. It takes preparation."

"Get moving, pretty boy."

At the back entrance, he considered not suiting up because they probably weren't coming back, but by the off chance they were, he took as much precaution as he could while holding to a timeline shorter than thirty minutes. Inside, the lab remained almost unchanged from when Wall entered it for the first time, which was to say, pristine and untouched by rust. All of their precautions paid off. The problem was that nature was about to make their diligence meaningless.

As soon as he touched the zipper of the inner lab's plastic door, Kayla noticed his presence and yelled, "Out! Now! What do you think you're doing?"

Ignoring her, he unzipped the flimsy bubble door. "We're abandoning ship. Time to pack up."

"What? No." She shook her head, eyes full of darts and daggers. "We can't leave. I'm on the verge of a suppressant for the HIV strain."

"Suppressant?" Wall asked, annoyed and dismayed. She hadn't mentioned anything about a suppressant, a medicine that would minimize the effects of Towning's HIV strain, not cure or inoculate the patient. Suppressants were poor substitutes, needing repetitive doses, not just one-and-done. They required a lifetime of taking meds. The technological infrastructure needed for a suppressant was far greater than a cure or vaccine, which would need more hard-to-resource materials and better distribution systems. He instantly recognized what happened. Kayla told him what he wanted to hear while doing her own thing, following her interests rather than doing what was best for humanity.

All the vaccines were in a clear plastic bag on the top shelf of the inner lab, well within Wall's reach but barely within hers. Already knowing the answer, he asked, "Did you even try any of the vaccines?"

"No," she said, the implied "obviously" communicated by her tone.

He stepped forward, only a twitch away from slapping a woman, something his upbringing told him to never do. *Focus on what's important,* he thought. "There's a fire. Either we leave or we die, if not by flame, then by smoke. We have to protect our research."

Eyes wide, she flinched at his use of the word, *our.* "I'm not going any-where."

He snatched the vaccines off the shelf and shoved them into his pack, thinking, *if only I had a good syringe full of valium.* He mentally kicked himself for not thinking of it earlier.

She attempted to grab the vaccines from Wall, saying, "Those are mine. They don't go anywhere without me, and I'm not leaving." Her newly acquired agoraphobia was going to get him killed.

"Kayla, consider it a backup plan. A contingency. We'll come back if Eugene survives."

"Fine," she said in a way that meant it was *not* okay at all. "Now, get out of my lab."

Not trusting her, especially now that she'd been lying to him about her focus, he said, "I'm here until we're ready to go."

Her cheek trembled and her lashes vibrated in a half-fearful and half-angry snarl. She grumbled something he couldn't make out.

"Kayla, let me help you."

"No!" she yelled, throwing her arms wide to keep him away from her bench. Her single word told of terror, fear for her life, and fear for her life's work. They stood, him looking down and her up at him. Letting her hands fall, she said, "Fine. But I'll do it. You stay back." With the slow, purposeful motions of a meticulous lab guru, she gradually filled his backpack with samples and vaccines. He noted that she didn't prepare any of her notebooks, the most important aspect of her research.

"Back up the computer," she said about three minutes into the evac, handing him a thumb drive. The data would be almost as valuable as her notebooks if Towning's computers were still functional.

About a minute into copying the files, his Spidey senses picked up on something wrong in his peripheral vision. When he looked, Kayla depressed the plunger of a clear syringe into her wrist. The motion was smooth, practiced, and too fast for Wall to stop.

Quickly recovering from a stunned mental belch, he said, "What in the bona fide nut-sack of hell are you doing?"

Defiant yet shaky, she said, "Isn't it obvious? I injected myself with the suppressant. It needs testing."

"What-what?" His eyes bulged. The sixteen-car pileup in his mind clogged the pathways for a moment, during which she affixed a small bandage to the injection site and disposed of the syringe. "Kayla, you didn't..." In the era of the FDA and all the other three-letter agencies, there were best practices to keep pharmaceuticals from killing human subjects. While some red tape might have been over the top, very few people died because of well-vetted medications.

She ignored him and jotted something down in a notebook.

His concern turned to anger. "How could you? You put everything at risk. What if you damaged your liver, kidneys, or heart? We can't risk your life." He couldn't believe he was about to say this. "Humanity depends on us—on you."

"Either I die in here or in the chaos out there," she said while taking her pulse. "I'd rather rely on my abilities than yours. Just look at you."

"Kayla..."

She tuned him out, scribbling in her notebook.

He waved his hand in front of her face.

She swatted it away.

"Kayla."

"I'm not talking to you."

"We need to leave right now." She represented their greatest hope of some recovery from Towning's downfall. He needed her. Alpha Bravo needed her. The world needed her. She could be as much of a primadonna as she wanted, but he wasn't about to let her stay and die from smoke inhalation.

The backup dinged, and he removed the thumb drive.

"Grab your notebooks," he barked, imitating a drill sergeant. "We leave now."

"No," she said, looking as if she might slap him.

Switch gears, he told himself. Attempting to lure her with logic, he said, "Kayla, we'll come back when the lab survives. Then you can continue your research."

"No! It's here or nowhere. I can't go out there. I can't."

Taking a different tack, he said, "You and I helped cause this mess. We owe it to the world to stop it. If you're dead, we can't do that."

Her face contorted, and she slapped him across the cheek. It wasn't a surprise. In fact, he had hoped she would and suppressed his instinct to block her feeble attack. By resorting to violence, it gave him an excuse to do what needed doing. He extended his long arm to hold her back while loading her notebooks into his pack.

"No!" she screamed, swinging at him wildly as he stiff-armed her. She changed strategies and scraped at his arm ineffectually, her short lab-friendly fingernails, blue lab gloves, and his long-sleeve shirt declawing her enough to ignore. As uncoordinated as a kid in a potato sack, she tried kicking him, only to fall on her ass. "You can't! They're mine."

"I can and I will," he said calmly as he zipped up his pack.

She stood slowly and dusted off her nearly assless rump with a few pats. As if he didn't anticipate it, she ran at him, or rather, at his pack. Using her momentum against her, he crouched low and twisted so he could dangle her over his shoulder like a fireman or father with an angry child. While the turn and squat maneuver came with the price of a thousand grievances from his muscles and joints, it worked, and he didn't collapse. If she had been more than a waif, he probably would have fallen on his ass.

An animalistic shriek filled the clean room, her legs pedaled uselessly in the air, and her arms pounded on his back, lacking the umph that Aspen would deliver, particularly because they landed on his body armor. "Let me down! Let me down!"

He might have laughed at their comical situation had the restoration of humanity not depended on his ability to extricate her from the lab. As he turned with her over his shoulder, her flailing feet caught the inner lab's flimsy plastic divider, tearing down the bio-curtain more with each kick.

"Damn," he said, unable to hear himself above her screams and cries for help. If they could return after the fire swept by, he had just compromised the inner lab. "Keep still," he growled. The irony wasn't lost on him. She tore down her own inner sanctum. "F'n tragic."

As a future olive branch, he paused in the outer vestibule to collect a few boxes of soylent. By the time he reached the backside of the building, his leg barely held him upright. Her screams raised in pitch, so shrill on his abused ears that it grated on his bones.

"What's going on?" Lucas asked, tilting his head up innocently the way only little ones can.

"We're leaving." Wall didn't know what else to tell the kid. "Come with me."

"Why is she yelling?"

"She's been a bad girl," he said. "We're going on a trip and she doesn't want to come."

"No!" Kayla wailed. "I can't be out here!"

"You can, and you will," he yelled, shifting to keep her from slipping.

"Sit Rep?" Plink said as he rounded the corner, as she rubbed down a new green Yamaha ultra-light motorbike from who-knows-where.

Wall stuck with the simplest explanation. "Kayla refused to evac. I refused to leave her. I won out."

When he stopped at Rhino's oversized bike, he gently set Kayla down. Predictably, she immediately tried to bolt, but Wall had other plans and grabbed her white coveralls from behind and easily held her in place. Carefully, he leveraged her onto her butt again, then pointed at the ground. "Sit."

She kept struggling and yelling incoherently like a wild animal in need of her burrow.

"Sit," he repeated. "Don't make me shoot you in the foot."

She froze in place, then curled into the fetal position, hands over her head, whimpering and pathetic, the opposite of a survivor. He was glad to see that she at least had some ability to understand. That had to count for something. As if talking to an ornery dog, he commanded, "Stay."

While keeping Kayla in his peripheral vision, he organized his gear and filled the remaining space he had in his pack, sanitizing each bit as he went. Always sanitizing.

The most important gear they were leaving behind–other than the lab–was their stockpile of disinfectant. During his ride back from the autosports store, he had recalled how to make high-percentage ethanol, an ideal cleaner, with the age-old process of fermenting grains and distilling alcohol. With a good amount of copper, he could create a still for potent moonshine, which would have "auxiliary benefits." The renewable nature of alcohol could also give them a long-term staple for bartering.

About sixty heartbeats from departure, Kayla started flailing again. Wall closed his eyes in frustration as she threw her temper tantrum. When he looked again, he realized she wasn't kicking in protest. She was mid-seizure, convulsing and rigid from face to toe, gurgling. He quickly knelt at her side and gently protected her head from ramming into the ground.

"This will pass," he told her gently, wishing he had known she was epileptic. He might have handled things differently.

She abruptly stopped convulsing, unblinking, eyes unfocused. He listed her stats as he went through a first-responder evaluation. "No breathing, no arterial pulse, no eye dilation." None of the aspects that belonged to the living. She was, for all intents and purposes, dead.

"Starting compressions."

He pumped her chest to the tune of "Shit, shit, shit," in imitation of Metallica's "Nothing Else Matters." He was supposed to use the Beegees song, "Stayin' Alive," but hated it so much he could never bring himself to use it as a metronome.

"What happened?" Plink asked, kneeling at his side.

"Seizure." Pump, pump, pump. "She was laying there." Pump, pump, pump. "Started shaking violently." Pump, pump, pump. "She fucking crapped out."

Plink asked, "Can you save her?"

The image of her plunging the syringe into her arm surfaced and he stopped CPR, knowing exactly what happened. "Gah!" In another reality, one where Towning never carried out his plan, she might have survived with the immediate application of CPR and a quick ambulance ride to the hospital. However, in Wall's universe, hospitals were ground zero for rusting, and there would be no help for her.

He clenched his fists and bunched his trembling lips together, blinking away tears of frustration. "Stupid, stupid, stupid!" He wanted to hit something and almost bashed Kayla out of frustration. "You self-centered, conceited..."

Professional and outwardly calm other than the one-two he was getting used to, Plink caught his attention and asked, "Did you obtain what we need?"

He didn't answer right away, eyes closed, the smell of smoke growing stronger.

She cupped his fist and repeated herself, with a bit of sympathy leaking into her cool demeanor. "Did you obtain what we need?"

This time, he patted his pack. "Yeah." What he didn't say was that it wouldn't do much good without Kayla.

"We move out in two minutes," she hollered drill sergeant-style. "Rhino, get Nellibi." She cupped her mouth and yelled, "Aspen, come down."

"Acknowledged," responded the teen-turning-miniature warrior.

After extricating himself from his white lab onesie, Wall hefted his pack to his front side so that Aspen would have space on the XR 400R to sit behind him.

Plink pulled down his mask and kissed him. "Kayla wasn't your fault."

He said, "I know," even though he didn't believe her. If he caught her before she injected the suppressant into her wrist... If he'd handled her more gently... If he'd known she was epileptic, if she was in fact, epileptic. *Pull it together,* he ordered himself. Based on the darkening sky and the increasing smell of ash, there wasn't much time to escape. Swallowing his frustration with Kayla and himself, two words gonged in his head. *Choices made.*

Aspen waited for him to start the bike before hopping on. The pistol on her hip and the purple bulletproof vest had transformed her into a miniature warrior. *No,* he decided. *She was a fighter long before they met.* Now, her outside reflected her core.

"Wrap your arms tight around me. No, here." He placed her hands around his belly, under the backpack. "There."

"We're moving," Plink said once she strapped Lucas to her front, and Rhino did the same with Nellibi. "I'm in the lead. Rhino, you're cleanup."

CHAPTER THIRTY-FIVE

Wall followed Plink off the road when they reached their downed helicopter, which could have been there for a century and not looked any worse. While Wall paid respects to the dead, Rhino collected a bundle of gear he had left behind, hidden inside a burned-out cavity of a tree.

Wall stretched his neck and leg, both of which cramped up during their short ride from Renegade Genomix. He didn't care for the prospect of riding four more hours, more if they encountered similar levels of abandoned traffic jams. The decision to abandon Renegade Genomix permanently was decided by Kayla's disastrous death. Between the glowing embers that fell around them as they rode and the draw of what they might find in Towning's lab, the decision was made all the easier.

With Lucas at his side, he returned to Plink who was looking at a map with a route marked in red with an "X" on the coordinates from the note. Standing inside her personal bubble, he asked, "How are you doing?"

"Like a pig in shit," she said with a false smile.

"Ha," he chortled. "But really, how are you?"

She faced him, searching his eyes. "You don't want to know."

He held her gaze. "Yes, I do."

"I warn you. You're opening a can of worms." Her face pulled taught with a complex combination of emotions he couldn't piece together. "I think my kidney is getting worse. I'm afraid we failed to preserve the future of humanity, demoralized by Kayla's loss."

She paused, and he let her take her time. Lucas ran to Rhino, who threw him into the air, both of them laughing.

"You must know how angry I am at Kayla for taking such a stupid risk. How could she?"

He nodded and pulled her hand into his.

"I want to kiss you again, which seems silly given everything that's happening."

He pulled her into a hug.

"Weeee!" Lucas yelled as Rhino threw him again.

"I'm stupidly committed to these kids. It goes against my training. They're operational risks. I'm supposed to leave them behind."

He patted her back.

"And so much more." He looked down at her while she looked up at him, her eyes glistening with half-formed tears.

Confused by which emotion to latch onto, he asked, "How can you carry all that and not collapse into a black hole?"

She snorted and pulled off her yellow shooting glasses to wipe away the tears with a blue-gloved hand. He almost pointed out that she contaminated herself but kept his big damn mouth shut. Inwardly he cursed Towning for the thousandth time. *You weaponized tears, you bastard.*

Plink sniffed, put her glasses back on, and she sprayed her hand. "Don't worry about me. I'm spec ops, Wall. We're tough and not a little bit crazy."

He smiled. "Kissing me, huh?"

"Yeah," she said, sniffing again, her eyes communicating something Wall couldn't decipher. She took on a grin, waved her hands down her body as if on display, and playfully said, "If you can handle all this..."

He leaned in and whispered in her ear. "I'm game." They kissed, her lips salty from tears, his hands around her waist. How she could be a badass one moment, then cry the next, then kiss passionately, defied the laws of nature.

"Get a room," Aspen said from behind, her voice heavily laced with disgust. "This isn't the nature channel, you know?"

Wall kissed Plink again, extending their closeness for a few seconds longer before they jointly withdrew. She twirled her hand overhead and said, "Mount up."

Then they were back on the road, alternating between open spaces where they throttled up and backups where they had to carefully dodge between infected vehicles. Plink and Rhino appraised every potential risk, prepared to act with lethal force at an instant's notice. Wall, while a good rider and an improving shot, wasn't used to a front pack or a passenger rider, even one as light as Aspen, so he mostly focused on avoiding car carcasses, slamming into road cuts, or flying off tall cliffs.

Wall slipped through time on occasion, coming out of a blink in fear. Each time he came to, he muttered something like, "I shouldn't be riding." But he kept his fears to himself. When he wasn't slipped out of memories, his mind wandered in and out of daydreams too often for comfort. He should have been focused on the present but found himself contemplating the future and the impossibility of finishing their mission. Kayla truly screwed them, a devastating blow that would have consequences that would ripple through time. She had been invaluable for the years to come. If Nellibi couldn't recover, his only hope was to study his ass off for a decade, maybe more, to learn what he needed before making headway.

During the empty stretches of road, questions chipped away at the inside of his skull. Would Towning's lab still be there? Would the cabin blow up with him inside? Could he keep the lab disease-free long enough to accomplish anything meaningful? Even if they created a vaccine, would the lab have enough materials to inoculate even a small population?

The first hour passed and they hadn't shot anyone, and nobody shot them, a mark in the bonus column as far as Wall was concerned. The routine of alternating between driving fast on empty roads and slowly while weaving between backups got easier with time, granting more room for his brain to haze over and dwell on possibilities, neither of which was conducive to surviving the here and now.

So, when the sound of gunfire from ahead knocked his senses back into focus, he was ill-prepared to respond. "Crank it!" Plink yelled over her shoulder, commanding and strong, leading the way through a particularly bad snaggle of cars. Seconds later, he nearly crashed when he looked to the side, where a man screamed on the ground, curled up, sure that his howls were a result of Plink's drawn P17.

A short while later, Wall sprang back into reality, nearly plowing into Plink when she stopped cold in the middle of a particularly bad traffic jam and yelled, "Turn around! Go back!" Wall's first thought was, *motorcycles don't have a reverse gear.* If Aspen weren't on his back, he might have tried to peel out and spin the bike, but it would have been risky even then. Awkwardly, he weaved past Plink and looped around a rust pile of a car.

That was when the first stone, a fist-sized piece of river rock, hit his forearm like a double-hard baseball, propelled by a good arm and the aid of gravity, nearly making him pull away from the handle grip, which would have sent him into the fishbones of a minivan. Instead, his hand twisted back on the grip, inadvertently revving the engine and rocketing the powerful bike forward, popping a wheelie from which he barely recovered. Aspen would have fallen off the seat if she weren't clamped onto Wall with her abnormal strength for someone so small. More rocks flew his way as he fled for safety, a nearly head-sized mass of sandstone hitting his good shoulder, and he nearly drove into the plastic bed of a wheelless yellow wheelbarrow.

"Piece of..."

From behind, rapid gunfire popped off along with a series of yells and screams, angry, afraid, and wounded.

"Eee!" Aspen yelled at such a high pitch that it gripped his core. Her hold around his belly momentarily loosened, then tightened even stronger than before.

A man dressed in a gray suit with a freshly pressed button-down shirt and red tie stepped into Wall's path with his arm cocked back, ready to throw a rock. Wall skidded to a halt with his front brake kicking in much harder than the rear, accidentally spinning him sideways. Struggling to keep the bike from falling over, Wall didn't see the throw but felt it on his helmet, a direct blow, which momentarily knocked his senses blurry.

He drew his pistol and fired at the double vision of the fuzzy-looking man, employing every bit of training that Rhino taught him over the last day or so. Awkwardly twisted at the torso as he was, Wall missed three times in a row. At least the man cowered behind a nearly pristine Subaru, so Wall could holster the pistol and pull the throttle, veering around the dust of a car and away into the clearing beyond. As he picked up speed, a rock hit the front spokes and spun off, glancing off his heavy boot.

Then he was out of the tangled mess of cars, away from the rock-throwing saboteurs.

With shots continuing back at the ambush, he skidded to a stop and torqued his body to see Aspen. "Are you okay?"

"Yeah," she said through what sounded like clenched teeth, now holding her cheek.

He hopped off the bike, nearly knocking her off with an involuntary kick, and only managed to soften the blow by falling onto all fours. Jumping up faster than a bouncy ball, he checked on her, peeling back her hand and desert scarf. His anger ignited upon seeing the redness and rapid swelling on the right side of her face.

"Ahhhh!" someone—no, multiple people—yelled from up the road as they ran toward him.

"Slow is smooth," he told himself as he raised his M4. "And smooth is fast." He aimed at the closest of three people running at him, the suit-wearing man who had perfectly quaffed hair, a clean shave, and fairy-tale good looks tarnished by a snarl. Wall raised his shoulder, kept both eyes open, leaned forward, and shot, center of mass. The banker or lawyer fell forward and face-plowed to a stop, creating a red skid mark, never to stand again.

Wall set the crosshairs on the next fast-moving rust zombie, a stereotypical soccer mom with a dark bob haircut, oversized sunglasses, a pilates enthusiast's body, and a huge diamond ring. If not for too much plastic surgery, her expression might have matched her rage-filled yell. She wound up to throw a rock mid-run. After double-checking his form, Wall pulled the trigger. Her silicon-enhanced chest flew backward, and her feet momentarily left the ground. She was dead before she hit the pavement.

"Never bring a rock to a gunfight."

The third oncomer, a good-looking blond teen who wore a green-and-white Sheldon High School track shirt, probably a sophomore, leapt over the woman, then canted his arm, preparing to pitch a fastball. With remorse, Wall shot. The boy stopped, his arms flopped to his side, and looked down at his chest disbelievingly. A hole punctured his left lung near the heart. Making a ruthlessly merciful decision, Wall shot again, offering the kid a quick death via a bullet to the forehead.

"Mercy," he said.

In about five heartbeats, he killed a family, man, woman, and child. "Stupid!" he yelled at them. It wasn't his fault that they grossly miscalculated their prey. Self-defense had dictated that he end them. More percussions from Plink and Rhino told of similarly necessary deaths. He recited one of his dad's sayings. "Never lay a trap if you can't handle the catch."

"Acknowledged," Aspen said as if the comment was intended for her. Instead of a hurt girl crying in fear, she was a small warrior with her pistol drawn and pointed down, the picture of preparedness. While she might have been physically capable and skilled enough to kill, she was too young to comprehend the significance. *No*, he contradicted himself. *There isn't an age limit on self-defense anymore.* The time would soon come, and she had to be conditioned to see and understand death. In a sick way, this skirmish was good for her, exposing her to what would come down the road.

He scanned in a 360, pivoting on his good leg, expecting a new assailant to materialize. Up the road, gunfire continued, quick double-taps from the tier-one operators. He awkwardly mounted up again, angered, amped, and itching to ride back into the fray. If not for Aspen, he might have re-entered the skirmish, though the net effect probably would have reduced Plink and Rhino's effectiveness, splitting their attention between defending their passengers, him, and killing their saboteurs.

Accepting his limitations and unaware of the situation up ahead, he said, "Know thy enemy and know thyself."

"Acknowledged," the mini warrior said again.

The last of the gunfire told of Plink and Rhino's final victims. A moment later, the SEAL sped back to Wall and Aspen, his right hand on the throttle and his left ready to shoot any late-coming threat with his P17. Nellibi was bleeding and slumped over unconscious, only held upright by the straps around the big man, who didn't heed her comatose state. Showing no outward signs of injury, not even his messed up leg, he asked, "Are you guys okay?"

"Yeah, but Aspen–" Wall started to say.

"I'm fine."

"Tough as nails," Rhino said, pride in his voice. "When we hear the signal, drive through the trap as fast as you can. I think we got them all, but you never know."

"What's the signal?" Aspen asked as she tightened her grip around Wall.

Both men started to say, "You'll know it–"

Boom! An explosion rocked their ears and resonated in their chests.

"–when you hear it." Rhino finished. "Now, go."

Wall throttled up until he couldn't go faster without smacking into rust piles. Plink waved him past a gap in a barrier that their ambushers had constructed of decaying metal scrap. The stone-age bandits chose a road cut with nearly vertical sides, a natural kill box. The slain men and women looked like everyday folk, decent people driven to drastic measures in horrible times.

Behind the roadblock, the spoils of the parasitic tribe resembled those on the bridge to the motorsports store. Suitcases, bags, clothes of all sizes, rusted gear, the works. Fifty paces later, amid a tangle of car-like lumps, they passed a huddle of cowering kids, from toddlers to a kid about Aspen's age.

"Stupid."

The parents not only risked their own lives but gambled the wellbeing of their children too. If he could have, he would have stopped and helped them. But, like in Africa, he couldn't. There were too many of them and he didn't have the resources to make a dent in their helplessness. Without adults to protect them, they would probably pass into the rust, or at least most of them, and their family lines would die out in the Darwinian struggle to survive.

Another fifty meters down, the smell of rotting flesh told of the effectiveness of the stone-age saboteurs' strategy. With over a hundred kills, they likely grew confident in their superiority over normal folks, a level of success that led them to trust their ability to overcome any prey. They couldn't have predicted the deadly skills of the SEAL and Delta Force operatives nor Wall's rapidly improving marksmanship.

And then they were in the clear, away from danger, on the lookout for the next threat with Plink returning to the bronze tip of their spear. About a minute later, she pulled behind a cluster of trees that mostly blocked the view from the road. She hopped off the Yamaha, set Lucas down, and dashed to Wall and Aspen.

"Are you okay?"

"Fine," Wall answered as he dismounted and pulled Aspen's mask down to check on her again. He could feel Plink's anger blazing beside him, adding to his own fury. Poking at her jaw, he said, "Nothing's broken. It won't be pretty, but she'll be fine." He was impressed that, while the teen's eyes grew glassy wet at his prodding, she didn't cry, yelp, or cringe.

When he was done, Plink pulled Aspen into a hug, then laid on her thick Mexican accent. "Nothin' tougher than a man except a woman. You remember that, Aspen."

The teen smiled through the pain. "I will."

"Momo!" Lucas screamed.

Wall instantly knew what happened, not how, but what. Rhino laid her down on her side, her normally comatose eyes turned another level of dull. A short-shafted, stone-tipped fiberglass arrow stuck out of her throat. Blood ran down Rhino's front.

"No," he whispered, his Adam's apple bobbing as his mouth went dry, both upset for the kiddo and for the future of humanity.

The big man picked up the kid with one arm over his shoulder before he reached her, careful not to get blood on him. With the other hand, he sprayed himself down. Wall and Rhino closed the distance between them with long strides, both ignoring the pain in their legs. They transferred the boy without word so Rhino could really clean himself and Wall could hold the boy close.

"I'm so sorry," Wall whispered with two meanings as he wrapped the boy in his long arms. He regretted that Lucas had lost both of his mothers in such a close timespan. *Such loss.* And just as deeply, he felt guilty that his research contributed toward their deaths, the consequences of which would have an untold reproduction on the boy's future worldview. He knew it wasn't his fault. It was Townings doing. *But if...*

"Come with me," he whispered, though he didn't give the boy a chance to do anything but. He carried the boy to his mother and set him down on his knee a pace away. Wall had no idea whether it was better to allow Lucas to see Nellibi or shelter him from her death. A few days ago, he would have taken the boy away, but post-rusting, things were different.

The kid tried to wiggle out of Wall's hold, arms extended toward the dead woman. "Momo!"

"It'll be okay," he said outwardly while saying the opposite inwardly. Nothing could be further from the truth. Nellibi's death wasn't only a blow for the boy. It was a blow for all of mankind.

After an interminable amount of time, the little guy stopped wailing and turned into Wall's chest, sobbing quietly with a case of the hiccups.

A while later, Plink set her hand on Wall's shoulder. "Okay, boys. We need you to spray down. I took care of the bike and your pack."

Wall stood and walked around a tree to where they couldn't see Nellibi and doused them in a thick layer. Lucas didn't protest, but he didn't stop sobbing either, though he ran out of rusting tears.

When he returned to his bike, the boy in his arms again, he checked on Aspen's chin and whispered, "I know you're tough and all, but how are you holding up? Not physically. Emotionally."

"Wall, no demons in the verse could shake me."

"Amen, sister," Plink said.

Not realizing he was speaking, Wall mused aloud. "The kids get to me every time."

Rhino solemnly responded that "They don't deserve the repercussions of their parents. History abounds with unending battles momentarily interrupted by peace won through bloodshed. War harms the kid. The kid grows up. The adult causes war."

"How do you handle it?" Aspen said as if asking for a friend.

"Me?" said the SEAL. "I'm not the person to ask. I bottle everything up and take my anger out on adults, perpetuating the cycle. You, Wall?"

While petting Lucas's head, which now rested on his shoulder, he took ten heartbeats to consider. "It's about protecting the person who has your back and the others who have your loved ones' backs. When it comes to life and death, nobody can handle more than that. In the times of peace that Rhino talked about, you can act in the service of a broader population. But I'm not the one you should ask. We see how much good my way of thinking did. The end of everything."

She turned to Plink and asked, "How about you?"

"Morality isn't black or white or gray. It is all the colors of the rainbow. Right and wrong are not an end-to-end scale but an interconnected knot of confusion that can't be unwound. If examined closely enough, morality vanishes in the face of love, love for family, love of country, love of a partner, any kind of love."

"You guys sound like philosophers," Aspen said.

"Many warriors are," the SEAL said. "It's an occupational hazard. Some were the best thinkers, like Marcus Aurelius. Others were the worst, like Hitler's Ernst Bergmann. My favorite is–"

"Time to get on the road again," Plink said, cutting short what was no doubt going to be a history lesson.

CHAPTER THIRTY-SIX

As the sun began to set, Plink pulled off the road, forming her own trail into the woods. This provided a new set of challenges for Wall, who didn't want to buck Aspen off the back. It was one thing on mostly smooth roads with avoidable potholes, but here, the uneven ground didn't mix with fatigue and too many wounds to count. Plink didn't rush him, and Rhino followed, giving Wall enough room to go at his own pace. At one point, it would have been faster for Aspen to hop off and walk, and he almost suggested it when Plink cut her engine and hopped down. "This is home for two hours. Hydrate, eat, and rest."

Aspen hopped off and said, "I was about to die on that thing." She stretched out like a kitten. "I need my own bike."

Wall had similar thoughts but kept them to himself, instead reciting something his dad used to say, "We have what we have. Nothing more. Nothing less." A bit late, he remembered that he hated when his old man repeated that line. In the last thirty-six hours, ever since he met Aspen, he'd been quoting his dad more than in the prior year. Either the strain was getting to him, his bashed mind was relying on deep-seated instincts, or she brought it out in him.

With a fifty-fifty-split of grouchiness and sarcasm, she said, "Obvious much?"

Wall took Lucas, who was sound asleep, into his arms as the fog rolled in so Plink could walk the perimeter of a natural camp formed by a ring of large trees. The thickening mist and a strong breeze chilled them faster than a blizzard, a damp cold. The heavy dew quickly covered their clothes and gear.

"Can we make a fire?" Aspen asked, already shivering and hopping about for warmth.

"The best security is invisibility," Rhino said. "And that ain't fire."

Wall handed her his sleeping bag. Within seconds, she pulled the cocoon up around her and sat at the base of a giant Douglas fir. Kneeling at her side, he whispered, "Share some heat with Lucas." After a flash of defiance from Aspen, she nodded and unzipped her sleeping bag enough for him to slide the boy in without waking him.

Wall divvied up portions of hickory Goose, which they ate greedily. They all needed the energy. With a mostly full belly, he leaned against the dry side of Aspen's fir tree and tried not to shiver.

Rhino, their massive sentinel, the only one outwardly unaffected by the cold, began a world history lesson from the lens of war and warriors. He would have made an excellent professor, weaving tales of intrigue and conflict through time and drawing connections and themes between cultures and governments.

Aspen settled against Wall, nuzzling under his left arm, her sleeping bag insulating him from that side. Before long, Rhino's deep voice and chosen subject drew Aspen into a twitching slumber. Plink tucked herself under Wall's other arm, claiming the need for heat as an excuse. Soon, her steady breathing and cozied-in state told him that she had also fallen asleep. The worry he felt for Plink and her kidney injury shouldn't have been far less considering the time they'd known each other, but things were how they were.

Nearly warm, he half listened to Rhino, who wasn't deterred by three-fourths of his audience falling asleep and the remaining fourth barely paying attention.

He tried not to read too much into the welcomed situation, an instant family of sorts. A new, instantly bonded ladyfriend. Two young wards. A giant uncle type. All warriors in one way or another. At the very least, their situation demonstrated a heightened level of trust.

Aspen occupied a foreign part of his mind. She attached to him quickly, something he assumed she didn't often do while moving from foster home to foster home. The skeptical demon on his shoulder told him that she was playing him, relying on years of experience in the art of manipulating adults to find safety. The hopeful demon on the other shoulder said that she was the genuine deal. He reasoned that Plink must have read her and wouldn't have let her join Alpha Bravo if it was all a lie.

The last few days created bonds like those who he served with in the Army, particularly the friendships forged in battle. Once in the family, you were always in. Alpha Bravo would ride the downfall as one.

"The downfall," he whispered. The demolition of society came faster than he thought possible, faster than anyone did. The zombie apocalypse had always been the joke, slowly spreading but gradually amassing biters like an erf function, then slowing down again as less and less human food became available. After some amount of time, the survivors would figure out ways to combat the zombies and eventually thrive, rebounding with gradually improving tactics and technologies, one day recovering their position as the apex species.

Deadly diseases worried everyone throughout history, a subject Rhino would no doubt expound upon someday. With Wall's understanding of manipulated DNA, he had been certain that COVID-19 was made by scientists in Wuhan for study. He blamed the facility's well-known lax safety protocols, not malicious intent, but it was easy to imagine someone going all Towning on the world. Even if a disease killed ninety-nine percent of the population, those with immunity would one day bounce back and retake their technological advantage.

Nuclear war stood out as an inevitable extinction-level event. Ever since the United States demonstrated atomic military power in Japan, governments occasionally threatened each other. Mutually assured destruction deescalated situations thus far, but things eventually would have gotten out of hand, not a matter of if, only a matter of time. Nuclear downfall would have devastated the world population, but in that case, pockets of society could have repopulated Earth and clawed their way back to their prior technological level.

Global warming would have displaced coastal populations and endangered crops, but humans would have migrated and adapted as they always did. With the brightest minds working on the problem, the damage could have been slowed and then stopped someday by scientists and engineers pushing toward the environmental singularity. Again, humans would survive and eventually thrive.

Towning's diseases ensured that humans could only recover to bronze-age sophistication, a population-limiting attack. And, if Wall didn't find a way to counteract the diseases, a giant "if," they might never return to pre-downfall capabilities. The time of iron, steel, and electronics would pass into mythology.

"No pressure, Wall,"

Plink stirred but didn't wake.

His minimal but only real hope was that other scientists around the world were working on vaccines and cures. He couldn't be alone in his pursuit of an end to Towning's pandemic. The problem was that the old man would have attacked most labs capable of combating the diseases. And few, if any, would have a spec-ops duo to defend them.

"Too many ifs," he mouthed.

A dark thought occurred to him. What if Towning was a closet racist? He was half-German, half-Indian, wasn't he? Would he have ensured natural immunity for those with similar genetics? Wall couldn't put it past a man willing to unleash the rusting diseases.

Around the time Wall's eyes drooped, Rhino stirred the four of them. In an otherwise pitch-black forest, the only light was the dim green of the big man's glow stick. "Do we have to?" Aspen asked while shifting a Lucas-shaped lump to her side. "It's fucking dark out. Witch's titties wouldn't go out in this cold."

Wall shimmied out from between the two women. "You sound like Jimmy Twenty."

"Jimmy Twenty?"

"There is always one guy in a platoon who cusses on a randomized loop. For mine, it was Jimmy Twenty. Swearing was like poetry to him. If there was a church of profanity, he would be an archbishop."

"Yeah," Rhino said as he plucked Lucas off the ground and handed him over to Plink. When he lifted Aspen, he spun her over his shoulders. "Johnson was that way in my unit. He even swore in his sleep."

Rhino handed Wall ski goggles, saying, "Christmas came early." Unlike their shape suggested, this matte-black device was heavy like a laptop. Four lenses at the goggle's corners told him what they were. "Night vision goggles."

"Do I get one?" Aspen asked with excitement.

Rhino handed her a pair. "Of course, my dear. But keep them turned off and packed away unless you absolutely need them. We need to save batteries and minimize contamination."

"Yes!" She said, then immediately disregarded his words and strapped them over her helmet, bouncing up and down. "This is way shway! Weeeee!" She ran around a tree and cartwheeled back.

The immersive nature of the goggles required a moment to grow accustomed to. While the fog impaired his view, he was amazed to not only see a flat display but a three-dimensional combination of thermal and light-enhanced vision. Not as good as sunlight but ridiculously impressive, another example of humankind's technological pinnacle.

"Time to move out," she announced after bonking Aspen and Wall's helmet with her own.

By the time they mounted up, many of the kinks in Wall's muscles had worked themselves out. Unfortunately, the fog hugged him in its cold embrace, portending an even colder ride. He envied Lucas, who Plink managed to strap to her inside the sleeping bag.

Then they rode away through the mist without headlights. In the cold, Wall appreciated the thin surgical gloves and his frontpack, both of which cut down on the wind and the dew.

In the dark, they passed groups on the side of the road, unwisely within hearing distance of less scrupulous travelers, though anyone else would have had a hard time sneaking up on them without a flashlight. Each batch of refugees was as pathetic as the last, often huddled together for warmth, a few with campfires. In a way, he envied them the opportunity to pool their heat and wait for morning.

They often stopped to wipe mist from their headgear. Wall welcomed the frequent breaks that allowed him to work the soreness out of everywhere. Their slower pace in the nighttime fog extended the trip. During one break, Rhino said, "Wall, can you tell us a few science jokes?"

"Uh, are you sure? Most of them are pretty bad."

"Hit us."

Wall thought for a second. "How often do we tell chemistry jokes?"

"How often?" the big man asked.

"Periodically."

Rhino laughed, his deep rumble warming them all. Wall couldn't see Aspen's eye roll, but her face told him all he needed to know. It was the equivalent of a dad pun. *In fact,* Wall thought. *Didn't dad tell me that one?*

"I don't get it," Lucas said.

"Another," Rhino requested.

"What's the easiest way to determine the sex of a chromosome?"

Rhino thought on it, his hand stroking his chin. "What?"

"You pull its genes down."

"Ugh," Aspen groaned.

Plink laughed. Not with Wall. At him. "I'm right there with you, sister. Make it stop. We surrender."

"Your jokes aren't very funny," Lucas said.

"More," Rhino urged. "More." Most of the jokes were met with scoffs and complaints from the ladies while the big man laughed. Lucas only understood a couple. He would have to learn some age-appropriate ones for the boy.

Rhino added a joke of his own. "What do you call a sapling oak who enlisted in the Army? The infant-tree!"

During another break, Wall tried to kiss Plink only to bump goggles, a gaff that entertained Aspen. "Smooth, Romeo. Very smooth."

The dead and abandoned bodies on the road told of brigandry and something more worrisome. From the lack of old people out and about he suspected that the diseases killed some part of the population. Any number of things could have taken down the elderly, from rusted pacemakers to impaired immune systems.

Wall couldn't help but think about those who received no ceremony like the dozen or so he left to waste. Were the individual men and women left along the road on their own? Or did their groups abandon them while fleeing for safety? Resource-deprived populations typically viewed death differently from resource-rich societies. It was a horrible loss either way but expected and accepted in one and railed against in the other. Their world flipped from abundance to scarcity in the past two weeks, and the cast-offs were evidence.

"How quickly we fall..."

All of their moods improved when they rose above the fog. Their speed picked up and their stops grew less frequent and shorter.

Near daybreak, they rolled close to the tiny town of Idanha, and Plink brought them to a stop.

"Roadblock," Rhino said, appraising the situation. "Not a trap."

About a football field ahead, a pile of logs obstructed their route. A head peaked above a car's hood and then disappeared. To the right, the steep roadcut eliminated any chance of working around the blockade. On their left, a river blocked any opportunity of circumnavigating the barricade.

"Someone knew what they were doing when they set this up," Rhino said appreciatively. "Hostiles at two and ten." Once pointed out, Wall saw that what looked like the small thermal footprints of critters like he'd seen all along the way were actually partially obscured men.

Plink killed her engine, handed the boy to Rhino, and signaled for them to stay while she walked toward the roadblock, pressing at her kidney like a pregnant woman. The idea of her walking into danger's nest didn't sit well with Wall, his concern more emotional than professional. She was a warrior and would certainly outlive him even if she was hanging in death's noose, but knowing that and feeling it were two separate things.

"Wall," the SEAL said. "Face the river to your left. Cover one-eighty degrees. I'll cover the rest. Aspen, keep your pistol low, facing back down the road."

Wall understood why he had her facing the wrong direction. In addition to putting her between them, he didn't want her bringing a pistol to a rifle fight. Not even the spec-ops badasses could shoot a man at that distance in the gray of dawn.

Wall's nerves remained surprisingly calm, his heartbeat smooth and steady. He trusted Rhino's assessment that this wasn't a repeat of the stone throwers. Either way, he had to wait and see. *After all, what else could go wrong?*

Rhino whispered, "No quick motions. Keep it smooth and easy. Don't spook them. Tips low but sweeping gradually in an arc."

Plink and a man from behind the barricade exchange slow words that Wall couldn't make out over the rush of the river and the whispers of wind. A minute later, Plink returned with a big-ass grin. In a thick full-on Mexican accent, she said, "Stand down, pendejos. You never gonna believe it. Small ass world."

"You know them?" Rhino asked for all of them.

Plink laughed. "That's Gunnery Puckerup."

"Puckerup?" the three of them asked in unison.

"Bad nickname. Good guy. He'll see us through town."

CHAPTER THIRTY-SEVEN

Puckerup guided them through Idanha, a grouping of homes that Wall wouldn't consider large enough to call a town. While they rumbled through on motorbikes, Puckerup rode one of the town's two horses. He rightly boasted of his home and its ability to adapt so quickly. The borough looked like an ideal haven for the happy and industrious, a strange combination of modern and old-fashioned frontier life. An altered version of a Mennonite village or a wild-west waypoint.

Rather than let their homes gradually fall apart and corrode one nail at a time, they were in various stages of building log cabins. The remains of their recently ended logging industry provided ample timber for their transforming hamlet. At the old post office, they set up a hunting depot with a coal fire for smoking deer and a bear.

Upon entry, Puckerup had pointed out the rotting corpse hanging on a telephone pole from a noose at the east end of town to remind everyone that crime would not be tolerated. Lesser misdeeds meant the loss of a finger or temporary banishment. More severe offenses or repeat customers earned permanent exile or, as they saw, death.

Idanha reached a reciprocal agreement with the town of Detroit, just seven kilometers up the road. Each protected its outer borders and therefore added protection for the other. Men and women could walk and trade freely between the towns, though Detroit had far more to offer because it was the larger of the two. They already collaborated on fishery efforts, including plans to stock the lake and rivers to maintain their renewable food supply. Several of the meadows near the river were tilled for winter and spring crops. As a whole, these towns transformed beyond what Wall thought possible so quickly, not collapsing like Eugene or Portland. Resilience and ingenuity were the words that came to mind as he rolled through.

Plink shared much of what they knew about the diseases and traded all but a few measly scraps of their duck jerky for three gallons of gasoline, what first seemed to be a generous deal on the part of Detroit's gas station owner. In truth, they wanted to rid themselves of gas before the tanks rusted and poisoned the grounds. Alpha Bravo was taking a risk by adding potentially contaminated gas to their tanks, meaning the bikes could fail sooner rather than later. As it was, his XR was hitching from time to time, and the shocks were stiffer, having sucked up road rust along the way. Regardless, they wouldn't have long.

Wall reluctantly left the towns of Detroit and Idanha. Each of the towns would be an ideal place to settle down and wait out the fall. His skill set as an overly-trained bioengineer didn't exactly give him the best position from which to negotiate for entrance into their community, but as a fast learner and in great shape—well, at least when he wasn't busted up—he could have made himself useful. Such dreams were for naught, though.

"The mission is all."

Ten minutes up the road from Detroit, Plink stopped at a pull-off that overlooked the North Fork Breiten River. Rhino said, "I'm impressed. They formed a city-state, like those that emerged around one thousand BC. They protect themselves and their food supplies, pool together resources, and make laws of their own, unable to enforce rule beyond their immediate surroundings."

"Hey, Rhino," Wall said, thinking of another joke. "Why did they call it the Dark Ages?"

"Why?"

"Because there were so many knights."

"Ugh," Aspen groaned while bouncing up and down for warmth or to release the excess energy she always seemed to have. "That was bad. A crime, really. I mean, finger-amputation-level punishment. After a few more like that, we might have to exile you."

Plink slapped Wall's ass and said, "Do we have to wait? We could rid ourselves of the trouble now."

Taking on a truly awful English accent, Aspen said, "I will have nothing of the sort. Not until we find a replacement chauffeur and personal butler."

Plink bowed low and apologized. "Sorry, m'lady. What was I thinking?"

"I have a joke," Lucas said. "Why did the chicken cross the road?"

"Why?" Aspen asked.

With pride, he said, "To get to the other slide." They all gave a courtesy laugh.

"Good, one," she said, messing up his hair.

Rhino lifted Aspen and Lucas over his shoulders like two straps of a backpack and pranced around on one leg, eliciting a bout of giggles. At that moment, Wall might have forgotten the global chaos. If not for the body armor and M4s it would–

"Hostiles. Up the road," Plink said sharply, cutting their fun short. In an instant, they transitioned from friends joking into a combat unit, alert and defensive, prepared to let loose extreme violence. "Mount up." Plink jumped onto her motorcycle and kicked the starter on the descent in one fluid motion, then roared thirty paces toward six people, a short man, a tall woman, and four kids ranging from five-ish to twelve-ish. The family ran into the forest toward the river, likely as leery of strangers as Alpha Bravo. Seconds later, they roared up the road, having left the frightened travelers behind.

As they continued onward, the groups of refugees grew less frequent, though no less miserable. Plink turned northwest onto a dirt and gravel road. Despite the common ruts and munched sections better described as trails, they made faster progress because they encountered almost no cars or refugees. Over the span of an hour, they only passed two groups. One family scurried off the road like frightened animals. The others held their hands high as if resigned to being robbed, which they probably had been, seeing as how they didn't have a backpack or a single water bottle among them.

It wasn't noon yet when they reached a trailhead at the bottom of a steep valley and ignored the no motorcycles sign, thus starting their true off-roading adventure. Aspen and Lucas hopped off whenever they hit tricky spots and leapt back on as soon as they reached the other side. Maybe half an hour later, the trail veered uphill and away from the meandering creek that would lead them to Towning's coordinates. The steep valley sides forced them to stop only a hundred meters off the path, bringing the motorized portion of their trip to an end.

After sanitizing and hiding the bikes under a sheath of underbrush, not that they'd work when they returned, they took one last break, or at least they hoped it would be the last. Aspen, whose mouth was like a vacuum, finished all but a couple of good jerky strands, then wrapped herself in their sole sleeping bag. Seconds later, she fell asleep leaning against Wall. Rhino fell asleep just as fast.

Plink leaned down and kissed Wall's forehead. "Catch some z's, big guy. Don't worry. I'll make sure nobody steals your frilly panties."

About two hours after noon, they set out cross-country along the untamed edges of a stream into an even sharper valley. The going was arduous even for Aspen, whose feet practically floated over branches and levitated over the loose-packed forest floor. Wall constantly argued with his muscles, forcing them to continue. Despite the big man's ability to withstand pain, Rhino was even slower, which occasionally gave Wall a moment to sit on a rock or a log. Lucas mostly stayed at Plink's side, talking her ear off. They had to walk through the stream from time to time and occasionally balanced across fallen trees to reach the other side. Brambles of bushes forced them to climb higher onto the slopes, only to drop down again for more sure footing.

"What's that?" Aspen asked, cupping her hands to her ears. Wall couldn't hear anything but the whoosh of blood pounding in his head and the high pitch wine of damaged receptors in his ears.

"Take cover," Plink commanded in a loud whisper as she darted behind a large tree stump, ushering Lucas with her. Wall turned and ran for the cover of a wide Douglass fir and slipped on a thick layer of wet soil, sliding into the creek bed under a recently fallen tree, which knocked the wind out of him and hammered his legs like a wrecking ball. As wet and uncomfortable as he was, it made for a reasonably defensible spot. The whoosh-whoosh in his head blocked his best effort to listen for whatever Aspen heard. He began to think it was the squeaking of a tree or a falling branch and that Plink overreacted but held his position anyway.

Then he heard it. The whir of something mechanical grew louder, higher pitch than their motorcycles, but moving just as fast. He raised his M4 and prepared to fire when it nearly flew over him. As broad as a man is tall, a camouflage drone hovered between the trees. Six booms held a large-caliber turret aloft, a modern machine of death.

"Towning," he swore under his breath, imagining how the gray-haired mega-killer must be smiling that he'd drawn Wall into yet another trap. As if things weren't bad enough, the father of rust had to extend another olive whip.

Two suppressed large-caliber rounds hit a nearby tree, possibly the one Aspen hid behind. The fact that the hovercraft barely rocked when it shot told of its incredible design. This was a serious military-grade weapon, as dangerous of a deterrent as he'd ever seen. No drone with that much control could have any rust damage.

A second later, two quieter bullets counterattacked, rewarding the shooter with the sound of *plink, plink*. The six-rotor hummingbird sparked but didn't budge. Instead, it returned a double volley. Both loud impacts hit the stump that Plink and Lucas used for cover, followed by a high-pitched yelp that he expected came from the boy, but could have been the badass warrior.

The drone arched right and shot another round at her tree, then kept firing once per second while rounding in a flanking arc.

Wall slowly turned, hoping that the smooth motion wouldn't draw attention, aimed with poor grounding on his backside, exhaled, and pulled the trigger at the camouflage drone. Once, twice, then a third time. The first round hit center of mass, the second missed, and the third hit the end of a boom. The six-legged helicopter turned into a five-rotared drone and fell about a meter as the damaged propeller ground to a stop but then quickly recovered.

Instead of firing at Wall, it kept targeting Plink's tree, slowly moving to the side, stalking her.

Rhino popped out from behind another tree and shot three times, two of which hit home with sparks, one center of mass and the other a propeller, dropping the sucker by a meter or more. The whine shifted higher still. Even before it righted itself, the drone returned fire, each bullet pounding Rhino's tree. At least the shots weren't as accurate and required more time to aim as it had to correct itself after each recoil.

Wall sent another trio, one hitting left-of-middle and another on a different boom, and the last completely missing. None of them seemed to affect the assassin on propellers. Again, the thing didn't return his fire, choosing to send brass up the valley at Rhino's tree. Plink fired again, hitting another rotor, causing it to drop and veer wildly to the side, only to recover a finger's distance from smashing into a tree trunk. Both of the tier-one soldiers sent fire at the thing, with the only effect being a slight set of jolts as it righted itself.

Recognizing the whirlybird's weakness, its propellers, Wall fired another trio, missing all three times. One of their shots disabled the motorized machine's third rotor, but it remained in the air, albeit wobbly and returning fire at Rhino wildly.

Trying to take the pressure off the superior marksmen, Wall let fly another two rounds. Instead of striking back, it alternated shots between the elite warriors, so he shot again and again and again until his magazine ran dry. Being the luckiest unlucky person known to humankind, he hit one of the last three rotors, and the thing spun wildly and rebounded off a large stump, landing topside down only a few meters from Wall.

Upside down, its turret kept firing at Plink, then Rhino, and back and forth. Emboldened by his miraculous invisibility, Wall reloaded his M4 and launched another attack at the mechanical beast, *tap-tap, ping, tap-tap, clink*, until he ran dry again. Still, the thing wouldn't die and didn't counterstrike. He reloaded again while the two elite soldiers tried to cover him, each landing shots on the tough-as-titanium drone.

Thoroughly pissed off that he couldn't draw the armored weapon's attention off the superior marksmen, he exposed himself, taking the stupidest risk of his life. To his amazement, it didn't blast him full of large-caliber holes, so he double-downed on idiocy and hopped over his protective log, then walked toward it without any cover. He flinched with every shot, sure the tough piece of shit would mark his end. It never even twitched his way.

Reasoning that its lateral cameras were damaged, he closed the distance and fired two rounds up a gap in a broken arm toward the thing's core. The drone's gun wound down, and its last functional rotor spun to a stop. For good measure, he grabbed hold of the turret and wrenched it from the chassis as he yelled like a wild man.

"What in the fucking name of Barney?!" Plink yelled. "You imbecile! What if it killed you?! You're our Hail Mary!"

"It didn't," Wall said, punctuated by an attempt at a world record in shrugs.

"We lost Ueskev! We lost Kayla! We lost Nellibi! We can't lose you!"

"I worked it out," he said, walking to her slowly as one might approach an angry dog.

"If it—"

The distinctive whir of another drone—no, multiple drones—reverberated up the canyon, rising above the new level of ringing in his ears.

"Retreat!" Plink hissed.

None of them needed clarification or reiteration, working their way up the valley as fast as the uneven canyon floor would allow. Given the drones' speed, they would be upon Alpha Bravo in a hot minute. Wall, now splashing through the creek on a bum leg, slow like Rhino, falling behind. Aspen ran with the ease of a wood elf. Plink was only a few paces behind, carrying Lucas.

"Hurry up!" she yelled as she set the boy down, spun, and backstepped her way up the canyon with her M4 drawn to cover him and Rhino from the oncoming drones. She didn't fire, and if Wall's blood-pounding ears were any judge, the drones stopped pursuing them. He ran-limped up the creek bed to her. No guns fired, no bullets hit trees, and he didn't look back to see why. She helped him around a bend, maybe a hundred meters from where they were ambushed.

"Hold," Plink said.

Wall toppled into the stream, panting too hard for his ribs to cooperate. Rasping, he barely managed to curse, "Towning."

"One home blows up," Plink said through clenched teeth as she sat on the bank and cut her shirt open to expose a prolific flow of blood. "He tries to kill us with drones at the other."

Wall barely registered her words as he scrambled on hands and knees to her side to examine her shoulder. He pulled the waterproof medical kit off his pack with remarkably steady hands for someone who just ran for his life and still heaved like a couch potato on a treadmill. Her wound wasn't from a large-caliber bullet, which would have blown her shoulder clean off, but from wood shrapnel, which stuck out of her, from minuscule splinters to a wrench-sized shard.

Rhino groaned as he sat and propped his ankle on a large, moss-covered rock. "Towning laid another trap."

"Not so much," Wall said as he quickly switched to sterile gloves, eyeing her wound.

"Explain," Plink said, tapping her fingers.

He pulled the largest piece of kindling from her upper bicep, smeared the spot with triple antibiotic, and patched it with a cotton ball. She flinched when he uncovered it and plucked out a pinky-sized splinter that hadn't come along for the ride. "Hold still, woman." Aspen huddled over his shoulder in morbid fascination. Lucas sat on Rhino's good leg, bawling.

"C'mon, Wall," Plink growled as he plucked another shard from the same wound. "Spit it out. How in the holy shit storm was that not a trap."

Dividing his concentration between mending Plink and reasoning, he said, "It was, and it wasn't. They're like border guards, guard dogs, to stop *you* from entering." He shoved his tongue into his cheek as he cleaned the mangled hole in Plink's arm with gauze and tweezers.

"They stopped coming for us after we fled," Rhino said, riffing off Wall. "We crossed out of their territory. And—"

"Quit it!" Plink snapped, batting at his hand.

Wall simply growled at her and pulled out a key-sized sliver before drawing a scalpel. "It wasn't a trap for me. The drone didn't shoot me. I can go into their protected zone. The rest of you can't. It's—Plink, this is gonna hurt." He dug out a crumbling chunk of bark, causing the wound to bleed even faster. Mentally, he said, *Please don't sever an artery.* Trying to keep the conversation going while torturing Plink, he said, "For some reason, Towning wants me and only me to enter."

Silence.

Plink smacked his hand again. "Do you even know what you're doing?"

He smacked her hand right back. "Does anyone else have experience digging chunks of wood out of someone?"

"Someone?" she asked. "How many kisses do I need to give in order to get to the center of your tootsie pop? Not a girlfriend? Not even a friend? Just someone."

"This many," he said, bonking helmets with her in an attempt to kiss her and shut her up. A second later, a blood-soaked fragment popped out and hit him in the eye. He groaned, wishing he hadn't lost his shooting glasses somewhere in the stream.

Plink sucked air in through her teeth.

"Gross!" Aspen cringed, immediately followed by, "That. Was. So. Shway!"

Rhino piped in. "Towning gave you his cabin, right? Do you have any idea what he wants you to do?"

"No," Wall said abrasively. His leg spasmed and nearly knocked him into Plink, needle first as he prepared to stitch her biggest wound. "At what stage of this shitshow did you think, 'Wall really seems to be on top of this? He's two steps ahead of that Towning, the mad-ass psycho who ended our way of life. Wow, Wall really instills a sense of calm and reassurance. These diseases have no chance against him.'"

"Sorry," Rhino said. "I didn't mean nothin' by it."

"No," Wall said, digging the needle into Plink. "I didn't–I shouldn't have..."

"All good, man," the big guy said as he cleaned Plink's M4. "This ain't no watermelon picnic."

"Are you done yet?" Plink asked as she stretched her neck. "I'll die of old age before you finish."

"You know what they say about life, don't you?" Wall asked.

"What?"

"If you have to ask, you don't have one." He tied off an ugly stitch and cut the string.

She leaned in and kissed him. "So profound, you are. I knew there was a reason I liked you."

"Guys," Aspen groaned. "If you want, we can go, so you have time for whatever this is." She waved her hand at Wall and Plink, her face one of "Adults are lame."

Wall ignored her. "Towning planned for me to come here. He said that choices made, as in multiple choices, were my burden to carry. He wants me to go in and make some decisions. Choice number one is whether to go in or not."

"Agreed," the SEAL said. "Do we have any clue what type of game Towning has planned for you?"

While Wall dug another stitch through Plink's shoulder, he said, "It's obviously about the rusting. Other than that, I couldn't tell you. Who knows what goes on behind the face of a man like him?"

Rhino grunted as he held Lucas's trembling body close. "Towning might be in there? He may want you to join him in his paradise."

"No," Aspen said, firm and strong, a fellow contributor rather than a child pushed to the sidelines. "The note said that Wall has a lot to do, right? Towning may be in there but staying doesn't sound like miles to go."

"For now," Rhino said, "the only decision Wall needs to make is whether to go in."

Plink flinched as he picked out a relatively small splinter, then said, "Whatever Towning has planned can't be good. I wouldn't go in if I were you."

"If I can get in there," Wall said, digging into another splinter. "I might be able to let you guys in. I could work on cures in the lab. It would take years, but it's possible."

"You're talking about a lot of *ifs*," Plink said, one blade angry and the other concerned.

He locked eyes with her. "I have to try. The only surviving lab is beyond those drones. If I go in, we have a chance, as slim as it may be. If I don't, there is no chance at all."

They settled into a quiet melancholy as Wall continued tending to Plink's many micro wounds.

The mission is all, he thought.

CHAPTER THIRTY-EIGHT

"I'll be back," Wall said, having kissed Plink, fist-bumped Rhino, dumped Aspen off his back, and ruffled the little guy's hair.

After a deep breath and re-gripping the quickly-fashioned walking stick he found a few minutes ago, he walked forty meters down the stream bed to find three drones hovering at an imaginary border. They reminded Wall of chained guard dogs, drooling for blood. While approaching their invisible boundary, Wall pictured becoming the proud recipient of supersonic high-caliber brass trophies. With his M4 dangling freely, he breathed heavily as he stepped through the intangible barrier. If they decided to kill him, there would be nothing he could do to stop them.

As soon as he entered the bounds of Towning's homestead, the central drone dropped too fast to track, terminating its descent with a blast of wind strong enough to topple a smaller man. The other drones remained vigilantly where they were. He let go of his breath when they didn't smite him for trespassing.

Wall followed the creek downhill, and, like a prison guard, the drone followed him. A minute in, he found a dead backpacker dressed in top-of-the-line gear punctured by a trio of massive holes through the chest. The guy, who recently died based on his lack of decomposition, lay on the sandy bank of the gentle stream.

"Damn." He bridged his nose. "The stream is infected."

About ten minutes later, the gorge transitioned from a steep V-shaped ravine to a U-shaped glacial valley with a nearly flat bottom. The trees here stretched taller with broader trunks similar to what Wall remembered of Towning's secret hideaway.

He blinked, and a well-groomed trail ran across the stream with a picturesque arrangement of stone he and Towning had walked over several times while they talked about science or the future.

The drone herded him toward the cabin with a few blasts of wind. "So much for choices. This is a one-way street."

The forest in the vale was truly spectacular, with broad trees towering impossibly high. The place embodied peace, a notion spoiled by Towning's deceit. He looked back up the stream, questioning his decision to play into Towning's game.

Several contradictory desires pulled at him. The concept of jackrabbiting in an attempt to escape Towning's trap kept bouncing around his skull. While fatigue called him to lie down and stare up at the forest canopy for a spell, two strong urges enticed Wall onward, the desire to reach Towning's cabin so he could let the others in and the hope of killing the old man. When he slowed, the drone fanned him onward.

"I'm in it now. No going back."

After another twenty minutes of limping, as the valley widened even more, Wall walked through a sunny clearing with an immaculately maintained vegetable garden, as wholesome as he remembered. Paris, the butler, took joy in manicuring the sustainable source of food, and its tidy state meant that she was still in the vale. Wall turned to pluck some strawberries, peas, and carrots, but the drone nudged him onward. The promise of living inside Towning's hidden paradise while creating cures or vaccines beckoned. If he could let the others in...

Then, he was upon the enormous log cabin, unchanged by the rusting, as tranquil and lovely as any place he'd ever been. He paused outside, recalling how the home's lookalike exploded so spectacularly.

Walking up the steps, he verbally reasoned that "Towning could easily have killed me a dozen times if he wanted to. I have nothing to fear."

The drone nudged him onto the front porch.

"Master Mathison," said Paris as she opened the front door with a formal nod that bordered on a bow. "It's my pleasure to see you again. Master Towning was confident you would come." The pale-skinned, black-haired woman dressed in a smart white-collar shirt, black pants, and a black tie had a characteristic voice belying her Norwegian upbringing and secondary schooling in England. On previous visits, she referred to Towning as Master, an oddity in the modern world, but never Wall. Being called "Master" sat as well as moldy cream cheese.

A pinch of relief and a dash of hope added to his recipe of contradictory thoughts and emotions. She emanated order and civility in a manner that he hadn't seen since before his camping trip. There was an organic structure to Towning's natural haven, from the groomed paths to the garden to this un-rusted getaway.

"Please come in, sir. May I take your luggage?"

"Ha," he chuckled, thinking it a stretch to call his sopping backpack *luggage*. Regardless, He didn't trust any pawn of Towning's. "Sorry, but I'd rather keep my belongings close."

"As you will, sir. This is your home, after all."

"My home?" Wall asked. He hadn't believed Towning meant for him to own this patch of land, especially after the old man's other home went up in flames. A certain giddiness filled him at the idea of being lord over such a spectacular slice of Earth, one protected from outside influence.

As he stepped inside, he gained a new perspective of the cabin. The door hinges were bronze. So were the fire tools. The pots and pans above the kitchen counter shined of copper. He couldn't see a single nail in the "cabin's" construction, all wood and stone, craftsmanship reminiscent of ancient times, immune to infection. An artisan built the furniture with dove-tail joints and dowels. Candles instead of lightbulbs. Not a bit of iron or steel exposed the house to rusting. Towning planned for this place to survive the downfall. In retrospect, Wall should have recognized the construction for what it was, a clue to Towning's plans.

"Yes, sir," Paris said, closing the door behind them. "The vale now belongs to you."

"And you?" he asked, not looking forward to the answer.

"I come with the package, sir, so long as you want me to remain. Might I recommend an Epson salt bath, sir?" She'd offered this luxury on his previous visits, and he'd never taken her up on it. This time, he was tempted. "Dusting off the dirt of the road and eating a balanced meal may help you consider the responsibilities Towning has placed upon you."

"Responsibilities?" Wall asked. "What are they?"

"That, sir, only Towning can tell you. He left a message in the lab, and I have no knowledge of its contents."

"A message..." Wall said, the words bitter on his tongue. His mind hurt with possibilities. Would it be another set of poems? Or new coordinates to hunt down? What sort of game had Towning drawn him into? Whatever it was, Wall wouldn't play along.

"May I draw that bath for you, sir?" she asked again.

"Yeah. That would be great. Thanks." Not only would a soak ease his aches and pains so he could think clearer, but a thorough cleaning was also absolutely necessary to preserve the lab, their only chance to aid humankind. "But first, let my friends in, okay?"

"Sorry, sir. I have no control over the sentinels." She waited for a moment while Wall processed, then said, "I arranged a snack for you. Why don't you have a bite to eat while I prepare your soak."

"Okay." While he sat at the long wooden table carved from the center of a massive tree, she disappeared down the hall. He picked at a charcuterie that included gamey sausage, goat cheese, pickled green beans, honey, strawberry jam, and apple slices. She even added bits of salty-sweet jerky.

Minutes later, Paris bade him follow her. In the oversized master bathroom, he found a steaming tub waiting for him along with a fresh pair of beige quick-dry pants, a synthetic sage long-sleeve shirt, undergarments, and a full set of hygiene products, not a fleck of exposed metal on any of it.

He felt guilty lounging in the bath while Plink and the others remained outside Towning's perimeter, hungry with no amenities but the cold stream. If it weren't for the excessive grit clouding the water, he might have soaked for an hour. After shaving with a bronze blade, brushing his teeth, applying deodorant, and dressing, he slipped the amenities into his pack–just in case.

Ready, he returned to Paris, who awaited him, hands behind her back. The valley offered opulence and luxury, while the world outside offered decay and pain. "Sir, shall I prepare a fire for you?"

The temptation to relax, kick his feet up and enjoy a finger of Scotch nearly won out over his need to call off the sentinels for his friends. "Thanks, but no thanks, Paris. I need to see Towning's message and get on with it."

"Excellent, sir. Please come downstairs." She waved for him to follow.

In the basement, Paris held the door to the lab's antechamber for him. "Are you ready, sir?"

"There is no future or past," he said by way of an answer. "Only the ever-changing present."

"Very good, sir." She followed him into the vestibule and closed the door behind them. Instantly, the inside door to the lab hissed, clicked, and opened. There wasn't even time for him to set his soiled pack down, not to mention take all the precautions necessary for coming into contact with finely tuned and immunodeficient equipment.

. *This is it,* he thought, his stomach twisting. *This is how Towning kills me. I'm infected with a lethal disease that will turn me inside out.*

The expansive lab gleamed white from within, brightly lit like the last time he visited, the memories of which he once cherished and now loathed. Nausea threatened to bring up the lovely meal Paris had arranged for him. The cavernous space contained nothing but a table, a large bronze hexagonal prism atop it, two sets of augmented reality glasses, and two stainless-steel chairs. Towning had removed all of his next-generation equipment, the tools Wall would need to research and synthesize a vaccine–if he ever could have. The impressive mix of machinery and electronics for the production of said vaccines no longer sat at the far end. The beakers. The centrifuges. All gone.

A few steps ahead of Wall, Paris pulled out a seat for him, which he very much needed, his head and knees unsteady. His hope failed. Atop everything else, Towning stripped him of hope, obliterated a path forward, and extinguished any sense of purpose. Before him, the dark bronze hexagonal block glinted in the brightly lit room, the single point of focus.

A yellow sticky note on the augmented-reality glasses read, "Put me on," in Towning's characteristic jagged handwriting. He tore the note off the glasses, crumpled it, and threw it like a baseball as hard as he could. He was tempted to leave and never come back–if the sentinels would let him. The simple act of donning the glasses felt like suckling at the teat of the devil. All the same, he slid the AR lenses into place.

The distinctive man appeared before him. Wall's urge to pummel the psychopath's very lifelike apparition nearly overwhelmed him. His lips twitched, and his fists clenched. His teeth ground and the throbbing veins on his forehead threatened to rupture. If ever there was a man who deserved a good beating, it was the man before him.

Towning looked older than he remembered, weaker, saddened. "I'm glad you made it, my boy."

Wall hated that he used to feel flattered every time Towning treated him like a son. It was as if he was the child Towning always wanted while he disliked all of his own children. Wall had swallowed all the fatherly approval that the genius fed him. Pre-rusting, Wall would have resorted to great measures to garner more favor. Now, he wanted to beat on the rendering of the gray-haired man for addressing him so familiarly. How could Towning think that Wall would still view such friendliness, such familiarity, as anything but a slight?

The message continued. "We achieved greatness, you and I. Our work averted the mounting threats that humans pose to the world's vibrant and tenuous ecosystems. Nuclear armageddon was inevitable. Global warming was assured by clumsy nations. China's lithium mining would continue poisoning the oceans. Deforestation continued."

"You fucking asshole!" Wall raged at Towning. "We were on the verge of righting wrongs."

Towning's avatar glitched, and he reappeared with hands held out. "Calm, my boy. I understand your frustration."

"Really?!" Wall yelled.

The older man glitched again. "Logical minds must prevail. I give you the gift of choice. But first, I must explain."

"Ahhh!" he yelled at the manifestation.

Continuing as only a pre-recorded message would, Towning said, "We were approaching a precipice. Half-measures and compromises weren't working. Overpopulation threatened everything. Too much damage was already done."

"There was time!" Wall yelled. "One solution, then the next, then on and on. Technology was the way forward!"

Towning glitched again. "Our technology was generations away from the environmental singularity we so often talked about. By the point we reached sustainability, if we ever got there, thousands of micro- and macro-biomes would die. Animals, plants, bacteria, everything destroyed."

Wall was tempted to draw his pistol and shoot the righteous pan-murderer. Understanding the futility of arguing with a recording, Wall said, "You don't know that."

Towning clicked into a different part of the interactive message. "Be honest with yourself, Wall. Governments and non-governmental agencies, as slow as they were, stifled environmentalism while lying about the great progress they made." He hand quoted "great progress."

Wall bridged his nose. "I know, but–"

"Exceptional individuals like us, visionaries in the environmental community, had to act, to take drastic measures, and that is what we did. Together."

Wall stood and turned his back on Towning, barely able to contain the furnace of anger within.

"I knew you would understand, my boy."

"Understand?!" Wall yelled.

"Together, we equalized the balance of man and nature, the environmental singularity. We returned Earth to an Eden."

"Those are people out there," Wall growled, his voice growing hoarser.

"Thank you, my boy, for agreeing that by culling the herd, those that remain will be healthier and happier."

"No. That was theoretical. Drunken musings." He couldn't believe Towning was pinning this on him. "What gave you the right?"

Towning shifted into another piece of the recording. "Good. To the point." He recited the note he left:

"Choices made, whether bad or good,
follow you forever and
affect everyone in their path.

You have many miles
to go before you sleep."

Wall shoved his tongue into his cheek. He would hear the message, then let the others in. The less he talked, the faster it would go. Even if there wasn't a chance to restore the order of things, they could live with a semblance of comfort. They might be able to find another mission like preserving books or protecting irreplaceable art pieces.

Towning gestured at the case on the table. "Here is one side of the equation, but reserve judgment until you hear me out." The augmented reality glasses displayed the interior of the bronze box, where seven syringes sat in stands, each virtually labeled with one of the metals and its associated disease.

"These, my boy, are the cures to our rusting diseases, a back door to eliminate each one."

Wall's heart beat faster. He couldn't believe it. Towning, the bringer of so much death and destruction, was handing him the ability to provide a rise after the great fall.

"Each of these syringes contains a virophage, a virus that will kill one of our environmental singularity viruses." Wall internally bucked at Towning's use of the word, *our*. These weren't his viruses. They were Towning's. He never wanted this. The avatar continued. Nevertheless, his head floated with hope. "These viruses will kill our rusters, both inside and outside of the host. Because I value your mind and your loyalty to both Earth and humanity, I present you the choice to reverse what we set forth."

Wall thought he might explode with excitement. He looked at Paris. "This is–"

"Wait, my boy." Towning set his virtual hand on the case. "Hear me out."

"What else could matter now?"

"Each of the virus killers is fatal to some of its human hosts." Fatality rates appeared above the syringes, ranging between 13% and 27%, meaning that cures would kill about one in four people.

"Some hosts?!" Wall's wide eyes darted between the numbers. The smallpox cure for Zinc ranked up there with the bubonic plague. The best odds were over one hundred times worse than COVID-19.

"What are the incubation times for these diseases?" he asked.

Towning's avatar shifted. "These are the incubation stages." New numbers appeared below each virus ranging from days to months.

Wall squeezed the bridge of his nose. "How long will each cure infect the hosts?"

"All of the virus killers are permanent infections."

"And the Ro?" he asked, referring to the number of other people a single infected person would spread the disease to under normal conditions.

"Their Ros are high," the old man said with a smile, speaking as if discussing the ingredients of chocolate chip cookies. "The actual values would depend on too many parameters to predict."

"What–" Wall stuttered over his own thoughts. "What–What kind of die-off is expected if we release them all?"

Towning stood still, and the answer appeared in the air. "99.3% fatality."

"Gah!" he yelled, swinging his fist upward through the old man's chin, nearly falling over for his efforts. "How about if we combine the cures for Iron and Steel?"

A new answer replaced the old one. "59% fatality"

"What about Iron and Aluminum?"

"62%"

Wall closed his eyes to think.

In the silence, Towning repeated, "Choices made, whether bad or good, follow you forever and affect everyone in their path."

"Fine," Wall said to himself. "Paris, help me pack this case up." Plink and the others could weigh in. The choice was too important for one person.

"You misunderstand, my boy. You may only leave the vale with the cures in your bloodstream. You can only choose once. All decisions are final. If you try to tamper with the box, the cures will be rendered inert."

He seethed. "So, there's a good chance I'll die?"

Without compassion, Towning said, "Your death is a possibility, though I've taken some precautions against that."

Wall sat down, exhaustion settling on him like a blanket of rust. "Is there anything else I need to know?"

Towning said, "If you leave, you can never return. Or you can choose to stay and live out your days, in which case the box will terminate the cures. The haven is your reward for everything you have done. Thank you, my boy."

CHAPTER THIRTY-NINE

Hours of circling around the same problem portended nothing but awful futures. Wall tapped a single augmented reality syringe, then waffled back to the idea of inviting his new family into the valley and living in peace. A moment later, he chose a combination of virus killers, one of the 5,040 possibilities. For the hundredth or thousandth time, he and Paris reviewed probabilities and statistics, weighing the pros and cons. He barely glanced at his latest answer, 39% fatality. The numbers on either side showed how uncertain the answer was. While the guess was 39%, it could kill anywhere between 29% and 84% of everyone.

He tried another, then another.

"This is it," he said. "Compromise. That's the key." Mathematically, it was a simple optimization problem where the main factors were 1) killing as few people as possible while 2) giving humanity the right metals to give society the best chance to rebound. The crux of the issue was deciding what was an "acceptable loss" and what was "worth saving." If he killed off too many people, humanity might not survive. If he didn't choose the right metals, humanity had one less tool for climbing out of the second bronze age.

Paris laid her hand on Wall's shoulder. "You need not decide now. Stay overnight, or live here for days, weeks, or months so you can make the right decision."

"If I stay, I might never leave, and I can't do that. Humanity needs metal."

"As is your privilege, sir."

He wouldn't exactly consider it a *privilege*. "Tell me again of Towning," he said, hoping to subconsciously make the decision while distracted, the way ideas came to him while showering.

To Paris's credit, she didn't sigh or roll her eyes. He'd asked too many times to count. "Master Towning took his own life, sir. He said that the world was not meant for men like him, warriors who would burn down the house to rid it of rats. I injected him with a concoction of drugs, including Rohypnol, cyanide, and fentanyl. He died peacefully of his choosing. I personally buried him in a beautiful field down the valley."

"Good," Wall said, both glad that the old man was dead and angry that he couldn't personally bludgeon him to death. "He didn't have the guts to see the world he created."

"Master Towning was brave in his own way, sir. And he was very proud of his friendship with you."

Wall's stomach growled. "Yet, he handed me this dumpster fire, forcing me to be just like him."

"Not like him, sir. You never would have unleashed the rusting diseases. The world and humanity are better for your existence."

"Ha!" Wall scoffed. "You don't know me. I've been busy killing and abandoning people for the sake of a doomed cause."

"If sir says so, then it is so."

Wall's eye ticked.

"Nobody will blame you for your decisions, sir."

"That's rich," Wall scoffed, his voice acidic with the rust of sarcasm. "If I stay, Plink and the others will know that I abandoned them and the rest of humanity. If I take a cure with me, they will know I killed millions, maybe billions."

"It was Master Towning that killed, not you, sir. He left the final decision to a better man, if I may be so bold."

"I made up my mind," Wall said, a sense of finality falling into place.

"Excellent, sir."

Wall tapped his selection in augmented reality, gulped uncomfortably, and hit submit. The box hissed and clicked mechanically. Circles opened on the top, releasing a quick puff of steam. The selected syringes rose slowly.

With remarkable composure for someone who witnessed a world-altering decision, Paris gestured to the syringes and said, "Sir, may I have the honor of assisting you?"

He almost said that there was no honor in this. He made the least bad choice. He chose one evil over another. He made a single decision for everyone. He chose quality of life over preserving lives, mass murder over squalor. What honor could there be in that?

Instead, he pulled up his sleeve. "Sure. Let's get this over with."

Paris prepped the injection site, squeezed his shoulder, and said, "This will pinch." She stuck him with deft hands and depressed the plunger. Such a simple act. One pinprick. "And...All done."

In augmented reality, Wall watched the hexagonal box flush the remaining syringes into a reservoir of acid. Now that there was no going back, Wall's sense of unease faded. The decision was made, both good and bad. Others might judge him for what he'd done, but that couldn't change the past.

"As I suspected, it is time for you to leave, my boy," Towning's avatar said, his face sad and sympathetic, so contrary to the old man's legacy. Perhaps he had some sliver of humanity after all. "I'm sorry you won't stay, happy to live out your days in the knowledge that we achieved the singularity. But I trust your judgment in all things, and so it is."

"Screw you. You psycho–"

"Wall, my boy, you have ten minutes to pack up and leave the cabin and twenty to leave the valley." A timer began counting down in the corner of his AR glasses. "Please go now." The implication was clear: death if he stayed.

"Here, sir." She said, handing him his gear. "We must hurry."

Wall turned and hop-skipped to the door, Paris on his heels. Normally it would have taken minutes to change in the antechamber, but the outer door opened as soon as the inner door closed. "Slow is smooth, and smooth is fast," he told himself, willing his legs to adhere to the adage. This was no time to fall, to injure himself, and to pick himself back up.

"Stupid leg," he growled as he limped up the stairs with the help of his walking stick.

"Keep moving, sir." The crack in her voice spoke of urgency.

At the top of the stairs, she ran ahead and hefted camping gear that matched the set Towning had given him a couple of weeks earlier. Towning, mentally sick or not, prepared for everything. If only Wall could have gone back and taken the "mad" out of "mad genius." But, what was done, was done.

While pulling his bulletproof jacket on, he tripped over the front door's threshold, landing on the porch like a sack of jelly and twigs, his walking stick broken under him. "Slow is smooth," he whispered to himself again. Only now did he realize that dusk had come and gone. He flicked on his M4's light and hopped down the front stairs.

"Here." Paris, who wore a headlamp, thrust Towning's walking stick into his hand, the one with a beautiful carving of a double helix that the old man would use on their outings. Wall nearly declined to take it out of hatred toward the old man but needed it for speed.

"Don't stop, sir." She nudged him onward. "There are several pounds of jerky in my pack. You can dine in style when we get there." A sentinel followed them several paces back, dangerous and sinister. It was the stick to Paris's carrot.

About fifty meters from the house, a shockwave pounded them from behind, blasting him forward onto his belly. While his brain spun inside his skull and his chest seized, heat flashed over him. He shook the rust from his mind and blinked as if to let dust spill from his eyes.

"What the?!" His words came out muffled and distant. The high-pitch feedback of a poorly miked rock concert rang through the colosseum of his head. "That wasn't nearly ten minutes."

Paris, who received scrapes on her hands and face, helped him to his feet. Behind them, the remainder of the burning mansion fell into a deep hole. Adjacent trees smoked with small fires of their own. For a man who loved this place, Towning apparently felt no misgivings about sending it into flames. He tossed the augmented reality glasses that broke during the fall.

"Keep moving, sir."

His leg was too heavy for speed, his ribs too abused to expand and contract, his head too concussed to balance. The cold, calculating sentinel behind him didn't care how he felt. If he didn't get to the property's edge, none of it would matter, so he–

He slipped forward in time, tripping into the creek, brought back by the cold shock of the water.

"Stand, sir!" Paris yelled, dragging him upright.

"How much time?" Wall asked as he slogged up the stream.

"Ten minutes, sir."

Around each bend in the ravine, Wall hoped to see the other sentinels that would mark the property boundary. Twice more, he skipped into the future. Each time afraid that he was awakening to death. After the fifth switchback, sure that his life was forfeit, he asked, "How long" gasp "do we have?"

She panted twice before answering. "One minute, sir."

The sentinels came into view after the next meander. With so little time left, he wasn't anything similar to confident that they would stay on the live side of the high-caliber meat grinder. *One last push.* He urged himself on, running full out, splashing through the stream, and sliding over a downed tree like a cop across the hood of a car.

The thrum of rotors ahead sang of death. "Twenty-seven seconds," Paris rasped. "Run, sir!" If not for his leg, he would have been out of danger minutes ago. As it was...There is nothing so motivating as death, whether for himself or a loved one. It was the necessary incentive that drove him in those final seconds.

"Ten seconds, sir." It was going to be close. Once again, a decision made by Towning could ruin all of Wall's best intentions. "Faster!" The drones' high-caliber turrets aimed at him, ready to declare his expiration date. Time sped up, each heartbeat coming too fast, each footfall blurring into the next, every stride shocking his neck like continuous lightning, the perceived changes in gravity throwing him off balance.

"Four," Paris said through a harsh exhale as they neared the drones.

Two paces later, with only two heartbeats of spare time, he passed under the sentinels and kept running until he tripped over a log and splashed into a pool. He landed face down in the stream with his lungs pulling in water and knocking his brain into a primal mode, an animalistic need to find oxygen. He pushed up and coughed water from his lungs, sputtering and spitting.

When his inner barbarian relinquished its hold over him, he realized that the sentinels hadn't filled him with giant holes. The impacts of supersonic projectiles hadn't rocked his body, thereby voiding his lifetime warranty. With his lungs burning and heart pounding, he rolled onto his back in the shallows. The sentinels hovered where they had moments before, a few paces behind.

His mind hitched upon seeing Paris still on the other side of the invisible boundary, panting, hunched over with her hands on her knees. The drone that followed them up the valley flew a meter behind her with its turret prepared to bring her life to an end. But it hadn't fired. Not yet.

"What, now?" Wall managed to say between sandpaper coughs. What great treat would Towning bestow unto the world this time?

"My arrangement with Master Towning was different from yours, sir. You had to leave. Years ago, I vowed never to leave under the penalty of death."

"What are you talking about?"

"Master Towning saved my life in so many ways. I owe him everything."

"No," Wall said, dumbfounded. "Not anymore." Wall gritted his teeth. "He's dead." Cough. "He destroyed everything." Gasp. "His actions broke every agreement, ever."

She looked all the sadder. "If only that were so. To have free will and purpose in life is a gift beyond anything except for the bonds we make. I bonded myself to Towning, vowed my life to him."

"But..."

She tossed Wall her high-tech backpack. "I don't know if this helps, sir, but you should know that Master Towning deeply respected you."

Without thinking, he drew his Glock and nearly shot the messenger. The sentinels jerked as if cocking a shotgun in warning.

Without flinching, she continued. "He valued your judgment, Master Mathison."

Wall regained his feet with the aid of Towning's stick. He panted a few times. "I don't-" he began to say.

"It was a privilege to serve you, sir," she interrupted. With a purposeful stride toward Wall, the sentinel behind her fired, ending her life even before her foot touched the free-will side of the border. She fell, Towning's marionette cut free of her master's will only to drop into the stream, red threads wisping away. Wall stared at her for a while, her only remaining act of free will cut down by the most ruthless of men.

Towning predicted all of this. The inevitability of Paris's last step, the only act of free will left at her disposal, only free in death. The old man knew Wall would venture forth, forced into action by his conscience. The psychopath had said, "You have many miles to go before you sleep."

"Wall," Plink called out, her voice echoing down the ravine.

He turned, lifting the ultra-light pack Paris had carried for him, and limped up the streambed to his compatriots, his new family. "I'm okay," he said. The bases of trees ahead flickered with the orange waviness of a campfire ringing Plink's silhouette with warmth.

He blinked and she pulled him into a hug, whispering into his ear, "You're alive. We thought..."

"I'm too lucky to die," he said, squeezing her tight.

She kissed him. "You're the luckiest unlucky-"

"Back!" he yelled and shoved her away, knocking her on her butt, while he stumbled back and also fell, holding his hand out to ward her off. He scrambled several meters farther up the valley's steep side as if fleeing a slow zombie

"What's wrong?!" she asked.

"I'm sick," he explained. "I'm not sure if I'm infectious yet, but I could be."

"Sick? How?"

"Towning's choice. His twisted, demented–" He yelled in fury. For the next half hour, he kept his distance and told them about what he saw and did while inside Towning's funhouse. Every several minutes he zoned out and Plink would draw him out of a waking sleep. While Wall changed into drier clothes, the others warmed themselves around a fire over which Rhino slowly cooked a leg from a deer he bagged.

"So," Rhino said, cutting off the outer layer of the cooking meat. "If I walk with you, there's a one-in-six chance I will die."

"Thereabout," Wall said. His first test of resolve sat across the stream from him, lives he might end simply by breathing too near them. It was one thing to consider populations in abstractions and calculations. The idea of killing Plink, Aspen, Lucas, or Rhino gutted him.

"The kids," he whispered. "Are always the hardest."

Rhino scrawled something with his finger in the air, then stated, "The odds of at least one of us dying is a little over fifty percent."

Wall closed his eyes. "There abouts."

Plink tapped at her pants and whistled. "Ain't that a bee sting on bare ass? At the flip of a nickel one of us dies."

Wall stripped off a sliver of Paris's hickory venison jerky, then said, "That, my friends, is why I'm over here, and you're over there. You can still live your lives, grow old and gray. You can stay here, and I'll leave. I can't go on knowing I killed you."

Plink swallowed a piece of Rhino's venison and said, "Wall, it isn't your choice to make. Would you deny us the gift of free will? The right to walk with you and share in your burden? My place is at your side."

"Me too," Aspen said.

"No!" Wall snapped at the teen. "You are too young to decide."

"What?! That's not–"

"He's right," Rhino said, deep and powerful despite not raising his voice, perhaps all the more commanding because he didn't.

"But–"

Rhino placed a bear-sized hand on her shoulder, gentle and kind. "But nothing. You're too young."

Undeterred, she raised her voice and spoke her piece. "I lived on my own long before I met any of you. I choose. Not you."

Now it was Rhino's turn to say, "But–"

"But nothing," she threw his words back at him. A silence grew between them, a case of David and Goliath.

"Either way," Plink said into the uncomfortable void. "A night's sleep will polish the pewter, make the reflection of truth clearer. We might see things differently in the morning."

CHAPTER FORTY

Wall woke warm and cozy, which let loose the sirens of fear in his head. He jolted to full consciousness, aware that Aspen and Plink were on either side of him, Plink's many-braided hair itching his nose as he spooned her and Aspen's sleeping bag insulating him from behind. Plink's head rested on his arm while his other draped over her.

"Morning," she whispered, snuggling her backside into him. Deep in the heavily wooded and steep-sloped valley, the sun wouldn't rise for several hours yet, but the cerulean sky visible through the tall forest told of daybreak.

"No," he gasped, wrenching his half-asleep arm from under her and jumping to his feet. "You can't..."

Plink rolled onto her back and yawned. "Yet, you can clearly see that I have." Then she gasped upon seeing Aspen slumbering within Wall's sickness bubble, the barrier they decided to honor until morning. The young woman stirred but didn't wake, an innocence on her slack face that wasn't there during waking hours. His heart fell out from under him when he spotted Lucas's bulge at the side of Aspen's sleeping bag.

Drawing her hand over her mouth, Plink whispered, "No. Aspen."

Wall backed away like a black widow, both fearful and deadly. "I'm not contagious yet," he told himself while not believing it. A secondhand infection might not be contagious for days or weeks, but a direct injection could have made him dangerous as soon as blood circulated through his body and reached his skin through sweat. Maybe twenty minutes under normal conditions. Less for him because of how hard his heart was pounding while fleeing. It was entirely too likely that Wall had already infected Plink with that single kiss, possibly murdering her. Overnight, the viruses in his bloodstream would have grown exponentially.

Wall coughed, compounding his fear of killing the ladies. Last night, during one of the times he woke with chills, he realized that he allowed Towning to weaponize his blood, his breath, and his life. He would spend what miles he had left combating rust and leaving a trail of death and hope in his contrails. His weapons were breath and sweat, handshakes and hugs, sullied dishes and shared food.

"What have you done?" he asked both of Plink and Aspen.

"Shut up," the teen said groggily, rolled over, and curled around Lucas. "Can't you see I'm sleeping?" How she could doze in the face of possible death clogged his mind as sure as rust in a filter. It was a clear sign that she couldn't fully grasp what she'd done, a sign that she wasn't mature enough to decide for herself.

Plink propped herself onto her elbows to see him better. "Wall, it's as simple as apples and sky. We did as you would have. Could you have walked away from this?"

He stretched his arms wide with clenched fists in animalistic anger. "But I didn't–don't want to be your killer. It's bad enough that I have to massacre strangers wherever I go. I can't handle killing you, any of you. It was supposed to be my burden, not yours."

"You didn't kill us," Plink said. Her worried and taught face lingered over Aspen and Lucas, her words carrying far less weight in light of their innocence. Wall didn't need her ability to read people in order to know what was going on in her mind. When her eyes met his again, his face ashen in the dim light. "We volunteered ourselves. We didn't shy away."

Rhino hopped over the creek, undeterred by Wall's bubble of death, penetrating the invisible boundary that divided the infected from the healthy. The big man nodded. "It's okay, Wall. What's done is done."

Nevertheless, he backed away from the SEAL. "Rhino, you aren't infected. Go live your life. Find what peace you can. Settle down somewhere."

Calm and undeterred, the warrior/historian stepped closer and said, "No matter where we go, the diseases are gonna find us. Do you want us to live as hermits, cut off from anyone and everyone? It's only a matter of time before we get infected."

"I'll go one way. You go the other. You can still have a full life."

The big man smiled. "Warriors don't cower and hide. We act. We make the hard choices so others don't have to."

"Yeah, but..."

Rhino continued. "We can't risk you dying before you have a chance to spread the virus killers far and wide. You're gonna need our help."

"Yeah, but..."

Rhino pressed on. "Do you think us unworthy?"

Plink rolled to her feet like a featherweight dancer and walked to Wall, who didn't back away. He nodded and pulled her into a firm hug, his lips pressing into her forehead. When she looked up at him, he kissed her soft and tender despite both of their chapped lips, then with deeper meaning, the fresh tingle of new lovers.

"Get a room," Aspen said as if slimed by ectoplasm. "I'm too young for porn."

Wall laughed, first lightly, then louder and uninhibited, coughing because of his ribs, or was it the sickness? Plink and Rhino joined in, adding deeper and higher tones to the orchestra of teen-induced happiness. In the face of the serious moment, laughter was the only option that didn't lead to a downward spiral.

Rhino closed the distance to Wall, spit into his hand, and held it out to shake. The big man nodded, his lips flattened, eyes reverent, respecting the importance of the moment. With an ingrained aversion to spreading germs, Wall had to fight his instincts in order to sully his own hand. With Plink under one arm, they shook, a shared agreement between them, marking the first time he intentionally infected anyone.

"Ooh!" Aspen called out. With agility far surpassing his own, she grabbed ahold of Wall's left arm and flung herself onto his back like a monkey. With

Plink's aid, he managed to keep his footing as the teen pulled herself up to his broad shoulders. Then it happened, something that he would deny no matter how many times she brought it up; Aspen licked his cheek, then up over the eyeball and onto his forehead.

"Gah!" he howled as he unwrapped her arms.

She managed to begin a second disturbing lick on his other eyeball before he could rid himself of her disgusting ways. They broke into side-splitting laughter while he wiped her saliva off.

"That," Rhino wheezed between uncontrollable heaves of his lungs. He was too busy laughing to finish whatever he was about to say.

Aspen danced around Wall with her tongue stuck out, keeping out of his reach. At that moment, he realized exactly how much he needed them. Three pillars and a child-sized anchor he could depend on just as they could depend on him.

After some time, they quietly settled around the fireside that Rhino re-stoked. While they warmed themselves, Rhino entertained them with the story of John Joseph Merlin, the inventor of roller skates. Merlin didn't practice stopping before demonstrating his new creation for the first time, so he ended up smashing through a giant mirror. The others were content to listen as he went on about the eccentric man and all the crazy and mundane activities that followed him. Another unfortunate rabbit.

Acceptance was the nature of their thoughts. Death and a nomad's life.

Surrounded by his four companions, Wall's purpose wasn't as formidable. Unaware that Plink could hear him, he whispered, "Everyone dies, either sooner or later. The question is, can we live with our decisions?"

Over the next few days, they shared venison and jokes, happy for the first time since the rusting began, waiting for the virus killers to incubate. Their wounds began to mend. Aspen collected mushrooms for Rhino to thumbs up or thumbs down. Plink and Wall stole moments to themselves, beginning to heal.

The elite warriors shared stories from their time in service, some fun and some harrowing. They honored their brethren among the armed forces, wishing them luck during the downfall. Their hopes of reuniting with their units went unspoken.

They often grew silent when one of them mentioned tools from the time of metal, mourning the death of technology. To protect their gear, they thoroughly cleaned every piece of metal and stashed it away for later use, giving them a sense of what they would lose in days or weeks to come. Then they would continue bantering and laughing.

The tier-one operators trained Wall and Aspen in the ways of urban combat, an education they would need in the days and years to come. While he blundered through the exercises, she took to it like a dandelion puff on the wind. He wanted to blame it on his beat-up body but knew better and praised her every time she excelled. Lucas learned the importance of respecting the danger of weapons and how to handle the wood knife Wall carved for him.

Late in the morning of the fourth day, Wall walked into the growing hut they built out of branches, mud, and paracord, to find Plink sweaty and pale, shoulders uncharacteristically slumped, not bothering to look up at him. "Are you okay?"

"Fine," she said, an obvious lie punctuated by a wet cough.

He recalled her words while fleeing the fires of Portland. "And you'll tell me before fine turns to fucked?"

"Yeah," she said, then slumped and fell sideways off a seat that Rhino fashioned from five sandstone boulders he found in the creek bed.

"Plink!" he called out as he jumped to catch her but was too slow with his wound still only partially healed. She didn't rouse when he tapped her cheek, saying, "Plink, come on! Wake up."

Nothing.

After laying her on her back, he ran through the steps of his first-responder training, observing an alarmingly hot and sweaty forehead, a racing heart, and shallow breathing. Upon closer inspection, her lips were chapped, which they hadn't been only an hour earlier.

Aspen ran into the hut, stopping on a dime with her amazing agility. "What happened?"

"She has a fever," he said, hollowed out, sickened. This was what he had feared. "The other blade of Towning's cure."

Aspen bounced nervously at his side. "What can I do?"

"Soak a shirt in the stream. We need to cool her down."

Two days later, while Wall watched Plink sleep in yet another long nap, he tried to take pleasure in the rabbit Rhino and Aspen caught in a snare but failed to enjoy it. Her breathing had grown even shallower and raspier over the last few hours, and no matter how often he replaced the cold wet cloth on her forehead, her fever wouldn't go down. No matter how much logic he clung to, no matter how important and measured his decision had been, Wall was terrified by what he'd done. Plink's sickness was his doing, and the way things were going, it was going to be—

Her crackling breath ceased.

"No," he whispered, kneeling at her side, placing a knuckle on each cracked lip to feel for airflow, and checking her carotid pulse. "No." She was the first casualty of Towning's cure. The penalty he had to pay for returning metal to humanity.

Wall immediately began compressions. "Don't do this!" he yelled at her as he mentally sang Black Sabbath's "Paranoid." Pump, pump, pump. *Finished with my woman 'cause couldn't help me with my mind.*

"Is she?" Rhino asked from the doorway.

"Not if I..."

Her rasping breath returned, weak like before, but there. Her eyes didn't open. Another examination, the count of which he'd lost track of over the last couple of days, he found that her eyes dilated, and she responded to pain stimulus, both good signs, not that there was anything good about her being post-heart attack without an ambulance or hospital.

"What can we do?" Aspen asked.

"Starting now, we keep an eye on her around the clock."

A day later, Plink sat wrapped in the sleeping bag, tucked under Wall's arm, staring blankly at the fire, her brown eyes reflecting the flames as dusk compounded the darkness of their hut. The bowl of rabbit and squirrel bone broth no longer steamed.

"Plink. You need to keep drinking." Between her loss of appetite and regular bouts of vomiting, she had lost too much weight and become dangerously dehydrated. But she was already getting stronger than before her heart attack, able to sit up for a while. She died, but came back, Towning's first fatality of the rebound, brought back to life.

"I can't," she whispered, pushing the bowl away. For anything to stop her, a fierce fighter, she had to feel as wretched as she looked.

"Please. For me."

She groaned. "Fine." Slowly, she shakily raised the spoon to her lips, then leaned over and vomited into the fire, immediately sending off steam with a foulness of burnt stomach acid, which almost made Wall follow her example. She coughed and spit, letting her head roll forward, and leaned dangerously toward the hot coals.

"Sorry, Plink. I shouldn't have pushed you." He gently rubbed her back in a counterclockwise motion. "Plink?"

Nothing.

"Plink?!"

He pulled her away from the flames. Her eyes were open and her face blank, dead.

"Damn it!" For the second time in just as many days, he laid her on her back and started pumping blood for her. "Plink. Don't do this." Megadeth's "Holy Wars...The Punishment Due" pounded through his thoughts.

"Plink," Rhino said as he dropped to his knees, ready to breathe for her once Wall counted to thirty.

Pump, pump, pump.

"Rhino, now."

The large man held her nostrils and puffed twice.

Pump, pump, pump.

He repeated this process, each passing compression reducing her chance of survival, each puff of air bringing her closer to permanent death. "No," Wall said. "You're stronger than this." After the fourth round, he gave up hope but kept pressing his palms into her chest.

"She's dead," Rhino said. "You have to let her–"

Her eyelids fluttered and she coughed. Her eyes drooped shut. He leaned down and felt her weak breath on his ear, barely alive, but alive all the same. The question was, for how long? Several terrible thoughts crossed through his head like a multi-car accident, colliding into an inseparable mess of metal, glass, and plastic. Did he bring her back because he needed her to live or because she would have wanted it? By continuing compressions, had he simply prolonged her suffering? Would she wake up wishing she had died, angry at Wall for resuscitating her, possibly scarred irreparably with reduced faculties or physical limitations?

"Thank god," Aspen whispered from next to him. As playfully snarky as she so often was, her depth of emotion was proving to be far greater than he expected.

Only time would tell if there was reason to be thankful. She might survive, but just as likely, she could pass in her sleep or wake up brainless. This hollowness was how too many mothers and fathers, brothers and sisters, friends and lovers would feel in the years ahead.

Two weeks later, they snuffed the fire for the last time and packed up their meager possessions. Together, they climbed out of the valley, neither hurried nor moseying, simply walking with Towning's backhanded gift in their blood, a morbidly purposeful life. The hike out proved far nicer than their way in, beautiful and serene, lighter of heart and mind, partially healed with time.

Their motorcycles had long since turned to waste, consumed by dusty roads and spoiled gasoline, a small blight on the land compared to what they would find on their travels.

Looking at the trail ahead, Plink said, "So, Wall, where to?"

He smiled. "Everywhere. Miles to go."

The End

Made in the USA
Middletown, DE
09 March 2024

51113424R00216